A beam of light stabs through the night sky, summoning from his cave the Protector of Gotham: BATMAN.

From the distant past to the near future, here are fourteen of the most baffling cases from the files of the Dark Knight Detective™:

"Death of the Dreammaster"—the Joker is dead. Batman watches as the Clown Prince of Crime is crushed to death between two huge stone wheels. But if that's so, who does Bruce Wayne see walking down the street the next day?...

"The Origin of The Polarizer"—there's a different kind of criminal loose in 1957 Gotham City, a mysterious figure who not only can control the Bat Signal and the BATIVAC Crime Computer, but who has even infiltrated the Dynamic Duo's utility belts! Will they be able to deduce the insidious villain's identity in time?

"Subway Jack"—a serial killer is rampaging through the subways, killing bag ladies and anyone else who gets in his way. It's up to Batman to stop him in this tale of terror and the supernatural.

And eleven more stories from the greatest authors of mystery, science fiction, fantasy, and horror!

The Further Adventures of Batman®

™

Edited by
MARTIN H. GREENBERG

BANTAM BOOKS
NEW YORK · TORONTO · LONDON · SYDNEY · AUCKLAND

THE FURTHER ADVENTURES OF BATMAN

A Bantam Book/July 1989

ISBN 0-553-28270-0

Published simultaneously in the United States and Canada

Bantam Books are published by Bantam Books, a division of Bantam
Doubleday Dell Publishing Group, Inc. Its trademark, consisting of the
words "Bantam Books" and the portrayal of a rooster, is Registered in
U.S. Patent and Trademark Office and in other countries. Marca
Registrada. Bantam Books, 666 Fifth Avenue, New York, New York
10103

PRINTED IN THE UNITED STATES OF AMERICA

0 9 8 7 6 5 4 3 2 1

Contents

The Further Adventures of Batman

Death of the Dreammaster

ROBERT SHECKLEY

Bruce Wayne would never forget the scene. He saw it again in his mind's eye, the grisly windmill in the low fen country outside New Charity Parish. Bruce himself, as Batman, was there. He was spread-eagled against a wide wooden door, his arms and legs pinioned by steel clamps secured with half-inch bolts. The bodies of the Joker's most recent victims had been stacked roughly against a wall like so much bloodstained cordwood. The torsos were in one pile, the arms and legs in another, the heads in a third. The Joker himself, his thin-lipped grin wider and more hideous than ever, his painter's smock stiff with blood, a bloodstained beret perched on his green-haired head, had just lifted up the last of his victims, little Monica Elroy. The child was still alive, but she had fainted. The Joker tried to slap her into consciousness because death was so much nicer when the victim was awake to appreciate it. Mercifully for her, the child did not respond.

"Well, she's being a poor sport about it," the Joker said. "Might as well finish her and get to you, Batman."

Death of the Dreammaster

The Joker carried the child to the center of the big high-ceilinged room. It was dominated by two enormous grindstones, set on axles contained within an open scaffolding. The great wheels turned slowly, propelled by the wide wings of the windmill outside. They were blood-stained, those wheels. The blood from the victims they had ground into a paste of flesh and bone had stained the granite deeply.

"We'll just feed her in one toe at a time," the Joker said. "Maybe she'll come around in time to say bye-bye."

Batman had been tugging at the clamp that held his right arm to the door. It had a fraction of give to it. Not much, but maybe enough. Enough to give him a chance, faint though it was.

In past years, Batman had learned a precise control of muscles and nerves in his advanced studies in Tibet. He remembered those studies now and forced his concentration to narrow and deepen, ignoring the scenes of horror around him and the overwhelming smell of blood. All his energy had to go into that arm, into his wrist, into the exact point of contact where the clamp pressed. He directed his force outward in a rhythmic fashion, timing it with his pulse beats, and, as he saw the Joker, unconscious child in his arms, mounting the three steps to the platform where the great grindstones touched their rough faces together, Batman drove at the clamp with every ounce of mental and physical energy at his disposal.

For a moment, nothing happened. And then the steel clamp wrenched free from the wooden door with a loud clear ringing sound, and the bolt that had secured it flew across the room as if it had been shot from a slingshot.

The Joker, who had just been lowering the unconscious girl toward the grindstones, was hit on the back of the head. Although the blow did not hurt him, he started violently, more shock than pain, and the girl fell from his arms. Off balance, he flailed, trying to regain his footing.

One hand, wildly gesticulating in its bloodstained white glove, came up against the grindstones at their point of contact. The hand was pulled in at once. The Joker howled and tried to pull free. The grindstones turned inexorably. The madman screamed and wrenched at his arm, and so violent was his movement that it seemed as if the limb might be pulled from his shoulder. But no such luck. The grindstones continued to devour him, and, as his forearm vanished between the stones and the rest of him was pulled in after it, the Joker, mad with pain, began to laugh, the high inhuman laughter of absolute insanity, and he continued to laugh as his body was pulled between the grindstone wheels, only stopping when his head came apart like a watermelon in a hydraulic press....

And so the Joker was dead.

But was he?

If so, who was that madcap and horrifying creature that Bruce kept glimpsing at the corners of his vision?

Who was Bruce Wayne seeing now, as he walked through downtown Gotham City, on his way to see his old friend Dr. Edwin Waltham?

Bruce Wayne shuddered slightly and resisted the urge to turn. The figure was never there when he turned around.

But he kept on seeing it.

This time, however, was different.

He was at the corner of Fifth and Concord in the heart of Gotham City. Across the street rose the tall tower with the famous polychrome façade that was the New Era Hotel. It was the newest and most sumptuous hotel in the city, built, it was said, by a consortium of foreign investors. It was a place where the rich from all over the world came to look and to be seen, the women to parade in their furs and silks, the men to blow smoke from their fine Havana cigars.

As he stood on the corner across from the hotel, waiting for the light to change, he clearly saw the figure he had glimpsed earlier. The man was long and skinny, dressed in a bottle-green swallow-tailed coat and tattersall trousers like an Edwardian dandy. But that was not what caught Bruce Wayne's eye. It was the man's hair, mossy green above a narrow, long-nosed, long-chinned face. The face looked at Wayne for a split second; the long, red, thin-lipped mouth stretched into a grin. There could be no doubt about it: it was the Joker.

But that was impossible. The Joker was dead. Bruce had seen him die himself; had even had a hand in it.

The Joker, or his look-alike, turned away abruptly, darted across the street, and went into the New Era Hotel.

Bruce Wayne came to an immediate decision. He darted out into the street. Cars screeched, and slewed out of his way. Picking his way across the wide boulevard like a fleet, broken-field runner, Wayne made it to the curb, pushed with unaccustomed brusqueness past a group of gabbling society women, and entered the lobby.

It was like stepping into another world. Outside was the modern-day rush and squalor of Gotham City. Inside, his feet sank into the deep-piled Isfahani rug made especially for the New Era. Overhead the central vault of the ceiling arched upward. Chandeliers, suspended from slender stainless steel threads, glittered with cut glass and blazed with light. The tall windows of the lobby were made of stained glass, giving the place a resemblance to a church for the worship of success.

Surveying the scene, Bruce noticed many men in long flowing Arab robes and headdresses. Some of the women were attired in the heavy veils of those where a form of purdah is still practiced. Scattered here and there were bellboys, smart in their Coldstream Guards uniforms.

Nowhere was there anyone who bore the least resemblance to the grinning figure Bruce had seen only seconds ago.

Bruce hesitated a moment, then went up to the front desk. An assistant manager, a large dignified-looking man in full evening dress with muttonchop sideburns and a bald, gleaming skull, asked if he could be of service.

Bruce described the man he sought.

The assistant manager pursed his lips in an imitation of thoughtfulness.

"No such person of that description has entered here, sir. Not now or ever."

"He might have sneaked in without being noticed," Bruce suggested.

"Oh, I think not, sir," the assistant manager said. He smiled a supercilious smile. "A person of the description you gave us could hardly go unnoticed in a place like the New Era. Green hair and bottle-green coat you said? No sir, not in the New Era."

Bruce felt like a fool. The man was eyeing him as though he were drunk or crazy. Bruce knew very well he was not drunk. As for crazy.... Well, that was one of the things he was going to Dr. Waltham to find out about.

6:15 p.m. Dr. Waltham looked at his watch. Batman was late for his appointment. Waltham had been the Dark Knight's physician for many years. Never before had Batman been this late.

Waltham was ready to close up. The physician went to draw the blinds. He heard a low laugh behind him and turned.

"Sorry I'm late," Batman said. "I ran into somebody I thought I knew. Hope you hadn't given up on me."

"No problem, Batman," Dr. Waltham said, peering at the tall cloaked man with the black mask. As usual, Batman appeared seemingly out of nowhere. Waltham had come to expect it—as well as you can expect the unexpected. "Anybody I know?"

"No longer."

"Beg pardon?"

"Nothing, Doc. Shall we get on with the examination?"

It was the time for Bruce Wayne's yearly physical. In his role as Batman, he required absolute physical conditioning of himself. He worked to his own exercise program, and spent hours each week honing his skills in the martial arts. Although he was always in perfect condition, he knew that ailments and conditions could sneak up on you. Hence this yearly physical with his old family friend, Edwin Waltham, one of the top physicians in Gotham City. Waltham was an independently wealthy man who maintained his office and apartment on Starcross Boulevard, one of the best locations in the city. Waltham was small and corpulent, with a head of curly gray hair, a face flushed from good living, and small alert eyes that, behind round glasses, glinted with intelligence. Clever though he was, however, it had never occurred to him that his old friend Batman was the same person as his father's friend, Bruce Wayne.

"You're in great shape, Batman, as usual," Waltham said at the conclusion of the examination as Batman adjusted his tunic. "You've got a heart like a steam locomotive. You'd have to, for some of the things you do."

Batman nodded, frowning slightly. Waltham, who had been his parents' physician, was like most of the people in Gotham City and knew him only as Batman, scourge of criminals and of evildoers everywhere. The doctor was always eager to hear about Batman's cases. There was no harm in it, but there was no need for it, either. Bruce Wayne handled the Batman portion of his life like a state secret.

As he expected, Waltham asked, "Are you working on anything now, Batman?"

"No, I'm still taking it easy."

"I haven't seen you with Vera recently." He was referring to Vera St. Clair, a pretty society woman whom Batman had been seen with.

"She's in Rio. For the Carnival."

"Lucky her! You should have gone yourself, Batman."

"I considered it." Batman didn't know how to tell it to Waltham, but a sort of lethargy had invaded his senses in the last few months. It had begun about the time he began having the hallucinations.

He didn't want to talk about that, but it was one of the reasons he had come to see the doctor.

Seeing him hesitate, Waltham asked, "What is it, Batman?"

Batman decided to take the plunge. "Doc, I've begun seeing things."

The doctor maintained his professional aplomb, but concern glinted from his eyes. "Tell me about it."

The tall, grim-faced masked man described his recent hallucinations. He had had them three times now in as many months. They were usually fleeting, no more than a glimpse of some old enemy from the past, now long defeated and safely buried.

Death of the Dreammaster

Most recently it had been the Joker. Dead, but Bruce had seen him entering the lobby of the New Era Hotel.

Dr. Waltham considered his words carefully. "Batman, I've given you the best physical money can buy. There is nothing wrong with you physically."

"But mentally?"

"I would almost stake my life on your being the sanest man I know."

"Almost?"

"Just a way of speaking. Have you had any unusual concerns on your mind recently?"

Batman shook his head. He couldn't tell Waltham that he had been thinking a lot about the past recently. About friends he had once known, now dead. Robin, Bat Woman, Bat Girl.... And dead enemies, too—the Joker, the Riddler, the Penguin. All of them, friends and foes alike, were his family, those who shared his deeds back when the world was younger.

He was older now. Still perfectly fit, a unique physical specimen. But older.

"No, no particular concerns."

Waltham took off his glasses and wiped them carefully. Before putting them back on he looked at Batman, his eyes a soft, unfocused myopic blue. "Tell me about the most recent."

"On my way here, I thought I saw the Joker."

"Somebody in the crowd, perhaps, a superficial resemblance...."

"No, it was him. I followed him into the New Era Hotel. But he wasn't there. The manager said that no such person had entered."

"A few hallucinations don't matter much," Dr. Waltham said. "You've been through some of the most difficult and terrible experiences known to man. A little psychomotor activity would not be unexpected. But tell me...is there any chance the Joker is still alive?"

"None whatsoever."

"I don't know the details of his demise, but I would remind you that the Joker escaped from many situations where death seemed certain. Why not this time?"

"I'm sure he's dead," he said.

"Well then, I don't know how to advise you," Dr. Waltham said. "The best thing would be for you to go down to Rio and join Vera. You need to get away, take your mind off these concerns."

"Thanks for the advice," Batman said. "I'll think about it."

"Some tea, sir?" asked Alfred Pennyworth, Bruce Wayne's butler. "It's the special Darjeeling that you like so well."

"Not right now," Bruce said. He had been going over crime reports at the antique table that served him as a desk. There were priceless antiques throughout the big, gracious old mansion that was situated on a landscaped knoll within view of Gotham City. "Is there anything else I can do for you, sir, before I retire?" Alfred asked.

"As a matter of fact, there is," Bruce said. He had been brooding all evening about the events of the day and his visit to Dr. Waltham. Now he had decided to do something. "I want you to pack a suitcase for me immediately."

"Certainly, sir," Alfred said, and his grave expression brightened. "I'll pack your lightweight shorts, sir, and your new tropical suits. Perhaps a mask and snorkel? They say there's good underwater swimming there."

"I beg your pardon, Alfred?"

"In Rio de Janeiro, sir. I assume that is your destination. To join Miss Vera for the Carnival. And if you'll excuse my saying so, it's just what you need, sir. A change, and a little amusement in your life. You have been rather on the gloomy side of late, sir, if you'll permit the observation."

Bruce smiled. "I'm touched by your concern, Alfred, but I'm afraid you've jumped to an erroneous conclusion. I will need no carnival costume where I'm going."

"I apologize for my incorrect assumption, sir. Might I ask where you're going?"

"The New Era Hotel, here in Gotham City."

"Indeed, sir?" Alfred's aplomb was unshakeable. Bruce could have told him he was going to the North Pole and the faithful servant would merely have inquired if he should pack ice skates.

"I'll need about half a dozen evening suits, and some casual clothing for daytime wear, and the usual shirts and socks."

"A wardrobe such as you describe is already packed and ready to go, Master Wayne. I packed the Charlie Morrison wardrobe for you, sir."

"Alfred, you anticipate well."

"Yes, sir. One thing I didn't know, sir. Will you require the Batman Suit?"

Bruce looked up sharply. Somehow he hadn't considered taking the Batman Suit. He hadn't quite brought himself to the point of considering that there were at least two interpretations of his hallucinations. One, that he was going crazy. Two, that someone was planning something clever and criminal and was trying to put a scare into him.

"Yes, pack the Batman Suit," Bruce said. "And put in the small leather bag marked OPS 12. And one of the standard utility belts."

"At once, sir," said Alfred. He didn't bother to mention that he had also packed those things in expectation of just such a trip. You don't stay Batman's batman for long if you can't anticipate his needs.

Despite all the advantages of his Batman persona, there were a few disadvantages, too. For surprising hoodlums and criminals, the shock value of Batman was great. But for everyday use, it was too noticeable. When it was necessary for him to go somewhere, it was often an advantage to go looking like an ordinary citizen. But there were problems to going as Bruce Wayne, and then suddenly appearing later as Batman. Someone might find it a little more than coincidence that Bruce was around whenever Batman appeared.

Because of this, Bruce had adopted several other personas, to be used when occasion demanded it. The most recent of these, whom he called Charlie Morrison, had been invaluable when Bruce had gone to Europe to detect and foil a counterfeiting ring operating in several cities of northern Europe. Bruce remembered how Commissioner Gordon himself had congratulated him at the end of the case when they met in the mayor's office in Hamburg. Gordon might have suspected that Charlie Morrison was Batman; but that was all right. He was supposed to think that. It helped keep suspicions off Bruce Wayne, the progenitor of both personas.

Working with Lafayette Boyent, one of the masters of classical drama, Bruce had mastered makeup, posture and voice. His impersonations could have earned him a place in the theater if the direction of his life had not been decided long ago.

When Charlie Morrison checked into the New Era Hotel, the assistant manager helped him sign in with no hint of remembering his earlier visit as Bruce Wayne.

The assistant manager was cheerful and helpful. Charlie Morrison was a man whose sapphire and ruby American Express card allowed him luxuries unknown to the ordinary citizen. Even among the crowds of visiting oil sheiks and heads of industrial parks, he was a welcome guest—tall, good-looking, quiet-mannered, and renowned for his liberal tips.

The assistant manager brushed back his muttonchop whiskers, a habitual gesture, and swiftly plucked out of a nearby tray a shimmering, plastic oblong slightly larger than a credit card. He held it out to Bruce.

"Your suite is penthouse A2, Mr. Morrison. It is one of our choicest suites, and I'm sure you will find it eminently satisfactory. This card will give you entry to all of the New Era's facilities—the health club, the restaurants and nightclubs, the solarium, the flying room, and so on. There is a complete list of our services in your suite. My name is Blithely. It is my ambition to serve you. If there is any complaint at all, please do not hesitate to call on me day or night."

Bruce thanked Blithely, picked up his key and went to the elevators. There was a special elevator for the penthouse suites. His luggage had already gone up. He pressed the button and stepped in when the heavy, ornate brass door opened. Just as the door was about to close, a woman slipped in with him.

She was tall, sleek and attractive, wearing a frock whose simplicity accentuated rather than belied its price tag. Her dark hair was tied back with a simple ribbon. She carried a small, richly brocaded purse that must have cost plenty, even in Hincheng, China, which Bruce remembered as the home of these objects.

"Yes," she said, following his gaze. "It's Hinchengese. Do you like it?"

Bruce shrugged. "It is quite attractive."

She looked at him boldly. He didn't like the intensity of her inspection. Yet there was something exciting about her, something forward yet subtle, and unashamedly feminine.

"You are also in one of the penthouses?" she asked.

"Yes. And you?"

"Of course. I always stay here when I am in Gotham City." He had detected her faint foreign accent. But what was it? Not German. Something farther east . . . Czechoslovakia, perhaps. "Dear old penthouse A1 has become something of a home for me. Do you stay here often?"

"My first time," Bruce said.

"You will like it here very much," she said, as the elevator came to a soft stop and the door slid open.

They walked together down the corridor. Penthouses A1 and A2 were opposite each other, the only apartments on the floor. They opened their doors with their cards.

"By the way," Bruce said, "I'm Charlie Morrison."

"Perhaps we will meet again," she said. "I am Ilona." She closed the door softly behind her.

Bruce's clothes were already laid out by the hotel staff, all except the one large leather case to which he kept the only key. In it was the Batman equipment he might soon need, if his instincts were to be trusted.

The suite was indeed beautiful, with a breathtaking terrace view of Gotham City. The city looked magnificent at this hour, a sleeping giant composed of the bodies and minds of its millions of inhabitants.

Was one of those inhabitants the Joker? Impossible. Yet he had seen something.

Or had he?

Death of the Dreammaster

He sighed and turned away from the terrace.

The living room of his suite was furnished with rare antiques from Eastern Europe and the Near East. There were Turkish wall hangings on one wall, a Picasso on another. A quick inspection told Bruce that the Picasso was genuine, worth perhaps several million dollars. The television was state-of-the-art. The VCR came with a complete tape library, and a catalogue of others that could be called up on a moment's notice. The music console was also impressive.

These things meant little to Bruce, however. This was the same sort of equipment he had at home. He knew from personal experience how difficult it is for the rich to buy anything really special.

He sat in an Ames chair and leafed through a magazine. He was preoccupied, morose. What was he doing here? What could possibly happen in a place like this? The New Era was one of the great bastions of safety with luxury. He was wasting his time.

He called room service and ordered a light dinner: eggs poached in Normandy butter, toast points, slice of Paris ham, fruit cocktail, demitasse. He showered and shaved and dressed in a lightweight evening suit. He had just finished combing his hair when a discreet tap at the door told him the meal had come.

The waiter wheeled the cart, with its high silver-domed salver, to the little table near the balcony. Bruce seated himself and opened the day's newspaper that the man had brought. The waiter deftly laid out the silverware, then whisked the top off the salver and set the plate down in front of Bruce. He bowed, said, "anything else, sir, please call," and started toward the door.

Bruce folded his newspaper and looked down at the plate. His expression froze. There, on the fine Spode china, was a mass of writhing snakes, little green ones and a few red ones. Among them were several small toads. They looked up balefully at Bruce with their evil pop eyes.

"Waiter!" Bruce called out as the waiter was going through the door.

"Sir?"

"What is the meaning of this?"

"I beg your pardon, sir?"

"Come here and tell me how you explain this."

Dutifully enough the man came back into the room. Bruce noticed now that the waiter was almost bald, and that there were faint tattoo marks on his shining skull.

"What seems to be the trouble, sir?"

"Just look here and explain it," Bruce said, indicating his place.

"Yes sir. I'm looking, but I fail to see anything amiss."

Bruce looked down. The snakes and toads were no longer there. What was on the plate now was what he had ordered: ham and eggs by any other name.

"It's the toast points," Bruce said, recovering quickly. "They're soggy."

"They look all right to me, Mr. Morrison," the waiter said, bending down to peer at the golden brown triangles of bread.

"You can see the moisture shining on them. And those eggs are practically hardboiled, not poached at all."

Bruce glared at the waiter, daring him to dispute, but the waiter was not there for that.

"Yes, sir, of course, sir," he said, his tone of voice indicating that he thought Bruce was acting a little peculiar but that he was prepared to humor him. "I'll have the order replaced at once."

He wheeled the cart out, closing the door quietly behind him.

It didn't take long to replace his dinner, and this time it underwent no change. Bruce ate quickly. After he was through he wheeled the cart into the corridor. As he turned to return to his room, he saw a figure vanish around the corner at the end of the long corridor. A familiar figure. Tall, emaciated, with green hair and a crazy smile....

It took Bruce Wayne only three strides to reach full sprinting speed as he raced after the figure of his old enemy, who was looking remarkably healthy for one who was well and truly dead.

The corridor was empty. On this side of the hotel there were no suites, no doors at all. The Joker, or whoever it was, had vanished into a blank wall.

Bruce inspected the wall closely. Beneath a light fixture he saw a thin, metal-lined slit. He slipped the card the hotel had given him into it. A panel in the corridor's wall slid back. Retrieving his card, Bruce went through the opening into the darkness within.

The corridor led down a long slope. Bruce hurried down it, just faintly hearing the sound of distant footsteps ahead of him. In another twenty yards the corridor branched. A faint swirling of dust in the left-hand branch told him which way to go. He plunged down a steepening incline. The corridor had at first been lit by fluorescent panels set into the ceiling. As Bruce proceeded, the corridor became dimmer. Some of the panels weren't working. The pitch was so great that he was having difficulty maintaining his balance. There was a blocked-up window ahead of him, dimly perceivable in the gloom. There was

Robert Sheckley

no place to go other than through that or back up the slope. Bruce picked up speed and rammed the window with his shoulder, crashing through it and tumbling into a brightly lit room beyond.

The room was done entirely in white tile and was lit by overhead fluorescents. It was steamy and warm. As Bruce rolled to his feet, he noticed that there were many men in the room, some of them wearing shorts, some towels, a few nothing at all. There were machines scattered around the room. Bruce was familiar with them. They were exercise machines of the sort he had himself in his workout room. He was in the health club.

If there had been any doubt, that doubt would have been cleared up immediately when a short, muscular man with a wrestler's build, wearing white slacks and a white T-shirt that read, New Era Health Club Instructor, strode up to him in a belligerent manner and said, "Say, look here, bub, what's the big idea trying to break in here through the ventilator system?" Then he noticed the card in Bruce's hand. "Oh, sorry, sir, didn't know you were a guest. Our clients usually come through the door."

The instructor was starting to grin. Bruce reached out and took the man's biceps in his hand. It looked like a friendly gesture. And his grip tightened only slightly. But the instructor went pale, tried to pull free, saw it was no use and turned to Bruce with a frightened look on his face.

"Did you see someone just enter?" Bruce asked. "A very tall, thin man with green hair?"

"Green hair!" the instructor said, and seemed ready to laugh. A slight application of pressure to his biceps convinced him that it was not really a laughing matter.

"No sir, I didn't. Really. I'd tell you if I did."

Bruce released the man. A quick glance around the room told him that nobody answering the Joker's description could possibly have come here.

Bruce said, "Get me a pair of swimming trunks, please. I think I'll have a dip before I go back up."

"Yes sir," the instructor said. "And which way will you be leaving, sir? Going by the ventilators again?"

"No," Bruce said, "they're only fast getting here."

Bruce felt better after doing a hundred or so laps in his explosive Australian crawl. He returned to his suite.

Mr. Blithely came to visit him a little later. Blithely wanted to know if there was anything the matter. By his expression, Bruce surmised that he really meant, is there anything the matter with you, sir? Bruce merely glared at him. Blithely explained that although it was not so posted, the management encouraged guests to stay out of the ventilation system. Bruce managed to hold his temper. Now was not the time for an outburst.

When the manager had left, Bruce went to the balcony and looked out at the night for a long time. He could hear music from the suite next door, and sounds of laughter and the clink of glasses. It sounded like someone was having a good time.

He was starting to get the idea that something was going on in the New Era Hotel. So far it seemed to be something done especially for him.

It was much later in the night that the noise woke him up. He sat bolt upright, moving instantaneously from deep sleep to immediate alertness. What had it been? A muffled thud from the next suite. It must have been something thrown against the wall, thrown hard enough for the sound to penetrate the soundproofing. Bruce dressed quickly in the dark. He was utterly silent, listening, his senses at full alert. Then he heard a scream. It was from the suite next door.

He hurried out to the balcony. It was about a fifteen-foot jump to the balcony of the next suite. Bruce could do better than that in the standing broad jump, but that was under ideal conditions. Here he would have to crouch on the very edge of his balcony and push off without the benefit of being able to swing his arms. And he would also have to be careful not to let his feet slip on the bevelled facing material.

He leaped. His calculations were not amiss, no matter what else might be wrong with him. His fingers closed crisply around the rail of the next penthouse. He used his back flip to vault neatly over the railing.

The terrace doors to the penthouse were open, but long fluttering white curtains obscured his view within. He moved forward into the darkened room. He felt something soft under his foot and recoiled sharply. Then he had found the light switch and flooded the room with light.

She had been beautiful in life, but death had taken something out of her. She lay with one arm thrown back, the other bent beneath her. Her eyes were open and she seemed to be smiling. This was remarkable in view of the fact that her throat had been cut.

There was nothing to do there. The woman, sole occupant of the suite, was dead. The telephone line had been cut. Her brocade purse seemed to be missing, but Bruce had no time for a complete search. Nor did he know what to look for.

He went back to his own suite. There he made two calls, one to Commissioner James Gordon, the other to

Assistant Manager Blithely. And then back to await further developments.

Soon thereafter, he received a telephone call from the assistant manager. Would Mr. Morrison come to the main office.

Bruce was already dressed. He paused only to check his attire, then went down to the lobby. Although it was the small hours of the morning, there were still many people there milling around. Fun ran late in Gotham City.

Blithely greeted him as suavely as before. But he had a curious expression on his round rosy face as he looked at Bruce. Could it be pity?

Also present in the office was Police Commissioner James Gordon. The tough cop had cooperated secretly with Batman on more than one occasion. Despite Gordon's skepticism, they often teamed up in their fight against crime.

"Hello, Morrison," James Gordon said. "Been quite a while."

"Hamburg, about three years ago," Bruce said.

"Tell me what you saw tonight, Charlie," Gordon said.

"But you've seen it yourself by now."

"Never mind. Describe it for me, please."

Bruce described the scene in the suite.

"OK," Gordon said. "Let's take a look."

Bruce, Gordon, and Blithely took the penthouse elevator to the top floor. There was the same corridor, with Bruce's suite on one side, the other belonging to the woman who had ridden up in the elevator with him.

"Is this the place?" Gordon asked, indicating the door through which the woman had passed.

"Of course it is," Bruce said. "What's the problem?"

Blithely opened the door with his pass card. He entered and turned on the light. The first thing Bruce

Robert Sheckley

noticed when he went in was the smell of fresh paint. Under the strong overhead lights, he could see that the whole suite had been freshly painted. Before painting, it had been stripped of furniture. A pile of dropcloths was stacked in a corner. Aside from that, the room was empty.

Gordon and Blithely waited while Bruce inspected the apartment. He checked out all the rooms. In none of them was there any trace of recent occupancy, and even less was there evidence that a brutal murder had been committed less than half an hour ago.

The two men waited while Bruce walked back to them.

Bruce said, "Gentlemen, my apologies. I seem to have been mistaken."

Gordon gave him a curious look and sucked at his unlit pipe. In his own brown gabardine suit and beige trenchcoat he looked like a private investigator of the old days rather than Police Commissioner of Gotham City.

The manager said, "Are you feeling all right, sir? It was a very startling incident you described. I do not wish to pry, but are you perhaps under the influence of alcohol or some prohibited drug?"

"Certainly not," Bruce said, his voice taking on a cutting edge. "Do you want to make charges against me, Mr. Blithely?"

"Heavens no," Blithely said. "I am only thinking of the reputation of the hotel. When a guest starts describing scenes of mayhem that have never taken place.... Well, it makes one fear ever so slightly for the safety of the other guests. That, taken with the various other incidents—"

"What are those?" Gordon asked, interrupting sharply.

Blithely described Bruce's first appearance at the hotel, when he was looking for a man with green hair, and then Bruce's unusual entry into the health club.

Gordon nodded when Blithely was through. He took off his heavy horn-rimmed glasses and cleaned them with a crumpled tissue. He put the glasses back on, then broke into a grin.

"Well, Charlie," he said, "you've won your bet." He took a ten dollar bill out of his pocket and handed it to Bruce.

"Thanks," Bruce said, following Gordon's lead, nonchalantly pocketing the money.

"I don't understand," Blithely said.

"I used to tell Mr. Morrison here he was too formal, too uptight. I said he was too well-mannered to start a commotion. Charlie bet me ten bucks he could get the manager of the best hotel in town to call me and complain that he was crazy. I never thought you'd go through with it, Charlie."

"Well, you annoyed me," Bruce said.

"So this has all been a practical joke?" Blithely asked.

"Of course it has," Gordon said. "Does Mr. Morrison look crazy to you?"

"Not in the slightest," Blithely said. But there was still a shade of doubt in his voice.

"Thanks for being such a good sport about it," Bruce said. "There'll be a nice bonus added to the bill for you, personally, for taking this in such good humor."

"Oh, Mr. Morrison, there's no need—"

But Bruce waved him away with a lordly gesture. When Blithely left, even he was chuckling at the joke.

When they were alone, Bruce went to the bar and poured Gordon a shot of bourbon, and accompanied it with branchwater on the side. He poured himself a glass of Vichy. Both men sat down on one of the couches. Gordon sipped his bourbon.

"Damn good bourbon, Charlie," he said.

"They have only the best here," Bruce said.

"So I see. Charlie, what in the name of Sam Hill went on here?"

"Nothing, apparently," Bruce said. "You should have taken me in. I'm obviously 'round the bend."

Gordon didn't reply until he had his pipe going. While malodorous fumes rose in the air, he said, "Even if you were crazy, I'd never let on to a guy like that."

Bruce nodded. "Blithely is not a sympathetic type, is he?"

Gordon shook his head. "I'd arrange to have you committed all by myself, if that was what was needed. Charlie, are you crazy?"

"Why ask me?" Bruce said. "How would I know?"

"I've gotten to know you pretty well over the years," Gordon said. "You and I were involved in one of the toughest cases of this century. Charlie, I lost my belief in organized religion a long time ago. And I think I've lost about half my faith in justice, too. But one thing I still believe in is Batman."

Gordon looked up from his drink. He saw that "Charlie Morrison" was smiling at him.

"What's so funny?"

"You. Police Commissioner of Gotham City and you don't even know a loony when you see one. But you know what, Jim? I'm just as bad. I don't believe for a moment I'm crazy. Tonight has proven it to me."

"How's that, Charlie?"

"I've seen the Joker several times in recent months. Just quick little glimpses, then he vanishes. It had me worried. I followed him into this hotel, or so I thought. I decided it would be worthwhile to check in myself and see what was going on. All these incidents, all in one night, convince me that someone is trying to put something over on me. I don't know how, or why—not yet—but I'm going to find out."

"Frankly, I'm glad you're doing this," Gordon said. "We've been getting a lot of rumors recently, nothing we can pin down, but stuff that keeps on popping up. About something going down that's both criminal and political. Something involving important people. Something involving the New Era Hotel."

"Interesting," Bruce said. "Anything else?"

"Nothing definite. Just a lot of ominous-sounding rumors. You always hear these crazy stories about new criminal combines from foreign countries. This time there just might be something to it."

"I'm going to see what turns up," Bruce said.

"I'm glad. The way I see it, we've got just one thing to worry about."

"What's that?" Bruce asked.

"I know you're sane and you know you're sane. But what if we're both wrong?"

Two days passed without incident. Charlie Morrison did all the things a wealthy young bachelor might do in a hotel like the New Era. He sampled all their nightclubs and watched the shows. He listened to the comedians and laughed as heartily as anyone else. He tasted the gourmet specialties in several exquisite restaurants. He drank sparingly and turned down the offers of drugs and women from the bellboys.

Early on the evening of the third day he saw her again. She stepped out of the New Era beauty parlor just as he was coming out of the magazine shop. It was her unmistakably, Ilona, the woman he had ridden up with in the elevator and later seen murdered in her suite.

She wore a dark silk dress, and had a turquoise scarf knotted carelessly around her neck.

"Excuse me, Ilona," he said. But she ignored him and hurried through the lobby, going through a door marked PRIVATE. Bruce followed. He was in a corridor that seemed to lead to the kitchen area. The lighting was bad, and there was deep dust on the floor: the New Eras spick-and-span look did not extend to the off-stage areas. Bruce decided he wouldn't eat here any more if this was a sample of their true housekeeping. He rounded a corner, and there she was.

"Stop following me!" she said.

"Just a couple of questions," Bruce said.

"Oh. Well, if that's all...." She smiled, then opened her purse and took out a cigarette. She found a small golden lighter in her purse. She flicked it once and a cloud of yellow gas sprayed into Bruce's face. She dropped the lighter and fled as soon as Bruce hit the floor.

You can fool all of the superheroes some of the time, but you can't fool any of them all of the time. Especially not Batman. Lacking Superman's invulnerability, Batman had to rely on cunning, foresight, and his preternaturally keen eyesight. He had seen at once that the object Ilona took from her purse was no ordinary lighter. Her very air of unconcern gave her away. He guessed what it was, but did not let on that he knew. He was holding his breath when she sprayed him. He fell to the floor and was gratified to hear the tinkle of the little gas container as she dropped it beside him.

He got up and picked up the little metal case. It was cunningly fashioned, turned on a metal lathe with a jeweler's precision. The curves of its surfaces were deep and complex. All in all it was one of the finest bits of machine work he had seen in a long time. And he was one to know: Bruce Wayne, Batman, had his own tool shop and his own metal-working equipment. He knew good work when he saw it.

Good work, yes. But who's work was it?

He didn't know. But he had an idea where to go to find out.

First, though, a change of attire.

Night fell, deep and dangerous, on Gotham City.

Darkness came down over the Northside docks, where sailors of a dozen nations traded with whores from half the continent. The gin mills of Gotham City were notorious from Montreal to Valparaiso. Recent defense contracts in Subiuz County adjoining Gotham City had brought many new people into the city. They came to work in the Subiuz County defense plants. At night, after finishing their shifts, they wanted some fun. They were not particular about how they got it.

Fun tended to get rough in the more noisome parts of Gotham City such as Limehouse. A man could get knocked on the head and rolled with little difficulty. If he was smart, he took his lumps and went away, a sadder but wiser man. If he tried to do something about it, he was due for an even more unpleasant surprise—such as waking up to find himself wearing lead-filled skiboots and sinking in the garbage-strewn waters of the Limehouse River in the company of eels and crabs.

Limehouse was an old industrial slum, a dark and dangerous place. The more upright inhabitants had been trying to get the street lighting back on for a long time, without success, because of a corrupt city administra-

Robert Sheckley

tion that sold all the lighting fixtures to a Mexican entrepreneur.

Darkness bred crime in the stews of the city.

Darkness bred all creatures of the night.

Especially bats.

It was close to midnight, and Limehouse was just coming into its fullest flower. The drunken and motley crowds of sailors parading the streets did not notice a shadow that passed briefly across the huge lemon moon before it dipped down to ground level and came to rest in one of the narrow backyards.

Batman, in full uniform and mask, folded the small batwinged Batcopter and stowed it in its compact carrying case. With a small but powerful Batlight he briefly consulted a map of his own devising. It was a flat tablet about the size of a sheet of typing paper, and less than an inch thick. Illuminated from beneath, it could be scrolled to reveal highly detailed maps of any part of Gotham City.

Batman checked his coordinates again. Yes, he was in the right location. It had been almost two years since he had come to this particular address. He hoped that Tony Marrotti was still in business.

Orienting himself, Batman moved silently to the back door of the sagging one-story frame house nearby. He moved like a shadow. The full moon picked up the white glints of his eyes beneath the black mask. That was all that was visible as he jimmied the door and slipped inside.

The house was divided into several rooms, just as he had remembered. He was in the rearmost, the storage room. Here, neatly laid out on greasy steel shelving, was a variety of metal tubing, cogwheels, nuts and bolts in steel bins, reels of electrical wire of various gauges, and many other things of similar nature. The door to the outer rooms was closed, but a yellow oblong of light shone from beneath it. Batman listened at the door. He could hear a radio softly playing jazz, and the scrape of footsteps as a man moved around within.

A few minutes' listening convinced him that only one man was inside. Batman opened the door and stepped into the room.

The man had been working at a small lathe. He looked up abruptly as Batman came through, his hand diving toward a rear pocket. Before he could draw the gun he kept there, Batman was across the room and had taken the weapon out of his hand.

"Not so fast, Marrotti," he said. "You don't want to plug your old friend Batman, do you?"

"Sorry, Batman," Marrotti said. "Didn't know it was you. I went for the rod before looking to see who it was."

"Do you usually shoot first without looking to see who it is?"

"When they come through my storage room after midnight, yes. But you're very welcome here, Batman. Can I get you a drink?"

"Not while I'm on duty," Batman said.

"But this is something special. My uncle, Lou, you remember him, don't you, sent over this bottle of liqueur from the old country. Try a shot with me for old time's sake."

"A sip, no more," Batman said.

Marrotti crossed the room and went to a cupboard. He took out a large long-necked bottle with a florid Italian label on it.

Marrotti was a short man, bull-chested and thick-necked. His head was round and covered in crisp black curls. He had a wide, generous mouth and clever, shifty eyes. He walked with a noticeable limp, a souvenir of the time some years ago when Batman had managed to save him from a gang that had trapped him on a tenement roof near his pigeon coop and shot out his kneecap.

"Good to see you, Batman," Marrotti said. "Whatcha been up to? Haven't seen any newspaper writeups about you in quite a while."

Batman ignored that. "How have you been keeping, Marrotti?"

"Pretty well, Batman, pretty well."

"Is crime still profitable?"

"Aw, come on, you know I don't do that stuff anymore."

"I know that you do," Batman said. "But I'm not here about that. You're not big enough for me to go after. No insult intended, but I need to reserve my time for the really big ones."

"I know that," Marrotti said, "and I respect it."

"I need some information."

"Sure," Marrotti said. "Shoot. Only kidding, I mean, what about?"

Batman took a pouch out of one of the pockets on his utility belt and opened it. He removed the small cannister with which Ilona had tried to gas him earlier and handed it to Marrotti.

Marrotti looked at it and seemed about to ask a question. Then he changed his mind, fished a pair of granny glasses out of a greasy vest pocket, put them on and studied the cannister carefully.

"Where'd you get this?" he asked.

"Never mind. Tell me who made it, and who for. I thought this might have been your handiwork."

Marrotti shook his head. "This is high-class machining. Takes better equipment than I've got to do this. See this beading? You need a zero-null drill press and hoe-line redactor to do that. I don't need that for my line of equipment."

"Can you identify it for me?" Batman asked.

"Maybe. Mind if I cut it apart?"

"Go ahead," Batman said.

Marrotti limped across the room and adjusted the overhead floodlights so that he could get a good look at what he was doing. He set up the casing in a vise, then cut it apart with a diamond-toothed saw. He examined the interior of the two hemispheres, frowning, then looked at them again with a magnifying glass. After studying both carefully he discarded one and turned his attention to the other. He gave a grunt when he found what he wanted.

"Look here, Batman. See this symbol?"

Batman peered through the magnifying glass and made out a tiny V with a crossbar stamped into the metal.

"That's a manufacturing symbol," Marrotti said.

"Do you know whose it is?"

"I've seen it somewhere but I don't remember. But I must have it here somewhere."

Marrotti went to a sagging bookshelf and pulled down a thick book. "Manufacturers' symbols," he explained. He leafed quickly through, his fingers going deftly to the right page.

"Here it is. One of the trademarked symbols of ARDC. That stands for Armadillo Rex Development Corporation. Says here they're based in Ogdensville, Texas. The plant manager and chief stockholder is Rufus 'Red' Murphy."

"Do you know anything about these people?" Batman asked.

"ARDC designs and sells special arms. They specialize in exotics, as they're sometimes called in the trade. They turn out anything from miniature spy stuff to complete missile launch systems."

Marrotti took off his glasses and put them away in a worn case. Then he turned to Batman and said, "What was in this cannister? Some kind of tear gas?"

Batman shook his head. "A gas evidently designed to make a man sleep. Or possibly kill him. I didn't inhale it to find out."

"Very wise."

"Do you know anything about this?"

Marrotti went to his jacket, hanging from a wooden peg on a wall, and fished out a cigarette. He fired up and said, "There's been talk about new development in anti-personnel gases. In some compounds they can put a man out for twenty-four hours without harming him. Change the formula slightly and you kill the man dead. All without telltale odor, mind you. In another formulation, LSD extracts are used to make a hallucinatory gas designed to disorient an enemy."

"Interesting, " Batman said. "Is that of interest to the criminal element?"

"You can bet on it. Can you think of a better way to stage a bank robbery? Get everybody tripping and seeing visions or horrors while you walk away with the loot. But nobody's got any of the stuff yet. Otherwise you'd be hearing more about it."

Batman could testify that someone, at least, had some of that gas. But there was no need to tell Marrotti that.

Bruce Wayne, disguised as Charlie Morrison, was at the Gotham City Municipal Airport at nine o'clock the next morning. He was booked first class to Ogdensville, Texas, with only one brief stop in Atlanta. His two suitcases of equipment made him overweight, but he was able to get them on the same flight. There was no inspection for in-country luggage, but even if an inspector had looked into it, he would have seen cases of industrial samples. Only when they were assembled would they constitute the essential equipment Batman found useful on many of his cases.

Atlanta was bright and steaming. Bruce had time for a coffee in the first-class lounge, and a look at the newspaper. Then it was time to board again. Miraculously, the flight was nearly on time.

The trip passed uneventfully. It was mid-afternoon, Central Time, when the big Boeing 747 put down at Staked Plains Airport serving Ogdensville and Amarillo. A telex sent earlier had alerted Finley Lopez, an investment consultant on energy and defense matters, with his main office in Houston. He was one of the foremost investment consultants in the Southwest, and someone Bruce often worked with in his Morrison persona. Lopez had taken a local flight to Ogdensville and was at the airport to meet him.

"How good to see you, Mr. Morrison!" Finley Lopez was a large man, suave and easy-mannered, his complexion a light olive. He had a narrow black moustache and bright brown eyes with dark pouches under them. A small scar above his left eye was the last reminder of a tough childhood growing up in the barrios of Brownsville.

"You're looking well, Finley. Not letting the señoritas take up all of your time, are you?"

Lopez grinned. His reputation as a lady's man was known from Bayou City, Louisiana, clear west to Albuquerque. "Not quite all, Mr. Morrison. Business comes first. But I could show you one fine old time if you'd let me."

"Good of you to offer," Bruce said, "but I'm afraid I'm here this time on business."

Robert Sheckley

"So let's get it done, then we can paint the town red. Or maybe you'd like a real old-style Texas barbecue at my ranch. My wife Esmeralda has a special way with beef ribs."

"I remember Esmeralda's cooking well," Bruce said. "Please give her my love. But I'm just here for the day. I return to Gotham City tonight."

"Well, tarnation," Lopez said with mock annoyance. "Can't get you to have any fun at all. What can I do for you, Mr. Morrison?"

"I'm interested in the ARDC corporation."

Lopez nodded. "Good solid output with a first-class reputation. Red Murphy's the chief ramrod on that spread, Mr. Morrison. You'd like him. He looks a little like Spencer Tracy, only not so pretty."

"I'd like to meet him. Today."

"Let's find a telephone," Lopez said.

Lopez found a phone in the airport and called. He left the booth shaking his head.

"I don't know what's getting into Murphy," he said. "Must be getting old."

"What's the matter?" Bruce asked.

"I spoke to his personal secretary. She said that Murphy isn't seeing anyone at the moment."

"For how long?"

"She couldn't say. Just that he was very occupied with important matters." Lopez scratched his chin, thinking. "Let me make another call."

Ten minutes later he had further news.

"I called Ben Braxton. I don't think you ever met him, Mr. Morrison. He's chief editor of the main newspaper here, *The Ogdensville Bugle*. I've done him a few favors in my time and he was glad to fill me in on Murphy. It's all public knowledge anyhow, but it saves us from having to dig it out of the newspaper's morgue. It seems that Murphy has been acting oddly for the past several weeks. He has a suite in the factory complex, you know, and he moved in there recently, him and his wife. Her name's Lavinia. She's a fine woman, Mr. Morrison."

"So they're both living in the ARDC factory complex?"

"That's right. And they haven't come out. They talk to family members by telephone from time to time. But they haven't been seeing anyone. Not even their son, Dennis, who was in town recently on his way to South America. He's a fire-fighting specialist and spends most of his time on the road. But Murphy wouldn't even see him. It's very curious."

"Curious indeed," Bruce said. "Well, Finley, let's have some lunch. I'll just have time to catch the evening flight back to Gotham City."

"You're going to come and go just like that? Come on, Mr. Morrison! Why don't you tell me what this is all about."

"It isn't about anything," Bruce said. "I've gotten some information about ARDC and I was considering making a large investment in the company. I thought I'd talk to Murphy, see what I think of him, before tying up capital. But if it can't be done at this time, it'll keep. You got any place good to eat around here?"

"Indeed we do!" Lopez said. "I hope you like barbecue, Mr. Morrison, because one of the finest restaurants in the state is just a few miles outside of town."

The restaurant, Las Angelitas de Tejas, was a beautifully restored building in Spanish colonial style. They ate on the broad terrace, overlooking the formal gardens that the restaurant maintained at great expense. Bruce ate enough of the fiery and savory barbecue to satisfy his host. Bruce's own taste was more for diets high in fiber and nuts, with plenty of salad and vegetables on the side. But he didn't want to insult Lopez's native cuisine.

Lopez drove him back to the airport and saw him aboard the four p.m. flight to Gotham City with a stopover in Kansas City.

When the plane reached Kansas City, Bruce got off and booked a private plane to take him back to Ogdensville. He arrived just after dark. His luggage was still there, in the locker where he had left it.

The ARDC complex occupied several hundred square acres of flat desert close to Ogdensville. It was surrounded by a double barrier of electrified fence. Armed guards patroled the perimeter at all hours.

At night, the place looked uncanny with its guard towers spaced every hundred yards, the entire line of fence brilliantly illuminated by searchlights. It looked like a concentration camp in the American desert.

Bruce Wayne, who had been Charlie Morrison, now became Batman. And Batman was not too impressed.

In his line of work, fighting some of the most ingenious and well-financed criminals the world had ever known, he had on many occasions had to get into places of strong security; places whose owners had gone to considerable expense and ingenuity to make Batmanproof.

ARDC would not be easy, but it was a long way from impossible.

Batman's first attempt was on the north side of the complex. Here, several of the floodlights had gone out; a sign of carelessness that might in itself mean something. Carrying a heavy suitcase of equipment with him, Batman observed the guards' routine for a while. Blending perfectly into the night, and with the gift of total immobility when he so desired, Batman watched for almost two hours.

He concluded that it would be difficult to get through the wire without someone noticing. The guards' paths meshed too well to allow even the ten minutes or so he would need to neutralize the electricity and get through the wire.

He turned his attention to burrowing beneath. Taking a small but powerful mass detector from his suitcase, he took an underground profile of the surrounding land to a depth of a hundred feet.

As he had feared, the ARDC security people had invested in an advanced sensing alarm system, which would detect movements in the earth to a depth of fifty feet. He would have to give up any thought of going under the wire. He would need earthmoving equipment if he wanted to get below the level of the detectors.

He decided that this break-in might not be as easy as he had expected.

He stood in the darkness and thought for a while, a tall, awe-inspiring figure dressed in black from head to toe. Even the little peaked ears of his costume seemed to be standing stiff in concentration.

At last he made up his mind. It was risky, but he had undergone worse.

Billy-Joe Namon and Steve Kingston were on the northeastern quadrant that night. Even in their dark blue guards' uniforms they looked like what they were—out-of-work cowboys filling in the time between rodeos with any work they could find. Guarding the place for Old Man Murphy was not bad work. Murphy was a fair man and he paid a decent wage. The only trouble with the job was, it was boring. So highly evolved were the protective systems that surrounded the factory that no one ever tried to get in. Night after night it was the same: the soft hiss of the desert wind, the occasional howl of a coyote, and nothing else. Ever.

Except for tonight.

Tonight was different. It began with a loud hissing sound that seemed to come from the desert.

"You ever heard anything like that?" Billy-Joe asked.

"Might be a gut-shot bear," Steve said.

"I doubt it. Not this far south."

They listened. The sound increased in intensity. Then a light appeared in the sky in front of them. It pulsed, a bright electric violet, unlike anything either man had ever seen before.

"You know," Billy-Joe said, "I don't like this one little bit."

"What's it up to now?" Steve asked.

The violet light had begun to move, traveling in easy swoops back and forth across the sky, coming closer and closer to the perimeter fence.

"You think we should shoot it down?" Steve asked. He had already cleared his sidearm.

"Don't go gettin' nervous," Billy-Joe said. "Ain't even nothin' to shoot at yet. Let it get a little closer."

They watched as the brilliant violet light advanced toward them. Billy-Joe had picked up his submachine gun. He clicked off the safeties as the violet light came directly overhead.

Then it burst into dazzling light like the simultaneous bursting of a million flashbulbs. At the same time it gave off a deafening noise like a howitzer going off about five feet from them.

Both men fell down, stunned and blinded. They got to their feet quickly, rubbing their eyes and trying to regain sight.

There was a field telephone ringing nearby. It was from the southern quadrant guardpost, several miles away on the other side of the perimeter fence. The guards there had picked up the noise and flash and wanted to know what was going on.

Billy-Joe pulled himself together enough to make a report.

"Cal," he said to the southern quadrant guard, "I hate to tell you this because you're going to call me a liar, but I think we just saw a UFO close up."

"My aunt May saw one of those last year," Cal said. "They are the dangdest things, aren't they?"

"Cal, I'm telling you, that's what we saw near as we can tell."

"Oh, I believe you," Cal said. "But I guess we'd better go on full alert just in case you boys been hittin' the bottle or chewing on devil weed."

Four Jeeps full of armed men roared out of the motor pool. They raced around the inner perimeter, helping out the Jeeps' headlights with handheld searchlights. They came across plenty of tumbleweed but nothing else.

Nothing they were able to spot, that is.

Darkness and silence again. No sounds but the moaning desert wind and the occasional call of a coyote.

No movement on the fenced-in land of the inner perimeter except for the wind, rippling the grass that the ARDC Corporation maintained at so high a cost.

Grass rippling in the dark.

Something flowing across the dark grass.

Something dark, shapeless, large, moving in a zigzag fashion, coming closer and closer to the main buildings.

In the high watchtower, Steve was watching the grass. There was something a little funny about it tonight. But that was the wind, blowing it back and forth in sudden flaws, taking unexpected turns and reversals, until you could almost swear there was someone or something moving through it.

But that was crazy.

Nothing could get through the fence.

"What you looking at?" Billy-Joe remarked beside him.

"Just watching the grass," Steve said.

"Old buddy," Billy-Joe said, "we're paid to look outside the perimeter, not inside. We already know there's nothing inside."

"Nothing except us chickens," Steve said, grinning.

Us chickens. And a very large bat.

Promptly at midnight, the Captain of the ARDC guards, Blaise Connell, a former Texas Ranger, reported to Red Murphy in his suite.

"Everything OK, Mr. Murphy."

"Thank you, Blaise. What was that bright flash a couple of hours ago?"

Although Murphy's suite was deep within the ARDC complex, and had no window to the outer world, Red Murphy had picked up the flash on one of the banks of tv monitors that were the eyes of the perimeter surveillance system.

"Couple of the boys think it was flying saucers," Connell said. "But that's crazy. I really don't know what it was, sir."

Death of the Dreammaster

"Does the perimeter fence show any signs of breaching?"

Connell shook his head. "Integrity intact."

"I guess we won't worry too much about it," Murphy said. "Good night, Blaise."

When his guard captain had departed, Red Murphy went to the sideboard and poured himself a drink. He'd been going to the bottle a little too much recently. He knew that, but he was under heavy stress. The worst of it was having to keep it all to himself. At least he could share it with his bottle, even if that was not such a great idea.

The apartment was furnished plainly in a typical Western motif. Piebald cowhides covered the chairs. The couches and tables were simple but well made. There were two original Remington oil paintings on the wall, the only touch of ostentation in the room. Aside from them, everything was plain and serviceable, even though the suite was larger than usual. Red Murphy was a man who didn't like to feel hemmed in. The Remingtons, with their sense of wide spaces and western subjects, helped him forget the reinforced concrete on all sides.

He held the shotglass up to the light and squinted at it. He had a tough square face, tanned to the color of saddle leather and seamed by many hours in the fierce sun and driving wind. Murphy was short, and so big in the chest and shoulders that he looked almost misshapen. He had done all the oil field jobs—roustabout, gantry walker, puddler, valve wiper. For years his hobby had been riding around the scrub country west of Ogdensville in his battered old land rover. Folks thought he was a touch loco, spending all those hours just aimlessly riding around the desolate land. They thought he was crazy for sure when he put up every cent of his earnings to take out a drilling lease on the old Double "O" Field. It had gone dry ten years before, and even though new deposits had been suspected in the area, not a drop had been taken out of it.

Red Murphy got up the money to hire an oil rig. He surprised everybody by first bulldozing the shack and corrals that had marked the headquarters building of the Double "O" Enterprise. Then he'd sunk his bits into a point not more than ten feet off the center of what had been the living room.

The ensuing guster was a beauty.

He'd found the basin. Just as his studies of the surrounding countryside, carried out during those so-called idle trips in the land rover, had predicted. The oil was there, in sufficient quantity to let him begin to build a fortune that was soon to be legendary even in this country of big men with big bankrolls.

When the bottom dropped out of the oil business in Texas, he anticipated it by almost six months. He got his money out and bought the ailing ARDC corporation.

ARDC had a list of bad debts as long as a polecat's shadow on Sadie Hawkins' Day, as the wits at Bernigan's Saloon and Pool Hall in Ogdensville used to say. Its machinery was out of date and mostly falling apart, and its senior personnel had given up on the company long ago, keeping their jobs for the paychecks, but looking around for something more interesting to switch into.

Against all these liabilities, the company had only two assets: a potentially lucrative assortment of defense contracts, and a team of the country's best weapons systems engineers.

Murphy thought he could parlay those into something interesting. He rebuilt the factory, replaced the worn-out machinery, fired the time-servers and gave wage increases

and incentive bonuses to the ones he kept. When he hired
new men, he hired the best.

Soon, ARDC, under its dynamic new management,
was turning out some of the best weapons systems in the
world. Their small arms division attracted the attention
of the British and French secret services, who were eager
to buy some of the products. And the Department of
Defense was very interested indeed. As were the police
chiefs of America, who saw in ARDC one of their best
hopes in the endless war against crime.

Red Murphy was liked and respected in business
groups all over the country. He was welcome in high circles in Washington. He used to attend Washington's special functions frequently.

But for the past months he had not been seen in his
usual haunts. He had begun staying in the factory suite,
talking to business associates, friends and relatives by
telephone. Only Blaise Connell the security chief saw
him. People wondered about it, but eccentricity is part of
the Texas tradition. As long as a man doesn't hurt people
or walk around naked, he can act as weird as he pleases.
Nobody's going to pay any attention.

Practically nobody.

Murphy finished his drink and quickly poured
another. He held up the shotglass and looked at the room
through its amber transparency. The room looked distorted. Murphy laughed and tossed down half the drink.

Then he heard a sound behind him and stiffened.

There was nothing there but the big double closet
where he stored his hat collection and his golf clubs.

"Somebody in there?" he said aloud.

There was no reply.

Murphy put down the shot glass. He reached to his
back and took out, from beneath his flowing Hawaiian

shirt, a chromed .44 Magnum automatic with rosewood handles. He cocked it and walked toward the closet.

"Come on out," he said. "This is the only time I'll say it."

No reply.

He leveled the big gun and pulled the trigger. Slugs blasted apart the light wooden closet door. A pile of hats tumbled out, some of them ragged from being shot through the headbands.

Murphy cursed softly when he saw what he'd done.

He was even angrier when he saw that he'd put a slug through his Ben Hogan Memorial Classic sets of woods.

"Damnation!" he said.

"Don't worry," a voice said behind him. "You only punctured the bag."

The sparse hair on Murphy's big skull lifted as he heard a voice from where no man could be. A tremor of fear swept over him. He forced himself to turn and wasn't surprised when the automatic was plucked out of his hand.

His second shock came when he faced the owner of the voice. He was looking at a tall man dressed entirely in black and gray. A wide cloak with many points flowed from the man's broad shoulders. The man wore a cowl and a half mask. On top of the cowl-like covering, there were small pointed ears.

"Batman!" Murphy cried, clutching at his chest. The pain had just hit him, the almost-forgotten pain in his chest and neck that he used to get before the triple bypass; the sudden attack brought on by the shock of seeing the legendary figure here, in the midst of his fortifications; the pain brought on by long anxiety and a guilty conscience.

Murphy collapsed suddenly, and wasn't aware that blue-gauntleted arms caught him before he hit the floor.

Murphy's eyes fluttered, then opened wide. "You still here?" he asked.

He was stretched out on the bed. His tie had been loosened and his shoes taken off. The tall figure of Batman stood near the bedside.

"Yes, I'm still here," Batman said. "How are you feeling?"

"Not bad, for a man who didn't expect to open his eyes this side of the Jordon. What'd you do?"

"I gave you an injection of hectomorphinate. It's one of the antidotes I carry in my utility belt. I couldn't be sure, but it seemed that you were having a heart attack."

"And what does this hecto whatever-you-call-it do?"

"It acts on the blood vessel walls, taking them out of the fatal spasms that presage death."

"My doctor never mentioned this stuff to me."

"He will. It will be coming on the market in the fall."

Murphy sat up cautiously. "I guess I don't have to ask who you are. I've heard about you for years, but never thought I'd meet you. I did meet Superman once, at a fund raising for crippled children in Washington. Seemed like a nice fellow."

"Superman's OK," Batman said. "But I didn't come here to discuss superheroes with you."

"I didn't think so. Do you think I can walk all right? No, don't help me. If I can't make it to the liquor cabinet myself, I'm washed up anyway."

He moved in a slightly creaky fashion to the liquor cabinet and poured himself a double shot of bourbon. It steadied him so nicely that he immediately poured another.

"Hitting that stuff a little hard, aren't you?" Batman said.

"So what are you? Murphy said belligerently. "An advanceman for the WCTU or something?"

"Just a concerned bystander," Batman said. "I need an explanation from you, Mr. Murphy."

"About what?"

"This." Batman produced the two halves of the little hemisphere with which llona had tried to gas him.

Murphy examined it. "Yeah, that's our trademark. Where'd you get this?"

"Somebody tried to use it on me."

"So? Is Colt responsible for every revolver that gets used on somebody?"

"That's beside the point," Batman said. "I know you know something about this because other weapons like this have been turning up. They've been traced to your factory."

"You can't prove a thing," Murphy said.

"Maybe I can't," Batman said. "Not yet. But I will."

"Go ahead and try," Murphy said, and put away half the shot, looking up startled when Batman slapped the glass out of his hand.

"What's the big idea?"

"Get hold of yourself, Murphy," Batman said. "You've got quite a reputation in this country. People consider you a brilliant operator and a straight shooter. You've always had a reputation for being forthright, accessible. Now suddenly you're hiding inside your own factory, you've got the place guarded like it was Hitler's hideout, and you're drinking heavily. You've got troubles, Murphy; something's turned your life around, and I want you to tell me about it."

"Why should I?"

"Because you've got to tell somebody, otherwise you'll explode. And why not me? If you can't tell your troubles to a superhero, whom can you tell them to?"

Murphy stared at him, open mouthed.

"And anyhow, Red," Batman said, "maybe I can help. I'd like to try."

Murphy continued to stare at him. Suddenly there were tears in his eyes.

He said, "When I was a kid, I loved the superheroes and wanted more than anything to be like them. Tarzan was the first for me, and then there were a lot after that. You were always special for me, Batman. I liked you because you were more human than most of them. For a while I tried to be like you....Funny, isn't it? You ought to get a good laugh out of this."

"I'm not laughing," Batman said. "And I don't look down on you. Talk to me, Red. Tell me what's going on."

Murphy looked uncertain. "I could get killed for talking to you."

"You're killing yourself by not talking to me."

"I guess that's so," Murphy said. "Yes, I'm in trouble, Batman. It all started about a year ago..."

Murphy told about how, a year ago, when ARDC went public for the first time, Teufel Corporation, a big Swiss-based corporation, made hidden purchases all over the world through designated nominees and acquired a controlling share of ARDC's outstanding stocks. Teufel had taken over ARDC, and they had the right to retire Red Murphy if they so desired. Murphy didn't figure out for a long time how it had happened. It all took place so rapidly that he was shocked and apathetic at a time when all his senses should have been on alert. The new owners never appeared. Operating behind on screen of lawyers, they proposed to allow Murphy to continue running

ARDC. They even promised him a chance to buy back a majority interest in the stock, and so reacquire his own company. But first, for a while, he had to do things their way.

"Several of my people warned me about them," Murphy said. "I should have listened. Especially when they started screwing up the research and production divisions. But I thought that playing along would get me back in control faster. I figured that with their sloppy methods and inadequate quality control they'd fail, you see. I didn't know then what they were really up to."

He reached for the bourbon bottle. Batman pushed it gently out of his reach.

"Might as well give it up now, Red. You can't keep on hiding here forever and drinking. You'll never find a better chance to quit than now."

Murphy looked at Batman and knew that the masked man spoke the truth; you don't get a superhero telling you to quit the booze every day.

Murphy reached out and grabbed the bottle. He threw it against the wall as hard as he could. It made a satisfying sound as it shattered.

Soon after that his telephone rang. Murphy answered it. "Blaise? Yes, I'm fine. Yeah, that was me firing the .44 earlier. And breaking the bottle now. I was having a little celebration. Yeah, sure, all by myself. Me and my bats. The bats in my belfry, I mean. Sure, I'm fine, see you in the morning."

He hung up the phone and said to Batman, "Suppose I make us some coffee. We've got a lot of talking to do, and not much time to do it in."

"What do you mean?" Batman asked.

"The Joint Chiefs are about to sign a contract with ARDC for a new computerized weapons system."

"What's so bad about that?" Batman asked.
"Let's get that coffee and I'll tell you."

In the morning, Red Murphy surprised his staff by announcing that he was going to Lake Sarmatian, the manmade lake that had been created by the recent damming of the North Pecos River. He had his staff pack the new Carlino–Gar Wood monohull, still in its packing case, onto the back of his heavy-duty pickup. The gates opened and Murphy sped through, waving to his guards.

Twenty miles down the road there was a grove of cottonwood trees used by the local high school and bible college for barbecues and song fests. It was deserted now. Murphy negotiated the steep dirt road and pulled out of sight of the highway. He got out and went back, pry bar in hand, to open the packing case.

Batman, who had been secreted within the packing case, had already worked his way out and was sitting under a tarpaulin, reading a plane schedule with a little penlight.

"Hope it wasn't too uncomfortable for you," Murphy said.

"I've been in worse," Batman said. "It was easier than breaking out of your factory again."

"What do you want me to do now?" Murphy asked.

"I'd like to leave you here for a while," Batman said. "I'll drive your truck to the airport alone, and arrange to have someone drive it back here."

"That's fine with me," Murphy said. "Lucky I brought along a newspaper. But why can't I drive you to the airport myself?"

"When I reach the airport," Batman said, "I will have changed clothes and become someone else."

Robert Sheckley

"And you don't want me to know who that someone else is?"

"That's it. Please understand, it's not that I don't trust you. But it should be obvious that there's no sense being an anonymous figure if everyone knows who you are in real life."

"Makes sense," Murphy said.

"Sometimes," Batman said, "the costume changes are more difficult to arrange than solving the case."

"I can imagine," Murphy said. "Here, Batman." He handed the masked man the car keys. "Is there anything else I can do for you?"

"Just a final point or two. You said that the Joint Chiefs are about to sign the contract with ARDC?"

"I got confirmation of that only yesterday. It ought to be signed into law by tonight."

Batman nodded. "I think there's still time to do something. I'm glad you let me have the facsimile plans for your production models. I'll have a chance to study them on the plane to Washington."

"My competition would do a lot to get their hands on those blueprints."

"Don't worry. I'll destroy them when I'm finished with them. Now, these people who took over your company. You really have no idea who is in control of them?"

"None at all. Whoever it is, they seem to have some friends in high places. I've never seen a contract go through so smoothly."

"One more question. Do any of your weapons systems make use of hallucinogens?"

Murphy looked surprised. "How did you know? That's the tightest secret of the century."

"I learned it from a man with green hair," Batman said.

"Come again?"

"Forget I said it. Goodbye, Murphy."

"Good luck, Batman."

"Thanks," Batman said. "I suspect I'm going to need it."

Batman drove another five miles down the highway. No cars passed him in either direction. That was just as well; your average cowboy might become curious if he passed a new red pickup driven by a man over six feet tall dressed as a bat. Not that that was likely. Batman had taken the precaution of spraying the windshield and windows of the pickup with a glare-resistant compound that did not impede vision from inside the vehicle but rendered it opaque from the outside. He had neglected to tell Murphy that the compound washed off with soap and water—an uncustomary lapse, but no doubt Murphy could figure that out for himself.

Batman stopped the pickup on a turnout and quickly changed to the sober and well-tailored suit of Charlie Morrison. He packed up the Batman gear in the folding valise he had brought along for that purpose, and went on to the airport.

Bruce decided not to take a commercial aircraft, since none were scheduled at a suitable hour. He quickly arranged to charter a plane for the trip to Washington. Although he was an experienced pilot, he also hired a pilot. It was simply easier that way.

The Batman gear, the two suitcases of special equipment, and the utility belt fit nicely into the Lear jet he had rented.

He had time for a quick brunch while the pilot fueled up and made out a flight plan. He had a small green salad and a side dish of guacamole, accompanied by plenty of strong black coffee. He had just paid his bill when he remembered a phone call he had to make. He telephoned Commissioner James Gordon in Gotham City and told him briefly where he was going. That was necessary in case anything happened to him. If Robin could be killed, then Batman could be killed, too. But crime fighting had to go on.

Then he went to the Personal Services Booth and arranged for a chauffeur to take Red Murphy's pickup to where he was waiting, reading a newspaper under the cottonwoods. And then it was plane time.

It was early evening when the quick little Lear jet flew into Washington's Reagan airport. The evening lights were on in the city; twinkling little fairy lights belying the skullduggery that went on in the nation's capital.

In the airport, taking a private booth in the first-class lounge's men's room, Bruce dressed again in the Batman outfit. This time he left off the mask and cowl, concealing his costume under a long camel's hair overcoat. He was going to need both of his identities if he hoped to get this job done.

When he emerged, he looked like any well-dressed young man.

The overcoat was loose enough to conceal the bulky utility belt. It was difficult to know in advance exactly which piece of equipment he would need.

He caught a taxi into Washington proper, directing the driver to take him to Old Edward's Chop House on Fifth and Ohio. It was a popular dining place for Washingtonians. It also was just across the street from the Gaudi Building, where, in the General Procurement offices on the fortieth floor, the contracts for ARDC were to be signed.

The Gaudi Building was not a simple glass tower like so much of the recent construction in Washington. It had been done in a florid neo-Baroque style, with pediments and gargoyles and odd curves and unexpected angles. The architect, Nino de Talaveres of Barcelona, the eccentric Spanish mystic who had won the Prix de Rome for architecture two years running, had predicted, accurately, as it turned out, that the Gaudi Building would introduce a new and popular style into the sterile skyline of the nation's capital.

This unique and unexpected building was liked by many.

Batman was not one of them.

Batman's judgment was not aesthetic, however. It was purely functional. He had worked out long ago a system and the necessary equipment to scale glass towers with great speed and sureness. Now, faced with a brand new version of an outmoded architectural schema, he saw that he would have to improvise.

The porous Carrara granite offered unreliable purchase for the quick-release suction cups that he usually relied on.

The laser glasscutters he had used so often to gain entry through the gigantic picture windows would do no good with windows shaped like slits and barred with wrought iron bars.

He sighed. It was hard enough staying up with new technology without having to reinvent ways of scaling ancient buildings.

He could try to get in through one of the entrances, of course. The thought was attractive, but impractical, he decided after giving it a moment's thought. There was an unusual flurry of activity around the building tonight. The streets were full of police SWAT teams. There were also a lot of men lurking around in simple seersucker suits and rep ties with bulges in their jackets. These, Batman knew from previous experience, were apt to be Secret Service men.

Had Murphy talked to the people who had such a hold over him? Had he given Batman away?

Batman thought not. But they might have become curious about Murphy's unusual actions of the night before, firing off his .44 Magnum and then, in the morning, driving out in his pickup. They would have to be extremely obtuse not to relate these discrepancies. Would they have time to do anything about them? He would have to wait and see.

Batman had had a chance to study ARDC's plans on the trip to Washington, concealing them within a newspaper so that the pilot, a cheerful Tennesssean named Cohen, would not get curious.

Bruce Wayne had a fair technical background. He augmented it with a great deal of mathematical and scientific reading.

He was able to supplement his insights now by using his laptop computer, built to his own specifications at high cost, but with the power of a third generation mainframe.

The insights he had gained into the blueprints had been eye-opening, to say the least.

If that contract were signed into law...

He studied the building again. Getting into it was never going to get much easier than it was right now.

Death of the Dreammaster

He finished his meal at the chop house, paid his bill, went to the rest room, and slipped out the back way.

He was in a noisome alley. Yowling cats slunk around overflowing garbage cans. The zebralike combination of strong lights and impenetrable shadows made the perfect milieu for a man on the run—or a bat in flight.

Within the Gaudi building, on the fortieth floor, in a special amphitheater with recessed lighting, the Joint Chiefs were meeting to consider the ARDC contract proposals. Admiral William Fenton was chairman for tonight's session. He was a squarefaced old seadog with iron gray hair and a bulldog mouth. General "Flying Phil" Kowalski, Commandant of the Air Force, sat at his right hand. Kowalski was tall and slim; his baby face, tousled blond hair, and easy laughter belied the fact that he had been an ace during the recent incident in the south Caribbean, piloting his own Thunderclap-class all-weather interceptor and shooting down four Trinidadian jets before it was discovered that the U.S. was not at war with Trinidad. Beside him was General Chuck Rohort of the army, his short, heavily built body displaying the concentrated attentiveness that a really good tank commander needs.

"Well," Admiral Fenton said, "we might as well call this meeting to order. I propose that we waive the reading of the minutes of the last meeting. There are entirely too many important decisions to make tonight without having to rehash any old ones. No objections? Good, let's go on. I believe that General Kowalski has a somewhat unusual request to make."

Flying Phil stood up, grinning pleasantly, twirling his goldleaf encrusted hat in his hands in an awkward motion that he had studied with some care.

"As I understand it, this meeting is to decide the issue of the ARDC contract, docket number 123341-A-2."

"That is correct," Admiral Fenton said. "As you would know if you had attended yesterday's meeting, those of us present weighed the pros and cons of the new ARDC system. Since we will be supplying these weapons to our own troops as well as our allies, I need hardly mention to you the seriousness of this contract."

"I know the weapons are good," said General Rohort, shifting his heavy body in an alert manner. But can ARDC be relied upon to deliver?"

"I think we need have no doubts about that," Fenton said. "But as a final witness, I have taken the liberty of calling in James Nelson, Deputy Director of the CIA."

Fenton gestured and a yeoman opened the door to the outer office.

In walked a tall tan man dressed entirely in shades of tan. Even his fingernails were tan; an extremely light tan, but a tan nevertheless.

Only his teeth were white; his teeth, and the whites of his eyes.

General Kowalski wondered if it meant anything that the first thing he noticed about James Nelson was the whites of his eyes.

"Good evening, gentlemen," Nelson said. "Please excuse my tan. I'm just back from Florida where I have been supervising our counterinsurgency program designed to bring Columbian cocaine dealers in line with current clandestine drug pricing policies."

"Have they been undercutting the government drug-supply programs again?" General Rohort said, a frown on his tanklike face.

"Indeed they have," Nelson said. "The loss of revenue for the government's various clandestine services has been

severe. And of course there is the loss of quality experienced by the end users."

"That foreign stuff doesn't meet FDA regulations,"
Admiral Fenton growled. "There really ought to be a law
against it."

"The President believes in free trade," Nelson said.
"Within limits, of course." He ignored the No Smoking
sign and lit a cigarette. The faint yellow cast of the tan
cigarette contrasted subtly with the faded rose tan of his
lips.

"Well, never mind," Kowalski said. "It's none of our
business what anyone does about drugs. We're here to do
something about this contract. I must say, Nelson, I've had
my doubts about a few of the details."

"Set your mind at rest," Nelson said. "This is one of
the best and most constructive contracts the U.S. government has ever entered into with a company from the private sector. What makes it even nicer is that several of our
foreign allies will also profit from the contract and give
this move a lot of good publicity."

A copy of the contract was taken out and passed
around. The Joint Chiefs peered at it and passed it around.

"Well, gee," Kowalski said. "I'm still unsure."

"Let me reassure you," Nelson said. "The President
himself wants this bill to be signed into law."

"Then why doesn't he tell us so?" Kowalski asked.

"Gentlemen, that is just what he is going to do. The
President is coming here to witness your signatures and
congratulate you on doing your patriotic duty."

"The President? Coming here?" said Chuck Rohort.

"You got it, Chuck," Fenton said.

"Then let me waste no further time," Nelson said.
"Gentlemen, the President!"

He nodded to the yeoman. The yeoman gulped and opened the door. In walked Marshall Seldon, the tall, stooped, gray-haired man with the lopsided grin known in every home around America.

The Joint Chiefs rose so as to crowd around the President. Nelson made them stay back.

The President held up a hand. Soon they heard his familiar tweedy tenor.

"Gentlemen, I have many important matters to attend to. Please sign the treaty, and let us get on with the business of confounding our enemies and comforting our friends."

The Joint Chiefs crowded around, each pushing to be first. They were interrupted by a clear baritone voice as the door opened again, this time without any assistance from the yeoman.

"Before you sign that piece of paper, gentlemen, I'd like a word with you."

They all fell silent. Even important men like generals and admirals were likely to give Batman a chance to speak.

Nelson was an exception to that rule, by virtue of his unique position. It was his duty not to be seduced by other men's words. He knew that Batman did not belong there. He pretended to listen, but all the time his right hand was snaking toward his belt, where a two-shot derringer, disguised as a Hickok belt buckle, awaited his touch.

Batman had had no insurmountable difficulties scaling the Gaudi at first. He hadn't been able to use the means that had gotten him over the ARDC fence. In that instance he had employed a whiz-bang, a simple enough contraption designed to make brilliant flashes of light and strange, unsettling noises, and to do so long enough to allow an attack to be launched from another quarter. The attacker had been Batman himself, climbing up and over the fence, protected from the electrical current by his insulated gloves and boots. For a moment he had blotted out the stars as he came over the fence and down the other side. During that brief time, Billy-Joe and Steve were blinking into the flash of the whiz-bang, blinded and deafened for critical moments necessary for Batman to land safely and secretly on the other side.

No such diversion could be used here. No distraction could be counted on to rivet the attention for the long minutes that would be needed to scale the Gaudi, and nothing in Batman's bag of tricks could propel him to the fortieth floor.

Luckily, there was a brilliant gibbous moon that night. It bathed one face of the building in its cold white light, but left the other faces in darkness. Using spring-driven crampons of his own devising that permitted him to get footholds on granite, the Masked Man swarmed up the dark side of the building. When he reached the fifth floor, where there was a row of gargoyles, an expedient presented itself. The next level of gargoyles was on the tenth floor, and each five floors after that. The Batarang presented a feasible opportunity, tied to a light line on the end of a coiled line. Batman was an expert at throwing the curiously shaped Batarang, similar to a boomerang but infinitely more useful in terms of angles that it could be projected along.

Batman's first cast was a few feet high. He retrieved the Batarang and threw again, cautioning himself not to overdo it—precision was called for, not brute strength.

This time the Batarang flew true and coiled around the neck of a stone devil.

To climb forty stories up a rope is, in its quiet way, a greater feat than many others the world deems more spectacular. Luckily, Batman had along a BatHoist to assist him on vertical assents by rope. The little device, powered by a miniature atomic motor, and operating through a cunning set of gears, was able to pull a man's weight up a rope at a steady four miles an hour.

When Batman gained the fortieth floor, he used a hand-held punch to take out the exterior window fasteners and let himself in. He took care not the drop the window, and refastened the fasteners again from the inside, reversing the hand-held punch and tapping the rivets in with great delicacy. After that, it was easy enough to skulk down the hall and find the main conference room where the Joint Chiefs were meeting.

"What is the meaning of this?" Admiral Fenton said. "I've heard of you, of course, Batman. It is said that you serve some good causes. But if you think your reputation is going to intimidate me, you've got another thing coming."

"I had no such thought," Batman said. "I merely wanted to present a few facts about the ARDC weapons systems with which you are proposing to arm our forces."

"You've got a lot of nerve," Fenton said, "trying to teach us our business. We've checked out those weapons to the hundredth decimal point. They're the best I've ever seen."

"Perhaps," Batman said. "But have you also checked out their computer-supported operating systems?"

"It's a new system," General Rohort said. "Supposed to be the best the mind of man has come up with."

"I'd advise that you look again," Batman said. "I have some documents I think you'll find interesting."

"What are you getting at, Batman?" Fenton said. "You don't expect to stop us, do you?"

The Masked Man did not answer.

"This place is filled with our men," Fenton went on. "You can't hope to delay us from signing for long. And to think you'd try something like this with the President here."

President Marshall Seldon had been standing at the far end of the room throughout this exchange. Now, smiling slightly, he said, "Let him show us his documents. This will be amusing."

Batman pulled his cloak close to him, and, from a pocket deep in its fold, he extracted a wad of computer printouts. They showed complex circuitry and were filled with tiny numbers and Greek letters.

"Gentlemen," Batman said, "please take a look at these."

Kowalski was the first to reach for one. "What are these?"

"Schematics for the main computer circuitry for the ARDC weapons."

Kowalski looked through them, his curly blond hair tumbling boyishly over his forehead. "Yes...yes, it all looks all right so far...Yes, that's a standard Sliger circuit....But what's this, it's tied into a resonator with a provision for switchable mirror reflectivity.... Hell, I see what you mean!"

"What is it?" the other chiefs asked, not being as adept at computer schematics as was the tall, young Air Force general.

Kowalski looked up and his face was grim. "You tell them, Batman."

Batman said, "I believe you've all heard of computer viruses."

"Of course," Fenton said. "They are those specially designed programs that some madmen or malcontents devise to feed into computers and so render them inoperative, sometimes for long periods of time, until a killer program can be devised and introduced to get rid of them again. Sometimes the computer virus program is so deeply ingrained that even the metals of the affected computers must be changed due to imprinting error. But nobody is going to introduce any viruses into these programs, Batman. This is a whole new generation of program and it is virus-resistant except to an as yet undevised new generation of computer viruses."

"That is true," Batman said. "But you miss the point."

"Which is?"

"The software for the ARDC programs is designed to generate its own virus which will first pervert its functioning, then destroy it."

"Create its own viruses?" General Rohort said. "Like tadpoles hatching out of mud?"

Kowalski nodded grimly. "It's there in the specs, general. We just overlooked it—as we were intended to do."

Rohort turned to Kowalski. "You understand these matters, Flying Phil. But I can hardly believe it. Can what the masked man is saying be true?"

"It's true, all right." Kowalski said, a note of iron underlying the lightness of his voice. "That's exactly what it is."

"Gentlemen!" It was the voice of President Seldon, and it brought every man in the room to attention—and the yeoman, too.

"Yes, Mr. President?" said Admiral Fenton.

Death of the Dreammaster

"First of all, I want to thank Batman," the President said, "for having brought this matter to our attention. As a matter of fact we have already corrected the design flaw, Batman, and now there is nothing standing in the way of the Joint Chiefs signing it."

"That document must not be signed," Batman said. "And these men must no longer take their orders from you."

"Why do you say that?" the President asked. "Stop this senseless charade now, Batman, and I think we can arrange a medal for you. How would you like an official position in my cabinet? Presidential Advisor on Superheroes. How does that sound to you?"

"It's fine, Mr. President," Batman said. "Except for one thing." He stepped forward suddenly, walking directly toward the President. Even Nelson of the CIA was caught off guard for a moment. He drew his sidearm quickly, not the beltbuckle derringer but a heavy Browning automatic that he reserved for dire emergencies. But by then Batman had stepped up to the President....

And then, in another step, he had walked through the President.

And the President continued smiling.

The Joint Chiefs stared at Batman, slack-jawed. Nelson stood with the gun at his side, momentarily frozen.

"The trouble is," Batman said, "I don't see how you can do anything, Mr. President. Because you're not the President at all."

"What in God's name is it?" Fenton asked, long-suppressed superstition bringing his voice to a reedy tenor. "A ghost?"

"Not exactly," Batman said. "It's a hologram."

Fenton was trying to understand. "How did you know?"

"Because the same people who produce this," Batman said, jerking a gloved thumb at the still smiling hologram of President Selden, "have also been throwing holograms at other people."

"Who are these people?" Kowalski asked.

"I think," Batman said, "that Deputy Director James Nelson here has the answer to that one."

Nelson looked at him with pure hate.

The image of the President winked out abruptly.

Deputy Director Nelson had come into prominence about six months before, when James Tolliver, respected head of the CIA, had fallen ill to an as yet unidentified virus that even the best specialists had been unable to cure. The disease had taken a great toll on Tolliver's strength and vitality. Bedridden, kept alive on support systems, Tolliver had been forced to turn over the day-to-day running of the agency to his assistant, Nelson.

Nelson was known as an extremely capable man with a grandiose personality. He had a reputation for ruthlessness, and more recently, and almost paranoid self-assurance. He had been known to take the law into his own hands when he thought he knew what to do better than his superiors. This, Tolliver would not tolerate.

There had been rumors that Tolliver had been planning to fire Nelson, or force him into early retirement. But now Tolliver was able to do nothing but lie in an oxygen tent and fight for his life.

Some in Washington circles considered Nelson more than a little dangerous, and more than a little crazy.

Like many another crazy and dangerous man, he had gathered a small circle of CIA operatives around him,

Death of the Dreammaster

whom he had seduced to his view. They were fanatical in their devotion to him. They would follow his every order.

These were the men who came into the meeting room now, moving slowly and alertly, hands near their concealed weapons.

"That contract is going to be signed," Nelson said.

"You must be mad," Admiral Fenton said. "You can't expect us to sign it after all this."

"I can, and you shall. But you needn't bother doing it in person, gentlemen, I have expert forgers who can do a better job on your signatures than you can do yourselves."

"What are you going to do with us?" Rohort asked.

"You will be given heroes' burials," Nelson said. "We have already established that Batman has been having hallucinations. His misadventures with Ilona and others in the New Era Hotel are on film. The public will believe it when we tell them that he massacred all of you before we could get here and kill him. We will release our news shortly before Super Bowl time, when no one will pay it any attention anyhow."

"And what about me?" Batman asked.

Nelson gave a short, unhappy laugh. "I tried my best to keep you out of this, Batman. I decided to work on you. With the aid of my organization I discovered your true identity. You are Charlie Morrison!"

The tall hooded figure stirred slightly. A smile appeared on the masked man's grim lips.

"Is that why you showed those holograms to Charlie Morrison in the New Era Hotel?" Batman asked.

"I was trying to convince you to stay out of this."

"Your sense of psychology," Batman said, "is as flawed as your sense of strategy. How could Batman resist a challenge like that? You set up your own defeat, Nelson."

"But Nelson, why are you doing this?" General Kowalski asked. "Why do you want us to sign the contract? The ARDC weapons system is obviously flawed. And it is vulnerable to infiltration by enemy computers. As soon as our enemies get wind of this, they can attack our weapons system with impunity. When we try to fight back, our own weapons will be programmed to act against us."

"That's what Tolliver said when I showed him the plan," Nelson said. "He couldn't see that its weakness was only the outer layer of a deeper scheme. Yes, our enemies will certainly learn about the deficiencies in our plans and try to make a profit from our weakness. But we also have another program, this one really secret, which turns our enemy's apparent gain into our advantage. It's a built-in computer-killing program that is initiated when they try to crack our codes. When our enemies try to stab us in the back by reprogramming our weapons systems, they'll find they've introduced the seeds of destruction into their own systems."

"Interesting," Batman said. "Ilona was a plant, I suppose?"

"Of course," Nelson said. "We faked her death."

The Joint Chiefs looked at each other in astonishment. Finally, Fenton said, "Nelson, this whole thing's crazy! Your plan is crazy! What if our enemies also discover the scavenger program?"

"We have other secrets!" Nelson cried. His eyes were quite mad. "You don't know how many secrets we have! Only my followers and I are aware of the power we can wield and the influence we can have upon events!"

Batman said, "What I do know is, you and your little clique stand to make a lot of money out of this contract. You are the secret shareholder behind the buyout of ARDC. Isn't that so?"

Nelson shrugged. "It doesn't matter that you know that now. There's nothing you can do about it. This contract is going through."

"Oh, I don't think so," Batman said.

James Nelson looked at the hooded figure and laughed. "Are you going to stop us? According to the standard biographical material, you are vulnerable to human weapons, unlike your hardshelled friend Superman."

"I puncture as easily as other men," Batman said. "But first you have to hit me."

Nelson raised his gun. Batman opened his hand. A flock of tiny motes flew out of the capsule at the end of his little finger which he had managed to puncture while Nelson was ranting. The motes flew toward the light sources. The lights flashed crazily, dimmed, and went black.

"Chinese light-suckers!" Nelson exclaimed. "You *are* clever, Batman. But it will do you no good. Shoot, men!"

The CIA men swung into action. Shots crashed through the room, ricocheting off filing cabinets, screaming off the hardened plastic walls like a swarm of enraged hornets. But Batman was already moving, an inky shadow in the darkened room. The Joint Chiefs, too, had dived under tables and were answering the CIA fire with their own sidearms.

The outcome was never really in doubt, but perhaps it was just as well that James Gordon at the head of platoon of New Gotham's finest burst through the door just then. The hard-bitten boys in blue made short work of the seersuckered government operatives.

"Gordon!" Batman said. "What are you doing here?"

"After you called me, I figured you might need a little backup," Gordon said. "So I brought a platoon of my Gotham City boys for a tour of Washington."

Robert Sheckley

"Don't kill Nelson!" Batman said.

"The rat deserves it," Gordon said, but held his fire.

"I know he does," Batman said. "But he has to take us to wherever he's hidden the President."

Nelson, in handcuffs, led them to a small storage room in the basement. There, haggard and unshaven, they found President Marshall Seldon.

"Batman," Seldon said. "I might have guessed it'd be you."

"I thought I had taken care of you, Batman," Nelson said. "I seem to have been mistaken." The tan man bit down hard and grimaced, then slumped to the floor. The acrid odor of bitter almonds filled the room.

"A cyanide capsule," Batman said. "Poor deluded fool. It's all over now, Mr. President. But I think you're going to need a new deputy director."

Back at his house in Gotham City, Bruce Wayne was reading the newspaper in the drawing room when Alfred came in with a letter on a silver tray. "For you, sir. From Miss Vera."

Bruce opened it and scanned it quickly. "She says she's having a wonderful time," he said, "but misses me and wishes I would join her."

"A very good idea, sir," Alfred said from the door.

Bruce Wayne needed less than a second to consider and make up his mind. "Alfred, pack my tropicals and book me the next flight to Rio."

"Very good, sir!" the butler said, smiling despite his

best efforts to maintain a grave face. "And the Batman Suit, sir?"

"Don't pack it. This time I'm really going to take a vacation."

Bats

HENRY SLESAR

I have always resisted the temptation to keep a diary. In my privileged position, a journal of my experiences would undoubtedly be of incalculable value, both commercial and historic, but it would also reveal secrets entrusted to me by the person to whom I owe my loyalty and my devoted service, to say nothing of my weekly salary. My name is Alfred Pennyworth, and I am Batman's butler.

It was only when that estimable person seemed lost to me (indeed, to the whole world) that I found myself in need of the cathartic that a diary often provides. I had a desperate yearning to share my pain and grief with someone, but my sacred vow of silence regarding Batman's secret identity left me with only one confidante: myself. And on that unhappy evening when I returned from the Pine-Whatney Clinic where Batman was languishing, I inserted a sheet of paper into a rather cranky portable typewriter (a sad reminder of Master Robin's school days) and made the first entry, beginning with an account of my visit to the hospital, an experience still vivid in my mind.

I have just returned from the Clinic, and Commissioner Gordon was kind enough to permit me a glimpse of Batman in his private room, in what he later described to me as his "antiseptic prison." I was impressed with the security arrangements the Commissioner had made to avoid any public disclosure of the fact that the legendary figure was a patient at the institution located in a secluded suburb of Gotham City. I was even more impressed by how zealously he had guarded Batman's concealed identity. Under the circumstances, he could easily have satisfied a long-standing curiosity concerning the face behind the Batmask, but the Commissioner did the honorable thing. The sedated man I saw in that hospital bed with those pitiful guard rails not only wore a hospital gown, he also wore his mask.

I had arrived in a disguise of my own. I came as an emissary of good will, from my employer, the wealthy Bruce Wayne, to offer whatever financial assistance necessary to provide Batman with the best of medical care. The ruse was of my own devising, but I soon learned from the Commissioner that I wasn't the first to extend a helping hand. Hundreds, even thousands of people, stricken by the news of Batman's breakdown, had volunteered their aid. It was a touching tribute from a grateful citizenry, and I felt a bit ashamed that my own offer was merely a subterfuge. Even though Batman's medical expenses were eventually paid by "The Wayne Foundation," Bruce Wayne was actually paying for his own care. Mr. Wayne, you see, is not only my employer and Commissioner Gordon's friend; he is also Batman's everyday identity.

It was during my visit to the Pine-Whatney that I learned the true details of the event that led to Batman's hospitalization. To this point, all my information had come from the lurid accounts in the press, including that ignominious headline that defaced the front page of the Gotham City Post:

BATMAN GOES BATS!

There have been many lies blazoned about Batman. But the shock of those words was heightened by my realization that the announcement may well have been valid. I was only too painfully aware of the troubled condition of Batman's mind ever since the death of Robin. His grief was understandable, of course, and while I am not a qualified psychiatrist, I have read enough in the field to know that his reaction may have been magnified by feelings of guilt. Robin's safety had always been Batman's first priority in all of their adventures, and Robin himself always recognized the perils he faced as Batman's partner in crime-fighting. Nevertheless, Batman may well have blamed himself for the loss of that brave young man.

There could not have been a worse time for Batman to fall into this "slough of despond," to quote Reverend Bunyan. Whether it was an evil conjunction of stars, or because the underworld had been emboldened by Robin's death, Gotham City was undergoing its worst crime wave in decades. The number of profit-motivated felonies, with all of their attendant violence, had risen sharply. A dozen banks had been robbed in a three-week period, two of them on the same day. The city's best and best-guarded jeweler had been plundered of almost ten million dollars worth of gems. Five payroll robberies had succeeded, in plants where the security systems had been vaunted as unassailable. Worst of all, a dozen innocent people had been slain or injured during the commission of these offenses. Despite their audacity, the police seemed helpless to prevent them or to apprehend their perpetrators.

I was privy to the abysmal depth of the law's frustration when Commissioner Gordon came to dine with Mr. Wayne only a few days before his breakdown. As I served their meal, I overheard him express his anxiety in no uncertain terms.

"I've never seen anything like it." he said, savagely attacking his *ris de veau*. "These hoodlums are acting as if there simply isn't any police deterrent in this city. Sometimes," he added gloomily, "I think it may be my fault, that perhaps I should offer the Mayor my resignation."

Mr. Wayne murmured some placating response, but I could see that his mind wasn't really on the conversation.

"There's organization behind it all," Commissioner Gordon said. "But we just can't determine where the leadership is, even though we've rounded up all the usual suspects."

Mr. Wayne smiled thinly at this echo of Captain Renault's line from *Casablanca*. It was the last smile I saw on his face for a very long time.

"What about Federal assistance?" he asked. "Two of the banks that were robbed were Federal institutions."

"I spoke to my friend from the FBI, Randolph Spicer. He offered his aid but he seems as baffled and helpless as I am."

"You've been under a lot of pressure, Commissioner," Mr. Wayne said. "Your wife's long illness, and the problems you've had with your daughter..." (Barbara Gordon was a handful, and Commissioner Gordon would have been even more upset if he knew of her secret life as Batgirl.)

"Yes," the Commissioner sighed, "I haven't been myself lately. And, for that matter, neither has..." He stopped, as if reluctant to complete his thought. Both Mr. Wayne and I reached the same conclusion, but since I was only the butler, I allowed Mr. Wayne to express it.

"Neither has Batman?" he asked lightly.

"Not that I blame the man," Gordon said. "He's obviously still in mourning for poor Robin. And I haven't been upholding my part of our bargain lately. He always relied on me for briefings, and I haven't been in touch with him for weeks...."

Of course, the Commissioner, unaware of Mr. Wayne's other identity, didn't know he was "in touch" with Batman at that very moment. If there was an anticipatory gleam in Mr. Wayne's eyes, I failed to detect it in the candlelight; he merely regarded Commissioner Gordon in solemn contemplation and said nothing.

I recalled that last encounter when I faced the despondent Commissioner again, this time in the cold white confines of the Pine-Whatney Clinic, and heard his pathetic description of Batman as he had been discovered just twenty-four hours before.

"It was in Wellman's department store," he said. "An alarm had sounded, signaling that a robbery was in progress. I personally dispatched a dozen officers to the scene. Somehow, they got to the wrong floor, and the criminals who were ransacking the company safe escaped with half a million dollars in cash receipts.... But this time, despite my respect for this mourning period, I decided to use my hot line to reach Batman. I told him what was happening, and he responded."

"But wasn't it too late?" I ventured. "Since the criminals had already escaped?"

"Batman isn't all brawn and acrobatics, you know. He has a keen intelligence, especially when it comes to crime detection. I hoped he might have some idea about tracking the culprits to their hideout. But—well, you heard what happened."

I confessed to a mistrust of the newspaper count.

"It was accurate enough," Commissioner Gordon said ruefully. "A woman on the Lingerie floor of Wellman's screamed at the sight of the costumed man who was wandering aimlessly down the center aisle. A saleslady approached him, recognizing him as Batman, and asked if he needed help. He looked at her blankly and muttered something incoherent. Then he sat down on the carpet and put his head in his hands and...wept."

I couldn't exhibit my heartbroken reaction without revealing my close connection to the Caped Crusader. Instead, I merely clucked in sympathy and, fighting tears of my own, asked the Commissioner about the current state of Batman's health.

"He's coherent again," Gordon told me. "But he has no recollection of the 'fugue' he suffered. He's refused to remain at the Clinic for treatment, but he *has* agreed to enter intensive therapy at once."

I expressed my gratification, and inquired about the sort of treatment indicated.

"I've asked my own therapist to take him on as a patient," Gordon said, "and she's agreed."

"*She?*" I said, with a raised eyebrow that didn't escape his notice.

"Yes," Gordon said. "*She* happens to be one of the most eminent psychiatrists in Gotham City. Her name is Dr. Letitia Lace, and she was recommended to me by Randolph Spicer of the FBI. She was enormously helpful to me during my wife's serious illness...."

"But what about...well, Batman's actual identity? Won't that be...compromised by psychiatric treatment?"

"Dr. Lace has agreed to respect his desire for anonymity. And even if his identity is...well, spontaneously revealed, you can be sure she'll protect his secret. Professional confidentiality and all that."

This time, I couldn't conceal my look of skepticism, but the Commissioner merely shrugged.

"Who knows, perhaps it would do Batman good to stop playing a dual role. Maybe he's suffering an identity crisis. Perhaps if he was one person, he could lead a more normal life, settle down, marry perhaps..."

"Oh, dear," I said, trying to envision a woman in the Batcave. Batman has always resisted commitment because of his dedication, and it has cost him the love of several remarkable females. But right now, I was worrying about the *new* woman who was about to enter Batman's life.

Of course, I wasn't present when Batman first stretched his magnificent costumed frame on Dr. Lace's leather couch, and began psychoanalysis. This account, however, may be considered quite veracious, since it came to me from Batman himself, whose memory is as formidable as his musculature.

The first thing that must be said about Dr. Letitia Lace was that she failed utterly to inspire confidence in her patients upon their first encounter.

The reason was simple enough. The doctor, in parlance, was a "dish." She made a serious effort to disguise her pulchritude by wearing almost shapeless lead-gray suits, but her curvacious figure insisted upon reshaping them into voluptuous lines. Her hair was as black as a raven's wing, and she wore it severely, but the style only emphasized the striking violet of her eyes and the perfection of her features. The eyes, by the way, were shielded by thick-rimmed spectacles, but Batman's own sharp vision detected the plate glass within the frames.

Batman, however, harbored no prejudices and was willing to give Dr. Lace the benefit of the doubt, even when she began their session with a shocking question.

"Can you tell me why you have no respect for the American legal system?"

"Now wait a minute—" Batman said.

"Taking the law into one's hands is opposed to everything our criminal code stands for. Who gave you the right to be judge and jury over your fellow men?"

"Listen, doctor, there are some things you must not understand—"

"I understand vigilante justice," Dr. Lace said cooly. "And can you deny that it *always* leads to a breakdown of constitutional guarantees? That it denies due process, harms the innocent more than it punishes the guilty, that it leads to anarchy and even fascism?"

Batman started to sit up, indignation stirring, but then he decided he was being deliberately baited and relaxed.

"I happen to agree with you," he said disarmingly. "I don't believe in vigilantism either, Doctor. That's why I was officially deputized by the Commissioner of Police many years ago. I don't judge criminals; I try to apprehend them, and then turn them over to the proper authorities. I'm simply another sort of police officer. Does that answer your question?"

"One doesn't see many police officers in cowls, skin-tight bodysuits, and capes shaped like batwings."

"I have a reason for this costume."

"Would you care to tell me what it is?"

Batman hesitated. It had been a long time since he had experienced the necessity of explaining himself.

"When I first decided to dedicate my life to fighting crime, something happened—something you might call ...symbolic." He smiled wryly. "You know all about symbols, don't you, Doctor?"

"Go on."

"A large black bat flew into the open window of my study.... Do you like bats, Dr. Lace?" She didn't reply. "I don't suppose you do. Most people are terrified by bats; they inspire us with superstitious dread, even though the majority of them are harmless creatures, quite useful in the ecological balance."

"Is that what you wanted to do? Inspire superstitious dread in people?"

"Not 'people,' Doctor. Only criminals."

"Like the ones who killed your parents?"

"I see you know something about my background."

"Not your background," Dr. Lace said. "Your legend, Batman. It is a legend, isn't it?"

"Are you implying that it isn't true?"

Batman was conscious of the psychiatrist's shrug even though he couldn't see her from the couch.

"I think you're determined to create a mythology," she said. "Isn't that apparent from your behavior? My only question is whether the myth was created to help you in your 'career,' or to rationalize away some secret iniquity of your own."

"You think I'm hiding something?" Batman asked, amused.

"I have no idea," Dr. Lace confessed. "That's why we're here, to find out what might be happening beneath the surface of your life. The Batcave of your mind, you might say."

"And just what do you think that might be?"

"If I had to venture a guess, which would be very unprofessional—"

"You're among friends."

"I'd say guilt was a possibility. The guilt you may have felt the night your parents were shot down by that street-corner holdup man.... You didn't do much to save them, did you?"

"I was only a boy. What could I have done?"

"You could have died with them," Dr. Lace said. "But you survived.... This coldblooded killer let you live. Isn't that the truth of the situation?"

Batman frowned.

"Yes," he said. "He heard the sound of a police whistle after the shots were fired, and ran away."

"And what did you feel after it happened? After you realized that both your parents were dead? Pain, rage, the desire for revenge?"

"I felt all those things. That's when I made my vow to conduct my life the way I have. I spent every waking moment from that night on in training my mind, my body—"

"Did it help? Did all the dedication, all the criminals you apprehended, ever make up for the guilt you felt when your parents died?"

"I can't answer that."

"Can you answer this? How well do you remember that night? What you saw, how you acted, how you felt?"

Batman hesitated.

"Not much. Only the darkness. The sudden appearance of the holdup man, demanding my mother's necklace. My father's resistance. The gun going off...twice. That's all I can recall."

"Never mind," Dr. Lace said softly. "All the details are still in your mind, deep within your subconscious. I'll extract them all, through hypnosis. Then we'll see if they have any relevance to this new guilt you're suffering, the one that caused you to weep in public...."

"New guilt?" She didn't reply, but Batman easily read her thoughts. "You mean Robin, of course."

"Yes," Dr. Letitia Lace said. "Robin. What did the press call him?"

"The Boy Wonder," Batman said.

"Yes. The Boy who died fighting for others...unlike the boy who *lived*, while others died...."

Well, it was apparent from Batman's account of this dialogue that he was dealing with a formidable personality, fortunately in a beneficent cause. I must confess that, for the first time since I became Batman's confidante, I realized that he was subject to the same human weaknesses that separate the rest of us from the gods. I should have accepted this sign of his humanity, yet I couldn't escape a sense of disappointment.

I can give an even more detailed report of what occurred at Batman's next session with his psychiatrist, simply because every word was transcribed.

It was Batman's first hypnotherapy. He was concerned about the procedure, of course, worried about what he might reveal about himself (meaning Bruce Wayne) under hypnotic influence. Dr. Lace assured him that hypnotic subjects will not behave in any manner antithetical to their convictions, nor reveal secrets they consider sacred. Batman wisely required her to provide more assurance than that. He asked that she record the entire session on audio tape.

In the following transcript, I have edited out those statements employed to initiate the trance state.

DR. LACE: I want you to go back to the night of your parents death. I know the journey will be painful for you, that you would rather not make it, but you won't be able to help yourself. You will be the boy you were then, and you will be walking home with your parents. Are you on that dark, dark street now? Tell me what you see.

BATMAN: We're talking. We've just seen a movie, and we're talking about it. I liked the movie. They aren't so sure. My mother thought it was too violent.... Wait! There's someone.

DR. LACE: Someone where?

BATMAN: Under the lamppost. He's pretending to be tying a shoelace. I can tell he's waiting for us.

DR. LACE: You're only a boy. How do you know?

BATMAN: I'm not sure. I always seem able to...know things about people. What they're thinking, what they're about to do. Their eyes tell me things. This man's eyes... he's frightened. He's terribly afraid. And that makes me afraid—

DR. LACE: Why?

BATMAN: Frightened people are dangerous.... Gosh, Dad, that man has a gun!

It was at this point that Batman's voice altered on the tape. One could swear it was the voice of a boy not yet in his teens. It was uncanny, and a bit unnerving.

DR. LACE: Go on. What happened then?

BATMAN: He said—it was a stickup! It didn't seem real. It was almost like the movie we had just seen.... He said he'd take the necklace my mother was wearing. He grabbed her, and my father cried out for him to leave her alone.... That was when he fired the gun.... My father fell...and when my mother shouted for the police, the holdup man shot her

too.... I ran to my parents, but I knew that there was nothing I could do, that they were both dead, that they had died
instantly...

DR. LACE: And the holdup man? Where was he?

BATMAN: He ran away. A patrolman heard the shouts...he
blew his whistle and came running.... The rest of that
night...is just a blank.

DR. LACE: Then we must dig even deeper, Batman. You
must travel back even farther into your subconscious....

The tape ran silently for the next five minutes while, I
assume, Dr. Lace attempted to deepen the hypnotic state,
but when she resumed her questioning, Batman was still
unable to recall more than he had already related about
that fateful night.

Even as Batman struggled to regain his emotional sta-
bility, the world outside Dr. Lace's office seemed to go
stark staring mad!

It was the *Gotham City Post* that orchestrated the madness. Its editor, Samuel Leaze, had thirsted for Batman's
blood ever since that irresponsible tabloid had tried to
increase their circulation with scandalous rumors about
Batman. First, there was a story implying that Batman had
deliberately allowed the Catwoman to escape the clutches
of the law because of a romantic involvement. Then they
had printed gossip trash about Batman and Catwoman.
But the final straw was the reprehensible item in a gossip
column implying an illicit relationship between Batman
and Robin. Batman had been outraged, of course, but he
was in no position to sue, as Leaze well knew. It was actually some members of the Batman Fan Club who took
revenge. When the newspaper launched a hot-air balloon
as part of a promotional stunt, they amended the written
message on the balloon to read: THE GOTHAM CITY POST—

NOTHING BUT HOT AIR. The editor, in an attempt to eradicate the offensive words, accidentally set himself adrift in the balloon and had the humiliating experience of being rescued by—Batman himself. The episode only made Samuel Leaze despise Batman all the more.

From the day of Batman's breakdown, not a single issue of the *Gotham City Post* appeared without a front page headline about Batman's "hopeless" condition. With no regard for the truth, the *Post* quoted "informed sources" and "hospital spokesmen" and "intimate associates" who reported that Batman was on the brink of total insanity. Distressed as I was to read these stories, I still had faith that the public would discredit these shameless falsehoods. To some extent, my faith was justified—until the "Batty Batmans" appeared.

I'm sorry to repeat that dreadful vulgar phase, but it became common currency in Gotham City, and not just by the *Post*. All the local media, the national press, the television newscasters employed the phrase. Soon, broadcasters all over the country were dispatching ENG crews to our fair city in the hopes of capturing an exploit of "Batty Batman" for the consumption of their audience. It was surely the darkest period of Batman's life, to say nothing of my own.

The first appearance took place at the opening of a new shopping center in downtown Gotham City, an event hardly significant to the advancement of mankind, but one that attracted several thousand people, lured by the promise of free handouts and free entertainment. Indeed, they assumed that the caped figure that swooped into their midst on what appeared to be genuine Batwire was part of the entertainment program. I was stunned to see the front-page photograph of that moment, and to read the accompanying headline.

BATMAN BECOMES FATMAN!

Indeed, the headline was justified. The caped figure swinging at the end of the wire was definitely on the stout side. Batman's usually skin-tight body suit bulged with excess poundage, including a pot belly worthy of another legendary figure, St. Nicholas. And yet, there was no attempt to conceal the fact that the bulges and belly were false; that they were the result of cotton wool and feather pillows, that it was all someone's idea of a jolly mad masquerade—and that "someone" seemed to be Batman himself!

It was an imposter, of course; I felt absolutely certain of it as I hastily brought the morning paper to the door of Mr. Wayne's bedroom and knocked gingerly. It had to be a prank perpetrated by the promoters of the new shopping center, or perhaps even the *Gotham City Post*. But a terrible shock awaited me. When Mr. Wayne failed to respond to my knock, I let myself into his room and saw his sleeping figure in the bed. The first thing I saw, draped over a chair, was his Batman costume, flagrantly displayed. But what startled me was the sight of wads of cotton wool lying on the rug, along with pillows that had obviously been used as padding. Badly shaken, I left the newspaper and closed the bedroom door behind me.

I said nothing to Mr. Wayne about what I had seen, and he made no comment to me, not even after perusing the morning newspaper. Indeed, he had been virtually incommunicado since starting his therapy with Dr. Lace, almost as if reticence had been prescribed as part of his treatment.

Then, just two days later, another "Batty Batman" appeared.

You may be familiar with the Gotham City Park monument that has been the children's favorite for more than fifty years. In life-size stone carvings, it depicts many of the beloved characters from *Alice's Adventures in Wonderland*. During clement weather, it is always garlanded by climbing, laughing, happy youngsters.

The weather wasn't clement on the Sunday that marked the one hundredth and twenty-fifth anniversary of the Lewis Carroll classic. Despite the persistent drizzle, a small ceremony was held at the base of the *Alice* monument. There was an unexpected celebrity in attendance. Just as the Mayor and a dozen other political luminaries gathered to pay tribute to the author and his creation— and to provide the press with a photo opportunity—Batman appeared triumphantly on the top of the monument, standing on the stone shoulders of Tweedledum and Tweedledee. Only it wasn't the Batman they all knew and loved. Because this caped crusader wore an enormous top hat that carried a price tag in its ribbon, clearly the hat worn by the Mad Hatter of Tea Party fame. Flinging back his cape, he spread out his arms to the crowd and cried out:

"Happy anniversary from...*Hatman*!"

He laughed wildly, the shrill, humorless laughter of the deranged, and as swiftly as he had appeared, disappeared again. With Batman's customary alacrity, he was out of sight before the photographers present could capture anything more than a blurred image of his departure.

The next morning, I stared at that image on the front page of the *Post* and shuddered. My "imposter" theory was weakening. Despite the lack of photographic detail, I recognized the hat. It had been a trophy of one of Batman's most famous exploits, his capture of Jervis Tetch, the "Mad Hatter" who had terrorized Gotham City before Batman ended his career. The hat had been locked away in Batman's private museum, but when I descended to his subterranean lair, there it was, lying carelessly beside the computer bank, still damp with rain....

In all my years of service, I had never ventured either advice or criticism to Batman, but I was sorely tempted now. It was obvious that he had gone from depression to dementia, and I had to discuss the matter with someone, no matter how obliquely.

Commissioner Gordon was the only logical person with which to share my concern. I decided to use the same ruse that gained me entry into Pine-Whatney Clinic, my master's concern for Batman's welfare. However, it was hopeless; the Commissioner was far too busy to take my call, and it was understandable. The criminals of Gotham City, showing their disdain for "Batty Batman," were intensifying their assault on public property. Commissioner Gordon was undoubtedly frantic, especially since the press was exhorting Mayor Paul Donovan to demand his resignation. Indeed, that action seemed inevitable.

Then another thought occurred to me. Perhaps it might be useful if I spoke privately with Batman's psychiatrist, Dr. Lace. Her fees were being paid through Mr. Wayne's bank, and that might provide enough excuse for a conversation.

Rather than risk another rejection by telephone, I made a personal visit to Dr. Lace, making sure that my timing didn't coincide with Batman's own scheduled daily visit. But there was still a surprise awaiting me. As I arrived, I saw someone else leaving Dr. Lace's quiet brownstone, a man whose face was immediately recognizable. It was Mayor Donovan himself.

I was still pondering this odd coincidence when I rang the doorbell. Dr. Lace's nurse-receptionist, a cold-eyed matron with the inappropriate name Mrs. Bonny, looked at me suspiciously. However, when she communicated my message to Dr. Lace, the psychiatrist amiably agreed to see me.

Her first question was why Batman's benefactor, Mr. Wayne, hadn't made this call himself. Wasn't it odd to send a butler in his place?

"Mr. Wayne is indisposed," I explained. "He contracted a virus of some sort." I didn't blink at the lie; there was actually some symbolic truth in it.

"Well, I hope your Mr. Wayne realizes that there is very little I can reveal about this case. It wouldn't be ethical."

"He understands that you have to respect your patient's confidentiality," I said. "But he's very concerned about this new development, these bizarre public appearances.... You *are* aware of your patient's... eccentric behavior?"

"I'm aware of it," the psychiatrist said coolly. "But why do you assume all 'eccentric' behavior is abnormal? Hasn't it occurred to you—that Batman may be merely expressing a long-suppressed sense of humor?"

"I never thought Batman's humor was 'supressed,'" I replied, just as cooly. Then, fearing that I was revealing too much, added quickly: "It seems odd that he would turn prankster so shortly after suffering a tragic loss..."

"The normal mourning period passed some time ago," Dr. Lace said. "This may simply be Batman's way of expressing his renewed zest for life, by playing games with his identity."

"That's exactly what worries me—Mr. Wayne, I mean. The game seems so pointless! Fatman! Hatman! Who knows what's next?"

I was soon to find out. The telephone on Dr. Lace's desk chirped quietly, and she picked it up. Her lovely face darkened as she heard Mrs. Bonny's voice. When she hung up, she said: "I'm afraid you'll have to excuse me. I have a patient in trouble."

It was only after I left Dr. Lace's office that I learned that patient was Batman himself. Fortunately, I passed a blaring car radio on the street, and heard the news bulletin. Batman had been spotted perched on a thirty-story ledge of Gotham City Towers, and police and fire brigades had been dispatched with ladders and nets in case of a suicide attempt.

I was horrified, of course. Batman was frequently referred to as a superhero, and many myths circulated about his superhuman powers. Whatever supreme qualities he possessed, he had earned by rigorous training of his body and mind. He had already demonstrated that that mind was all too vulnerable, but so was his body. I sped to the site of Gotham City Towers.

Speed was impossible, however. Every street within a twenty-block radius of the skyscraper was clotted with people and vehicles. It was an irresistible attraction: not just a potential jumper, but a jumper who was surely the most famous individual in Gotham City. Perhaps now they would learn if their "superhero," like Superman, could fly; or perhaps their thirst for gore would be satisfied by the sight of Batman's crushed and bleeding body. As you can see, I entertained the most morbid thoughts as I finally came within viewing distance of Gotham City Towers. There, as promised, was Batman, sitting nonchalantly on the ledge, holding a white object in his blue-gauntleted hand.

I didn't know what the object was until Batman, apparently satisfied with the size of his audience, got to his feet and lifted it to his lips. Then his voice boomed out through the bullhorn, chilling me to the very marrow.

"Ladies and gentlemen! Introducing... *Splatman!*"

I knew what was going to happen next, but my mind refused to believe it. Batman stood on his toes, fanned out his batwing cape and dove gracefully into the air. For a single breathtaking moment he was poised in midair, almost as if he really could fly like the nocturnal creature he emulated—but gravity won the contest. A collective scream of horror and dismay rose from the crowd as Batman plunged toward them from that great height. The police and fire squads, their rescue equipment still aboard their respective vehicles, looked on helplessly. As for myself, I could only close my eyes and pray for my master's immortal soul.

Suddenly, time seemed to stop!

I didn't realize what had happened until another astonished cry from the spectators caused me to open my eyes and see Batman suspended above the ground as if caught by a stop-motion camera. His precipitous flight to oblivion had been halted abruptly. The almost invisible batwire tied to his leg had stopped him less than six feet from the pavement; a man of lesser strength would have had that leg torn from its socket by the sudden impact. Batman merely laughed at the "success" of his practical joke, and leaped lightly to the ground. Then, with a farewell wave to the stunned crowd, he hurried to the waiting batmobile and was soon tearing down the street, his wild laughter fading with the roar of the engine.

There was a videotape of the event on the six o'clock news that night, and the facetious commentary by the newscasters indicated that they shared the same opinion as the rest of the world: Batman was certifiable.

It wasn't the only item on the telecast. There was also a related story on the upsurge in crime in Gotham City, and a taped interview with Mayor Donovan, who stated flatly that he still had complete confidence in Commissioner Gordon; there would be no request for his resignation. Even though I was relieved for the Commissioner's sake, there was still something about the development that troubled me.

That night, I decided that I would risk my entire relationship with Batman by breaking a sacred rule. I was going to ask Mr. Wayne a direct question about the situation.

I couldn't sleep that night. I was sure sleep would never come until I had unburdened myself. I tossed aside the bedclothes, slipped on a robe, and went to Mr. Wayne's door. I didn't bother to knock; I simply walked into the room. It was in darkness, illuminated only by the pale moonlight that fell across his sleeping figure. He stirred slightly as I approached, and for a moment, I almost lost my nerve. Then I spoke softly.

"Mr. Wayne?"

There was no answer, but my determination was so great I decided to waken him at all costs. I touched his shoulder lightly and realized...*I wasn't touching flesh!*

Swiftly, I drew back the covers and saw that I had been deceived by a cleverly constructed dummy, an artificial man so lifelike that it even contained a breathing mechanism. Then I recalled the time when Batman, threatened with disclosure of his dual identity, had created a "Bruce Wayne" robot to take his place while Batman performed his deeds. Now, Mr. Wayne was using the dummy to fool me, the one person in the world entrusted with his most important secret! I was so baffled that I spoke the word aloud to the darkness:

"*Why?*"

Of course, madness was the Great Explainer of all mysteries, but the least satisfying. Even madness has method in it, and what lunatic reasoning could Batman have for this deception of his loyal servant? Irrational as it sounds, I felt a tinge of anger, and that emboldened me to make still another clandestine trip to the cave beneath Wayne Manor.

I detected nothing out of the ordinary—if "ordinary" can describe the Batcave, a combination of computer room, laboratory, museum, and central headquarters. I understood enough of Batman's methods to know that his starting point is often at his liquid-cooled Cray computer console. Its workings were a mystery, but on one occasion Batman, in another location, had needed some stored data in a hurry, and had instructed me in the technique of "booting" the device. I did so now, and I was in luck. There was a program still in memory, and it asked:

Do you wish to see list again?

I hesitated, then punched the Return key. There on the screen, appeared the following:

```
PENTOTHYL DIAZINE
CHLOROPAM E.
ALPRAPROXIDE
TRITOPHENOZENE
```

I was unfamiliar with the names, but they sounded like pharmaceuticals, perhaps prescribed by Dr. Lace? Surely Batman couldn't take them *all*, although that might explain his erratic behavior. I had little time for speculation, because I heard the distinct whine of the Batcave elevator and realized that Batman was coming down!

I confess to a moment of sheer panic. Batman never denied me free access to the Batcave, but I would be hard pressed to explain why I was tampering with his computer. I decided to hide. The first place of concealment that met my eye: the back seat of the Batmobile.

It was not the most fortuitous choice because Batman went straight to the Batmobile and climbed into the driver's seat. A touch on the dashboard, and the camouflaged door of the Batcave opened, the Batmobile engine growled, and with a burst of speed that made my ears ring, we roared off into the night

You can imagine the trepidation I felt, clad in robe and pajamas, at the mercy of a man who was almost certainly mentally unsound. After the department store break down, the emergence of Fatman, Batman, and Splatman, I could no longer deny that "Batty Batman" was the correct appellation for the former superhero of Gotham City. Who knew what lunatic visions were driving him now, or me, for that matter?

The ride lasted no more than twenty minutes, but it seemed an eternity until the powerful vehicle slowed to a purring halt and grew silent. It was only when Batman left the Batmobile that I ventured to steal a glance at my surroundings. We were in the suburbs, in a parking lot behind a looming square structure with only one or two lighted windows.

Finally, I made out a sign that read:

PINE-WHATNEY CLINIC
Physician Parking Only
Violators will be prosecuted

That sign was innocuous beside the one I discerned on the tall wire fence surrounding the building.

WARNING!
ELECTRIFIED FENCE
DO NOT TOUCH

Then, as if once again demonstrating the loss of his reasoning powers, I saw that Batman was preparing to scale that very fence!

As I watched in horrified fascination, he removed an instrument from his belt that appeared to be a small snub-nosed revolver. He aimed it at the roof of the building and fired a tiny grappling hook attached to a length of batwire. It draped right across that electrified fence, evoking a shower of sparks, but Batman began his climb just the same.

To my great relief, nothing happened. It took me a moment to realize that Batman's rubberized boots and gloves were acting as insulation.

Then Batman disappeared into the darkness above the roof of the Clinic, and I was left alone to ponder the mystery.

Why did Batman return to the Pine-Whatney, the clinic he had once called "that antiseptic prison?" Was there some sub-conscious desire to seek help for his pathetic mental state? Why was he using stealth? Most of all, was there any rational explanation for his behavior?

I decided that my best course of action was to leave the Batmobile and make my way back home. It was probably the worst decision of my life. When I unfolded my frame from the back seat, a space never intended for passengers of my size, I lost my balance and fell forward toward the dashboard. I reached out to steady myself and my hand slammed into the Batmobile horn!

That sound, in the stillness of the night, was as penetrating as the wail of an air-raid siren and caused as much alarm among the residents of the building. I heard shouts that rose to a chorus so cacophonous that I felt sure it came from the throats of the inmates. Then some of the voices became discernible, and what they were saying was alarming indeed.

"We got him! We got Batman!"

I didn't know *who* was celebrating this victory; I hoped it was merely some hospital authority, but there was something distinctively malevolent about the tone. When I saw the two white-coated figures emerging from a back door, my instincts sent me back to my hiding place in the rear of the Batmobile.

Once again, I found myself an involuntary passenger. The two men chortled over finding the Batmobile, but their delight was tempered when they discovered they couldn't start the motor. No one but Batman could, of course; its ignition would respond only to the palmprint of Batman at the wheel. But that didn't prevent them from pushing the vehicle down a ramp and into a garage beneath the hospital. Then they took the stairway to the upper floor, leaving me to my anxiety and indecision.

My indecision didn't last long. I couldn't leave under the circumstances; I simply had to know what had become of Batman. I tried to tell myself that he was in compassionate custody; that this was a hospital, a place of healing, and the people who "got" him had acted out of humanitarian motives. Still, I couldn't shake a feeling of dread. I left the Batmobile and followed the route of the two attendants to the upper floor.

I climbed eight flights in all, pausing at each landing to open the door barely a crack, looking for a scene of activity.

It was on the topmost floor, when I was almost entirely breathless from fatigue and apprehension, that I heard the raised voices. I entered a dimly lit corridor and made my way to the source of the sound. It was apparently some kind of medical conference room, and judging from the medley I heard, there were at least a dozen men in heated discussion. The thought of eavesdropping was frightening, but, as my old grandfather used to say, in for a penny, in for a pound. I put my ears to the white door and listened.

"You're sure he can't use any of his tricks on us?" a grating voice asked. "He's smarter than a dozen foxes, you know."

"Don't worry about it," another man replied. "We've got him in our camisole. He's helpless as a baby."

It took me a moment to deduce that a "camisole" was what they used to call a "straitjacket."

"All right, then," the first man said. "Bring him in and let's find out how much he knows."

There was the sound of half a dozen chairs being scraped back on a hard wooden floor, and then an excited murmur that must have been produced by Batman's entry. I could no longer resist the opportunity of peering into that room. With agonizing slowness, I turned the knob and opened the door a fraction of an inch, enough to catch sight of my poor master strapped into a white restraining garment, being unceremoniously shoved to the head of a long conference table around which sat what appeared to be a strange convocation of doctors in their hospital whites and patients in their robes and pajamas.

"Go on, Batman," the grating voice said, its owner not in my line of sight. "Tell us how you got here."

"Maybe he missed the place," another voice said, and there was a rumble of unpleasant laughter.

"I didn't want to miss this meeting," Batman said, in a clear, steady voice. "There hasn't been a conference like this since Appalachin."

The reference meant nothing to me, but it caused a stir among the seated figures.

"We all know you've got bats in that belfry of yours, Batman," another voice said. "This is a hospital, remember? We're doctors."

"And patients, I see," Batman said dryly, confirming my own suspicion. "Do you let the inmates run this asylum, too?"

"Why are we listening to this maniac?" someone else said. "Let's give him a healthy dose of Alpaproxide and throw him into a rubber room."

"No," the grating voice said loudly. "Let's here what he has to say. Go on, Batman. What's all this crap about Appalachin? That's in the mountains, ain't it?

Strange grammar for a physician, I thought.

"Yes," Batman said. "It's in the Catskills. Back in 1957, it was where the biggest crime boss meeting in history was held. Also the most embarrassing, since it was broken up by the police."

"And is that what you think you're doing, Batman?"

I gasped at this implication.

"I knew this conference was going to take place because I overheard your boss making the arrangements. Where is the Big Boss, anyway?"

I didn't expect them to answer Batman's bold challenge, but someone did. Astonishingly, the voice was female. Even more incredible, it was a voice I recognized!

"I'm right here," Dr. Lace said composedly. "But I can hardly believe you 'overheard' anything, Batman, since you were well under the influence of a hypnotic drug at the time."

Batman's smile was wide beneath his mask.

"Sorry, doctor. Whichever delightful concoction you introduced into my system had no effect whatsoever. You see, I made sure I was immunized against all your hypnotics some time ago. At the beginning of your treatment, as a matter of fact."

"That's impossible!"

"The nice thing about Alpaproxide and Chloropram and the rest of those drugs—they can all be nullified by one compound. Of course, I had to be my own guinea pig before I could offer the same remedy to your other patients—like Commissioner Gordon, and Randolph Spicer of the FBI, and of course, your latest victim, Mayor Donovan."

"Hey, what is this?" The grating voice was harsher than ever. "What's going on here, Doc? I thought you said Batman was completely under control?"

"He was!" Dr. Lace said, and I detected a nervous quaver in her voice. "You know what he's been doing, acting like a complete lunatic, just as I ordered . . ."

Batman laughed, without a hint of nervousness.

"I enjoyed those little charades you devised for me, Doctor. It was fun carrying out your 'hypnotic' suggestions. Almost as much fun as becoming your patient in the first place."

"Wait a minute!" one of the others cried. "Are you kidding us? You *didn't* have a nervous breakdown?"

"Sorry to disappoint you," Batman said. "I simply thought it was the best way to find out if what I suspected was true—that Commissioner Gordon and others were being strangely influenced *not* to do their jobs. I've known Gordon a long time, and he never gave so many wrong orders, or followed such wrong leads, or reacted so wimpishly to a crime wave. I knew there was something wrong with his attitude, and I began to wonder if that 'attitude' wasn't being formed by somebody else."

"He is lying!" Dr. Lace said defensively. "The man was an emotional wreck when he came to me."

"Actually, you *did* do me good," Batman said with a grin. "You took my mind off my problems, Doctor. You gave me something to look forward to—like seeing all these illustrious gang bosses locked up in Gotham City jail."

"I've heard enough!" the harsh voice exploded. For the first time, I saw its owner, a huge man with barrel chest and hands like two sides of beef. I recognized Tough Teddy Thomas, once the most notorious crime figures in the country, long believed to be part of the asphalt in the Gotham City thruway. "This guy made a jackass out of you, Doc! He was the one playing games, not you! Only I'm making sure the game is over—"

To my horror, he drew a revolver from a shoulder holster, aimed it point blank at Batman, and fired! The force of the bullet sent Batman flying back against the wall of the conference room, and then limp as a rag doll, he slid to the ground and rolled over on his face.

Before my very eyes, Batman had been executed.

The stunning event electrified the assembly. Suddenly, chairs were pushed back and overthrown. The air was thick with cries and imprecations, and then there was a mad rush for the exit. The doors of the conference room were slammed open so precipitously that I was momentarily concealed behind them. Even when I could no longer remain hidden, my presence went completely unnoticed by the mobsters. Then I realized the reason. I was dressed just like most of the hoodlums posing as hospital patients, in robe and pajamas. They assumed I was one of them!

When the room was emptied, I hurried to Batman's side, certain that I could do no more than pay my last respects. I was already in tears, deeply regretting that I could never tell the fallen hero how sorry I was not to have trusted him from the beginning, not to have understood the elaborate game he had been playing to defeat this terrible criminal conspiracy. It was painful to realize that all his valiant effort, his willingness to humiliate himself for the greater good, was all in vain, that the villains had escaped leaving Batman to History.

Then I heard the sirens, and realized that Batman had foreseen this possibility, that he had arranged for police action before his arrival—but would they be in time?

"Don't worry, Alfred," Batman said. "I've wired all the exit doors shut with Batwire. The only way out of this building is through the garage, and they'll run into quite a number of squad cars there."

I could only gape at Batman as he rose to his feet and began to work his way out of the camisole.

"I've heard Houdini could do this in four minutes," he said lightly. "Let's see if I can beat his record."

I must record that he did not. Batman was free of his restraint in four minutes and fifteen seconds. The cloth garment hit the ground with a metallic thud.

"It's a bullet-proof shield," Batman explained. "I slipped it into a camisole before I allowed myself to be captured. Just to be on the safe side."

"You *wanted* to be caught?" I gasped.

"I thought it was the best way to get a confession from Dr. Lace." He removed the tiny tape recorder attached to his belt, and smiled. "Now I have it."

I must have collapsed suddenly, because the next minute was lost to my memory. I found myself in a chair, with Batman administering to me with a glass of water.

"I'm sorry," I said. "The truth is, I thought it was entirely my fault that you were captured."

Henry Slesar

"I'm the one who has to apologize to you, Alfred," he said. "I simply couldn't confide in you or anyone else about what I was doing; I couldn't afford to ruse the slightest suspicion about the state of my mental health."

"Then—it was all a ruse? From the beginning?"

"Only a game," Batman smiled. "There was definitely a method in my 'madness.'"

"Yes, sir," I said. "I understand perfectly. And I'm sure everyone in Gotham City will deeply appreciate the sacrifices you made."

"However," Batman said amiably, "no matter what the news media say about all this, don't be surprised if some people persist in believing that I really *am* 'bats.'"

Of course, it was the truth. It's human nature, I suppose, to believe the worst of others. To this day, there are people who think Batman is some schizophrenic with delusions of grandeur. There are others who think Batman is only a figment of someone's fevered imagination. Batman doesn't mind. He's willing to let the criminals of this world continue to live in fool's paradise, until that dark night when they see the black shadow of batwings against the circle of the yellow moon.

Subway Jack

A BATMAN ADVENTURE

JOE R. LANSDALE

OLD GOTHAM CITY CEMETERY (early October)

The moon...

The cemetery was at the top of the hill and dead center of the hill was the grave. It was marked by a stone cross covered in dark mold and twisting vines. There were other graves, of course, and all of them in a state of equal disrepair, but this was the one Jack Barrett wanted.

He climbed to the top of the hill and leaned on his shovel with one hand and held his flash with the other. The beam played across the stone marker but revealed little. Age and mold and vines had taken care of the writing there. Still, Jack had researched enough to know this was the spot.

He turned off the flash, put it in his coat pocket, and looked around. The hill the grave was on was high enough that it stood above the stone walls of the cemetery and afforded a look at the city; the city that had grown up around it over the years and now blinked its neon eyes over this pile of dirt and stone and bones.

Subway Jack

Jack could hear the cars roaring along the city streets, and he thought he could hear the rumble of the subway nearby. To the left of the hill was a great, brittle-looking oak, and he looked up through the branches to watch the moon coasting through the sky behind a veil of clouds. A cool wind blew through the cemetery, rattled the limbs of the tree, ruffled Jack's hair, and blew leaves before it.

Jack took a deep breath, put the shovel to the dirt and began to dig. The sound of the wind, the cars, and the subway died for Jack, and all he heard was the whistle of the shovel sliding into moist earth.

He dug until he came to a cracked stone slab about which were wrapped some rusty chains held fast by a corroded padlock. He put the shovel to the chains, and they snapped as easily as if they had been twine. He worked the point of the shovel into a crack in the slab and lifted out huge chunks until he revealed a short row of dark, narrow steps.

He put the shovel aside and took out his flashlight and went down the slick steps and into the tight, dank tomb. He played the light on a rise of stone covered in dust with a collapsed skull on one end of it and a small, rectangular, metal box on the other. There were a few fragments that might have been bones lying about the stone platform.

He went over and took hold of the box. In spite of the rust that covered it, it felt firm and heavy. He took it gently and felt and heard something move inside. He put the box in his huge, coat pocket and climbed out of the tomb.

He put the flash in his other coat pocket, and then grabbed the top of the cemetery wall and pulled himself over. He scrambled down the narrow, gravel path that led through a clutch of brush and trees and delivered him to the sidewalk. He walked along until the sounds of the city filled his ears and the lights filled his eyes.

Joe R. Lansdale

He walked on faster, his hand in his coat pocket, caressing the box there as gently as he might a woman's thigh.

JAMES W. GORDON, Police Commissioner (mid-October)

It was only natural that the whole bad business would blow into Gotham City like an October wind with ice on its tail, and I guess you could say it was only natural a dark-minded guy with dark-minded plans would take to the subway the way he did; take to it and do what he did.

So this cold wind blew into Gotham and women started dying—bag ladies, those who hugged the underground for warmth and scrounged or begged for the things they needed.

As if things weren't bad enough for them, along came this guy with a plan and a blade he knew how to use. He cut up women so they didn't look like women anymore; didn't look like much of anything human anymore. Then when he finished with them, he dipped his fingers in their blood and wrote on the subway walls: COMPLIMENTS OF SUBWAY JACK, then the number of the victim.

When he wrote Number 3, I got a firsthand look at his business. I was home in bed when the phone jangled me out of the blankets and into the kitchen to talk on the extension there. A beat cop named LoBrutto said, "Detective Mertz told me to call. Said you wanted to know if there was another one. Said you wanted to check things firsthand."

"Send a car," I said.

I had some instant coffee, then the black and white came and drove me over there. The subway entrance was marked off and there were a few people milling around and a lot of uniforms trying to turn them back. A couple of good detectives, Mertz and Crider, were waiting out front.

Subway Jack

Mertz took me by the elbow and we went down the subway steps and walked along for a ways, and I could smell the vomit and urine smells that were always there, and something else too.

Blood.

When we got to the body it was covered by a yellow tarp and was lying against the subway wall.

"We got photographs and everything," Mertz said. "Not a thing you can mess up if you want to take a look. I've had all I want."

I went over and pulled back the tarp and held my breath. It's bad enough seeing this kind of thing in photographs or in the morgue, but to see it on cold concrete, the blood still drying, the stench of death in the air, well, it gets you, gives you the willies, and I don't care if you've seen death a thousand times. It gets to you if you're normal.

Then too, I'd never seen death quite like this; never seen this kind of violence done to a human being. Maybe someone run through some kind of machinery could be expected to look this bad, but.... well, you get the picture.

"All the king's horses and all the king's men...." Crider said. He wasn't looking at the body. He had his back to it. Mertz was over by a concrete support smoking a cigarette and looking out at the subway tracks.

The coffee moved around in my stomach and turned sour and rose up, but I fought it down. I've had some experience.

I got down on one knee just outside the circle of drying blood and looked the body over, trying to be as cool and objective about it as I could. When I was through with that I looked up and took a breath and read what was written in blood on the subway wall: COMPLIMENTS OF SUBWAY JACK, NUMBER 3.

Crider glanced over his shoulder at me and said, "Shame he didn't put his address there, huh?"

I pulled the tarp over the body and got a cigar out of my coat pocket, and when I lit it with my lighter I saw my hands were shaking. I got a good snootful of smoke to dilute the smell of blood and walked over to where I could look down at the tracks with Mertz. Crider joined us. He got out his pipe and lit up. We stood there smoking for a while, then I said, "Don't guess anyone saw this happen?"

"Just like the others," Crider said. "Wasn't that many people around to see anything, but there was some. Seems like they'd have at least heard a scream. Guy can't do what this guy's doing without taking some time. You'd think someone would walk up on him."

"Might be best they didn't," I said.

"Yeah, but you'd think so," Crider said. "Hell, it isn't even that dark over there, a little shadowy maybe, but not that dark. Wasn't·like he did this in hiding. Guy must move like a rocket and be made of smoke."

"Any idea who the victim is?" I said.

"Bag lady probably," Mertz said. "But who can tell looking? A scrounger found the body. We've run him in for vagrancy and petty theft coupla times in the past. Name's Bud Vincent. Says he was walking along and found a shopping cart full of stuff, and he admits he was going to steal it, but he hadn't pushed it far when he came on the body. He called it in then, and I guess a guy like this calling in just shows how bad it is. These people don't usually want anything to do with us, not in any kind of way. In their book we're the bad guys."

"Until this fella showed up," Crider said. "He sort of put bad into perspective."

"You believe this Bud Vincent?" I said.

"Yeah, we believe him," Mertz said.

I didn't go home then. I had a black and white take me to my office. I went in and sat behind my desk in the dark, looked at the hot-line phone on the left of my desk. Looked at it a long time.

The files on the ripper case were locked in my desk drawer; I got my keys and unlocked it and got the files out. I spread the files in front of me and turned on my desk lamp. What I had there was on the first two victims, of course, but I assumed when the information on the third victim was put together, it would say pretty much what was said here about the first two. That the victim was a woman, a street person, that she had been cut to pieces with a sharp instrument and that the killer was very strong. Lastly, clues to the killer's identity would be minimal to none. So far, all we had was a little clay that we had found at the site of the first murder, maybe off the killer's shoes, and maybe not. It could have been from a passerby, and it wasn't really that much help anyway. It was a fairly common kind of clay.

I closed up the file and turned off the light and sat looking at the hot-line, thinking that this Subway Jack stuff was stranger than usual. I could feel it in my bones like some kind of cancer, and when you got into the territory of the strange, you got into Batman's territory.

I guess I didn't call because of a kind of pride. There had been serial murders before, and there would be again. The department had solved most of them, and sometimes they had just stopped. Maybe the killer moved on, maybe he or she died—but women were dying and that had to stop, and if anyone could stop it, Batman could. All I had to do was reach over and pick up the phone and it would ring, and without bothering to answer, he would come.

Joe R. Lansdale

BRUCE WAYNE (Batman)

The bullet.

It tumbled.

It shone in the street light like a silver rocket out of control.

The bullet. The first of two.

Bruce tried to freeze it with his mind and succeeded. It stopped tumbling. It froze in midair. But he couldn't hold it. It began to push at his will and move again, and this time, no matter how hard he willed it back, it tumbled onward.

It was going to happen again.

He was just a boy and moments before he had been happy, but now the bullet would end all that. Lord have mercy, it was going to happen again.

He and his parents had come out of a revival movie theater where they had seen The Mark of Zorro, and around the corner of the theater, waiting in the dark with a gun and no patience, was a thug who cut short their talk and laughter and sent Zorro from their heads with a demand for money.

But before his parent's could comply, the thug got nervous and pulled the trigger and the bullet leapt out.

The bullet.

It tumbled.

Bruce was amazed he could see the bullet. It was very clear; slow motion. He was also amazed that this time he had been able to stop it, but his will was not strong enough to maintain the situation. The bullet started to move again. Slowly forward, and now no matter how hard he willed it to stop, it kept straight on toward his mother.

His father stepped in front of her and took it and went down and didn't move, then his mother screamed and the thug fired again and the bullet split her pearl necklace and the pearls went in all directions and his mother fell across the body of his father.

Bruce looked up, and discovered he was in a balcony seat, like the one in the theater where they had watched *The Mark of Zorro*. He was watching the murder of his parents play out in the street below. He could see them lying dead and he could see himself standing there, stunned. The would-be robber panicked, turned, and fled down the street and was swallowed up by darkness like a fish sliding down the throat of a whale.

Bruce realized there was someone in the balcony with him. Someone breathing hotly against his neck, leaning forward to put a heavy arm across his shoulders. Then a voice that seemed to come from a great distance through a pipe said, "You are mine, and you will become me... I am your true father... and you are my son."

Cheeks wet with tears, Bruce whirled and saw the speaker had tall, leathery ears and a face full of long, sharp teeth. The arm around his shoulders moved away and it was attached to a dark serrated wing. The thing's fingers were tipped with great claws.

It was an enormous man-bat.

It beat its wings, rose from the balcony and into the upper shadows as Bruce sat up in bed and screamed. The shadows in the balcony were pushed aside by the softer shadows of his bedroom, they in turn split by a golden wedge of light split by a long, thin shadow that said, "Are you quite all right, sir?"

"Alfred?"

"The dream, sir?"

"Same one. Only this time I could see the bullets coming out of the gun, and it looked as if I could freeze them, stop them from killing my parents. But it still happened.

Even in a dream I couldn't make things come out the way I wanted."

"The man-bat again, sir?"

"In a balcony this time, overlooking the street."

"I'm quite sorry, sir."

"I'm learning to live with it. At least the dreams vary a little."

"Not just the dreams, sir. I was coming to wake you when you screamed."

"The hot-line?"

"Yes sir."

"Good."

SERIES OF PANELS, RICH IN SHADOW AND MOVEMENT

(1) BATCAVE—INTERIOR

Background: Blue-black with stalactites hanging down from the cave roof like witch fingers. There's enough light that we can see the wink of glass trophy cases. Their interiors, except for two—one containing a sampling of the Penguin's umbrellas and another containing Robin's retired uniform—are too dark for us to make out their contents. But we can see the larger, free-standing trophies: a giant Lincoln head penny from the "Penny Plunder's" case. The life-size mechanical dinosaur from the "Dinosaur Island" case, and the mammoth playing card bearing the likeness of Batman's arch enemy, the green-haired, white-faced Joker.

Foreground: Batmobile, long and sleek, a dark needle to sew through the night. Tinted bubble glass to hide the driver from view. Great fin attached to the rear. A large triangular bat head ornament attached to the front. The headlights bright as minature suns. Motion lines on either side of the craft to show us it's really moving.

(2) BATCAVE—EXTERIOR—NIGHT

Background: Full moon rising above the scene like a burnished shield. Tufts of dark cloud threaten to roll over it. Full view below of secret batcave entrance/exit as a mechanical door with its facade of rocks and brush is closing down; interior of the cave is as dark as a witch's heart.

Foreground: Batmobile (right angle, right side of panel) racing from the cave, looking very much like a prehistoric fish.

(3) GOTHAM CITY STREETS

Background: Straight view of the street, bordered by tall, dark buildings. Street is uncommonly empty. Moon rising dead center at the rear of the street, looking more like a gold ballon now than a burnished shield. No clouds threatening anymore. Clear, dark sky.

Foreground: Street split by the Batmobile racing forward, spreading wind lines before it like straw. A newspaper has blown across the street and stuck to the left headlight. Visible across the face of the headlight is part of a headline that reads: SUBWAY JACK.

JAMES W. GORDON

Batman opened the door to my office and stood framed in the light from the hallway. His costume never fails to strike me with a feeling of awe. The dark cowl with its tall ears and connected cape swirled around him like something alive. I saw the golden circle with a flying bat in the middle centered on his chest. I saw the man himself. Big, real big. Muscled. Yet lithe as a gymnast.

He closed the door. He didn't turn on the light. He likes it dark. He came over and sat down in the chair in front of the desk and smiled. That smile of his could be a frown upside down. He said, "My guess is Subway Jack."

"Good guess."

"I was going to get in on it anyway."

"I thought you might."

"I've been reading about it in the papers, seeing it on the news."

I slid the files across to him and turned on the lamp and positioned it where he could see. "There's extras there if you want them," I said. I leaned back and got out a cigar and lit it.

He reached out with a gloved hand and took the file and opened it and without looking up said, "Nasty habit."

"It's this Subway Jack stuff," I said. "Got me puffing my pipe more than usual, smoking these cigars. I'm nervous as a long-tailed cat in a roomful of rocking chairs. I'll be chewing and dipping next. I saw number three tonight, and I'll tell you, you saw what I saw, you might be taking up some things yourself. Those photos in there don't do these murders the bad justice they deserve."

"Just the same, Jim, I'd prefer not to breathe your smoke."

"You probably eat just the right amount of bran and prunes too, don't you?"

"Just the right amount."

I put out the cigar.

When he finished reading I said, "And number four probably won't be much different."

"Always the subway," he said. "Always bag ladies."

"Shrink might have something to say about that. We don't have a psych file on him yet. It could just be the subway's close and the bag ladies are easy prey.... But I tell you, there's something different about this one. Something odd. I feel it in my bones."

"Could be rheumatism, Jim."

"That's funny." He put the lamp back the way I had it and turned it off and stood up. He took spare copies of the file and stuck them somewhere in his cloak. "We'll get him."

"Yeah," I said, but I had my doubts. They never got Jack the Ripper. They haven't got the Green River Killer yet. There's some doubt they got the right man for the Boston Strangler crimes.

Sometimes they got away.

"They got a sample of that clay for you down at the dispatcher's office. You want it, they're supposed to give it to you."

"Thanks, Jim." He went out then. I had a sudden urge to tell him to be careful, but he had moved too fast. I got up and went over and opened the door and looked down both ends of the hallway.

He was gone.

He always did move like a ghost.

OLD GOTHAM CITY CEMETERY (after third murder)

Jack went out there after each of the murders and tried to put it back, but it wouldn't let him. Each time he went into the tomb and put the box down, the razor would cut through the metal and cut his hand. It would sing to him, high and pretty, and he knew he couldn't put it back. It owned him, and in the fleeting moments when his mind was his own and he could think clearly, he thought of the damnable book and how it had led him here.

Joe R. Lansdale

He had gone to Gotham City Library to do research on his criminology paper, "The Psychopath and Modern Society," and while searching through the reference section for *Psychopathia Sexualis* by Richard Von Krafft-Ebing...

FLASHBACK: SERIES OF PANELS, DARK AND FOREBODING, ANGLES SHARP AS BLADES

(1) GOTHAM CITY LIBRARY—INTERIOR—DEEP IN THE STACKS

Background: Not much. Rows and rows of books disappearing into darkness.

Foreground: Prominent is Jack (tall and lean with a blond brush-cut, dressed in stylish white, high-top, tennis shoes, slacks, and a red-and-white-striped, long-sleeved shirt) standing on tiptoes reaching for a book. His hand is on the spine of one, but the book next to the one he wants has dislodged and is starting to fall.

(2) LIBRARY FLOOR

Closeup: Jack's hand reaching for the fallen book, which has landed spread open, spine up. The book is old and gray in color and on the spine in dark letters is *Followers of the Razor* by David Webb.

(3) LIBRARY

Closeup: Jack standing, holding the book open. We have a thought balloon that reads: "My God, a book on ripper murders that goes back to the 1800s. I didn't know there was such a thing."

(4) LIBRARY

Overhead (Bird's-Eye) View: Jack seated at a long, wooden table, stacks of books at his right elbow, his head bent over the one he picked up from the floor. Long view of him at the table is the central focus of the panel, but as we move to the edges of the panel, it darkens. The shelves of books that surround him can be made out, but they are shadowy and appear to lean toward him, as if they are living things sneaking a peek over his shoulder. There is a large yellow caption box at the top of the panel that reads: BY THE TIME THE DAY SLID INTO NIGHT, JACK HAD MADE A REMARKABLE DISCOVERY. Within the panel itself is a thought balloon coming from Jack. "Man, what a research paper this will make."

FROM JACK'S JOURNAL (destroyed later by James Gordon)

(Entry written mid-September)

Wow, have I come across something that will make old Professor Hamrick pass out. This should be the research paper to end all research papers. It's got your true crime, it's got your hint of the mystical, it's got your weird legend that can tie in with all kinds of mythology and famous murders. And ultimately, what we're talking here, is a serious high mark on the old research paper for yours truly.

Strikes me it might be a good idea for me to synopsis what I remember from my reading here and now, so I can get down my hotter impressions, then later when I outline the paper, I can review this and transfer those impressions to my paper. And besides, have I ever denied myself what I'm excited about by not writing it down in this journal? The answer to that is, No Sir.

I found this book and it's called *Followers of the Razor* and it was written by this guy named David Webb in the early 1900s, and he had been researching it all his life. He was kind of ahead of his time on his interest in this sort of thing, but his conclusions are a little screwy to say the least. Still, it makes fascinating reading, and he has an interesting bibliography of books and articles and interviews he draws from. I looked at some of those things when I was in the library, and since the Webb book, and the most interesting of the ones he cited, *The Book of Doches*—which is some old English book written in the 1600s—couldn't be checked out, I sort of borrowed them by taking them out under my coat. When I finish my paper, I'll return them.

Webb's theory is that the world we know is occasionally crossed up with other worlds, or dimensions, and this is where we get our ideas about gods and monsters, and it explains some disappearances. Seems this dimension he's referring to is populated with all sorts of horrible people and critters. He explains the disappearance of the *Mary Celeste* crew this way, suggests that the murders Lizzie Borden were blamed for were committed by someone, or something, from this other dimension, which possessed and used her. He claims the same for Jack the Ripper.

But I'll come back to that. Let me note one of his more interesting ideas, the tying of witchcraft to mathematics, geometry, and the movement of the planets and the moon.

He talks about this character that through the centuries has been referred to as the God of Swords, the God of Blades, and during the time he was writing, as the God of the Razor. He says this thing isn't really a god, but a powerful being from this other dimension, and for some reason, when certain mathematical symbols are drawn up, it can open the gate to this world of his, and he can escape from it to possess someone and make them do his bidding.

There's this crude drawing of this dude in the Webb book, and I'll tell you, I wouldn't want to meet him in a dark alley, or a lighted alley for that matter. But the written description Webb gives creeps me even more. He says it's varied a bit over the centuries, but it's pretty much like this: The God of the Razor is very tall and broad and wears a kind of top hat (a helmet in some accounts), has a metal hat band and needles or daggers for teeth, wears human skin and human heads for shoes—has little cloven feet that fit right down into the mouths.

Anyway, these mathematical symbols can call him up if blood is involved. He also claims that there's a blade from this other dimension that can open the gate. Says it was once a sword but was somehow broken and made into two daggers, and later on one of the daggers turned up made into a barber's razor and the ivory sword hilt had been made into the razor's sheath or handle. On it are written these mathematical symbols, and if the blade tastes blood, and it doesn't kill who it cuts, then that person is possessed by the God of the Razor and the razor becomes his instrument of destruction. It sucks blood and makes whoever is possessed a berserker. (He ties this in with the Vikings and their wild madnesses in battle.)

Let's see, what else. Oh, Webb says Excalibur, King Arthur's sword, was originally from the same dimension as the God of the Razor, and that it belonged to him. He claims that this is the sword that got broken and made into a razor. (I wonder what happened to the rest of the blade.) He says that eventually the razor fell into the hands of this barber in London, and that the barber accidentally cut himself with it and the God possessed him and made him commit the murders in Whitechapel.

Webb suggests that this possessed man may actually have died or committed suicide, but not before the razor was somehow passed into other hands. He shows evidence of similar murders throughout the U.S. right after those in London, and the last murders he records in his book end right here in Gotham City in 1904.

And get this. His final verification is that he actually saw the God of the Razor with his own eyes, and that he and a policeman managed to dispatch the old boy, which of course freed the man possessed, but also led to his death. He says they were able to defeat the God when the moonlight was affected by cloud cover, one of the few things that dilutes the monster's strength. I guess I should add to this that he says that they did not actually kill the God, merely dismissed him to his own dimension.

Final bit of neato material here is that the murderer Webb claims was possessed by the God of the Razor is buried right here in Gotham City in the Old Gotham Cemetery. According to Webb, the razor was put in a metal box and buried with this fellow so that it will forever be out of the hands of man.

If Webb had thought things through, if he really believed this razor had power, he wouldn't have mentioned that in his book. Because eventually someone is bound to try and find out if there really is a razor in that grave. Someone like me. But maybe as a writer he just couldn't resist telling all he knew.

Might be the razor has already been stolen from the grave. Or perhaps the book has been thought fiction or the ramblings of a madman, as they say in all the gothic horror fiction.

But if there is a razor, think of the kind of presentation I could make. My paper on the God of Razor, and a little bit of show and tell to go with it.

(Entry written early October)

From the book I've figured out which grave the body of the possessed man and the razor is in. Webb never comes right out and says where he's buried, but there are enough references there, that I think I've narrowed it down.

I'm going to get a shovel and go back and dig that grave up. I was a little worried about how I could walk along with a shovel without being noticed, as I figure grave robbery will not be looked upon lightly, but then I realized that in this city a man with a shovel may be a bit unusual, but nothing compared with the stuff you see every day. Besides, if the cops ask I can say I'm taking it to pawn or something. Not the best story in the world, but who's to prove otherwise.

(Entry next day)

When I opened the grave, I was amazed there really was a razor. That's what I wanted to find, but I guess a part of me thought I was being silly. But when I found that box where it was supposed to be and got it back here and opened it and found the razor, I got a case of the spooks, you know. Not that I believe the razor is the door to another dimension and will let this demon into the body of whoever is cut and doesn't die from the would, but hey, Webb thought that, and there really is a razor....

I'm trying to figure a way around the grave robbing angle now. If I'm going to use this for show and tell, I can't admit I went out there and dug up a grave to get it.

Man, that razor is sharp and bright. You wouldn't think it would be after all this time. I figured it would be rusted to almost nothing. I guess I didn't have a hold of it good, because when I opened it, it shifted in my hand and I slid a finger onto the blade and knicked myself. Nothing bad, but I hardly touched it. It sure does sting.

(Entry written later that day)

Thought about the razor all day. Was terrible in class. Didn't get a third of the notes Professor Hamrick gave. My finger hurt like hell, and still hurts. Razor and paper cuts are the worst.

Decided to take the razor back. Couldn't think of a satisfactory way to explain possession of it. Besides, I don't like it. Guess Webb's book is getting to me. I'll still do the paper, but without show and tell. Sooner I get rid of the razor, the better.

(Entry written later that night)

Carried the razor with me in the box. I walked part of the way then caught the subway over to Center Station and got off since it's not too far a walk to the cemetery from there. When I got off at Center, I saw all these homeless people

Joe R. Lansdale

hanging around. I've always felt sorry for them, especially the bag ladies. But today I got to thinking different. There's really nothing that can be done for them. They really shouldn't be allowed on the street. They ought to be run in, or maybe put to sleep, like a sick dog or something. Isn't that what we do when the animal population gets out of hand? We exterminate the strays. I keep thinking of what it would be like to ... well, we've all had those kind of thoughts from time to time, haven't we?

When I got to the cemetery the razor sang to me. It wouldn't go back in the tomb. It cut me through the box. I rode the subway back and it sang to me all the way. I don't think anyone else can hear it. Just me. It sings very pretty. It has suggestions. My cut finger hurts so badly right now I can hardly write; it throbs like a blister and from time to time it opens up and bleeds.

Need to get some sleep. All for now.

(Last entry, mid-October)

Webb was right. I'm not myself. The singing is louder and more frequent; the songs tell me to do things I don't think I want to do. Can't be clear on that. I find my thoughts and *his* mixing together. Makes a bad jumble. Moment ago I took a sheet of paper and pulled it over my bare legs until I had a dozen paper cuts. Can't fathom why, unless it's the singing making me do that. The cuts hurt so good.

There's a full moon tonight; the singing told me that. Told me too that the razor's edge is the mouth of the God of the Razor and that the mouth needs feeding.

I think about the bag ladies a lot.

THE BATCAVE (day after meeting in James Gordon's office)

"Excuse me sir, I've brought your tray."

Bruce Wayne looked up from the computer screen. "Thanks, Alfred, but I'm not hungry."

"You asked me to prepare your dinner and bring it to you, sir."

"I did?"

"You did. Said you wanted to eat down here, that you had some work to do. Now please eat the clam chowder so I won't be inclined to break the bowl over your head, Master Bruce."

"Put it here and I'll get to it."

"Yes, put it there. That way you can appease poor old Alfred, but you'll leave it set and it'll get cold, then you won't eat it. Matters not that I've worked my fingers to the bone—"

"You opened a can for this."

"Well, yes sir, I did, but I pinched myself on the can opener. Making headway, Master Bruce?"

"Maybe. That clay they found. I ran it through my lab, analyzed it, and I've been running cross checks on it, and Jim was right."

"Common as dirt."

"A little joke, Alfred?"

"A small one, sir."

"But the thing is, common as dirt—clay actually—is, there really aren't that many places in the city it could have come from. I'm going to cross-hatch information in the computer, find all the spots closest to the city where the clay might have been picked up, and try to narrow the list from there. You see, it was carried in on the murderer's shoes."

"Thank you, sir. I thought perhaps he brought it in in a parcel."

"I don't mean to patronize you, Alfred."

"Of course not, sir."

"It's just that to narrow this down, to take the Sherlock Holmes approach, you determine where the clay might have come from and—"

"This last murder, sir...all the murders. They occurred at Center Station, did they not?"

"Yes, but it's the clay I'm concerned with. That's what—"

"The location of the murders is not too terribly far from the Old Gotham City Cemetery, sir. The murderer might well have gotten the clay on his shoes there. It seems a logical possibility to me. Or am I being too presumptuous in my untutored way to suggest such a thing? What he might have been doing there I've no idea. A picnic, perhaps.... You have a very ugly look on your face, Master Wayne."

"That will be all, Alfred."

"Yes, sir, eat your clam chowder. I'll come for the tray after awhile. Shall I serve tea in your study later?"

"I don't think so."

"Very good, sir." Alfred walked to the elevator that led up to Wayne mansion.

Bruce said to the old butler's back. "You're a smart aleck, Alfred, but I couldn't do without you."

Alfred stepped into the elevator and clasped his hands in front of him, and just before the elevator door closed, said, "Of course not, sir."

BATMAN CASE FILE A-4567-C, informal notes (computer entry—October 20)

In the late afternoon I got in contact with Jim and picked him up at his home and drove him over to the Old Gotham City Cemetery. We climbed over the wall because the gate was locked with a chain and padlock and I didn't want to pick the lock because it looked old and I thought it might go to pieces. Jim fussed when I boosted him over the wall. He claims I pushed his face into the wall to smash his cigar. I told him it was an accident. I told him he should look at photographs they've taken after autopsies of smoker's lungs. I told him the nicotine stains his mustache. He told me to go to hell.

We looked around and found a shovel and an open grave. I couldn't make out much about the marker, but the clay there was the kind found at the murder sites; I ran it through lab work when I got back. I bet Alfred's guess was correct, that the murder site clay came from the cemetery. Its close proximity to the murders was just too much of a coincidence. Add to that the uncovered grave, and I thought we'd got some interesting connections.

I got the grave marker cleaned off with some mild acid from my utility belt while Jim held the flashlight for me and cursed. Patience is not one of Jim's virtues. I worked on the marker until I could make out a name—Rufus Jefferson.

Jim promised to run it through his computer at the station and I came back here and did the same. What we both came up with was that Rufus Jefferson died in 1904 at the hands of a Gotham City policeman after committing the fourth of a series of murders, all of them quite like those being committed now by Subway Jack.

Jim said that when his computer records played out, he went downstairs and checked through the old files, the ones not on the computer. He found out that Jefferson was tracked down by a Sergeant Griffith and was aided by a writer named David Webb who later wrote a book that contained his experience in the matter. The book was titled *Followers of the Razor*.

I checked with the public library, as well as some of the smaller libraries in the city, and Gotham City Library said that they had a copy listed in their files, in the reserve section, but that it was missing—stolen perhaps.

Curiouser and curiouser.

Joe R. Lansdale

I got back on the computer and tied in with libraries across the country and found that Stephen F. Austin University Library in Nacogdoches, Texas, had a copy of the book in their rare book section. I have made arrangements through Jim to have it sent to us by overnight mail.

Maybe there's something there that can help us, something that might explain our current murderer's connection with that old grave and Rufus Jefferson.

(Excerpts from later A-4567-C file entries—October)

...book is fascinating, and in spite of its incredible subject matter, is convincing. Up to a point. I'm not sure I'm ready to accept a dimensional murderer, but I've seen some pretty strange things, and if nothing else, there may be a psychological tie-in with...

...the librarian said that after I called she started a little investigation of her own. She says that a young man by the name of Jack Barrett checked out a lot of books in that section, and told her he was looking for material on psychopathic killers for a research paper. She said she wasn't accusing the young man, but I might want to check him out and ...

...discreet inquiries show that Jack Barrett has been an excellent student, until this month. His professor in criminology told me in confidence that he had been acting strangely, and suddenly started cutting classes. He thought it might be problems at home or with a girl...

...University has provided Jack Barrett's address, and I plan to notify Jim so we can follow and check out...

JAMES W. GORDON (one week later)

I have a feeling we're both right and wrong about this Barrett guy, but can't explain it. There's been something funny about this case, right from the start.

We stationed men outside Barrett's apartment and we've been following him around all week. Batman's working the rooftops a lot. When Barrett goes out, Batman moves across the tops of the buildings like a shadow, like a spider... well, like a bat.

What we got here is a guy that doesn't do much. He's quit the University, and about all he does is walk to the subway entrance and ride the subways all day. He goes over to Center Station and stands around and looks at people, especially the bag ladies.

That part is interesting, of course, but there's a look about this guy like he really doesn't want to be there, that it's all against his will. He walks like his knees are being lifted by puppet strings, and until he gets to the subway he doesn't notice much.

Then he notices plenty about the bag ladies, and he seems to have a thing about the moon. It's always dark when he comes back, and he often stops to look at it. Or what he can see of it. It's been cloudy lately and the clouds cover the moon most of the time. It's little more than a sliver anyway, but he stares at it like he hates it. He keeps one hand in his pocket at all times.

Batman says he thinks he's waiting for a clear night. The idea of the moon being bright ties in with Webb's writings in *Followers of the Razor*. He says the weather report says tomorrow will be a little better, especially early morning—some clear moments with a slight threat of rain. He feels things just might break tomorrow.

I don't know about the moon stuff, but I have a feeling he's right—just one of those gut things. If Barrett does make his move tomorrow—if he is in fact Subway Jack—I hope we'll be ready.

Joe R. Lansdale

GOTHAM CITY STREETS (2 a.m., October 31)

Jack Barrett came out of his apartment and down the steps and onto the street. The tension inside him beat like a drum. He tightened his hand around the razor in his coat pocket and looked at the late night (early morning) moon. It had grown brighter and slightly thicker, and tonight the cloud cover was thin, though the forecast called for rain. The air had a mild tang to it, like the sting of a too-close shave.

He went down the street, walking briskly, not looking at much, except the moon from time to time, and then he heard a horn blare and he turned and looked at the street. There was a taxi rolling along slowly and the window on the passenger side was down. The driver leaned across the seat and called, "Looking for a ride somewhere?"

Barrett shook his head.

"Bad night for walking. Might get wet. You'll sure get cold."

"No money," Barrett said, and walked faster.

The taxi kept coasting. the driver said, "Heck with it, buddy. I hate to see a man walk on night like this, and I'm not getting any action anyway. This one's on the house if you want to get in. What am I doing anyway, huh?"

Barrett stopped walking and the taxi stopped moving Barrett looked at the moon. It was clear now, and he felt the urge swelling up inside him. The taxi would be better than grabbing the subway at Maynard Street and taking it over to Center. It was still a long walk to Maynard. He looked at the driver and said, "All right." He got in the back of the taxi and took a sideways look at the driver. He was big, old guy with a touch of gray whisk-white hair, a rubbery mouth, and wrinkles deep enough to hide quarters in. Maybe he reminded the old guy of his grandson or something. "Take me to Center Station, if that's okay."

Subway Jack

"I invited you," the driver said, and pulled away from the curb. He glanced in the mirror at his passenger and said, "You look a little under the weather, buddy. You been sick?"

"I been sick all right," Barrett said. "You wouldn't believe how I been sick."

"Another reason not to walk. Nights like this are criminal."

"Tell me about it," Barrett said as he leaned back and closed his fevered eyes.

"You know," the driver said, "You got some problems, there's guys you can see. If it's not just physical, there's people you can talk to."

Barrett didn't hear him. He was thinking of the bad things he had to do, and of the ultimate darkness on the other side, a darkness split by the shine of a razor.

"Center Station," the driver said. "Hey, Center Station."

Barrett opened his eyes. He didn't feel rested. His heart was beating faster. He was hot and his head was full of fuzz. He put his hand in his pocket and felt the razor. It was warm. It was starting to sing. He knew the driver couldn't hear it. It only gave its notes to him.

He wanted to take the razor out of his pocket and throw it away. He wanted to take it and slash someone—the driver maybe. He wanted to do all those things, yet none of them.

He said, "Thanks," and got out of the taxi. He went down the subway steps and out of sight.

The taxi driver drove around the corner, found a spot with a few shadows, and parked there. He took off his face by grabbing his hair and ripping up. The mask came free with a sound like a grape being sucked. He ran his hand through his dark hair and over his handsome features; the mask had pinched his face some. He slid out of his jacket and pulled at the tear-away pants and kicked off his shoes. He pulled the cowl over his head. He leaned back in the seat and opened the glove compartment and took out a walkie-talkie, switched it on and said, "He's down there, Jim. He looks rough. I tried to get him to talk. Thought he might spill his guts and I could get him to give up. No soap. You can almost feel the heat coming off this guy, and I got a feeling tonight's the night. If he's the one, and I think he is, and if he's going to do it, I've put him right in your lap."

"We're waiting," Gordon said.

Batman clipped the walkie-talkie to his belt, got out of the taxi and stood leaning against it. He wanted to go down there after Barrett, but he had made a promise to Gordon to try not to get involved. If possible, it was a promise he wanted to keep.

JAMES W. GORDON

I was dressed like a bum. I hadn't shaved in a few days, and my hair was mussed and the overcoat I was wearing had been in police storage so long it smelled mildewy. To add to that, I had poured a little Mad Dog 20/20 over the front of it. The stink of the mildew and the wine gave me motivation for my role. Maybe I could start a new career in the movies. I could play winos. The hours couldn't be any worse.

I put the walkie-talkie in my coat pocket and got out one of my cigars and lit it. Maybe a bum ought not to have a good, whole cigar, but you got to draw the line somewhere. It was either smoke some of my rope, or start pacing.

Subway Jack

I thought of Batman topside, and wished suddenly we hadn't made a deal for him to try to stay out of things so the department could claim the collar. Now and then I got the heat from the folks upstairs saying we relied on Batman too much. Could be.

Anyway, I had just gotten the cigar lit good when I saw Barrett coming down the steps, into the subway. He was weak and tired and sick-looking. He wore a ring of sweat beads around his forehead like a band of pearls. He staggered a little. He looked mostly at the ground.

I leaned against the subway wall and tried to appear drunk. He went on by me without looking up. I let him go on a ways before I took a gander and saw him walking along the edge of the subway landing. I kept thinking he might fall over onto the rails.

Still, there was something about him, a kind of mood in the air that made me reach inside my coat and touch the butt of my .38 for luck. I make a quick, soft call on the walkie-talkie, warned my people up ahead, then went on behind him at a distance, moving as smoothly and silently as I could.

Finally, I saw the bag lady pushing her shopping cart, coming about even with Barrett, humming to herself. Mertz looked good in the disguise, if a little bulky and broad-shouldered for a washed-out bag lady. He had his head down and the gray wig hung around his face and his his constant five-o'clock shadow.

I went over behind one of the concrete supports, leaned against it, spat my cigar out, and stepped on it. I peeked around the edge of my hiding place and put my hand in my coat and felt the .38, then waited.

Barrett went right on by Mertz.

Well, we had another "bag lady" plant on down a ways, and Crider had the far end cut off with three plain-

Joe R. Lansdale

clothes if things got nasty. I have to admit, I was disappointed. I didn't get out in the field much these days, and when I did, I was there because I expected something to happen. I began to think that mood I had felt in the air was old age.

I was about to step from behind the support and start walking toward Mertz when Barrett turned abruptly and started back.

Mertz pretended not to notice, but I knew he had because he stopped pushing the cart and put his head inside it, burying it under the junk he had there. I assumed he had a hold of his revolver.

I was about to pull my head back out of sight when I saw something that kept me from it; something that froze my eyes to Barrett and his shadow.

His shadow jutted out long and thick to his right, and suddenly Barrett fell to the left, flat as a cardboard cutout, and the shadow rose upright to take his place—only it wasn't a shadow anymore. It was a huge, top-hatted figure with a face as dark as tailpipe corrosion, eyes that sparked like shorted-out electrical sockets and this mouth overpacked with teeth as thin and sharp as knitting needles.

His loose coat and pants were ragged and the color of water-stained rawhide. He was wearing human heads for shoes; his ankles tapered like those of a goat and slid snuggly into the open mouths. When he walked, the heads came down on the cement with a noise like overripe fruit falling. To his left, floating flat against the cement, was a pale, pink shadow with the general appearance of Jack Barrett; it twitched in mimicry of the dark man's moves.

The dark man's right arm went up and I could see a flash of metal in his jug-size fist. The arm came down as Mertz jerked the revolver from the cart, turned, and fired.

The dark man soaked the bullet up and kept coming. The razor flashed and I saw Mertz's hand fly onto the subway tracks. It twitched there momentarily like a spider trying to crawl.

Then the world went hot and kaleidoscopic. There was a sensation of reality collapsing in upon itself, of a malignant universe pushing into our own, like a greased weasel attempting to navigate a tight tunnel.

Blood spurted from Mertz's wrist, made an arc, and hung in the air like a twisting tube of red neon. Shadows fluttered damply and the light flowed as if it were boiling honey. The subway rails quivered and writhed. The support I was leaning against turned soft as a sponge. The inside of my head was on fire and I was melting. The air screeched.

Then it all went away. I felt solid again. The rails quit moving. Shadows ceased to flutter. The light was firm and bright. Blood from Mertz's wrist shattered its neonlike tube and splattered to the cement and blossomed into rosy puddles.

The razor wove through the air like a conductor's baton during a tense musical movement. Mertz, without time for so much as a wimper, went to pieces.

Then the dark man came for me. I pulled the revolver and snapped off six shots. It didn't bother him. I fumbled for my speed loader and pushed in six more. I shot straight at his face now, all six, rapid fire. I could see where the loads were striking him on the cheeks and chin and below the nose, but the holes closed up rapidly as if his flesh were quicksand and my bullets were no more than a series of sad little victims who had stumbled in.

He was so close I could smell him. An odor like exhaust fumes, factory smoke, and open sewers.

The razor went up and caught the light. I ducked low, leaped, and rolled and tumbled over the subway landing, hitting my back across one of the rails. The impact sent a jolt through my spine, and momentarily I was paralyzed. I expected to look up and see the leering face of that big bastard looking over the landing at me, showing me his razor.

That didn't happen. I felt a vibration in the rails that told me a train was coming. I managed to get up and limp to the far side, nestle myself into an indention there with my back against the wall.

I still had my .38, but I was out of shells, and besides, what did it matter? As a matter of habit, I put it in its holster.

Crider and the three plainclothes had heard the shots and they came running. They were almost on the big guy. They were firing their guns, and not having any better luck than I had.

I yelled, "Run for it," but they didn't hear me above the shots and the thunder of the oncoming train. Just as that top-hatted behemoth grabbed Crider by the throat and lifted him above his head and slashed at one of the plainclothes with the razor, the train jetted in front of me and all there was for me to see was its metal side and its many lighted windows—a rickity-tick-tack of glass and steel.

I pushed back as tight as I could against the wall and felt the wind from the train and heard the screech and rattle of the rails, trying not to imagine what horrors were occurring across the way.

It seemed like a century, but the train finally went by and I saw that the big man was gone from the landing. Crider and the plainclothes were spread all over it. It looked like a slaughterhouse floor. On the wall, written in large, bloody letters was: COMPLIMENTS OF SUBWAY JACK—5

MORE AND THAT MAKES 8. I DON'T JUST DO THE LADIES. Some distance away, heading topside up the steps, I could see Barrett. He was stumbling. The razor dangled from his hand as if it were a long, silver finger.

I got out the walkie-talkie and tried to make my voice firm. "Batman. He's coming up. He's Barrett now. It's like that book says. It's for real. He changes."

"I got him, Jim."

Under most circumstances I would have believed that. I've seen Batman take some weird ones. But this time...even Batman might not be enough.

I got my feet under me and went across the rails and pulled myself onto the landing, then started toward the steps after Barrett.

BATMAN (topside)

Batman, he's thinking about what Jim said, about how Barrett changes, about that book, *Followers of the Razor* and about the God of the Razor; he's thinking if Jim says it's so, then it's so, and he feels something rare for him, something that matches the moments in his dreams when he sees his parents die and feels the presence of the man-bat at his back, and that rare thing is almost impossible for him to identify—but that rare thing is fear. A quick skuttle goes up his backbone and hits his brain, and then melts away as all his experience and training takes over and he sees Barrett coming out of the subway, wild-eyed, looking up at the sky, trying to spot the moon.

Instinctively, Batman cranes his neck and sees that the moon is behind those rain clouds that were promised, and then he looks back at Barrett who is racing across the street at a lumbering run that makes him look like a puppet being jerked along by strings.

Joe R. Lansdale

Traffic is nonexistent at this early morning hour, and Batman crosses the street easily, making good time and gaining on Barrett. Then everything becomes lighter, touched with silver, and Batman knows the moon is out. He sees that when Barrett puts his right foot forward it is dressed not in a shoe but in a head, and then the left foot goes forward and it is the same, and then the man running before him, moving much faster, is not Barrett, but the dimensional creature Webb called the God of the Razor.

The God of the Razor leaps more than he runs, and Batman thinks of the legends of Spring-heel Jack, then pours it on, trying to close, wondering in the back of his mind what he'll do with this thing if he catches it.

Up they go, the God of the Razor leading Batman through a narrow, twisting path that winds its way through brush and shrubs and trees, and Batman knows they are fast approaching the top of the hill where the walls of Old Gotham Cemetery stand.

The God is really moving and he's almost to the cemetery wall, and with a flex of his whip-thin legs he leaps up and out and over it, effortlessly as a kangaroo, and the weak little shadow of Barrett follows after him and slips over the wall like a wet, pink sheet.

Batman reaches the wall, jumps and grabs and swings himself over. And the clouds have done their trick again. Standing by the stone cross that marks the grave of Rufus Jefferson—the dark open tomb yawning to his right—is Barrett, head hung low, the razor held loosely against his leg.

"It isn't me," Barrett says, his voice weak as a signal from space. "I got no control. Nothing stops the power of the moon but the clouds. Just the clouds. Long as he's got the moon and the need, he's got control. You got to know it's not me. It's him."

Barrett waves the razor at the God's shadow that is thin and watery, bent, and partially out of sight down the open grave.

"I know, son," Batman says, and he moves quickly toward Barrett. "Give me the razor and we'll set you free."

"Not like that," Barrett says. "Can't give it to you. Not the way you want anyway. Not the way I want. Just the way he wants. I..."

The clouds twirl away from the face of the moon.

JAMES W. GORDON

I saw Batman cross the street and head toward the brush and trees that bunched at the bottom of the cemetery hill. I went after him.

I couldn't keep up with him, he was moving too fast. The cigar smoke that lived in my lungs wasn't helping either. When I got to the cemetery wall I saw the last of Batman's cape going over. Then I saw Barrett topping the rise of the hill inside the cemetery; the hill that was higher than the cemetery walls.

My back was killing me. My sides felt as if they were being skewered. I couldn't help myself. I dropped to one knee and tried to get my wind.

When the skewers quit twisting, I got up, staggered to the wall, and dragged myself over.

When I hit the ground it wasn't Barrett standing on the hill, it was the big top-hatted monster. The little pale shadow of Barrett was thin as watered milk and getting thinner. I guess the God of the Razor was growing stronger and stronger, and Barrett weaker and weaker, with every transformation.

Batman was charging up the hill with his head slightly bent, charging like a locomotive. His cloak fanned out high and wide behind him like a Japanese fan. Then he

ducked and the cape dropped down some and I could see
the faces of the monster and the flash of his razor as it
sliced off part of Batman's cape and sent it fluttering away.
Then Batman leaped high as the big guy bent low and
swiped back at Batman's ankles. When Batman came
down, he brought his fists together at the back of the big
guy's head.

It didn't seem to do much. Maybe it made him mad.
The big guy jerked upright and his top hat didn't even
sway. He raised his arm above his head and brought the
razor down like a hammer.

Batman shot out a hand and grabbed the big wrist,
stopping the blow. The big guy used his other hand to grab
Batman's throat and—

SPLASH PANEL

*Complete Side View Body Shots of Batman and the
God of the Razor*: The scene is dark, but not too dark.
(Don't forget that cold slice of moon.) Batman's head is
being pushed back and his teeth are clenched and we can
see the muscles swelling in his jaw. His muscles push out
his costume in the shoulders, arms, and legs. He has his
left hand up, holding back the hand with the razor, and
he is using his right hand to push at the God's other wrist,
trying to break the strangle hold the God has on his throat.
Batman's cape is twisted and we can see it hanging limp
and touching the ground as his knees are bent and he is
forced back.

The God of the Razor looks happy as a winning politi-
cian. His smile is so wide his teeth are brushing his ear
lobes. His left eye (the only one visible to us) appears to
be lit from within by a hot, red bulb. His ragged coat is
bulging with muscles. His thin legs are knotted with the
same, and his prominent head-shoe is splitting across the

forehead and teeth are popping out of the mouth like pop-corn because of the pressure of his left-leg-forward stance. Barrett's pathetic, near colorless shadow is flowing loose and distorted into the darkness of the open grave.

In the background is a great oak tree. Through its naked branches we can see the silver curve of the moon, and to the right of that, a dark cloud.

A yellow block at the bottom of the panel alerts us to what Batman sees as his head is being slowly pushed back:

IN WHAT SEEMED LIKE HIS FINAL MOMENTS, BATMAN SAW A DARK RAIN CLOUD ABOUT TO SLIDE OVER THE FACE OF FRAG-MENTED MOON LIKE A WOOL MASK.

JAMES W. GORDON

—I pounded up the hill toward them and dove for the big guy's leg, grabbing him just above the knee.

I might as well have been a flea. He kicked me off and I tumbled away.

I was on my hands and knees, about to try it again, when suddenly it grew darker, and in that same instant, Batman, still clinging to the big guy, dropped to his right side and stuck out his foot to catch the creep's knee and send him flipping forward toward the open grave.

Just before he disappeared into the darkness, I saw that it was Barrett falling, the big guy's shadow following after him like black silk sliding over polished bone.

From inside the tomb came a snapping sound, and Batman rolled to a squatting position and produced from his utility belt a little penlight. He shone it into the grave. I went up the hill and stood behind him and looked down into the little pool of light. I watched as Batman moved it up and down Barrett's body.

Joe R. Lansdale

Barrett lay face up with his back across the steps. His head was pointing down, and his legs had swiveled so far his buttocks were pointing up. You didn't have to be a doctor to know his spine was snapped.

His right hand was outstretched and open. The hilt of the razor was in his palm, the blade gleamed against a damp, moss-covered, stone step.

It started to rain.

BATMAN CASE FILE A-4567-C, last of the informal notes (computer entry—November 1)

The Barrett boy was boxed up and sent home to his parents. I don't know what Jim told them—an accident of some kind, I think. Whatever he said, it wasn't enough. No one could say enough, but at least Barrett won't be charged for his crimes. It won't look good on Jim's record that Subway Jack got away. The files will read OPEN, but that's fair play for Barrett. The killings have stopped and it wasn't Barrett anyway. It was the God of the Razor, and he's gone to his dimension to wait for some other fool to let him loose.

That won't be as easy next time.

Jim and I carefully stored the razor in a metal box and hid it. After Barrett and what was left of Jim's men were hauled away, we took the box and put it in a metal drum and filled the drum with concrete. We let it set and harden. The next night we met at the docks and took a police launch out to the middle of Gotham Bay and pushed the drum overboard.

It's deep there. I like to think that's the end of the bad things the razor can do. It won't bring Jim's men back, and it won't bring those bag ladies back, and it won't bring Jack Barrett back, but at least it's out of sight and grasp of others.

Subway Jack

When we were through we sat there on the boat and looked at the water, watching the bay gather in drops of rain. I thought about my parents and how their deaths had led me to become Batman. I thought about my strangest cases. I thought about the God of the Razor, over there safe and happy in his wild dimension. I thought about a lot of things.

Then, just before morning, the light rain stopped and I looked out at the water where we had pushed over the barrel, and there on the face of the bay was the wavering reflection of

the...

...moon.

This story is for Keith Lansdale

The Sound of One Hand Clapping

A BATMAN AND ROBIN STORY

MAX ALLAN COLLINS

The Joker sat on his playing-card throne behind a grotesquely grinning desk and frowned. His frown was as exaggerated as his (currently absent) trademark grin, and it reflected both emotional and physical pain: to summon a frown from a face frozen into a grin by a long-ago acid bath required effort, and concentration.

On those rare occasions when the Joker was depressed, when there was no news of earthquake devastation, school bus collisions, or toxic-waste spills to cheer him— he had to work hard at his despair.

"What is the *point* of it all?" mused the white-faced, green-haired, purple-jacketed psychotic. "Where is the *joy* in my life?"

He stood.

And paced.

And spoke to himself: "The pointlessness of my existence is no laughing matter."

He returned to his throne, his frown as down-turned as his usual crazed grin. He shook his elongated head, and wrung his purple-gloved hands.

The Sound of One Hand Clapping

The dreary castle from which this melancholy monarch ruled was a run-down, deserted toy factory near the slum area called Crime Alley. Jester Novelties had closed down years before, and stood condemned, even as was its current occupant by every local, state, and federal law enforcement agency you might name.

But the surroundings within the old factory were considerably more cheerful. On this rainy Gotham night, the clown prince of crime rested moodily on an oversize throne sculpted in his own harlequin image. The interior walls of the condemned factory were gaily, if not sanely, appointed with oversize playing cards—jokers, one and all—and bright yellow wallpaper smattered with hearts, spades, clubs, and diamonds.

No, it was not his castle that depressed him; it was his kingdom itself that had dimmed the demented devil's droll disposition—a kingdom of the mind in which a jester ruled.

"The boss is really depressed," whispered Kennison, a heavyset stooge in a long flasher topcoat and a black knit beret. "I'm afraid the boss is havin' a mid-life crisis."

"Th-th-that's only part of the problem," whispered back a second stooge, one "Bobcat" Goldman, a disheveled nervous wreck in tattered sweatshirt and tennies. "Th-th-that letter the Penguin sneaked outta stir to the boss—braggin' up the *joys* of bein' in love—has really, like you know...bummed him out."

Even now, the sour, self-pitying Joker stood behind his desk, reading the letter for perhaps the thousandth time. The Penguin had met his true love—Dovina—through the mail, a lonely heart's club friendship that blossomed into romance and impending wedlock.

"If that tuxedoed twerp can find happiness," the Joker pondered aloud bitterly, "why not *moi?*"

The Joker looked skyward, summoning his considerable powers of self-pity. He gestured to himself theatrically, a fourth-rate actor putting the ham into Hamlet.

"Here I stand at the midpoint of my life—and what have I to show for it?"

Kennison took a tentative step forward. "You've had a brilliant career, boss!"

"Well, that's true," the Joker said absently, as he casually plucked up three hard balls, not unlike those used in the game of croquet, and began to juggle.

"Y-y-yeah, Joker," Bobcat said, with a stupid nervous grin. "You've had a *wonderful* life!"

"Also true," the Joker admitted, juggling with lazy skill. "But who do I have to *share* it with?"

Kennison glanced at Bobcat and gestured with two big open hands and risked saying, "Us?"

It was a risk not worth taking.

"Precisely my point!" the Joker sneered, and savagely hurled the hard balls at the two stooges, who scurried away into the darker recesses of the warehouse-room, one hard ball bouncing off the head of the wincing, whimpering Bobcat.

"Where is the female companionship that could give my life resonance?" the Joker asked the sky—or, to be more precise, the skylight. "Where are the progeny who might carry my great tradition into the future?"

The Joker's long legs flashed like swords in a duel as he exited his inner sanctum and moved down a hallway, where framed portraits of famous comedians—from Eddie Cantor to Steve Martin—hung askew. His two stooges fell into step behind him—but at a safe distance.

"Boss," Kennison said, "you gotta cheer up—we gotta get back to work—"

The Sound of One Hand Clapping

"W-w-we haven't pulled a job in weeks," Bobcat said. "We're *broke!*"

The Joker glanced back at them with tragic self-pity as he entered the dark protective womb of his viewing room.

"Leave me to my solitude," the Joker said. "Perhaps Rodney will show me the way out of the slough of despond."

The Joker settled himself into a plush seat in his personal theater and summoned the image of Rodney Dangerfield on the giant television screen before him. As Rodney tugged at his tie, complaining of the lack of respect he received, the Joker remained unamused.

"I told my doctor I wanted a second opinion," said Rodney. "He said, 'Okay—you're *ugly!*'"

"Bah!" the Joker said, and he shot the screen with his remote control. "Even the great Rodney gives me no relief."

But the clown of crime, in turning off the VCR, had inadvertently filled the screen with another image, courtesy of a local news broadcast.

The image of a beautiful woman.

A woman in a black leotard, her face white, her lips bright red, her cheeks dotted with bright red circles, her long-lashed eyes dark and hauntingly sad.

This image—apparently that of a street mime—struck the Joker hard, like a loose board in a wooden sidewalk, leaving him awestruck. His mouth yawned open like a skillet awaiting eggs.

"Oh my," he said.

On the screen, a plump, middle-aged, balding blond male newscaster stood, microphone in hand, in front of a massive modern building.

"...Bellew, Eyewitness News," he said, "on the scene at the Gotham City Civic Center..."

The image suddenly shifted as, amazingly, that sweet haunting slip of a girl was shown grabbing two rock musicians by their wrists, shocking them senseless.

"...where the criminal known as the *Mime* has attempted to disrupt a rock concert—"

A still photo filled the screen now, of a beautiful, pale, dark-haired woman.

"The Mime is believed to be, beneath the greasepaint, Camilla Comeo, heir to the Ortin Fireworks fortune."

Then the screen was filled with file footage of Camilla and several other mimes as they gracefully performed on stage.

"Cameo's acclaimed mime troupe reportedly exhausted her inheritance and was disbanded, after government funding for the arts was withdrawn."

Then the screen was filled with the image of the taxi whose windshield had been spider-webbed from a gunshot.

"The recent shooting of a taxi driver in a noisy traffic jam is also believed to be the work of the Mime, whose crimes are thought to be a protest against the cacophony of sounds that litter the urban landscape."

The Joker, starry-eyed, was no longer frowning; he was smiling at the screen, a smile enormous even for him. His hands clasped to his heaving bosom, he said breathlessly, to no one in particular and to the universe in general, "She's—she's beautiful—beautiful...."

On screen, the newscaster continued to speak into his mike, while behind him the lovely sad Mime, hands cuffed behind her back, was led off by the cops.

"The Mime has made no public statement," the newscaster said, "but her captor *has*."

The Joker cringed at the next image that filled the screen: a tall, muscular figure in cape and cowl.

The Sound of One Hand Clapping

"Miss Cameo," the Batman said, "is a gifted artist who has suffered a great deal of stress. It is my hope she will be given suitable medical treatment."

Enraged, the Joker, his nostrils and eyes flaring, thrust an accusatory finger at the screen.

"You!" he cried. "*You!*"

"The Dark Knight," the newscaster was saying, "is often thought of as a cold avenger, but his compassion here is evident. Goodnight for..."

"Compassion!" the Joker screamed. He fired his remote control at the big-screen TV, killing it with a KLIK! "Compassion my lily-white ass!"

He stalked out into the hallway, where his two stooges cowered at the sight of him. He lifted them each off the ground by the back of their collars, holding them up like puppies plucked from a cardboard box; they looked back at him with confused looks befitting plucked-up puppies.

"The most beautiful, sensitive soul in creation has been incarcerated!" he explained at the top of his voice. "And it's the cape cretin's doing!"

He dropped the pair to the cement floor, and looked up at nothing in particular, and stretched out his arms and hands and began to laugh: HA! HA! HA! HA! HA! HA!

Between laughs, he made a pledge: "*I* will rescue her! I will *woo* her—and *win* her!"

The stooges looked at each other and shrugged.

🦇

The next morning, on the street outside the Gotham City jail, the costumed vigilante who had earned the trust of a city spoke to the police commissioner who regarded him as a friend and ally. At Batman's side was Robin, the colorfully attired youth who accompanied him into battle.

"The staff psychiatrist agrees with you, Batman," said Commissioner Gordon. "Ms. Cameo's being transferred to Arkham Asylum for observation."

Max Allan Collins

Indeed, even as Gordon spoke, a jail matron was turning over Cameo to a pair of cops near a squad car.

"Good," Batman said. "If nothing else she'll be able to find some peace and quiet."

Her makeup washed unceremoniously away in the city jail shower the night before, the Mime—a.k.a. Camilla Cameo— sat in the backseat of the squad car; but now she would meet the world minus the whiteface mask she so loved to hide behind.

Soon the jail, Batman, and the city had been left behind, as the squad car cruised a quiet, shady country road on the way to the secluded asylum. Camilla Cameo sat stony-faced behind the wire mesh. The young cop looked back at her and said to his older partner, who drove, "She's a quiet one."

"Hey, don't knock it," the older cop said with a smirk. "It's what I look for in a broad."

The country solitude broke apart with the sound of a siren—RRRREEEEEE—and the young cop glanced curiously out his window. A helmeted cop on a motorcycle was drawing up alongside the squad car, waving them over.

"What the hell's that all about?" the older cop, behind the wheel, asked.

"Must be an emergency or a change of plans or something."

Camilla Cameo, behind the wire mesh, winced, and covered her ears at the piercing siren.

The squad car drew to a stop.

The motorcycle cop dismounted, placing his hand on his helmet, to remove it as he walked toward the squad car. The young cop leaned out his window, concerned.

"What's the problem, pard?"

The cop's helmet came off and his white face and red lips and green hair were revealed; he bent down and grinned at the two true cops seated within, and reveled in the beauty of Camilla, who wore an exaggerated expression of wonderment.

"Why, there's no problem, officers," the Joker said cheerfully. "Life is wonderful this sunny morning—don't you agree?"

He showed them the gun in his hand, which was no joke.

"Hands up, now," he said. "You're about to release your charge into my protective custody, gentlemen."

A bright red convertible rolled up alongside the squad car, driven by Kennison with Bobcat riding shotgun.

Bobcat helped Camilla out of the squad car and into the convertible while the Joker trained his automatic on the two dismayed cops, whose hands were raised. In the Joker's other hand now appeared a small, round, red object that might have been a Christmas tree ornament, but wasn't.

"And now, before we go on our merry way, and just to brighten up your morning, gents, so that you might start out the day with a *smile*..."

The Joker tossed the red bulb in the front seat between the two men, and it began to sizzle and smoke.

"...here's a little party favor for you. Ciao."

As if in joyful appreciation of the Joker's gracious gesture, the cops began to laugh uproariously. Tears rolled down their eyes, as their faces bobbed in a cloud of gas.

Camilla, sitting alone in the back of the convertible, looked with wide, bewildered eyes toward the Joker, who stood beside the car near her, pulling apart the Velcro stays of the cop uniform to reveal his "normal" attire.

"They seemed depressed, my dear," he explained, running a hand through his green mane, which had been matted down unattractively by the helmet. "I thought a smidgen of laughing gas might cheer them up."

Bobcat squealed away on the motorcycle, while the Joker slid into the back of the convertible, easing an arm around the confused Camilla's shoulder; Kennison drove them away.

"I know you must feel positively *naked* without your makeup, my sweet," the Joker said, heady with the closeness of her. He leaned toward a shell-like ear to confide: "I myself would never *dream* of going out in the world sans pancake, lipstick, and rouge,"

As the car roared back toward the city, the Joker gestured expansively, while Camilla silently recoiled.

"You will soon see, my sweet, that I've provided for your every need. Your smallest whim shall provide meaning to my meager existence!"

Camilla said nothing.

The Joker said, charmingly, "You may call me 'the Joker'—or 'Joker,' for short. Shall I call you 'Camilla'? or 'the Mime'? Or simply, 'Mime'?"

Camilla said nothing.

Several silent minutes later, the Joker was escorting the shell-shocked young woman regally to the door of his condemned castle, his two stooges tagging along.

"Well," he said, working the key in the lock, "you're shy. I can understand that." He opened the heavy wooden door, which swung open creakily. "For the nonce, we'll make it 'Ms. Cameo.'"

Camilla took in the surroundings with wide eyes—the motif of playing cards, toys, and clowns clung to the walls, even the furnishings. She stared hollowly at Harpo in a gigantic framed photo of the Marx Brothers as the Joker escorted her through his palace, gesturing solicitously.

The Sound of One Hand Clapping

"You'll be my guest until you've had a chance to reorder your, uh...affairs."

With pride, the Joker swung open a doorway, gesturing within. The young woman, walking zombielike, entered. It was a bedroom, a feminine bedroom decorated in black-and-white harlequin masks in keeping with the Mime's style. Prominently on one wall was a mammoth portrait of her pasty-faced host, signed "with gobs of love—Joker." On the theatrical dressing table, light bulbs framing its mirror, were several framed Joker portraits of varying sizes and coy poses.

"We've taken the liberty," the Joker said shyly, "of preparing this suite for you—hope it suffices...."

The Joker stood behind her, both hands on his heart, while Camilla sat at the dressing table, compulsively applying her mime's makeup.

"My dear," he said, "I don't mean to be forward—but I must speak my heart."

Camilla continued to apply her makeup, fingers gouging her cheeks.

"Since the moment I first gazed upon you—why, it seems like only yesterday—well, actually, it *was* only yesterday...."

Her face was white now. She stared at herself in the mirror.

"But, be that as it may, I must say that I do admire you so...your style, your grace, your poise, your very essence."

Now, as she looked in the mirror at herself, the Mime once more, she saw the Joker's grinning face beside hers, and there was reflected in her eyes the horror of recognizing that there was, indeed, a similarity.

"Is it my imagination, my dear, or were we *made* for each other?"

The Mime said nothing.

The Joker moved gently away, gestured with one hand in the air, as if painting a picture, his other hand resting on the nearby shoulder of his blank-faced beloved.

"We have so much to discuss—the arts, philosophy.... 'What is the sound of one hand clapping?' 'If a tree falls in the forest, is there...'"

The Mime spoke.

She said, "AIEEEEEEEEEE!!!"

The Joker reared back, stunned.

The Mime rose from the dressing table and leaned into him, her tiny hands clenched.

She said, "Will—you—please—*shut*—up!"

She forcibly pushed the shocked Joker out the bedroom door and into the hall.

"But my dear," he said. "My love..."

The door slammed in his face.

The Joker, confused, shrugged pitifully to himself and spoke to the closed door.

"Was it something I said?" he asked.

Once again gloom descended upon the king of jests. He sat moping on his throne while his nervous stooges stood before him.

"She won't come out of her room, boss," Kennison said.

The Joker leaned forward and with utter sincerity asked, "Tell me, boys...and be brutally frank: do I *talk* too much?"

"Oh, *nooooo!*" Kennison said. "Are you kidding?"

"O-o-oh, no, *no*, boss!" Bobcat said.

Lying through their teeth.

The Sound of One Hand Clapping

"Perhaps," a thoughtful Joker posed, "I moved too quickly."

"Y-y-you gotta court her, boss," said the Bobcat. "G-g-get her a nice present or something."

The Joker snapped his fingers gleefully. "A present! Yes! What *better* way to express my esteem?"

"W-w-what are you going to get her, boss?" Bobcat asked.

The Joker smiled.

The sleek, black custom car glided along the Gotham City shoreline. Behind the wheel of the Batmobile was the Dark Knight himself, his face thoughtful behind the mask. Next to him, Robin wore a puzzled expression. If Batman looked foreboding in his dark attire, the Boy Wonder in yellow cape, with his red-breasted vest and emerald-green sleeves, gauntlets, and trunks, looked strangely festive.

"What do you suppose possessed the Joker to spring Camilla Cameo?"

"It's a mystery to me, Robin," Batman said, wheeling the machine into two parking spots in the lot of the Sprang Marina. "Their facial complexions may be similar, but their complexions as criminals couldn't be more dissimilar."

The night was cool and the moon reflected off the rippling water of Gotham Bay like the bat signal hugging in a dark sky. The pair jogged along a gravel path toward the docks. The police radio had said the Mime was sighted at the marina.

"You mean," Robin said, jogging, "the Joker breaks the law for fun and profit, while the Mime is a sort of social protester?"

"Yes," Batman said, "but it's also a clash of styles."

Robin and Batman came to a stop on a buoyant walkway and looked out at a maze of similar boardwalks; the vast moonlight-bathed marina was filled with pleasure craft.

"The police call mentioned the Mime," Robin said, "but not the Joker."

"Perhaps once the Joker got Camilla out of the authorities' hands," Batman said, surveying the scene, "they went their separate ways."

"Or maybe somebody spotted *a* mime," Robin suggested.

"A possibility," Batman admitted. "Lots of street performers around an area like..."

"Batman! Look..."

Running down one of the dock walkways, with boats in the nearby background, was a slender figure.

The Mime.

"I'll handle this, Robin. Keep an eye out for the Joker and his pals!"

With impossibly long strides, the Dark Knight streaked down the gravel path to the boardwalk where the Mime ran with easy grace.

"Camilla," he called, "stop!"

But this mime was not Camilla, though Batman did not yet know as much. This mincing mime was male, his back to his pursuer, hiding a grotesquely grinning face under a wig that resembled Camilla Cameo's hairstyle.

"Stop!"

The Joker hopped onto the deck of a craft, a good-size boat outfitted with sail and a motor. He nodded to Kennison and Bobcat, lurking in the shadows, holding on to a rope that extended upward.

The deck appeared empty when Batman hopped aboard. No sign of the Mime. The Dark Knight stood on the deck of the ship and looked around.

The Sound of One Hand Clapping

But not down: beneath him, spread out on the deck, under his feet, was the heavy crosshatch of a fishing net.

"Camilla?" Batman said.

The Joker's two stooges yanked hard on their rope.

Batman, caught in the sack of a fishing net, was pulled bodily up off the ground.

Still in the Camilla-like wig, the Joker peeked up from a trapdoor in the deck to look gloatingly at the netted Batman.

Exasperated, Batman hung in the fishing net and suffered the Joker's taunts.

"Batman, Batman, Batman...you should've *known* there'd be a Joker in the deck!"

The Joker climbed out of his hole and leaned over, with mock sympathy, to smile at the upside-down Batman, the fierce scowl of his square jaw turned into a bizarre grin.

"You must be lonely," the Joker said, "hanging around the marina on a dark night like this."

"You only *think* you've caught me, Joker."

"My! What a good imagination I must have!" The Joker yanked off his wig and walked to the wheel of the craft, a faithful stooge at either side. "Well, boys, let's head for home. I think we've caught the limit!"

Robin, who had witnessed this from a distance while running along the boardwalk to intercede, found himself standing at the end of the dock, cape flapping, fists raised in midair, watching with infinite frustration as the boat headed out, an unjumpable distance away from him.

The Joker stood, hands clasped, bending forward, listening at Camilla's bedroom door.

"My dearest one," he said tenderly, tentatively, "I have a surprise for you...a gift...a very *special* gift."

Within the bedroom, Camilla—the Mime—stood with her back to the door, captured by curiosity.

The Joker's voice from behind the door was supplicant. "And if it doesn't convince you that I'm your soulmate, if it doesn't touch you, move you...I'll gladly step out of your life—*forever*."

Hesitant, Camilla exited the bedroom; the Joker bowed grandly to the supple figure in black and white face.

"Ah—accompany me, my love, if you would," he said, offering his arm. "And I must say you look *lovely*."

The Mime pulled away, looking at him with suspicion and obvious dislike. The Joker ignored the reaction and gestured theatrically. He walked along and she followed, reluctantly.

"Now," he said, "consider that your run-of-the-mill suitor might have brought you chocolates—or perhaps said it with flowers."

In his main chamber, the Joker gestured with both hands as the Mime approached with puzzlement and even fear a huge package wrapped in colorful playing-card wrapping paper and a large red bow.

"Instead," the Joker said, "I've given you something much more...*personal*."

The Mime stared at the package, which was much taller than she.

"Open it, precious..."

She began to tear off the wrapping paper, haltingly at first, but soon with the enthusiasm of a small child on Christmas morning. Curiosity made the eyes in the white face seem larger than life.

Shortly, her present was revealed; an unconscious Batman strapped to a chair, a big red ribbon and bow around him; a brightly painted Joker face could be seen carved into the high back of the chair, rising above its slumbering occupant.

The Joker touched the shoulder of the shocked Mime, who viewed the unconscious, bound Batman without her usual expressiveness; her masklike face was blank.

"My gift of love," the Joker said, with a sweeping bow. "Our mutual nemesis!"

Camilla stood frozen.

The Joker placed a gentle gloved hand on her shoulder. "Shall I kill him for you, now, my sweet?"

She did not reply; ever so gently, he turned her to face him, gesturing grandly with one hand.

"You see, we really must decide quickly—he's a resourceful one."

Camilla touched her lips with one hand, confused, while the Joker walked to the desk before his joker-throne.

"We tranquilized the beast, my love...and we removed the porcupine's quills." The Joker displayed Batman's utility belt, lifting it from the desktop. "But even weaponless, he's troublesome—he won't remain groggy long."

Camilla stared at her present, which seemed to be coming around slowly.

"So, my precious...help me choose an artistic, a colorful means of demise for my love offering."

While the Joker gloated within his crumbling castle, Robin prowled the back streets of Gotham in the Batmobile, watching the dashboard computer screen on which a street map glowed and a dot blipped.

As long as they haven't tossed out Batman's utility belt, the youth thought, *I can track the signal.*

Max Allan Collins

Within minutes Robin was stepping out of the Batmobile, facing the entrance of the tumbledown building
that had once housed the Jester Novelty Company.

Inside, the Joker held up a small gas canister with an oxygen mask attached; his two stooges smiled their approval.
Batman himself, fully awake now, wore a faint, wry smile.
The disturbed, frightened Mime wore an exaggerated
expression of dismay.

"Might I suggest, my sweetness," the Joker said, "a
lethal dose of my laughing gas?"

The Mime blinked.

"I think the Joker likes you, Camilla," Batman said.

The Joker, unable to contain his excitement, painted
the air with his hands, while Batman listened, unim-
pressed, smirking.

"Imagine it, my love—the bat boob is convulsed with
gales of laughter...laughing till his heart bursts—his face
frozen in a grotesque, eternal grin!"

At this the Mime recoiled.

But the Joker, caught up in himself, in his love for the
Mime and his hatred for Batman, failed to notice. He
approached the Mime, touching her shoulder tenderly.

"And all for you, my dear—for your *love*."

The Mime screamed silently, but the Joker did not hear,
or see, for that matter.

"For my...dare I say it...future *bride*."

The Mime slapped the Joker.

Hard.

The sound rang out like a rifle shot.

The Joker touched his face with splayed fingers and,
with the expression of a child who has suddenly had a

The Sound of One Hand Clapping

nagging question answered, said, "The sound of one hand clapping!"

The Mime sat on the floor, huddling, despair-ridden. The Joker hovered over her, trying to keep his distance at the same time. He was crushed, truly dumbfounded by her rejection. He did not notice, behind him, that Batman had struggled to his feet, despite being tied in the chair.

"I don't understand," the Joker said pleadingly. "I gave you a present! Why, I'd have shared it all with you—made you my queen!"

With those words the king of comedy was crowned, as Batman, still tied to the chair, bent forward forcefully and conked the clown with the upper portion of the high-backed throne, hitting the Joker hard on the top of his head with his own grinning image.

The Joker, stunned and sitting on the floor with his knobby knees pointing north and south, respectively, winced as Batman, bound in the chair but on his feet, sneered down at him.

"Oww!" the Joker said, rubbing his head.

"You're no king," Batman said. "Just the court fool."

The mad jester's nostrils flared and his eyes filled with rage as he pointed a long purple finger up at Batman.

"Get him!" the Joker cried.

But the Joker's two stooges were busy.

Robin had come up behind them, tapping them on the shoulder to ask, "Excuse me—shouldn't you get me first?"

For a moment, they looked stupidly, blankly back at him.

The Joker was on his feet again, fiercely commanding his boys, "Get the brat! I can handle that caped clod with—"

"Both hands tied behind my back," Batman sneered, just waiting for the Joker, chair or no chair. The Mime, standing once more, took all of this in, not quite sure what to make of it.

Robin ran down the hallway where the gallery of framed comedians hung off-kilter. He smiled, the two stooges in close pursuit.

"You guys are really wearing me out," he said over his shoulder.

Robin dropped to the floor, saying, "Mind if I stop for a rest?" while Kennison and Bobcat tried to put on the brakes. Both of them tripped over Robin and hit the floor hard, with twin WHUMPS! Robin, resting on his stomach, stifled a yawn.

Then the Boy Wonder stood over the pair of dopes, his arms folded, and said, "Gee—I guess you hoodlums are a little worn out yourselves. Take five, why don't you—*years.*"

In the main chamber, the Joker stood before Batman, his purple fists pumping the air before him, ready to defend the honor of his ladylove.

Batman conked him with the chair again.

The Mime stifled a smile as the groggy Joker staggered, regrouping to try again. Purple fists pumping.

Only to be conked once more.

Knocked goofy, the Joker sat on the floor, counting the planets and stars that revolved before his vision.

And the Mime broke her silence with laughter worthy of the Joker himself: "HA! HA! HA! HA! HA! HA! HA!"

"I think she liked that," Robin smiled, as he untied Batman.

Tears streaked the white makeup off her face as she roared with glee, her laughter echoing through the old factory.

"Yes," Batman said, rubbing his arms where the ropes had been, "but I know something she *won't* like."

The Sound of One Hand Clapping

"What's that?"
"Her new home."

The next morning, within the sprawling, stern gothic
structure of Arkham Asylum, a guard escorted a wide-
eyed, shell-shocked Camilla Cameo—once again stripped
of her mime's makeup—down the asylum hall. Walking
along beside her was a frequent resident of the facility, a
man whose whiteface could not be washed off.

"You'll like it here," the Joker was assuring her. "I'll
put in a good word for you with my *therapist*, you'll make
friends...there's plenty to do..."

Camilla said nothing.

But she wore a big, wide smile, not unlike the Joker's.

Only Camilla's seemed rather glazed.

Neutral Ground

MIKE RESNICK

Kittlemeier's shop was in a poverty-stricken area of town. To say that it was unimpressive would be an understatement. Its windows were patched with plywood, and its door handle was so rusty it almost posed a physical threat.

The shop was not listed in any telephone book. Its door bore no street number. No sign proclaimed what it sold. Those who peered into it from the doorway saw only a dimly lit room with an ancient counter, an old-fashioned cash register, an out-of-date calendar from the local service station, and a curtained doorway leading to another room that opened onto the alley.

One would think, to look at it, that Kittlemeier's shop could not possibly attract any customers, and in truth it did not attract many. But those who needed Kittlemeier's particular services always seemed to know where to find him.

It was five o'clock in the afternoon when an elegant black limousine pulled up in front of Kittlemeier's shop and a tall, well-dressed man emerged from the backseat.

Lithe as a jungle panther—his custom-made suit barely concealing his heavily muscled frame—he walked the five steps to Kittlemeier's door, paused for just a moment, and then entered the shop.

A bell tinkled gently and old Kittlemeier, a measuring tape slung over his shoulder, a pencil tucked behind his ear, pushed past the curtain and greeted his customer.

"You are late," he said.

The tall man shrugged. "It was unavoidable," he said, and Kittlemeier noticed that the knuckles of his right hand were badly swollen.

"We must hurry," said Kittlemeier. "I have another appointment in fifteen minutes."

The tall man's interest was aroused, but he refrained from asking any questions. That was Kittlemeier's rule, and he honored it.

Kittlemeier reached below the counter and withdrew a yellow belt that was lined with exterior pouches.

"You see," he said, displaying it to the tall man, "I had to eliminate the container for the explosives in order to make room for the modified gas mask you will be using. You are quite sure of its dimensions?"

The tall man nodded.

"I took the liberty of making another slight change," continued Kittlemeier, showing him a different section of the belt. "The miniaturized winch for your silken cord was wearing against the leather here, and so I reversed the inset angle."

"I approve," said the tall man.

"A tungsten cord would be just as strong and take up less room," suggested Kittlemeier.

The tall man shook his head. "I prefer silk. It causes less damage to the hands."

Mike Resnick

Kittlemeier shrugged. "You might think about it in the future. You could add an extra twenty yards to its length, and I could always reinforce your gauntlets."

"Perhaps in the future, when the need for a longer cord arises," said the tall man. "You have something else for me?"

Old Kittlemeier nodded and reached beneath the counter again, this time withdrawing two long, dark blue gauntlets.

"Where is the power source?" asked the tall man.

"A lithium battery, sewn into the lining of each."

"And these will insulate against a temperature of a hundred degrees below zero Fahrenheit?"

"At least," said Kittlemeier.

"Good. I will be needing them to—"

"I don't want to know," interrupted Kittlemeier, holding up a hand. "What you do when you leave my premises is not my concern."

The tall man nodded, and for a moment he was aware of a clock ticking in the dusty stillness.

"I'll take these with me," he said at last, indicating the gauntlets.

"Have you considered the boots?"

"Yes. I very much like your suggestion."

"Good," said Kittlemeier. "Of course, I will need molds of your feet before I can equip them with springs enabling you to leap the required distance. Shall we make an appointment for, say, two o'clock on Thursday?"

"Why not now?" asked the tall man.

Kittlemeier shook his head. "I have another appointment. You must leave before my next client arrives. You know the rules."

"As you wish," said the tall man indifferently.

Kittlemeier set to work wrapping the belt and the gloves, then placed them into a nondescript shopping bag and handed them across the counter to the tall man.

"That will be..." He thought for a moment, then named a sum that did not seem too exorbitant to him. "In cash, as always."

The tall man grunted, withdraw his wallet, took out a number of large bills, and laid them on the counter.

"Until Thursday, then," said Kittlemeier.

"Until Thursday," said the tall man. He picked up his shopping bag, walked out the door, and entered the back-seat of his limousine, which immediately pulled out from the curb and was soon lost from sight in the rush-hour traffic.

Kittlemeier put the money in his cash register, then checked his wristwatch. He badly wanted a cigarette, but his next client was never late, and so he remained behind the counter.

At precisely 5:15 p.m., a wiry man with thinning blond hair entered the shop, looking furtively into the shadows before he approached the counter.

"Well?" he demanded. "Are they ready?"

"Four of them are," answered Kittlemeier. "Two were completely beyond repair. I will have to make entirely new ones."

"Do it. And last time you gave me only eighty question marks. This time I want at least one hundred, and I want you to know I will count every last one."

Kittlemeier pulled out a pad of paper and began scribbling in his almost illegible scrawl. "One hundred question marks each," he muttered as he wrote.

"And the material must be strong, and the dyes waterproof."

"Waterproof dyes," said Kittlemeier, while scribbling furiously.

"Can you do it?"

"Of course," said Kittlemeier.

"I must have them by next Monday, because on Tuesday..." He threw back his head and giggled hysterically.

"Monday," said Kittlemeier, nodding. "Ten o'clock in the morning?"

"Ten o'clock," said the man.

Kittlemeier placed four neatly folded green costumes in a brown paper bag from the local grocery store. He then took a fresh sheet of scratch paper and scribbled a figure on it.

"This is more than we agreed upon."

"My original figure was for repairing six costumes. I did not plan on having to make two from scratch."

"You kept the old devices for the new costumes?" queried the man. "I would be very unhappy to find that I was paying for new weapons when the old ones were in perfect working order."

"I kept them," said Kittlemeier. "You can inspect them when you return next Monday."

The man stared at him distrustfully for a long moment, then pulled out a roll of bills and placed them on the counter.

Kittlemeier counted them carefully, then looked up. "Please bring another six hundred dollars with you on Monday, and then your account will be up to date."

The man nodded almost imperceptibly, then grabbed his bag, turned on his heels, and left.

It had been a long day, and old Kittlemeier was getting hungry. He sighed; it was satisfying to be known as the very best in your trade, but your time was so seldom your own.

He checked his watch again, and decided that he had just enough time to go out for a quick sandwich before Selina arrived for her fitting.

Batman in Nighttown

KAREN HABER and ROBERT SILVERBERG

When the masked and caped figure walked into the black-and-white marble entry hall of the Wayne mansion thirty minutes before midnight, excitement ripped through the mass of party-goers.

"Can you imagine! It's Batman. Someone call the police," Alice Chilton said in feigned alarm. Resplendent in her gilded Indonesian dance garb, she strode forward to get a better look at him.

"Oh, no. Don't call the police," Mara Osuna said. "Call Channel Five news. I think he's exciting." And, sinuous in a black spandex cat costume, she too prowled closer, gliding through the splendid ballroom with barely concealed eagerness.

Trial attorney Carlton Thayer, done up as a British Redcoat, raised his glass in mock tribute. "Somebody's got to deal with crime," he said. "Certainly the courtrooms can't handle it all. I say, more power to him."

"He's just a damned vigilante," Alice Chilton retorted. "We can't have people taking the law into their own hands. Even if they are wearing blue silk gloves."

She turned to their host, who was standing quietly to one side, a bemused expression on what was visible of his face.

"What do you think, Bruce?"

Bruce Wayne had been watching the doppelganger of his crime-fighting alter-ego with amusement, and perhaps with a little perplexity. He swung about now and smiled at his aunt.

"I don't know if this Batman is a criminal or a saint," Wayne said. "But I do know that he's late. Alfred, see if our unexpected guest would like a drink."

"Very good, sir," the butler said in his clipped British accent. "And perhaps the gentleman would like me to take his cape as well? No?"

"Batman" shook his head.

When the newcomer accepted a glass of champagne, Wayne lifted his own flute in a toast.

Clever, he thought. And a damned close replica. If that's how I look, the effect is even better than I'd hoped. The cape is very good.

"Batman" moved into the main ballroom, joining the assorted demons and sprites, witches and warlocks. Wayne tracked him for a moment in deepening fascination.

It was a little dreamlike, he thought. As though I'm standing outside my own body, looking at myself arrive at a party. He admired the stranger's audacity. Did he know whose house he was at? Probably not. Or perhaps he knew very well, Wayne told himself. Who is he? I'll find out at the unmasking.

Wayne circulated through the party, playing the part of host to perfection. Initially, the young millionaire had regretted his offer to let the masked ball be held at Wayne Manor. But Aunt Alice had been so persuasive, wheedling

Karen Haber and Robert Silverberg

until he gave in. He certainly owed her a favor. Dear Alice. All those holidays, home from prep school, which he'd spent in her warm, gracious company. After his parents' murder, Alice Chilton had been very good to him. An "aunt," yes. Though not a blood relation, she was almost a second mother. The least he could do was provide a place for her Women's Auxiliary Charity Ball. Besides, he wanted to deflate his growing reputation as a hermit. And so the cream of Gotham society, bewigged, bejeweled, and by now pretty well inebriated, was crammed into his mansion, awaiting the toll of midnight to unmask.

With a quick motion of his hand, Wayne reached behind his own mask—a grinning, red-faced devil—and wiped the sweat from his jaw. Through the mask's narrow eye-slits, he peered at his jeweled Rolex. The time was 11:40 p.m. Only twenty minutes to go. He adjusted his sleek red tuxedo. Perhaps he should have come as Batman, too. But that would have been too easy.

"Swell party, Wayne," said a brown-cowled figure sporting an owl mask, with a long, thin cigar poking bizarrely through its mouthpiece. The tones were the bass rasp of Police Commissioner Gordon. "Nice to see the old mansion lit up like this."

"All for a good cause," Wayne said. "I don't mind, as long as nobody breaks the Ming vase. Or," he said, staring meaningfully at the Commissioner's stogie, "uses the Egyptian urn for an ashtray."

Gordon exhaled a large, malodorous cloud of smoke. Wayne coughed.

"Is your life insurance paid up?" he inquired pleasantly. "I'd hate to see your lung x-rays."

"And I'd hate to see the bill for this party," Gordon said. "But it's not my problem, I guess. How long have you been back in town now, anyway?"

"Six months, Commissioner."

"Gstaad lost its appeal?"

Wayne forced a debonair chuckle. "The world is filled with all manner of delights and distractions, yes. But occasionally one needs to come home."

The gray eyes behind the owl mask fixed him with a shrewd gaze.

"I don't know, Bruce. If I had the money and time, there's plenty of places I'd be happy to call home besides Gotham City."

With a shrug, he moved off.

A good man, Wayne thought. A good cop, too. Perhaps too good. He had a deep streak of keen curiosity, Gordon. Way too much curiosity. Did he suspect the truth?

Wayne walked across the ballroom toward the door.

"Don't just walk right by me like that," said a throaty female voice.

Wayne turned. Ellen Harring was standing by the window, her white-gloved hand resting coquettishly upon her hip. Her blond hair fell loosely down her back, gleaming like a dazzling cascade in the lamplight. She was dressed as a houri, all golden veils and shimmer.

Very apt, Wayne thought. Since his return to Gotham City, Ellen had found one pretext after another for coming by, leaving messages, indefatigably pursuing him with social hunting skills burnished by long use. Each time she made a move, he managed to extricate himself. One step forward, two steps back. For a time, he'd found it amusing, but the *pas de deux* was becoming all too intricate. Now she walked toward him as though oiled, all fluid motion.

She hooked her arms around his neck and leaned forward until her chest rested on his.

"Why don't you come tell me all about your erotic weapon collection?" she crooned.

Wayne smelled bourbon on her breath. Gently, he freed himself from her grasp.

"You'd miss the prize for prettiest costume," he said. "We can't have that."

She seemed unperturbed by his amiable coolness. Her expression was all too frank, her eyes all too explicitly intense. He cast around for escape. And found it as the mysterious blue-caped figure in the bat mask moved past them.

"Why don't we ask Batman about his exploits?" Wayne suggested, stepping back to include the stranger. "Even a costumed vigilante could use a beautiful assistant like you, Ellen."

She turned to gape just long enough for Wayne to slip past her and out through a hall door into the servants' quarters.

Safe.

Wayne leaned against the plain white wall and shook his head. A shame, really. So attractive, Ellen. He could feel the heat of her against him even now. But her kind never let up. If he invited her into his world, into his bed, he knew that eventually he would regret the decision. It would all end badly, with him prying her fingers, one by one, away from his life. And he had no time, no room left for any sort of serious entanglements on that level. Europe had cured him of such things.

He moved through the dim passage, his footsteps echoing on the concrete floor, and emerged from behind a bookshelf into the gaming room. Here, the noise of the party was muffled by teak paneling and thick russet carpeting. Two amber-shaded swag lamps cast warm circles of light on the greensward of an enormous pool table. A footman in white powdered wig and purple waistcoat was making an intricate carom shot, studied intently by his challenger, an imposing sultan in flowing black robes and an enormous, bejeweled turban.

"Super soiree, Bruce," the footman said as he watched the sultan ponder his next move.

"Harry—still hanging out by the pool table. I should have known." Wayne paused. Even in prep school, Harry Thornton had never been able to resist a pool game. Fifteen years had only honed his appetite.

The sultan looked up. It was Wayne's accountant, Jim Weatherby. He gestured broadly with his cue stick toward the scattered balls on the table.

"Got any tips?"

Wayne nodded. "Sure," he said. "Don't play Harry. He's a semiprofessional pool hustler." He gave them a half smile and moved on, restless. Surrounded by this swirling horde of friends and acquaintances, he was still alone, concealing his agitation, his alienation, behind clever patter and the aloofness that wealth conferred.

Wayne had come back heartsick from Europe, tired of the gambling tables and rich widows. He was weary of the same faces seen at the same spas, those hungry faces avidly scanning the crowd. All of them looking for the same thing. Fresh meat. He'd done his own share of predatory stalking, and with no little success. Long ago, he'd learned that his trim body, dark hair, and blue eyes were quite acceptable to women of all shapes and sizes. Of course, the money helped. And he'd inherited one of the largest fortunes in Gotham City.

But now he hunted different prey. He'd come back home to search for meaning. To do something useful. To avenge the past. It made little difference to him how Batman was perceived, whether as vigilante or folk hero. All

Karen Haber and Robert Silverberg

he knew was that he felt alive and connected with the world when he was wearing that blue-caped costume, and hollow and remote when he was not.

He slipped through the door into the library.

Three generations of Wayne bibliophiles had amassed a collection of rarities that filled two stories' worth of bookcases. The room, rich with its smell of antique leather binding and musty pages, its graceful cherrywood railings and ladders, was one of Wayne's favorites. He'd hoped to take a few minutes here, alone. But he saw now that the library was already occupied. Somebody wearing a blue silk mask and cape was wandering about by the far shelves, nineteenth-century French literature. The Batman masquerader.

For an eerie moment, Wayne felt as if he were looking into a mirror. As though he were a stranger standing across the room, watching himself. Then he shook off the dream image. With an effort, he managed a jocular tone, a tight grin, as he said, "Well, so how's the crime-fighting business these days?"

The impostor turned, nodded. He looked tense.

"Could be worse," he said in a tenor voice that perhaps was roughened a little around the edges by drink.

Wayne moved closer. He could see now that the outfit he wore was virtually an exact replica of his own Batman suit. "Nice costume," he said. "Who does your tailoring?"

"This little thing?" "Batman" shrugged. "Oh, I just picked it up someplace. Midnight blue has always been my favorite color."

"And mine."

"Want to switch costumes?" the impostor said. "I wouldn't mind being in your shoes for a while. Even if they are red. It'd be worth it, to find out what it's like to be a millionaire."

There was a wistful tone to his comment. And just a hint of menace.

Wayne was growing impatient to discover whose face lay behind that mask.

"You wouldn't like being in my shoes. Since I have an unusually shaped foot," he said, "all of them are hand-made. They aren't likely to fit anybody else."

He stared at "Batman," his annoyance growing. This joke was rapidly losing its charm. How dare some gate-crashing creep show up in, of all costumes, this one.

"I think I need a refill," the impostor said. "Excuse me."

His cape rustled like dry leaves as he brushed past Wayne and walked out of the library.

Slowly, the grandfather clock in the entry hall struck, twelve dolorous notes.

On the twelfth tone, the lights went out.

At first, the conversations and music continued. But as the darkness extended its hold on the party, the convivial noise began to ebb into silence. What had seemed like a gag was starting to feel odd. Disquieting. Aside from an occasional nervous giggle from a guest, an unbroken hush prevailed.

Alarmed, Wayne groped along the wall toward what he hoped was the door. Where were the auxiliary lights? The generator below the house should be working...

"My pearls!!" a woman shrieked.

In the dark, other cries joined hers.

"My watch!!"

"Thief!! Stop him!!"

"Lights!! We need lights!"

Wayne found the library door and began working his way toward the basement stairs. He'd have to throw the circuit breakers himself. If that didn't work, the next step was to find some hand lamps. Where was Alfred when he needed him?

Then he heard the hum of the auxiliary generator, and the lights came on, flickered uncertainly a moment, grew brighter again, and this time held. Wayne breathed easier. Better head off a major panic, he thought.

"Relax, everyone," he said. "Nothing to worry about. That was a little prank I thought you'd enjoy."

Laughter and applause met his words. With a bow, he moved toward the front door.

A small knot of people gathered there, Ellen Harring and Alice Chilton among them. Wayne's aunt was close to tears.

"Bruce, it's ghastly," she said. "Do you know what's happened? Someone's stolen Ellen's pearls. And Harry's watch. And even the brooch from Jim's turban."

Wayne pursed his lips. "You mean all of that stuff was real?"

"Of course," Ellen said sharply. "How could you think otherwise?"

"And you wore them to a costume party?"

He wanted to shake her.

Commissioner Gordon shouldered brusquely into the group, his mask pushed up off his face, its yellow owl eyes goggling the ceiling weirdly.

"Anybody get a sense of who the thief was?" he demanded.

"None."

"Nope."

"I heard something," Harry said. "Like a woman walking by in a satin dress. Then a yank at my sleeve, and my watch was gone."

"Somebody must see very well in the dark," Wayne said.

"Yes, with eyes like a cat," Gordon added.

Or the sonar of a bat, Wayne thought. Quickly, he glanced around the room, but saw no sign of a blue half-mask, ribbed cape, or golden utility belt. The bogus Batman had vanished. Of course.

A cold breeze drifted into the room, lifting the edges of Wayne's tuxedo jacket, setting Gordon's brown corduroy feathers dancing.

Wayne swung around. In the dining room, a leaded window yawned open, permitting a narrow rectangle of night sky to break the symmetry of the beveled glass wall.

Escape route, he thought. And precious minutes had already been devoured by chitchat. He had to get out of here.

He clutched his brow dramatically.

"Damn! The quotes are coming in from Tokyo." He turned to the group. "Auntie, I've got to run upstairs for a while and check the ticker. Would you see to the guests and close down the party?"

"Of course, Bruce. But what about the robbery?"

Wayne shrugged.

"That's Commissioner Gordon's department. I'm sure he'll handle it well."

He hurried up the stairs, ignoring the shocked looks on their faces.

Hurry, damn it. Through the door by the guest rooms, down the staircase to the back door, and out into wintry November darkness.

A car motor rumbled to life. Wayne recognized the sound and scowled. It was his car. Where was the alarm? That damned "Batman" was not only good at robbery, he was skilled at hot wiring as well. And the front gate was open. Even if Wayne reached the remote controls, he'd never close it in time.

The cave, he thought. Get the new motorcycle. Change into costume. No. No time. Go as I am.

He took the stairs in twos, grabbed the keys to the cycle, and leaped onto the powerful Harley.

The cycle roared to life, its headlight a white beacon spilling light on the path to the front drive. Wayne switched on the tracer. A small red light pulsed on the schematic map set next to the odometer. His quarry was heading out of Wayne's imposing suburb through the newer, cheaper neighborhoods toward the freeway.

Wayne frowned. If he'd had more time he could have radioed the police and told Gordon to put some cars in pursuit. Now he'd have to go it alone, chasing his own car into nighttime Gotham.

The wind cut through his red silk suit like sharpened icicles. The chill glow of streetlights flickered through the bare branches of the oak trees that lined the boulevard. Wayne reached behind, pulled goggles out of the cycle's side box, and strapped them on.

He began to feel more confident.

Cutting across Elm Street, he detoured through the parking lot of the First Episcopal Church and jumped its hedge, shearing seconds off his ride. The schematic showed his quarry entering the freeway. Wayne pressed harder on the accelerator.

Dark streets whizzed past, punctuated by patches of frozen water reflecting light onto the slick pavement. Houses went by in a blur—large, dark shapes looming behind carefully manicured hedges.

Motor screaming, the Harley hit a wet patch of leaves and fishtailed. Desperately, Wayne fought for control as the cycle skidded around and began to go off the road.

"Brake. No, don't brake, stupid. Steer into it," he muttered.

The cycle kept sliding. A massive oak, its limbs knotted with age, loomed on the right. Wayne braced for bonecrunching impact. Break collarbone at least, he thought. Hospital casts. Eight weeks to heal...

A patch of dry pavement caught the front wheel. With a whine, the bike pulled out of the skid at the last moment and righted itself.

Wayne sighed with relief. He glanced down, checked the map. His car was still on the freeway. In a moment, so was he, the wind screaming past his ears, trying to rip the back off his red tuxedo.

Exits flashed by: Hawken Street, Euclid, Morton. Ahead, the lights of downtown twinkled in their concrete and steel firmament.

The tracer showed his quarry at the Main Street ramp.

More lights, red and blue, caught his attention—a police car behind him. The mournful howl of the siren chased its way up his vertebrae. Belatedly, Wayne remembered that motorcycles were illegal on the freeway.

"Damn!"

No time now for playing tag with a squad car. And no utility belt, no bag of tricks to aid him. Have to tell Alfred to pack a spare in the cave.

He checked the gas tank. Three-quarters full. Good. The Harley could easily outpace any V-6 engine on open road. Once they were in the city, well, Wayne would worry about that later. They had to catch him first.

At the exit, he downshifted nimbly and squeaked through a yellow light turning red. The squad car was right behind him, tires squealing. He cut around a stalled car, sped between a double-parked delivery truck and a sedan, and made a hard right down an alley.

The police siren faded into a faint whine. Wayne glanced over his shoulder. The alley was empty, save for shadows. His pursuers must have gotten stuck behind the truck, trapped by the slow reactions of the driver. Good. Better speak to Gordon about upgrading driver training for his rookies, Wayne thought, grinning.

The red dot on his map turned onto Market. Came to a halt.

Wayne dialed up the address.

225 Market, just past the corner of Hayes.

Odd neighborhood. Just a few bars, grocery stores, and car-parts places. Wayne pulled the Harley out onto Market, searching his memory. No record of any fences in this neighborhood, as far as he knew. They were all in the East End.

He parked the cycle at the corner of Hayes and walked the two blocks, past locked, barred storefronts and shuttered windows.

There was his car: a low, dark shadow by the curb. Silent—the motor had been cut off. No sign of movement within, although the smoked-glass windows were difficult to see through. Wayne yanked the driver's door open. The gray Spencer was empty.

A trickle of music, bluesy and lonesome, pulled his attention from the car. Where was it coming from? He turned toward the dilapidated brownstone behind him.

Up two stone steps and he was in the hallway of an old flophouse. A row of tin mailboxes set into the wall bore tattered nameplates, all of them sad. faded ribbons save for the third box from the end. A new label had been glued to box 405 with red tape.

Club Astarte, it said.

In this dump? Must be an after-hours bar, Wayne thought. Moves its location regularly to avoid the cops. Probably operates without a liquor license and cleans up, charging five bucks a drink. Wouldn't Gordon enjoy being along for this one?

I'm beginning to miss him, he thought.

He climbed the stairs, each step squeaking, four flights up toward the growing sound of a bass guitar pulsing rhythm, women laughing a bit too shrilly, a horn player worrying a note.

Fourth floor. Dark as hell, he thought. Where's that music coming from?

He rounded a corner and saw light spilling through the cracked transom above the door to room 405. Club Astarte. Wayne pulled his devil mask down over his face and leaned against the door. It gave.

The room was filled with smoke and the cloying aroma of stale beer. Pink spotlights cut weakly through the murk. There was no band. No live music of any kind. Men and women sat slumped at tables, or moved slowly to taped music or their own internal drumbeat, leaning against each other on the tiny dance floor. They ignored him.

Maybe a man in red silk and a devil's mask comes in at this time every night, Wayne thought.

He shouldered through the crowd, searching for a sign of his quarry.

A long hallway, garishly painted green and orange, led back toward the bathrooms. One of them was in use. He leaned against the wall, waiting.

A woman in a short blue dress ran by, giggling tipsily. She disappeared into the empty bathroom.

The other bathroom door flew open. Wayne tensed.

A second woman, short, with a cloud of red hair, strode out of the john. She was wearing a tight, black, low-cut dress that showed a little too much. She stopped in her tracks when she saw him.

Karen Haber and Robert Silverberg

"Hey, devil," she said. Her smile was an unambiguous invitation. She lit a cigarette and inhaled, green eyes taking shrewd measure of him. When he failed to respond to the invitation, her eyes narrowed. She gestured, indicating his costume.

"What is this," she asked. "Mardi Gras?"

"I thought it was a bar," he said.

The redhead leaned back against the wall and crossed her arms. Smoke tendrils snaked around her head like a halo.

"First the guy in the cape," she said. "Now you with the red tux." She gave him a look of blunt approval. "Not bad. How about a peek behind the mask?"

"I'm shy."

"Want a drink?"

"Maybe later."

He started to move past her.

Mockingly, she rubbed her shoulders, shivering.

"Brrr. I thought you devils were supposed to be hot stuff. Guess you're just interested in buying souls. And Ricky is probably selling."

Her words stopped Wayne in mid-step. He turned to face her. "Ricky?" he asked.

She laughed, a high jagged sound. Her pupils were huge.

"Suddenly you're interested," she said. "Yeah, Beelzebub. It's Ricky you want, is it? Then keep going down that hall until you can't go any farther. That's my personal philosophy, too. See ya later, Satan."

She winked at him broadly and headed back to the other room.

Wayne followed the hallway. It came to an end in a flat, purple wall.

No exit? What did she mean, then?

He frowned and pushed against the wall. It swung back smoothly, spinning on recessed hinges.

Hidden doors were always useful for quick exits during police raids, he thought. I should have known.

He walked through into a dim corridor. The wall closed behind him.

Halfway down the hall, light glimmered under the crack of a door. He pressed his palm against the door and felt it move. Pushed harder. Hinges grating, the door opened.

Inside, a man with three days' growth of beard and a sour expression looked up from a desk littered with small plastic bags and a pile of ledgers. So there *was* a fence on Market Street. Wayne bit back a smile.

The fence sighed. "Not another one."

"Are you Ricky?" Wayne pitched his voice low.

"Who's asking?"

"The redhead sent me."

"Donna?"

"Who else?"

The fence's face relaxed into something midway between a scowl and a grin.

"Okay then," he said. "That last comedian made me jumpy. Comes in here with that goofy cape and wants to sell big jewels. Jerk. I only work in computer parts."

Wayne nodded. "So he left?"

"A minute ago. Weird son of a bitch. Wouldn't take off that bat mask."

"Which way?"

"Huh?"

Wayne grabbed a handful of the fence's shirt and pulled him halfway over the desk toward him. Between tightly clenched teeth, he asked again.

"I said, which way did he go?"

Karen Haber and Robert Silverberg

"T-that way." The fence pointed to a dark staircase across the hall. Shoving hard, Wayne released the man and dashed out the door. The stairs led down into blackness.

Grappling in his pocket, Wayne pulled out the infrared goggles from the cycle and slapped them on. Gray shadows were transmuted into hellish red and black geometry. He bolted down the stairs. One flight. Two flights.

Below him, he could hear the sound of footsteps running. He quickened his pace, using the handrail for balance. He missed a stair, started to fall, recovered, and kept going.

Three flights.

But he was still too far behind. Wayne bent one knee, grabbed the banister with both hands, vaulted up, over, and down to the final row of stairs, landing on the balls of his feet.

Thank God for that acrobatic training in France, he thought.

Wayne could see the front door swinging wildly. In three strides he was through it and on the street.

The Spencer had come to life again, motor rumbling. Wayne reached for his belt. A shame to have to slash my own tires, he thought. His hands closed on his red silk cummerbund.

He looked down.

And remembered that the only person wearing a utility belt was the man he'd been chasing.

Before he had time to curse, the Spencer moved. Tires squealed as the sleek, dark sedan pulled away from the curb, accelerating from zero to ninety in thirty seconds.

Wayne pounded down the sidewalk to the alley, kicked the cycle into overdrive. He was beginning to get annoyed.

It took fifteen minutes to trail his car back onto the highway, heading out of town.

Giddy with fatigue, Wayne watched the red blip move across the screen of the schematic monitor. He's going back to my house, he thought. Probably wants to drop off the car and have a drink. When I get there and ring the front doorbell, "Batman" will invite me in for a nightcap. Offer me a bed. Show me the gun collection.

The map shifted to a new quadrant as the Spencer took the exit back to Oakhurst. Wayne pressed the accelerator harder, and roared down the exit ramp and onto Oakdale Avenue. Trees flew by, street lamps, empty intersections. He was five minutes from Wayne Manor. Then the blip turned east on Vanderheel and continued on toward Huntington.

Where in hell was this clown going?

The red blip turned down Radison Drive. Pulled into number 211. Stopped.

Alice Chilton's house.

Was she in on this? Sweet, gray-haired Mrs. Chilton setting him up in his own home? Wayne was ready to believe anything.

He gunned the motor and made it to his aunt's driveway in two minutes.

The Spencer sat abandoned in the cul-de-sac near the front door. It was empty and the driver's door hung open. Out of habit, Wayne paused to shut and lock the door. Not that it would do him any good.

His aunt's taste in architecture ran to mock-Tudor. Wayne had always thought her house was attractive and inviting. But not tonight. Now each window was shuttered against him. The front door was dark. Odd. Alice usually left her light on all night.

He tried the front entrance. Locked. Well, no surprise there. But precious minutes would be wasted if he jimmied it open. Besides, what if it was armed? He imagined the look on his aunt's face as she came down the stairs to discover the host of the costume ball breaking into her house at a quarter to two in the morning?

Maybe he should ring the doorbell.

Surely she was home, in bed, the party an hour or so behind her. And if she wasn't in bed, if she was in league with this fraudulent Batman, it might shake her up to receive a visitor while she was busy counting the loot.

But the doorbell could also act as a warning.

Wayne sighed. Better try the windows.

He worked his way two-thirds around the house before a pantry window creaked open. He struggled through it, landing lightly, with practiced grace.

Tight fit, he thought. Better spend a few more minutes in the weight room.

The kitchen was dark. Wayne held his breath, listening. Footsteps, along the squeaking floorboards of the second story. Was it his aunt? The intruder menacing her? No time to guess. Move.

Lunging out of his hiding space, he made for the front stairs. Even in gloom, the house was familiar. The smell of freshly cleaned carpet and cedarwood summoned memories.

Christmas. New Years. Laughter.

Grimly, Wayne shoved the thoughts away.

On the second floor, he paused by an open doorway. This had to be his aunt's bedroom. Pink curtains and bedcovers. How she loved that color. The scent of her cologne hung in the air. The Indonesian dance costume was neatly folded over a chair. The room was empty.

A prickle of suspicion halted him in his tracks. Where was she, so late at night?

Moving past the open door, he walked down the hall. The first door he came to was a utility closet. The second, a study, empty save for a walnut antique desk and red easy chair. The third was a pastel-hued guest bedroom. Apparently, a guest had been using it for some time.

The pink chaise lounge was covered with scattered newspapers. Dirty clothing lay in wadded heaps on the yellow rug. The bed was unmade. Empty beer bottles huddled on the nightstand. The room smelled like an old ashtray that someone had forgotten to clean.

A pile of photo albums lay on a yellow bed pillow. Wayne flipped through them. Instead of photographs, each page held a newspaper or magazine clipping. The subject of each clip was the same. Batman. At the back of the last album were several sketches of a Batman costume.

Who would be living with Alice and keeping a record like this? Someone who also came to masquerades, uninvited, impersonating a masked vigilante?

Frustrated, Wayne threw the books down on the bed. The house was empty. His quarry had gotten away, possibly stopping to pick up his accomplice, the gracious Mrs. Chilton.

He was at the landing between floors when a harsh beam of light snapped on. He froze.

"Isn't it a bit late for trick or treat?" said a rusty tenor voice.

The light pinning Wayne down came from a flashlight. Behind its glare, he could just make out the pointed ears of a Batman mask.

"Who are you?" he demanded. "If you've hurt Alice in any way..."

Karen Haber and Robert Silverberg

"Hurt Alice?" The impostor sounded astonished. Then he laughed. The sound had a high, thin tone that climbed swiftly toward hysteria. "Are you nuts? Why would I hurt Alice? You're the one who's breaking and entering."

"I'm not the only one. You have no right to be here."

Again, the laugh.

"I have every right to be here," "Batman" said. "But that doesn't matter. You've made it so easy for me, Wayne. Very thoughtful. I should thank you."

"What do you mean?"

The flashlight beam was pulled back. Now Wayne could see a snub-nosed pistol pointing directly at him.

"Eccentric millionaire robs his own guests at fancy masked ball. Breaks into home of noted philanthropist to rob her as well. Discovered and shot in the act. It's perfect."

The madman's tone was gloating, triumphant.

Wayne played for time.

"Who are you?"

"Just call me Batman. Soon, everybody will."

"How did you get in here?"

"What difference does that make? I remind you, I'm holding a gun on you."

"But you really don't want to use it."

"Oh, but I do."

"Batman" tensed, took aim.

"No! Don't!" cried a woman's voice.

As he fired, a blurred figure cut in front of Wayne and fell back against him, propelled by the force of the bullet, knocking him to the ground. Aunt Alice.

"Damn you!" the false Batman cried. "See what you made me do!" He fired again, wildly, and bullets tore through the silk wallpaper above Wayne's head. Then he turned and fled upstairs. The light retreated with him.

For a moment, Wayne lay there, stunned, with Alice slumped against him. She'd taken the bullet meant for him.

Come on, man, move.

He set her gently against the wall, groped his way to the hall light switch, and flicked it on. She half lay, half sat, eyes closed. A dark red stain was widening across the front of her rose-colored nightgown.

Tenderly, Wayne knelt and touched her face. She stirred, opened her eyes.

"Bruce? Dear boy, is it you?"

"Yes. Don't try to talk."

There was a trickle of blood at the corner of her mouth. Wayne's insides turned to ice.

"Let me call an ambulance..."

"No time. Did you catch that phony Batman?"

"Dammit, Alice..."

He tried to set her down, but she clung to his lapels with surprising determination.

"Hush. I'm done for. That's all right. As long as you catch him. He came rampaging in here..."

She paused, coughed raggedly, bringing up blood.

Wayne cleaned her lips with the edge of his sleeve.

"Alice, let me get a doctor."

"Hush, dearie. Almost through. Catch him, Bruce. I know you can do it."

Wayne stared at her, astonished.

"What do you mean?"

Alice gave a feeble chuckle. "Don't play innocent with me, boy. You never could. It takes the real thing to catch an impostor." She leaned back and closed her eyes. Her voice was barely a whisper. "This crime fighting—good job. Parents would be proud."

She opened one eye, feebly touched his face.

Karen Haber and Robert Silverberg

"But what about love, Bruce? Don't forget love."

With a sigh, she was gone.

Wayne put his head against her shoulder, tears slipping from beneath clenched lids.

What about love? The little he had known of it lay lifeless in his arms, gone forever.

He pressed his lips to his aunt's forehead and set her down gently, taking care not to touch the seeping wound in her chest.

Tears turned to rage.

The Batman impostor would regret this evening in spades before Wayne was through with him.

He raced up the stairs.

"Batman" was in Alice's bedroom, opening the French windows that led out to the deck. Night wind caught the sheer curtains, swirling them about the gunman, ensnaring him long enough for Wayne to cross the room.

His first blow knocked the impostor against the doorframe. His next doubled him over. "Batman" wobbled, taken by surprise. Then he straightened up.

"You can't hurt Batman," he cried, and smashed his fist into Wayne's collarbone.

Wayne staggered backward, the wind knocked out of him. The impostor tore loose from the curtains and dashed past, through the bedroom door and out into the hall.

Come on. Get up. You're not going to let a phony Batman get the best of you, are you?

Gasping, Wayne half ran toward the stairs.

"Batman" was on the landing. In a moment, he'd be out of the house. Free.

Wayne bent at the knees, jumped, and catapulted himself over the railing. He came down two steps in front of the masquerader, cutting him off.

Savagely, Wayne launched a flying kick and caught the gunman in the shoulder, knocking him into the wall.

"Who are you?" he demanded.

"I told you," the impostor said, gasping for breath. "Batman."

The words were maddening. How could he be so crazy? With renewed fury, Wayne pulled him to his feet and flung him against the banister.

"There is only one Batman," he said coldly. "You're either a lunatic or an impostor. And a murderer!"

"Liar!"

For a moment, the gunman struggled in Wayne's grip. Then, seemingly exhausted, he relaxed, hanging his head.

That's better, Wayne thought. He pulled one hand back to wipe sweat from his chin.

With a violent heave, the impostor butted Wayne under the chin, shoved him aside, and ran down the stairs.

Got to stop him before he gets to the car, Wayne thought. He took the stairs in threes, praying for balance. For time.

The impostor had pulled the front door open.

From five stairs up, Wayne leaped. He tackled "Batman" hard, knocking him to the floor. Desperately, they struggled. The impostor seemed to have endless reserves of mad energy.

He kicked Wayne in the knee. Then he punched him savagely, a sharp blow to his kidneys.

Gasping, almost paralyzed, Wayne fell back. He heard the sound of footsteps moving up the stairs. Now what?

"I'll prove to you I'm Batman," the impostor shouted. His voice was high, wild.

Still immobilized by pain, Wayne opened his eyes. "Batman" was pulling a cord out of his utility belt. It glittered oddly.

"Sure," he said. "You think I'm just Joey, Alice's son. But I'll prove it to you. I'll prove it to everybody. I'm really Batman."

Alice's son? Wayne winced. Now he remembered. Her eldest son. Suffered from delusional episodes. Institutionalized years ago. Wayne had forgotten all about him. The whole world had. But Alice must have brought him home.

"I'm going to escape by swinging out the door," Joe Chilton announced. "That should convince you. Only the real Batman could do that."

He prepared to lasso the crystal chandelier with his glittering rope.

"You fool," Wayne cried. "Don't! Wait!"

The cord hooked around the light fixture. Faceted crystal teardrops danced and tinkled crazily. There was a flash. A pop. Joe Chilton screamed and kicked convulsively, like a puppet being jerked upward by its strings. A plume of smoke rose from the chandelier, and then the light went out. "Batman" tumbled forward, over the banister, down to the first floor, landing with a thud. He didn't move.

Slowly, painfully, Wayne pulled himself to his feet. His kidneys throbbed. His knee felt like it was on fire. With one hand on his lower back, he limped over to where Chilton lay, taking care to avoid the dangling rope. He didn't have to touch Chilton to know the truth. He was dead. Electrocuted. That shiny rope was metal cord.

The impostor lay on his back, his blue silk cape rayed out under him. The missing jewels lay by his side, jarred out of his pocket in the fall.

Again, Wayne had the uncomfortable sensation of looking at himself, dead. His head swam strangely. He felt a chill.

I'm alive, he told himself fiercely. I'm Batman, and I'm alive.

Taking hold of the blue silk mask, Wayne yanked it upward. For one eerie moment, he almost expected to see his own face revealed. The face behind the mask was sharply featured, though, with high cheekbones and sandy hair. It didn't even remotely look like him.

But the suit was a good copy.

Straightening up, Wayne lifted his head toward the stairs where his aunt lay and blew her a kiss.

Then he picked up the phone and called the police.

The Batman Memos

STUART M. KAMINSKY

MEMO FROM: David O. Selznick

TO: All Executives, Selznick International Studios

DATE: December 14, 1942

Follow-up projects to *Gone With the Wind* and *Rebecca* are moving much too slowly. Submit reports immediately on status of projects. Did we ever get the copyright on *Mein Kampf*? What about the ghost novel? Is Ben Hecht wrapped up? And what about the Batman story discussed at the Friday meeting? Is there something there? Is it a hoax? Harry, what about the rights? Is Walter back from Gotham City? Did he bring the clips? Ed thinks Errol Flynn would be willing to play Batman, but it would take a trade with Warners and they might want too much. Let's get some action on this one before MGM picks up on it. Fleming says he would consider directing but I think it's more a Woody Van Dyke project, which means another deal with MGM. Ivan, where is the report on Joan Teel? Have your people found her? We have four more weeks of

The Batman Memos

shooting on the Leslie Howard movie. Jess tells me she has two more scenes that can be shot on the last day. If you don't turn her up, we'll have to have a fast rewrite. Has anyone gone to the police with this? Ivan, if you don't turn her up by the 6th, go to Murchison in the Los Angeles Police Department and ask him to make some discreet inquiries. Or should it be discreet? What does publicity think about letting the information get to the press? Good promo for the Howard movie? Bad taste? Feedback on this one. What's going on with Phyllis Walker name change?

MEMO TO: David O. Selznick

FROM: Walter Schlect, Story Development and Rights

DATE: December 17, 1942

Batman is the real thing. I interviewed Gotham City's Police Commissioner Gordon, who's high on the guy and suggested I talk to Bruce Wayne, one of the town's social and business leaders. Wayne is into textiles, construction. Inherited a bundle and keeps his investments local. Wayne's a little stuffy, lives with a kid about sixteen whom he calls his "ward." Setup seems odd to me but so does the whole setup in Gotham. Wayne claims to be able to make contact with Batman and says he can get Batman to let Wayne represent him. Wayne didn't seem too interested in the whole deal but he said he'd be willing to talk. I've attached some newspaper pictures of Batman and his kid sidekick, Robin. We've got nothing in color but I've had Sheila in art fill in. I've also asked Dr. Benjamin Pinesett at U.C.L.A. to send you a psychological profile on Batman based on the clips and interviews attached. I billed the trip and profile to my department. A copy of the billing report is attached.

Stuart M. Kaminsky

MEMO TO: David O. Selznick

FROM: Ivan O'Connor, Security

DATE: January 3, 1943

Nothing to report on Joan Teel. Check of her apartment
indicates she hasn't moved out. Clothes are still in the
closets. Food in the refrigerator. I've talked to Lieutenant
Murchison of the Los Angeles Police Department as you
requested. He is making inquiries.

MEMO TO: David O. Selznick

FROM: Benjamin Pinesett, M.D., Ph.D.
               Professor of Psychiatry,
               The University of California, Los Angeles

DATE: January 4, 1943

At the request of Mr. Walter Schlect of your story department and based upon (a) biographical information provided by Mr. Schlect, (b) newspaper and magazine
clippings also supplied by Mr. Schlect, (c) photographs,
and (d) interview transcripts provided by Mr. Schlect, I
can draw some tentative, but only very tentative, conclusions about Batman. I would be happy to interview Batman if and when he is available for a more conclusive
study at my usual fee. As you will note, the bill enclosed
takes into account that Mr. Schlect informed me that the
report was needed urgently and his insistence that the
report be no more than three pages. I therefore worked on
it over the New Year weekend. I will also include a few
observations concerning the disappearance of Joan Teel,
which Mr. Schlect also mentioned to me and for which

he supplied me with studio biographical information and a private investigator's report.

It is my opinion about Batman that we are dealing with a case of infantile fixation combined with a Messianic complex. The two often accompany each other as your experience and mine with actors will bear out. Whoever this man is he is fulfilled only by wearing a Halloween costume. Fortunately, this need to hide his identity behind a costume is combined with a belief that his intervention is necessary to protect the city of Gotham from criminals. I say "fortunately" because under other circumstances such a man might well become a transvestite or join the Ku Klux Klan or, to put a better light on the situation, he might join an institution or organization that would allow him to wear a uniform—the police, the postal service, hospital service. However, such institutions would not allow him to preserve his identity. That the man is, in lay terms, mentally disturbed is self evident. What disturbs me even more is that the entire community of Gotham City including the Police Commissioner has embraced and supported this delusion, allowing "Batman" to not only feel that he is above the law but give him structured support for such a delusion. It is possible that such an unstable personality will eventually lose the distinction between right and wrong. Untreated and unchecked I would say institutionalization is inevitable. What disturbs me even more is that he has enlisted a young man in his delusion. The damage may already be great for the young man.

Note that Batman is garbed in the dark vesture of a bat, a night creature. Note the shape of the costume, the cowl as helmet, the dark phallic imagery is undeniable. In contrast, Robin is identified with a vulnerable bird, a bird of light hues. The relationship is dangerous.

My recommendation is to enter into no negotiations or correspondence with this man other than to suggest that he seek professional consultation which, I am sure at this point, he will not seek.

As for the Joan Teel situation, I'd suggest you place a call to her parents' home in Dixon, Illinois. It is not unusual for a 20-year-old girl in her first pressure situation—a 20-year-old girl who has been nurtured, supported, and given awards and prizes by parents and those surrounding her in a small, isolated community—to find the pressure too great and simply return to the "womb."

MEMO FROM: David O. Selznick

TO: Walter Schlect, Story Development and Rights

DATE: January 7, 1943

Our boys are dying around the world. I think they could use a Messianic hero. The whole country can use one and F.D.R., while he fills the emotional need, doesn't address the physical. I've called Bruce Wayne in Gotham City and said the same thing to him. I think I've persuaded him and he is willing to make the trip to Los Angeles to discuss the project and to bring with him a letter of consent from Batman. Wayne has even indicated an interest in investing in the project and serving as consultant. Danny has talked to Errol Flynn. He is *definitely* interested. I'm not sure what our alternatives would be. Gable is an Army private.

Ty Power is a Marine private. Hank Fonda is a sailor, and Van Heflin has just been drafted.

MEMO TO: David O. Selznick

FROM: Ivan O'Connor, Security

DATE: January 7, 1943

Joan Teel did not return to Illinois. Dead end here. Lieutenant Murchison of L.A. police is checking girlfriends, boyfriends. So far, nothing. Might turn into a touchy one. Check of unidentified DOAs and hospitals has also turned up nothing.

MEMO TO: David O. Selznick

FROM: Harlan Turkbekian; Turbekian, Zimmer and Kitt, Attorneys

DATE: January 8, 1943

We'll have to move cautiously on this one. I'm not sure the signature "Batman" on a contract will be legally binding since, we assume, Batman has another, legal identity. We have done our own profile on Bruce Wayne of Gotham City. He is, indeed, a man of both substance and, apparently, integrity. In spite of his considerable business interests, there has never been a major suit brought against him or any of his companies. If Bruce Wayne is willing to sign a contract or letter of indemnification holding him responsible should "Batman" bring suit or contest any movie, book, play, or story based on his exploits, we feel it safe and reasonable to proceed. It is also my opinion that in case of litigation Selznick International could claim that Batman's exploits are in the public domain. In that case, however, you might be compelled to present a past exploit of Batman drawn from newspaper and other accounts rather than create a fictional tale. Ross Zimmer and I will both be available after Friday for further discussion on this.

As for the Joan Teel situation, her departure, whether by her choice, "act of God," or circumstances beyond her control, releases Selznick International from any financial obligation should you decide to replace her or alter your working script. The situation is much the same as the Warner Brothers/Bette Davis case last year.

MEMO FROM: David O. Selznick

TO: Myron Selznick

DATE: January 10, 1943

Proceed with Flynn negotiations for Batman picture. I've just met with Bruce Wayne. Like most successful businessmen he has eyes like our father. He looks as if he has a secret that puts him one up on the rest of the world. That's fine with me. He brought a letter of release from Batman that I have sent to Turbekian. One sticky point. Wayne wants script approval for Batman. I don't like it but I don't see how we can get around it. I think we can live with it. Let's see if we can get Ben Hecht on a treatment and script right away. Keep the cost down in case we can't get script approval from Wayne and have to pull out. This means no signing for Flynn though talk seriously to him. How about Thomas Mitchell to play the police commissioner? Villains: Alan Hale, Basil Rathbone? Love interest—this is a sticky one. Who does Flynn want to work with? We don't need a big one but I'd still like Lana

Turner, Ida Lupino, or Phyllis Walker. How about Jennifer Jones as the new name for Walker?

I've got a favor to ask. Can you find a spot for Alice Feigner in your office? She's a good worker, fast typist but less than brilliant. She burst in when Bruce Wayne was in my office and said there was a call on the phone from someone who claimed to have kidnapped Joan Teel. Whoever it was hung up before I could pick up the call. I had to tell Wayne about the situation. He seemed interested but we went on with the negotiations. Nothing was lost but I'd appreciate finding a less sensitive position for Alice.

MEMO FROM: David O. Selznick

TO: Ivan O'Connor, Security

DATE: January 14, 1943

The Teel situation is getting out of hand. As you know, I've had two calls from a man who claims to have kidnapped Joan Teel. A woman did come on the line weeping and claiming to be Teel. I couldn't tell if it was Teel. Since talking to you I've discussed the situation with our attorneys. There are several possibilities here. Teel may be a part of this attempt to extort money from us. It isn't likely but we both know situations in which normally decent people have been tempted by love, sex, or confusion to do things they wouldn't normally do. That's the basic plot of half of the pictures Warner Brothers makes. If the threat is legitimate, it's from someone who doesn't know the picture business. He seems to think we'll lose millions on the Howard picture if she doesn't come back to it. I did not disillusion him. He wants $150,000. I see no alternative but to pay it. You are at liberty to discuss this with Lieutenant Murchison and get back to me this afternoon. If I'm in conference, give me a memo.

One more point. Let's dispense with the services of Dr. Pinesett. His fees are too high and his advice is about as far off as Tojo is from Washington.

Letter to David O. Selznick
From Bruce Wayne, The Beverly Hills Hotel
January 15, 1943

Dear Mr. Selznick:

It was a pleasure meeting you. As I told you, I admire your work and am particularly fond of *Gone With the Wind*. Your invitation to have me meet Miss DeHavilland was and is most gracious. I've decided to remain in the Los Angeles area for a while on business. You can reach me here. There is a chance that Batman will be joining me briefly. I mentioned the missing young actress to him and he, as do I, felt great concern and offered his services should they be needed.

I have spoken to my attorneys and instructed them to prepare a contract of indemnification as you requested. I assure you I am not in the least offended by this request. On the contrary, I think it a matter of sound business practice.

I look forward to hearing from you.

Sincerely,

Bruce Wayne

The Batman Memos

REPORT TO: David O. Selznick

FROM: Lieutenant Tom Murchison, Los Angeles
               Police Department

DATE: January 19, 1943

Ivan O'Connor tells me you plan to pay $150,000 to the supposed kidnappers of Joan Teel. I think this is a mistake. At this point we don't even know for sure she's been abducted. My advice is to stall, then set up a meet with the supposed kidnappers with me and two of my men ahead of you at the site. The decision is yours but I think our chances of getting Miss Teel back are better if we act rather than if we rely on the good graces of kidnappers.

This whole situation is complicated, as you know, by the reports of sightings of a man dressed like a black umbrella at Miss Teel's apartment last night. The custodian swore the man wearing a black hood and black wings came out of the Teel apartment. That's not the strangest costume I've seen around this town over the past thirty years but it rates right up there with Barrymore in his birthday suit and a top hat.

I tried to reach you by phone but couldn't get through. I'd prefer you destroy this letter after you read it.

Sincerely,

Tom Murchison, Lieutenant,
Los Angeles Police Department

MEMO FROM: David O. Selznick

TO: Ivan O'Connor, Security

DATE: January 19, 1943

The Teel situation is taking too much of mine and the studio's time. I'm concerned for Miss Teel's safety and the fact that you and Lieutenant Murchison have made so little headway in finding her. I'm willing to take your advice and not have Murchison set a trap for the kidnappers when the money is delivered. I am concerned, however, that the kidnappers insist that I personally deliver the money. What's to keep them from kidnapping me and making an even greater demand?

No, at his next call I intend, as you suggested, to tell the kidnapper that an emissary, you, will be delivering the cash. I'll tell him that this is the only way I will deal with the situation. Then, God help us, I hope they agree and that we deliver the money and get her free, after which I want you and Murchison to find this person.

MEMO TO: David O. Selznick

FROM: Ivan O'Connor, Security

DATE: January 21, 1943

This is to confirm our telephone conversation this morning and your instructions. I will pick up the package from you on Wednesday night, your office, take it to the tiger cage at the Griffith Park Zoo at midnight and trade it for the merchandise agreed upon.

MEMO FROM: David O. Selznick

TO: Janice Templeton

DATE: January 21, 1943

I've just come into my office this morning and discovered that someone has been through the copies of my recent memos and papers. No one is to go through my papers without my direct approval.

MEMO TO: David O. Selznick
FROM: Janice Templeton
DATE: January 21, 1943

I have checked with the night janitors and with night security. Both sources report no one entered your office during the night. I've also checked with the secretarial pool. No one entered your office and I assure you I did not. I am most distressed and should you wish my resignation it will be on your desk within an hour of your so informing me.

I hesitate to add this but feel I must. One of the night janitors, Baylor Riggs, who has been on several occasions reprimanded for intoxication while at work, reported that a "big fat black owl, big as a man" was prowling around the building after midnight. It is possible Mr. Riggs may have seen someone but security and his supervisor doubt it.

MEMO FROM: David O. Selznick
TO: Janice Templeton
DATE: January 21, 1943

I value your service very highly and have no intention of asking for your resignation. These are both difficult and interesting days for all of us and I rely upon your discretion and judgment and expect that you will continue to participate in our creative growth in the future. I would appreciate your arranging for locks for my files this after-noon. One set of keys only. I'll carry them with me.

NEWS ITEM: *THE LOS ANGELES TIMES*, January 24, 1943

—A large bird reportedly escaped from the Griffith Park Zoo some time after midnight last night, according to reports of an overnight caretaker at the zoo and a patroling police car.

In spite of the reported sightings, zoo officials report that no animals are missing from the zoo.

Dr. Leon Santucci, a veterinarian with the zoo, speculated than an eagle attracted by the caged animals may have flown down from the Hollywood Hills. "It's happened before," said Dr. Santucci. "Not often but it has happened."

The caretaker, Oliver Palmer, reported the sighting of the bird near the large mammal cages. According to Palmer, "the bird seemed to be attacking a man with a suitcase." Palmer says he shouted and tried to come to the assistance of the attacked man, but both bird and man were gone when he got there.

Another explanation of the strange events came from Lieutenant Tom Murchison of the Los Angeles police who was in the vicinity of the zoo after midnight on an unrelated matter. Murchison said that he saw two men emerging from the zoo, approached them and determined that they were "a couple of drunks playing games in the zoo."

Zoo officials promised a complete investigation and a tightening of zoo security though zoo officials said it is difficult to get sufficient help with so many men and women serving in the armed forces or engaged in work vital to the war effort.

The Batman Memos

MEMO FROM: David O. Selznick

TO: Tom Murchison

DATE: January 23, 1943

I have destroyed your note to me as you requested. I ask that you do the same after reading this. I am pleased that Miss Teel is free and unharmed after her ordeal and imprisonment in Ivan O'Connor's basement. I'm not sure how Batman figured out that Ivan O'Connor was involved in her abduction, but I'm glad he did or O'Connor would have gotten away with the money and, in spite of his protests, might, as you have suggested, not have allowed Miss Teel an opportunity to tell her story. If possible, I would like to keep the entire episode as quiet as possible which, my lawyers tell me, means making a deal for a reduced sentence and a plea of guilty by O'Connor. Please work with our attorneys on this. As you know, Mr. O'Connor's departure leaves an opening in our security section. I would be pleased if you would consider the post.

Letter to David O. Selznick

From Bruce Wayne, The Beverly Hills Hotel

January 25, 1943

Dear Mr. Selznick:

Batman and I truly appreciate your hospitality but he informs me that he would like to withdraw his offer to participate in a film based upon his endeavors. He informs me that his decision has something to do with the handling of the abduction of Miss Teel and the subsequent handling of the case. Batman does not believe that he is sufficiently prepared to deal with Hollywood at this point. Should a time come when he feels differently, he assures me that you will be the first to know.

Please give my regrets to Miss DeHavilland. Should she or you ever get to Gotham City, please consider staying at Wayne Manor.

Sincerely,

Bruce Wayne

MEMO TO: David O. Selznick

FROM: Harlan Turbekian; Turbekian, Zimmer and Kitt, Attorneys

DATE: January 26, 1943

I have copies of the reports, memos, and data you forwarded to me along with your very persuasive conclusions concerning the identity of Batman. I and my associates are not certain that we have sufficient evidence that Batman indeed broke into your office though the circumstantial evidence is certainly overwhelming. We will, as you instructed, hold the documentation concerning Batman's identity until such time as you wish it or wish, as you indicated, to turn it over to another production company.

Wise Men of Gotham

EDWARD WELLEN

Bruce Wayne wore a bemused smile as he mingled with the other guests aboard billionaire real estate developer Jack King's luxurious yacht. He also wore his Batman outfit.

It seemed a risk worth taking, for this was a costume ball—and he had already spotted three other Batmen. And—truth to tell—his outfit, somewhat the worse for wear after his latest adventure, looked the least authentic of all.

That, however, was not the cause of his bemusement. It had suddenly struck him how ironic it was that such a glittering occasion had such a sad cause.

Jack King and his wife Queena were throwing a benefit bash for the homeless of Gotham City.

On his way here to the yacht basin, under the neon that fogged the stars, Bruce Wayne had passed many ragged shapes huddled in stinking doorways or nestled in cardboard cartons or crumpled over steaming sidewalk grates, and he had dropped here a dollar and there a dollar. He looked around now at the other guests; they too had seen the homeless—but the homeless seemed already far away and forgotten in the babble and clink and band rhythm.

All about him in the dazzling ballroom, the men as well as the women flaunted their jewels and stuffed their faces. All appeared well-clothed, well-fed, well-housed.

Handsome Jack King and beautiful Queena King most of all. He knew them behind their gem-encrusted masks. Jack was the eye-patched pirate and Queena was the harem slave.

Others of the elite were also easy to spot. Hizzoner the Mayor moved about, glad-handing. Mayor Ned Notts and developer Jack King were at political odds, and had had their shouting matches by way of newspaper headlines and talk shows. However, the plight of the homeless— toward which neither had demonstrated any particular sensitivity—now drew them together in this fleeting show of care. Their teeth gleamed in big smiles at one another for the benefit of press flashbulbs and television lights. The charity ball brought Jack King favorable publicity to offset the bad, such as evicting the poor—and so adding to the homeless—to make way for his grandiose projects, and no doubt allowed him to charge off considerable expenses against taxes. The charity ball afforded Mayor Notts, who was running for re-election for the nth time, a welcome opportunity to put a new gloss on his tainted administration and to shore up his eroding popularity.

Keeping close company with Hizzoner were his political backer, Rudolph Newkirk, the newspaper magnate; Hizzoner's crony Housing Commissioner Sam Rubin; and Hizzoner's temporary ally in the election campaign, environmentalist Glenn Dubois.

Wayne marveled at the rampant hypocrisy. It seemed an ego thing between Nott and King, because Mayor Nott

had cosied up to other developers of luxury housing; Nott
and King each appeared to covet the role of Numero Uno
in Gotham City. Newkirk's papers were doing a hatchet
job on King, printing exposés of King's projects, hinting
at big bribes for permits and tax abatements, and inter-
viewing the poor harassed out of buildings standing in
King's juggernaut path—while Newkirk himself was an
insatiable gobbler-up of papers and television stations.
Commissioner Rubin had done little to rehabilitate abandoned buildings to house uprooted families; for some
unfathomable reason he found it more practical to cram
them into rundown-but-expensive, rat-and-roach-infested,
single-room-occupancy hotels. Environmentalist Dubois
had stood in the way of building out into the bay because
of what that would do to the fish population, but had
offered no alternatives. And here all of them joined with
the Kings to raise money for the homeless.

Another personage Bruce Wayne easily picked out was
his old friend Police Commissioner Gordon. Gordon's
presence took away much of the bad taste in Wayne's
mouth.

Commissioner Gordon had come as a musketeer, but
security seemed too much on his mind to let him play the
part with ease. He kept up the pose with gallant flourishes
and courtly bows whenever he met someone he knew, or
was introduced to someone new. But his knuckles were
white on his sword as he checked the placement of his
men and women, and he jerked around whenever a voice
grew too shrill or a glass suddenly crashed to the ballroom
floor.

Wayne smiled wryly. He knew what preyed on Gordon's mind. This past week the media had been full of the
fevered auction at which King outbid even the Japanese
for a Rembrandt. The battered gavel had finally knocked

the masterpiece down to King for eighty-six million dollars.

Commissioner Gordon's big fear had to be that someone would use the swirling confusion of the charity ball to steal the Rembrandt from under his patrician nose, for the famous painting hung in a stateroom here aboard the Île de Joie.

Some of the secrecy about it evaporated for a favored few. Wayne grew aware of this when he realized that Jack and Queena King were taking turns leading the more privileged of the guests—identified by discreet face-card pins that had been sent along with tickets when those invited to the ball RSVP'd with a fat check made out to the charity—on guided tours of the yacht's treasures, of which the Rembrandt was the highlight.

Bruce Wayne sported such a pin, and now found himself tapped by Jack King personally for such a tour. King patted him on the shoulder and nodded toward an elevator.

Wayne found himself matching stride with a sweaty musketeer wearing a face-card pin as they followed King to the elevator.

"Enjoying this nice little party, Commissioner Gordon?" Wayne asked.

The musketeer shot the Batman a sharp look. "Is that you, Bruce?"

Wayne nodded.

Gordon sighed almost explosively. "How I wish you were the real Batman instead of ..."

"Instead of a useless rich idler?"

"I didn't say that."

"No, you bit your tongue. But no matter. What's got you wishing for Batman's help?"

Edward Wellen

Gordon leaned close. "Let's keep this hush-hush—I don't want to panic all of Gotham City. Riddler's back in town."

Wayne's senses quickened at the mention of his old foe. The pointy ears of his cowl seemed to stand up on their own. "How do you know?"

Gordon drew a color photo from the pocket of his cloak. "Here's his handiwork. An unidentified corpse found floating in the harbor. One of his damnable riddles tattooed on the body."

Wayne took the gruesome picture and stared at a naked chest and read the rhyme printed on it. The period at the end of the rhyme was a lurid bullethole.

Art thou?
How now!
Art not
When shot.

    —Yours truly, the Riddler

Wayne handed the photo back and they caught up with the small party and remained silent in the full elevator as it descended two decks.

They brightened a bit at sight of the treasures King guided them by. Few monarchs had in their lifetimes garnered so great a hoard. King's prizes would outlast him, but while he held them he took full pride in them.

The Rembrandt drew the greatest hush. It hung in a well-lit alcove; a velvet rope kept viewers at a distance.

It was the famous *The Would-Be Bride*, sometimes called *The Coscinomancer*. The painting showed a young girl seemingly in the first awareness that her sexuality gave her power—and finding it both exhilarating and frightening. She held a pair of shears with a sieve hanging from the points of the blades, and she stood frozen hopefully, prayerfully apparently having just called the name of a suitor and now waiting to see if the turning of the sieve would tell her he was the one for her.

The viewers stood similarly frozen by the power of the painter.

SSWISSHHH-THUNNKK!

A blow dart whizzed through the open doorway and into the masterpiece, landing dead center on the robust breast. A note was impaled on the shank of the dart.

Wayne whirled with a black flutter and dashed to the doorway. Too late—a like black flutter had vanished up the companionway at the far end of the passage.

He turned back to the room. No one else seemed to have glimpsed the black-caped vandal. At least, no one spoke of having seen another Batman blow the dart and flee. Wayne breathed thankfully.

Commissioner Gordon had produced a walkie-talkie and was calling for assistance.

Wayne shot a glance at King. It seemed to him that King looked singularly unperturbed for one whose eighty-six-million-dollar prize possession had just sustained damage.

But he had no more time to ponder that. Gordon's call had brought a plainclotheswoman who swung into action Wayne closely observed.

Plainclotheswoman! Detective Sergeant Heather Mortimer, as Gordon introduced her, wore an elegant Empire gown, and more than fulfilled her role.

She swung briskly into action. From somewhere on her person she produced plastic gloves and put them on. Carefully, she removed the dart from the painting. She had

Edward Wellen

to pull hard to free the dart, and in doing so rubbed her forearm against the canvas. As her hand came away with the dart gripped firmly in it, Wayne noticed a faint smudge on her bare forearm. The smudge might have been there beforehand, but he doubted that. Forensics might find spittle on the dart and from it determine the blood type, and even the DNA pattern, of the vandal. Before putting it into an evidence bag, she slipped the note off the shank. She slid the note into a clear plastic envelope and handed the envelope to her boss.

Wayne read the note over Gordon's shoulder.

The sage—so-called—
Of Brought-Home-the-Bacon
Will drop off to sleep
And never awaken.

    —Yours unruly, the Riddler

He imprinted it in his memory.

Wayne smiled crookedly. So that had been the Riddler he had glimpsed—and wearing a Batman outfit! But villainous as the man was, the Riddler had not pinned the vandalism on Batman. The Riddler had too much ego to give credit to another for anything he himself had done.

Gordon's detail, and King's own security people, had sealed off all exits, but Wayne felt sure the Riddler had already made good his escape—had found some way off the yacht or some hiding place aboard it.

And so it proved.

After his own identity had been checked—and vouched for by Police Commissioner Gordon himself—Wayne descended the gangway and headed thoughtfully home. The Riddler had given him much to think about.

Alfred, the English butler, shook his head mournfully as he put the Batman costume away. He tsk-tsked and tut-tutted at its deplorable state.

"I feel dreadful about having let you go out in this, sir. I did do my best, though, on short notice."

"Yes, I'm afraid I waited till the last minute to advise you of the ball."

Alfred, once started, had to finish his bill of particulars. "I bespoke a dozen new outfits from our Saville Row tailors—using the safe address for delivery—but they were booked solid. Meanwhile I thought to make do locally; I tried all the costumers in the yellow pages, sir, but it seems they had rented out every one of their Batman suits."

From the bedroom window of the penthouse suite, Bruce Wayne could make out the lights of the Île de Joie at its slip in the yacht basin. "Somehow I guessed that might be the case, Alfred."

"If I may say so, sir, I'm afraid you have only your own popularity to blame for that."

Wayne turned from the window to eye Alfred. "Alfred, let me pick your brains."

Alfred looked alarmed. "Beg pardon, sir?"

"Tell me about Gotham."

Alfred's alarm increased. He looked out the penthouse window at the millions of lights. Where to begin? What to describe? How could he possibly do Gotham City justice?

Wayne followed Alfred's glance and laughed apologetically. "I mean the English Gotham, the place our Gotham gets its name from. The Wise Men of Gotham and all that."

Edward Wellen

"Oh, *that* Gotham, sir." Alfred looked first relieved, then severe. "That Gotham is a village in Nottinghamshire. I've never been there myself." He conveyed that he wouldn't be caught dead there. "'Wise Men' is a misnomer, sir. A jest, as it were. The Gothamites appear to have been quite a collection of fools." By his tone he washed his hands of them.

"Hmmm. And that's all you know?"

"Afraid so, sir. Will there be anything else?"

"Just wake me early tomorrow."

"As you wish, sir."

Alfred winced as the master crunched the toast so thoughtfully that crumbs spilled all over everything.

As soon as the hour approached decency, Wayne dialed Dr. Amicia Sollis and invited her to breakfast. She accepted sleepily, seeming both pleased and puzzled.

He picked her up at Gotham City University and took her to the Skyways Building and to the restaurant atop it.

They talked of this and that as they ate—Amicia seeming as always to seek some glimpse into the true nature of Bruce Wayne, for it was clear she did not take him at face value but sensed some depth to the shallow man-about-town. At last she shoved the dessert plate aside and put hand on chin and elbow on table and looked into his eyes.

"Time for me to sing for my lunch. What's the tune?"

So, while the restaurant revolved high above the streets of midtown Gotham City, he told the sleek, dark-haired professor of linguistics about the Riddler's having pinned a note to the Rembrandt. He recited it to her.

"That's scary," she said. "What do you make of it?"

He frowned. "'Brought-Home-the-Bacon' seems an obvious play on 'Got-ham,' and it follows that the Riddler is threatening the lives of the Wise Men of Gotham—whoever *they* may be. I've heard about the Wise Men of Gotham—the Nottinghamshire Gotham, I mean—but I don't know the story behind them. You're the authority on folklore, so give."

She took a moment to gather her thoughts before she answered. "Some say it goes back to King John in the 1200s. This was the tricky, greedy, cowardly king who was forced to sign the Magna Carta. The story goes that King John planned to seize some of the Gothamites' land for a hunting ground and to cut a highway across their pastures. That would have been bad enough, but in addition the people would be expected to provide services to the court and to the flock of courtiers. The townspeople got together and plotted to change King John's mind. They engaged in idiotic pursuits to fool the king's messengers into thinking the local yokels would make unsuitable neighbors. Things like trying to drown an eel in a pond; burning down a forge to get rid of a wasps' nest; hoisting a wagon to the top of a barn to shade the roof; planting a hedge around a cuckoo's nest—or, in another version, joining hands around a thornbush—to shut in a cuckoo so it would sing all year long."

"And it worked?"

"It worked. At least, so far as I know, there's no royal hunting lodge at Gotham." She smiled. "That's the legend. But the real source of tales about the fools of Gotham may have been the absurd customary services attached to land tenure there."

"Such as?"

She shrugged. "I can't tell you off the top of my head. Perhaps such things as still obtain right in our own neighborhood. Do you know that in one of the suburbs of *this* Gotham, the town must come up with 'one fatte calfe' each year forever if the descendants of the original owners of the land demand it?"

They had finished the meal but she had given him much to chew on.

He drove her back to the campus. As he watched her walk gracefully into the gothic building he felt his face burn. His Batman preoccupations got too much in the way of Bruce Wayne's life. Why hadn't he thought to invite Amicia to attend the ball with him? Why had he thought of her only after the fact? Not only did she deserve better of him but it was his great loss. Next time...

He phoned Commissioner Gordon's office and got through to Gordon, though the man sounded bothered and beset.

"Afraid I don't have much time, Wayne. Another of Riddler's notes."

"A threat?"

"A particular threat—but I don't think I should say any more about it. If only I could get word to Batman."

"You have some way of signaling to him, don't you?"

"Yes, but how can I be sure he's on the lookout for it?"

"He has a bat's radar. Anyway, you have no choice but to try."

"True." Gordon sighed. "I'll get on it." Then he said wearily, "did you have something you wanted to speak to me about?"

"Nothing that can't wait. You have enough to worry about. Let me get out of your hair. Goodbye."

"Thanks for being so understanding. Goodbye."

Wayne had a weather eye out to the night sky and Commissioner Gordon did not signal in vain.

Wise Men of Gotham

Sitting out on the terrace of his penthouse suite though March made itself felt, Wayne spotted the searchlight beam. It swept the heavens with a bat silhouette. The bat flew due east, then south–southwest. That formed a 7, and meant a rendezvous at the corner of Seventh Avenue and Seventh Street at seven p.m.

Wayne checked his watch. He had a half hour to get there.

The beam had switched off at the end of the 7; it switched on again and repeated the figure. It would keep on doing that until seven o'clock, when Gordon would give up if Batman failed to keep the rendezvous.

Wayne leapt inside. "Alfred!"

Alfred was ready, the Batman outfit folded on his arm. He helped Wayne get it on. Alfred had done his best, laundering and steampressing the cowl and the cape, but was still disdainful of the outfit's shabbiness.

Batman smiled to himself. Clothes did not make the bat.

Commissioner Gordon started as the black figure slid from the shadows. Then he gave a groan of relief. "Batman!"

"It's about the Riddler?"

"How did you know?"

"Bats have good ears."

"That's almost what Wayne said."

"Who?"

"Never mind. He doesn't really matter. Nice fellow and all that, but..."

"I know the type." Batman grew brisk. "What's our old friend the Riddler up to now?"

For answer, Commissioner Gordon drew three pictures from an inner pocket.

Edward Wellen

Batman unclipped a penlight from his belt and examined the topmost photo. It showed the punctuated message tattooed on the torso of the floater.

"We've identified him as a promising young art student," Gordon said. "Classmates told our homicide detectives that he had been flashing money and dropping hints about having received some mysterious commission. Then he himself suddenly dropped out of sight."

"Ah! That explains the 'Art thou?' and 'Art not.'" Batman's mouth went grim. "The Riddler, with his twisted logic, took someone whose subject was art—and made him into an object of art!"

Batman turned to the second photo. What it showed was also familiar, but he let Gordon explain it.

"This is a picture of a note Riddler pinned to the famous Rembrandt on Jack King's yacht."

Batman nodded. "Here he's threatening the Wise Men of Gotham."

Gordon stared at Batman's shadowy face. "Amazing! It took the best brains of the Department all night and all day to figure that out!"

Batman gave a modest wave of dismissal and concentrated on the third photo.

"That," Gordon said, "is a copy of Riddler's latest message." His voice shook with mixed rage and fear. "I found it on my own desk in my own office at headquarters. How he could penetrate that fortress—"

"Every fortress is penetrable," Batman said absently. He was busy with the message.

Smoking the beehive is best
For combing out honey.
Burning both house and wasps' nest
Is stupid but funny.

—Yours bluely, the Riddler

Wise Men of Gotham

Gordon was peering at him prayerfully, as one hoping for a miracle. In a hushed voice Gordon asked, "Well, Batman? Do you have any idea what this means?"

"It means trouble," Batman said. Then, with a smile, he lifted Gordon's gloom. "Yes, I have a pretty good idea what it means."

Before Gordon could ask further, Batman took a step back and was one with the shadows.

The Valley Forge Club was the last stronghold of male elitism, an exclusive organization with a policy of admitting none but White Anglo-Saxon Protestants.

A meat truck was making a delivery. The driver and his helper were unloading it. Batman waited his chance to shoulder a ham, and bent under it so that it obscured his face and upper body as he walked inside. He jettisoned the ham before he reached the meat locker, leaving it for others to wonder how it had got into the chef's clothes closet.

Batman flitted unseen through the corridors, looking for sign of the Riddler's machinations.

Nowhere did he find anything to back his hunch, though this *had* to be the latterday counterpart of the forge and the wasps' nest in the legend of the original Gothamites as told to him by Dr. Amicia Sollis.

He reached the head of the fire stairs on what sounds told him was the floor housing the game room and the smoking lounge. He cracked the door open and sneaked a look down the hallway.

A man in blue paced away from him. Batman raised an eyebrow. Had Commissioner Gordon reached the same conclusion—that the Valley Forge Club was the Riddler's target—and provided protection?

Edward Wellen

Batman was about to call to the policeman, with the object of joining forces, when—*BONNGGGG!*—an alarm went off in his head.

It had struck Batman that the man in blue was not so much patroling as prowling. Batman, himself prowling, knew the difference.

The next minute he was not so sure. For a pair of members, cocktail glasses and cigars in hand, emerged from a room and the man in blue straightened up and gave them a snappy salute that they casually returned. Batman recognized one of them as environmentalist Glenn Dubois. If these men accepted the policeman's presence without question...

But after they had crossed the hall and vanished into a room that emitted the clicking of billiards, the man in blue once more looked on the prowl. Batman's gaze hardened.

A man in blue had entry everywhere—even into the Police Commissioner's inner sanctum.

And the Riddler had signed his challenge "Yours *bluely.*"

A shiver passed through Batman. The avenger of evil knew evil when he saw it—though it were clothed in the vestments of good!

But he bided his moment to see what the Riddler meant to do.

The man in blue came to a stop at a point where a shelf jutted from the wall. He looked around, then slid open a small door just above the shelf. Batman realized that this was the opening of a dumbwaiter. The false cop lifted a jerrican down out of the dumbwaiter.

Quickly he uncapped the jerrican and splashed its contents along the hall toward the door of the game room.

Wise Men of Gotham

Batman caught the odor of gasoline and waited no longer.

Before the Riddler could finish emptying the jerrican and strike a match, Batman had hurled himself from the stairwell, straight at the arsonist.

"Hold it right there, Riddler!"

The Riddler froze. Then his face twisted in a sneer, and he whipped out a knife.

"Steel *this* thunder, Batman!"

SWOOOSSHHHH! The Riddler's knife slashed Batman's cape. Batman felt anger on Alfred's account. Alfred would be really put out.

Batman smiled fiercely. "Close—but no scar!"

Then, launching a savage attack of his own, he kicked the Riddler's wrist and the knife flew flashing out of his hand. But as he moved to grab the Riddler, he slipped on a gasoline slick. The Riddler took advantage of this and pulled the dumbwaiter box higher so that it cleared the shaft. Then he dived into the opening and escaped down the rope.

Batman had to comfort himself with the knowledge that he had foiled the Riddler's attempt on this one of the Wise Men of Gotham.

They met at the corner of 11th Avenue and 11th Street at 11 p.m.

"Great work, Batman!" Commissioner Gordon said, but worry and foreboding overlay his pleasure and gratitude. "Do you think you can pull it off again?"

"Another Riddler threat?"

Gordon nodded and produced a photocopy.

Batman—with the Riddler's knife slash in his cape neatly stitched, though Alfred had bitten off the thread with a most unbutlerish snarl—stepped out of the shadows to examine the latest challenge from the Riddler.

High now chuck the wain
To shade the roof.
Why not the mare, too,
In its behoof?

    —Yours coolly, the Riddler

Batman felt a chill sharper than the night's. The outmoded word *wain* for *wagon* had struck home.

Could the Riddler have pierced Batman's identity, Bruce *Wayne*, or was it merest and purest coincidence?

"Are you feeling all right, Batman?"

Batman looked at Gordon's worried face, made ghastly by the streetlight, and forced a smile. "I feel fine."

He had to put thoughts of his own peril out of his mind. He had to fix his wits on puzzling out the threat to another Wise Man of Gotham.

With a swirl of his cape, he melted into the darkness.

Unaware of affronting Alfred, Wayne let the breakfast crepes grow cold while he rifled through the morning papers. The Riddler appeared to be targeting public figures on the order of environmentalist Glenn Dubois, whose life Batman had saved...together with the lives of many innocents who would have perished had the Valley Forge Club burned down. What were the latest doings of such public figures?

Wayne frowned as he scanned the pages. The words *chuck* and *wain* had suggested to him that *chuck wagon* might be the key to what the Riddler had in mind. Wayne perused the columns in hopes of coming across some public event involving something even faintly hitched to a chuck wagon—a rodeo, Meals on Wheels, a dude ranch, a new fast-foods eaterie...

BINGO!—and none of the above.

This very afternoon, Hizzoner, the Mayor, would be attending the opening of a new display at the Planetarium.

That started a whole new line of thought, and prompted a call to Dr. Amicia Sollis.

She seemed not to mind that this was getting to be a habit. She smiled across the restaurant table at him. "Yes, 'Chuck' is a recognized nickname for 'Charles.' And yes, there is such a thing as 'Charles's Wain.' Though I hardly think the 'mare' in the rhyme would be a Charley horse."

Wayne nodded. He thought it likely that "Mare" was a play on "mayor." But he did not voice the thought, he merely gestured for Amicia to go on.

Which she did after taking a sip of claret to moisten her lips. "Let's stick to 'Charles's Wain.' Some say it's named for Charlemagne, some for Charles I of England. In either case, it refers to the group of seven stars in the constellation of Ursa Major, which we in the U.S. call the Big Dipper. That group of seven stars is supposed to resemble a cart without wheels, but with a shaft horses could be hitched to." She tilted her head. "Does that help you?"

It did.

Afternoon outside, but midnight inside.

Edward Wellen

Batman lurked in the darkness under the great starry dome. His gaze roamed the auditorium, with special attention to the section reserved for the mayoral party. Grimly, he noted that those seats were directly beneath the stars of Charles's Wain.

An agitated huddle of Planetarium officials drew Batman's attention. He slipped nearer to listen and caught mention of the air-conditioning system. From what they said, it was malfunctioning. Indeed, now that his attention was on the condition of the air, the place did seem stuffy.

Just then a coveralled figure bustled up to the group.

The Planetarium director heaved a sigh of relief. "It'll be all right. The air-conditioning serviceman is here."

Batman narrowed his eyes in thought. *Air conditioning.* The Riddler had signed his challenge "Yours *coolly.*"

"I'll have a look at the vents on the roof." The voice of the coveralled figure sounded familiar.

The mayor's party arrived just then, and the officials went to greet Hizzoner. The coveralled figure stood watching until Hizzoner was seated, then made for a door marked MAINTENANCE.

Batman gave him a moment, then followed him through the door into a dimly lit space between the inner and outer shells of the great dome. The place hummed with machinery and smelled of grease. Batman caught sight of the coveralled figure already halfway up a ladder that climbed the inner shell of the dome. Batman waited at the foot of the ladder until it stopped vibrating, then climbed it in turn, careful not to shake it and give away his presence.

He reached the top in time to see the coveralled figure fit a wrench to a nut on a bolt and begin to loosen it. No doubt about it—this was the Riddler at his deadly work!

From the care with which the Riddler worked the wrench, and from the give of the whole section as the nut on the bolt loosened, Batman could tell that the Riddler had previously loosened most of that section of the dome and that it would plummet to crush the mayoral party once this last bolt came free.

"Hold it, Riddler! You're one nut too many!"

The Riddler froze. Then, with a curse, he flung the wrench at Batman.

Batman did not flinch or duck. Instead, he made a neat one-handed catch. In almost the same motion with which he plucked the wrench out of the air, he hurled the wrench back at the Riddler.

BONNKK! The boomeranged wrench glanced off the Riddler's skull and caromed downward with a heavy clatter.

"Seeing stars, Riddler?"

If the Riddler was, he quickly shook off his daze and pushed himself away from Batman's—and the ladder's—side of the dome and with a prolonged and pronounced Y-E-E-E-O-W-W-W!!!! slid and slithered down the curve of the dome to the bottom. There was a SPLAT!, then silence.

By the time Batman scrambled down the ladder the Riddler was gone.

Alfred would find the grease stains on Batman's cape highly lamentable.

They met at the corner of First Avenue and First Street at one a.m.

Commissioner Gordon jumped a foot in the air. "Batman! I was expecting you, but not swooping down the guywire of a crane."

"Sorry." Maybe he should've been direct instead of derricked, but it had seemed a good idea to get a bird's-eye view of the rendezvous area beforehand and make sure they would be alone.

"Quite all right." Gordon harrumphed. "Thanks to you, Batman, Mayor Notts is still around. He had a severe heart attack when he learned of the close call. That made it another close call. But he'll pull through."

"Glad I could be of help. But you didn't summon me here so that you might deliver a bulletin on Hizzoner's medical condition. It's the Riddler again?"

Looking hopeful, Commissioner Gordon handed Batman a photocopy of a note in rhyme.

Have you heard the lewd word?

What does the cuckoo sing?

Is the wing on the bird—

Or the bird on the wing?

> *—Yours billet-doux-ly,*
>
> > *Yours bill-and-coo-ly,*
>
> > > *The Riddler*

Batman frowned but not too severely. Once again he needed Amicia's expertise.

"What's your interest in these riddles, Bruce? Are they merely an intellectual exercise?

"That's how it started out, Amicia. But my findings got passed along to Batman, who appears to have made good use of them."

"You make quite a team, don't you? She leaned forward avidly over the avocados. "What's Batman really like? I'd love to meet him."

Wayne smiled. "I'm the last one to tell you what he's really like. Commissioner Gordon has yet to introduce us. But if we do meet, I'll be sure to mention your interest."

Amicia flushed. "Don't you dare!" She spooned up the last of her dessert, then touched her napkin to her mouth. "I sing for supper, the cuckoo sings for summer. The Cuckoo Song is the oldest English song set to music." She sang softly in a voice that did not reach the other diners.

"'Sumer is icumen in,
 Lhude sing cuccu!'"

She smiled. "*Lhude* doesn't mean 'lewd'; it means 'loud.' But the Riddler seems to be leering. The female cuckoo lays her eggs in the nests of other birds, who hatch them and rear them. That's how 'cuckold' came to denote the husband of an unfaithful wife. Centuries ago, in England, people would call out 'cuckoo!' to warn a husband when a known adulterer came near. Somehow, the term stuck to the husband."

Wayne leaned back. "Ah. Then I—rather, Batman—would have to look for adultery."

"You won't have to look far," Amicia said. "I'm afraid the avocados were adulterated."

Alfred woke up Wayne. "Precisely seven a.m., sir."

Wayne opened one eye and cocked it. "How do you know—*precisely*?"

Alfred gestured to the French windows giving on to the terrace. "The clock tower of the Nest Egg building, sir."

And Wayne heard the last dying note of the chimes.

Edward Wellen

He swept the covers aside and leapt to his feet. He pressed his nose to the glass and stared at the clock tower that shouldered above the clinging mists of morning. *Nest Egg*...

The Nest Egg Investment Corporation, a subsidiary of Fidelity Trust, ranked among Gotham City's most respected institutions, financial or other. The Riddler surely would count its head among the Wise Men. Foster Cavendish, the Nest Egg's CEO, had to fit the Wise Man profile—a citizen of standing and power. Was Cavendish involved in adultery? Was the Nest Egg clock a cuckoo clock?

"My Batman costume, Alfred."

"But, sir. Do you really care to be seen in it? Shouldn't you prefer to await the bespoke costumes?"

"My Batman costume, Alfred."

"Sir, do you realize this is Easter Sunday and all will be attired in their best?"

"Alfred, my Batman costume."

"Very good, sir."

Batman was a creature of the night, but the canyons of Gotham City afforded shadow by day. And where that shadow did not reach, the latest model Batmobile, with its chameleon paint and dark windows, afforded cover and concealment for stakeouts. So it was that Batman found it feasible to pick up and tail Foster Cavendish without arousing Cavendish's suspicions.

The Foster Cavendishes lived in a high-rise condominium on fashionable Eden Avenue. At half past ten a.m., Foster Cavendish emerged from the elegant front entrance and the doorman hailed a cab. Just before stepping in, Cavendish looked back and up, shifted his carry-on to his other hand, and waved. From a window near the top, a wide-sleeved arm returned the wave.

Batman followed the cab to Fitzgerald Airport and watched Cavendish pick up a ticket to Red Wing, Minnesota, then board the plane a good ten minutes before takeoff. Batman smiled.

The bird would be on the wing and away from danger at the hands of the Riddler, for the Riddler would want— as a matter of pride if not honor—to carry out his threats within the borders of Gotham City.

Then Batman thought again. A bomb set to go off while the plane was still in Gotham City's airspace would fulfill the Riddler's self-imposed guidelines.

Batman had no certain knowledge that the Riddler had planted a bomb on this flight—but then he had no certain knowledge that the Riddler had not planted a bomb.

Better to be safe than sorry, as his parents had been wont to tell him before their untimely deaths at the hands of a holdup man—his eyewitnessed event that had turned him into the fearsome Batman striking terror into hearts of criminals.

He darted to a pay phone, beating out a yellow-bonneted, green-gowned woman. She folded her Easter parasol and hammered his shoulders with it while he dialed 911, but when she heard the word "bomb" in his anonymous tip she shrieked—OOOOHHH!!!—and let up.

Batman, again in the Batmobile, watched the plane disgorge its passengers and crew, a pale and trembling Cavendish among them.

ULPULPULPULPULP!!!   EEPWEEPWEEPWEEPWEEP!!!   The bomb squad arrived in its ululating van and searched the plane with dogs and electronic sniffers.

No bomb.

Edward Wellen

But the nonevent had shaken Cavendish. After a few drinks at an airport lounge, he got himself and his carry-on into another cab and headed home.

Batman followed, weighed down with responsibility. The anonymous tip had backfired, putting Cavendish squarely back in danger of death at the Riddler's hands. Now Batman would have to stay almost as close as Cavendish's skin if he were to protect him from the Riddler.

While the doorman assisted Cavendish and his carry-on out of the cab and into the building, Batman scooted around to the back and let himself in through the basement door. He had counted the stories to the window Mrs. Cavendish had waved from, and knew what button to press. The freight elevator took Batman to Cavendish's floor before the passenger elevator arrived.

With seconds to spare, Batman located the Cavendish nameplate, drew a lockpick from his belt, opened the door, and slipped inside.

He squeezed inside the hall closet, behind raincoats and boots. He had barely done so when the front door opened again, this time with the rattle of keys and a loud BANG! as it slammed shut and the THUMP! of the carry-on hitting the floor.

From a rear bedroom came a banshee wail. EEEEEE!!!

"It's only me, honey," Cavendish called out. "I just had a bad scare."

"You had a bad scare? What do you think this was?"

Batman peered out cautiously and glimpsed a frizz of hennaed hair and a filmy peignoir.

"Wait till I tell you, Bathsheba. Mine was a bomb scare. I let the plane take off without me. Brrr. Boy, I could use a stiff one."

Bathsheba's voice turned concerned. "Poor baby. Go into the living room and I'll pour you a tall glass."

Wise Men of Gotham

Batman waited until they had gone into the living room, then he stole out of the closet and prowled the apartment in search of a better hiding place, one that would allow him to keep a lookout for the Riddler.

As he stepped into the bedroom Bathsheba had come from, he stopped dead in his tracks. His senses told him of another presence.

He attuned himself and caught muffled breathing from beneath the king-size bed.

Moving softly, he drew near enough to the bed to grip the footboard, then with a sudden jerk and thrust he swung the bed in an arc. Then he pounced upon the form thus laid bare, before it could move.

"Got you, Riddler!" he gritted through clenched teeth as he tightened a chokehold on the man beneath him on the floor.

"Aarghh!" The man was trying to tell him something. To deny being the Riddler.

Batman took his first good look at the man, eased his grip, and slowly got to his feet. The man was Housing Commissioner Sam Rubin.

Batman quickly recovered. Rubin was sitting up, gently massaging his throat where wheals showed. He looked around and started to croak something. Batman spotted a shirt and trousers on a chair. He shoved Rubin flat, tossed the clothes onto him, and swung the bed back into place.

He owed Rubin nothing, not the covering up of Rubin's cuckolding of Foster Cavendish, not even the saving of Rubin's life—it seemed clear now that the Riddler's target was not Cavendish but Rubin. Batman would do whatever fell in with foiling the Riddler.

A buzzer sounded, and Batman listened to talk over the intercom. The doorman announced a postman with a special delivery package for Bathsheba Cavendish that she had to sign for, and Cavendish told the doorman to let the man in.

Batman's heart pounded. *This was it!* The Riddler had signed his challenge "Billet-doux-ly"—and here came a letter carrier. It must indeed be a special delivery that brought a letter carrier on Easter Sunday.

The doorbell rang.

"I'll get it, dear." That was Bathsheba.

Batman debated with himself whether to act now or to hold off until the Riddler made his move. He decided to hold off.

The door opened.

"Why, what a lovely package!" Bathsheba called over her shoulder. "Thank you, dear. Here, you take it and open it."

"Sign here, ma'am."

"I didn't send it. You must have an unknown admirer."

"Sign here, ma'am."

"And wouldn't that be nice. Open it. I want to see what my secret lover sent me."

"Sign here, ma'am."

Before Batman could shout not to open the package, he heard paper rip.

"It's a big chocolate Easter egg!"

"How sweet!"

He did not hear another "Sign here, ma'am."

Evidently the Riddler had chosen not to wait.

Batman hurtled into the living room, grabbed the chocolate egg from Foster Cavendish, and dashed out of the apartment.

TICK-TICK-TICK-TICK-TICK

The egg was clutched close to his heart, which went *thumpthumpthumpthumpthump.*

Wise Men of Gotham

Foster Cavendish stared at Bathsheba Cavendish. "With *Batman*?"

Bathsheba stood with folded arms and lifted her chin.

Oblivious to this byplay, Batman raced down the hall with the Easter egg as though heading for a touchdown. The Riddler, dressed as a letter carrier, was alone in the cage. Their eyes met as the door closed.

Batman skidded to a stop, and with one arm forced the sliding door open enough to drop the chocolate egg through; the egg fell toward the top of the descending elevator cab. Batman pulled quickly back and flattened against the wall. Even so, he found himself flung to the floor while splinters of wood and steel pierced his cape.

B-A-R-O-O-M!!!

Then SWOOSHHHH-THUDD!!! as the blast severed the steel cables and dropped the cage several floors to the basement.

A singed and battered postman limped out past the doorman and hobbled away.

A quarter hour later, Sam Rubin slipped out from under the bed and pretended to have come with the police and fire personnel now swarming the scene. Foster Cavendish was touched that Rubin had responded to the news of the explosion—not just as a Housing Commissioner concerned about damage to habitable buildings, but as an acquaintance concerned about the Cavendishes. Cavendish hadn't realized how good a friend of the family Rubin was.

Batman dreaded the thought of facing Alfred with the cape in the state it was.

Wayne phoned Sollis. "Do you happen to know how many Wise Men of Gotham there were?"

Edward Wellen

A pause, then Amicia said, "I could journey to England and look up Gotham in the Domesday Book, and in the Pipe Rolls that carried on the census, but I doubt I'd find a breakdown of the male population into wise and foolish."

A pause at Wayne's end, then he said, "You're taking me too literally. I'm talking about the Wise Men in the legends, not necessarily about men who lived and breathed."

"You're right, Bruce. I ought to lighten up. Let's see . . . Well, there *is* a nursery rhyme:

'Three wise men of Gotham
Went to sea in a bowl.
If the bowl had been stronger,
My story had been longer.'

But it doesn't say '*The* three wise men.' So that leaves it open-ended."

"What I was afraid of," Wayne said.

Even though Bruce would have continued cause to consult her—which she didn't mind at all—Dr. Sollis shared his fear.

"You have to go out again, sir? I haven't finished spotting the cape." Alfred reluctantly fetched the Batman costume. He hesitated before handing it over. "If I may suggest, sir, mightn't you wear Master Dick's Robin costume while he's in England on his Rhodes scholarship?"

Wayne worked his shoulders. "It wouldn't hang right." He patted Alfred reassuringly. "Don't fret, Alfred. Darkness covers a multitude of sins."

Wise Men of Gotham

Alfred remained stiff. "I thought it was Charity, sir, that did the covering."

"We're told to do good deeds in secret, aren't we? That's darkness." Batman flung this and his cape over his shoulder and did not wait for Alfred's comeback.

They met at Fourth Avenue and Fourth Street at four a.m.

"That was a near thing with Foster Cavendish," Comissioner Gordon said.

"That it was," Batman said. He did not add that not Cavendish but Rubin had been the Riddler's target. He said quickly, "The Riddler again?"

Gordon nodded grimly. "He keeps bouncing right back." He handed Batman a photocopy of a rhymed note.

Fool's cap for a crown,

Would'st see the dunce drown

An eel in a pond?

Then come and be conned.

   —*Yours cruelly, the Riddler*

Like a cold cold finger the word "cruelly" touched Batman's spine to ice. The Riddler seemed bent on making up for the past near-misses. Batman did not let Gordon see the dismay he felt. He smiled, then faded to black before Gordon could tell the smile was frozen.

Dr. Amicia Sollis had words for the words. "'Foolscap' is a size of writing paper large enough to twist-and-paste into a dunce cap. It gets its name from a watermark in the form of a jester's cap with bells. 'Drown an eel in a pond' is of course the Gothamites' playing at being fools. 'Come and be conned' invites Batman to be suckered by a con— or confidence—game. Then, too, there's 'conn' with a double en, from cond for conduct; 'to take the conn' is to take over the steering of a vessel, to watch its course and direct the helmsman."

"Then Batman has only to find the fool, the eel, and the pond."

"You got it." Amicia dug into the sole. "This is delicious."

But Wayne had lost his appetite. Glumly, without thinking, he sipped water.

CLICK! A light bulb went on in his head.

He held the glass to the light of the chandeliers. Water was the key.

Could the Riddler's "pond" be the yacht basin? Could the Riddler's "eel" be the *Île de Joie*? Could the "fool" be Jack King?

Batman would go and take the conn.

Alfred looked flushed but defiant. "Master Dick is in his room unpacking."

Wayne shot Alfred a look and made for his protegé's room. Dick Grayson looked fit save for signs of jet lag.

They thumped one another, then Wayne eyed Dick keenly. "I thought you planned to hike through the highlands on your Easter holiday. What gives?"

Dick shrugged. "Alfred called me last night and said that you had let yourself go in your preoccupation with the Riddler. I figured you could use my help, so I Concorded right over."

"I'll speak to Alfred later. But I must admit I feel surer and stronger now that you're here. Let's change, and I'll fill you in on our way to the yacht basin."

Batman pedaled to the Batmobile's metal. The sleek vehicle whizzed through Gotham's canyons.

SCREEEECHHH!!!

Only their seat belts saved them.

Robin turned to stare at Batman. "Why did you brake?"

"It hit me. I *am* being conned by the Riddler. Jack King is not his target. In fact, Jack King is the mastermind behind the Riddler's attempts on the Wise Men of Gotham."

He ticked off on black-gloved fingers. "First, the floating corpse with the tattooed Riddler rhyme had been an art student mixed up in something mysterious at the time he turned up missing. That mysterious something could well have been the copying of a particular painting—the $86 million Rembrandt. Second, that would explain Jack King's curious composure when the Riddler vandalized *The Would-Be Bride*—Jack King was exhibiting not the original but a recently painted copy. Because, third, I noticed a faint smudge on Detective Sergeant Heather Mortimer's forearm after she pulled the dart from the canvas. The paint had not yet dried hard! Four, the Riddler found it awfully easy to get on and off the Île de Joie. Five, the Wise Men the Riddler has been after have all stood in Jack King's juggernaut path."

Batman made a fist. "It adds up."

Robin nodded. "Seems to. But now what?"

Batman eased out of the Batmobile. "You cover the Île de Joie just in case the Riddler is pulling a double con."

Robin shifted to the driver's seat. "While you—?"

Edward Wellen

"Look for the right eel in the right pond."

"Good fishing!"

Robin's voice thinned away on the Batmobile's exhaust.

Batman moved to the sidewalk, looking for a newsstand—a bit late, now, to be scanning the paper for some hint as to where the Riddler might strike.

Robin slowed as he neared the yacht basin. He spotted the *Île de Joie* and parked the Batmobile in a space preserved by fluorescent-orange traffic cones. It struck him that they looked like dunce caps.

"Keep the change," Batman said absently. He was already perusing the paper.

"Gee, thanks Batman!" the blind newsstand operator said.

Batman gave a start. "How do you know who I am?"

"Who else wears a cape these days? I heard the swirl."

"Oh." Batman moved away, reading as he walked.

The paper was thicker than usual for a weekday. It had a special Boat Show section.

Batman stopped in his tracks.

"You all right, Batman?" the newsstand operator called.

"Fine, fine." Batman hurried away.

He headed for Exposition Center, the venue of the Boat Show.

It all fell into place. "Fool's cap for a crown." Foolscap was paper. Gotham City's leading newspaper, the one in

Batman's hands, was the crown of Rudolph Newkirk's media empire. Rudolph Newkirk stood in Jack King's way, therefore representing a Wise Man for the Riddler to bump off. According to the special section, which must have brought the paper millions in advertising revenue, Rudolph Newkirk would be at the Boat Show this evening.

Batman quickened his pace.

Exposition Center had ways of ingress unknown to ticket buyers.

Batman made entry into the labyrinthine basement of the complex. Others had done so before him. As he moved through the vaulted chambers he glimpsed shadowy forms in the dim recesses. Scores of the homeless had taken up residence here.

He moved carefully and quietly to keep from disturbing them. Even so, some stirred and muttered at his passage.

"YOWW!" Skeletal hands with dirty claws waved threateningly in his face, red eyes glared into his, and foul breath assailed his nostrils. A ragged figure, thick with layers of clothes rather than with meat on its bones, had sprung out of an alcove at him. The raspy voice followed up on its shout. "Stay away! This is my place!"

Batman gestured placatingly. "Right! It's all yours!"

He made to pass by, but the claws gripped his cape at the throat and held him fast and the red eyes bored into his. "You wear a mask, but I've seen those eyes. Where have I seen those eyes?"

Batman tore free and shoved the man as gently as he could back into the precious alcove. "I don't know, my friend. We'll have to puzzle that out another time. Right now I'm on urgent business." He hurried on toward stairs going up.

He did not notice that the ragged figure followed him, fear and fascination in its bloodshot eyes.

On the exhibition floor, a vast arena filled with boats of all sizes and decked with flags and bunting, Batman hid himself from the crowd behind a motorboat booth and studied a program sheet he had picked up. Rudolph Newkirk's name jumped out at him. The publisher was scheduled to award best-of-show trophies at ten o'clock— a quarter of an hour from now. The handing out was to take place at the Caribbean display.

The reverse of the program sheet had a map that showed the Caribbean display to be a detailed scale model of the Caribbean area—clay islands in a steel-framed pool of water. Batman stretched to see over the crowd and found the display where the map put it—at the other end of the hall.

Batman consulted the program again. Just before Rudolph Newkirk's big moment, an expert from Anguilla in the Leeward Islands would demonstrate spearfishing in the same display. Batman's synapses sparked. Anguilla meant eel or snake. L-e-e was e-e-l backwards...

Crews from the local channels were already setting up lights and television cameras, clearing space for the thick cables snaking across the floor.

Nearby, on a bench for the weary of soles, a woman sat embroidering away with a long-eyed sharp needle and worsted yarn, as if waiting patiently for her man to get his fill of the exhibits.

Wise Men of Gotham

Batman only had eyes for the Anguillan spearfisher, a bronzed man wearing goggles and swimming trunks. Speargun in hand, he waded calf-deep into the pool, stirring up the live fish swimming there. He mounted the replica of his native island, and balanced on this tiny foothold. Now Batman saw Newkirk arrive with an entourage and stand in the wings. How easy it would be for the spearfisher (the Riddler in disguise?) to kill Newkirk as the one left the spotlight and the other entered it!

Batman edged around to the Caribbean display. He stood next to the bench where the woman—who might have been Mme. Defarge knitting as the guillotine lopped heads—sat working needle and yarn through an embroidery hoop.

A sprightly program chairwoman introduced the spearfisher as Captain Jacoby. In an accent of the Islands, Captain Jacoby described the technique, then speared some half-dozen wriggling blowfish in rapid order.

To a smattering of applause, Captain Jacoby splashed out of the Caribbean Sea. Greater applause attended Newkirk's introduction.

One eye on the spearfisher, who stopped by the side of the pool to towel his legs, Batman watched Newkirk goodsportedly take off shoes and socks and roll up trouser bottoms before stepping into the pool.

Newkirk lifted one foot into the pool and then the other. Batman tensed. Now the Riddler would make his move.

Captain Jacoby straightened and turned to look at Newkirk. Batman set himself to leap at the spearfisher.

But the move came from the woman knitting. She rose from the bench, dropped her crewel embroidery, and bent to pull the male plug of a floodlight from an extension cord snaking from the wall socket. She whipped the female end of the extension cord at the pool.

Crewel...cruel... flashed through Batman's mind. The Riddler!

Everyone stood stunned as the length of cord, like some slick-backed electric eel, arced toward the water. Everyone but Batman.

He lunged for the extension cord, grabbed hold, and pulled it from the wall socket just as the other end was about to hit the water with a terrible hissing and sparking. Newkirk stood frightened but unharmed.

With a curse, the Riddler—with wig askew, his identity now clear—dove for the embroidery, grabbed the crewel needle, and thrust the sharp point straight at Batman's heart.

A ragged figure hurled itself between the needle and Batman.

Batman let others give chase to the Riddler. He bent to the ragged figure that had taken the deathblow meant for Batman.

He strained to hear the homeless man's last gasps. The man stared into Batman's eyes.

"The eyes...the eyes of the kid...who watched me...knock off his folks...in the stickup..."

It took a moment to sink in, then Batman felt a rush of rage. But the man's eyes had closed. The man was past Batman's hate, past everything except, perhaps, peace.

Bruce Wayne held a sort of postmortem, a gathering of himself, Dick Grayson, Commissioner Gordon, and Dr. Amicia Sollis.

Alfred had a riddle of claret at the proper temperature, and they were doing justice to at least the magnum.

Wise Men of Gotham

Batman's string of victories over the Riddler had had swift and amazing consequences.

Gordon looked darkly through his half-full glass. "Jack King overreached himself—with no golden handshake at the end. When the Wise Men of Gotham lived to frustrate his grandiose project, his whole house of cards collapsed. Even his Swiss and Caribbean assets were frozen, and the Île de Joie was attached for back taxes, together with all its treasures—including the *real* Rembrandt discovered rolled up in the wall safe."

Dick said, "I happened to be at the yacht basin at the time news of the attempt on Newkirk came over the radio. I happened to see Jack King leave the Île de Joie and zoom away in a speedboat. I'm surprised he didn't take the Rembrandt with him."

"Had other things on his mind," Wayne guessed.

Amicia smiled wryly. "He didn't think to take Queena with him. I hear Queena filed for divorce, asking huge alimony. Fat chance she'll collect, with all his creditors— wolves, sharks, and vultures—seeking him by land, sea, and air, but at least she has all her jewels."

"A Wise Woman of Gotham?" Wayne asked. He looked at Amicia. "I know a wiser."

The Police Commissioner and the Avenger of Evil met one more time about the affair of the Wise Men of Gotham, just that Gordon might thank Batman—and update him on the hunt for the Riddler.

"He's escaped us again. We've looked high and low. First place, of course, was low—the basement of Exposition Center." He shivered. "What a pesthole! It'll take some doing to clear those creatures out of their nests and burrows and to squatter-proof the place."

Batman put a hand on Gordon's arm. "Let them be. From what I hear, Jack King will be needing somewhere to lay his head."

Northwestward

(BLACK WIDOWERS #61)

ISAAC ASIMOV

Thomas Trumbull said to Emmanuel Rubin in a low voice, "Where the devil have you been? I've been trying to reach you for a week."

Rubin's eyes flashed behind the thick lenses of his spectacles, and his sparse beard bristled. "I was away at the Berkshires for a week. I was not aware I had to apply for permission to you for that."

"I wanted to speak to you."

"Then speak to me now. Here I am—that is, supposing you can think of something intelligent to say."

Trumbull looked about hastily. The Black Widowers had gathered for the monthly banquet at the Milano and Trumbull had managed to arrive on time because he was the host.

He said, "Keep your voice down, for God's sake, Manny. I can't speak freely now. It's about," his voice dropped to a mere mouthing, "my guest."

"Well, what about him?" Rubin glanced in the direction of the tall, distinguished-looking elderly man, who was conversing with Geoffrey Avalon in the far corner.

The guest was a good two inches taller than Avalon, who was usually the tallest person at the gathering. Rubin, who was ten inches shorter than Avalon, grinned.

"I think it does Jeff good to have to look up now and then," he said.

"Listen to me, will you?" said Trumbull. "I've talked to the others and you were the only one I was really worried about and the only one I couldn't reach."

"But what are you worried about? Get to the point, will you?"

"It's my guest. He's peculiar."

"If he's your guest—"

"Sh! He's an interesting guy, and he's not nuts, but you may consider him peculiar and I don't want you to mock him. You just let him be peculiar and accept it."

"How is he peculiar?"

"He has an idée fixe, if you know what that means."

Rubin looked revolted. "Can you tell me why it's so necessary for an American with a stumbling knowledge of English to say idée fixe when the English phrase 'fixed idea' does just as well?"

"He has a fixed idea, then. It will come out because he can't keep it in. Please don't make fun of it, or of him. *Please* accept him on his own terms."

"This violates the whole principle of the grilling, Tom."

"It just bends it a little. I'm asking you to be polite, that's all. Everyone else has agreed."

Rubin's eyes narrowed. "I'll try, but, so help me, Tom, if this is some sort of gag—if I'm being set up for something—I'll stand on a stool if I have to, and I'll punch you right in the eye."

"There's no gag involved."

Rubin wandered over to where Mario Gonzalo was putting the finishing touches on his caricature of the guest. Not much of a caricature at that. He was turning out a Gibson man, a collar ad.

Rubin looked at it, then turned to look at the guest. He said, "You're leaving out the lines, Mario."

"Caricature," said Gonzalo, "is the art of truthful exaggeration, Mannie. When a guy looks that good at his age, you don't spoil the effect by sticking in lines."

"What's his name?"

"I don't know. Tom didn't give it. He says we ought to wait for the grilling to ask."

Roger Halsted ambled over, drink in his hand, and said in a low voice, "Tom was looking for you all week, Manny."

"He told me. And he found me right here."

"Did he explain what he wanted?"

"He didn't explain it. He just asked me to be nice."

"Are you going to?"

"I will, until I get the idea that this is a joke at my expense. After which—"

"No, he's apparently serious."

Henry, that quiet bit of waiter-perfection, said in his soft, carrying voice, "Gentlemen, dinner served."

And they all sat down to their crab-leg cocktails.

James Drake had stubbed out his cigarette since, by general vote, there was to be no smoking during the actual meal, and handed the ashtray to Henry.

He said, "Henry's announcement just now interrupted our guest in some comments he was making about Superman, which I'd like him to repeat, if he doesn't mind."

The guest nodded his head in a stately gesture of gratitude, and having finished an appreciative mouthful of veal marengo, said, "What I was saying was that Superman was a travesty of an ancient and honorable tradition. There has always been a branch of literature concerning itself with heroes; human beings of superior strength and courage. Heroes, however, should be supernormal but not supernatural."

"As a matter of fact," said Avalon, in his startling baritone. "I agree. There have always been characters like Hercules, Achilles, Gilgamesh, Rustam—"

"We get the idea, Jeff," said Rubin, balefully.

Avalon went on, smoothly, "Even half a century ago, we had the development of Conan by Robert Howard, as a modern legend. These were all far stronger than we puny fellows are, but they were not godlike. They could be hurt, wounded, even killed. They usually were, in the end."

"In the *Iliad*," said Rubin, perfectly willing, as always, to start an argument, "the gods could be wounded. Ares and Aphrodite were each wounded by Diomedes."

"Homer can be allowed liberties," put in the guest. "But compare, say, Hercules, with Superman. Superman has x-ray eyes, he can fly through space without protection, he can move faster that light. None of this would be true of Hercules. But with Superman's abilities, where is the excitement, where's the suspense? Then, too, where's the fairness? He fights off human crooks who are less to him than a ladybug would be to me. How much pride can I take in flipping a ladybug off my wrist."

Drake said, "One trouble with these heroes, though, is that they're musclebound at the temples. Take Siegfried. If he had an atom of intelligence, he took care never to show it. For that matter, Hercules was not remarkable for the ability to think, either."

"On the other hand," said Halsted, "Prince Valiant has brains and so, especially, did Odysseus."

"Rare exceptions," said Drake.

Rubin turned to the guest and said, "You seem very interested in storybook heroes."

"Yes, I am," said the guest, quietly. "It's almost an idée fixe with me." He smiled with obvious self-deprecation. "I keep talking about them all the time, it seems."

It was soon after that that Henry brought on the baked Alaska.

Trumbull tapped his water glass with his spoon at about the time that Henry was carefully supplying the brandy. Trumbull had waited well past the coffee, as though reluctant to start the grilling, and, even now, the tinkle of metal against glass seemed less authoritative than customary.

Trumbull said, "It is time that we begin the grilling of our guest, and I would like to suggest that Manny Rubin do the honors this evening."

Rubin favored Trumbull with a hard stare, then said to the guest, "Sir, it is usual to ask our guest to begin by justifying his existence, but, against all custom, Tom has not introduced you by name. May I, therefore, ask you what your name is?"

"Certainly," said the guest. "My name is Bruce Wayne."

Rubin turned immediately toward Trumbull, who made an unobtrusive, but clear, quieting gesture with his hands.

Rubin took a deep breath and managed a smile. "Well, Mr. Wayne, since we were speaking of heroes, I can't resist asking you if you are ever kidded about being the comic-

strip hero, Batman. Bruce Wayne is Batman's real name,
as you probably know."

"I do know," said Wayne, "because I *am* Batman."

There was a general stir at the table at this, and even
the ordinarily imperturbable Henry raised his eyebrows.
Wayne was apparently accustomed to this reaction, for he
sipped at his brandy without reacting.

Rubin cast another quick glance at Trumbull, then
said, carefully, "I suppose that, in saying this, you imply
that you are, in one way or another, to be identified with
the comic-strip character, and not with something else
named Batman, as, for instance, an officer's orderly in the
British army."

"You're right," said Wayne. "I'm referring to the comic-
strip character. Of course," and he smiled gently, "I'm not
trying to convince you I am literally the comic-strip Batman, cape, bat symbol, and all. As you see, I am a three-
dimensional living human being, and I assure you I am
aware of that. However, I have *inspired* the existence of
the comic-strip character, Batman."

"And how did that come about?" asked Rubin.

"In the past, when I was considerably younger than I
am now—"

"How old are you now?" asked Halsted, suddenly.

Wayne smiled. "Tom has told me I must answer all
questions truthfully, so I will tell you, though I'd prefer
not to. I am seventy-three years old."

Halsted said, "You don't look it, Mr. Wayne. You could
pass for fifty."

"Thank you. I try to keep fit."

Rubin said, with a trace of impatience, "Would you get
back to my question, Mr. Wayne? Do you want it
repeated?"

"No, my memory manages to limp along satisfactorily. When I was considerably younger than I am now, I was of some help to various law-enforcement agencies. At that time, there was money to be had in these comic strips about heroes, and a friend of mine suggested that I serve as a model for one. Batman was invented with a great many of my characteristics and of my history.

"It was, of course, distinctly romanticized. I do not, and never have, gone about with a cape, or had a helicopter of my own, but I did insist that Batman be given no supernatural powers but be restricted to entirely human abilities. I admit they do stretch it a bit sometimes. Even the villains Batman faces, although they are invariably grotesque, are exaggerations of people with whom I had problems in the past and whom I helped put out of circulation."

Avalon said, "I see why Superman annoys you, then... There was a television Batman for two seasons. What about that?"

"I remember it well. Especially Julie Newmar playing Catwoman. I would have liked to have met her as an opponent in real life. The program was played for laughs, you know, and good-natured fun."

"Well," said Drake, looking about the table and carefully lighting a cigarette now that the meal was over (and cupping it in his hand in the obvious belief that that would trap the smoke), "you seem to have had an amusing life. Are you the multimillionaire that the comic-strip Batman is?"

"As a matter of fact," said Wayne, "I'm very well off. My house in the suburbs is elaborate, and I even have an adjoining museum, but you know, we're all human. I have my problems."

"Married? Children?" asked Avalon.

"No, there I also resemble my alter ego—or he resembles me. I have never been married and have no children. Those are not my problems. I have a butler who tends to my household needs, along with some other servants who are of comparatively trivial importance."

"In the comic strip," said Gonzalo, "your butler is your friend and confidant. Is that right?"

"Well—yes." And he sighed.

Rubin looked thoughtful, and said, "Tell us about the museum, Mr. Wayne. What kind of museum is it? A headquarters for science and criminology?"

"Oh, no. The comic strip continues successfully, but my own day as an active upholder of the law is over. My museum consists of curios. There have been a great many objects made that have been based on the Batman cartoon and his paraphernalia. I have, I believe, at least one of every single piece ever made in that fashion: Batman notepaper, large-scale models of the Batmobile, figurines of every important character in the strip, copies of every magazine issue featuring the character, cassettes of all the television shows, and so on.

"It pleases me to have all this. After all, I am sure the strip will survive me and it will be the part of me that will be best remembered after my death. I don't have children to revere my memory, and I have done nothing very much in my real life to make me be part of history. These evidences of my fictional life are the best I can do to bring myself a little nearer immortality."

Rubin said, "I see. Now I'm going to ask a question that may cause you to feel a little uncomfortable, but you must answer. You had said—oh, for God's sake, Tom, this is a legitimate question. Why don't you let me ask it, before you start jumping."

Trumbull, looking both abashed and troubled, sank back in his chair.

Rubin said, "A little while ago, Mr. Wayne, you said that you, too, have your problems and, almost immediately afterward, when you mentioned your butler, you looked distinctly uncomfortable. Are you having trouble with your butler?—What are you laughing at, Tom?"

"Nothing," said Trumbull, chuckling.

Wayne said, "He's laughing because he bet me five dollars that if I just answered any questions asked me, and did so naturally and truthfully, the Black Widowers would have this out of me within twenty minutes, and he's won."

"I take it, then, that Tom Trumbull knows about this."

"Yes, I do," said Trumbull, "but I'm dealing myself out of this one for that reason. The rest of you handle it."

"I would suggest," interposed Avalon, "that Tom and Manny both quiet down and that we ask Mr. Wayne to tell us of his troubles with his butler."

"My butler's name," began Wayne, "is Cecil Pennyworth—"

"Don't you mean Alfred Pennyworth," put in Halsted.

"No interruption," said Trumbull, clinking his water glass.

Wayne said, "That's all right, Tom. I don't mind being interrupted. Alfred Pennyworth was indeed my butler originally and, with his permission, his name was used in the strip. However, he was older than I and, in the course of time, he died. Characters do not necessarily age and die in comic strips, but real life is rather different, you know. My present butler is Alfred's nephew."

"Is he a worthy substitute?" asked Drake, softly.

"No one could ever replace Alfred, of course, but Cecil has given satisfaction"—here Wayne frowned—"in all but one respect, and there my problem rests.

"You must understand that I sometimes attend conventions that are devoted to comic-strip heroes. I don't make a big issue of my being Batman, and I don't put on a cape or anything like that, although the publishers sometimes hire actors to do so.

"What I do is set up an exhibition of my Batman memorabilia. Sometimes, my publishers set up the more conventional items for sale, not so much for the money that is taken in, as for the publicity, since it keeps the thought of Batman alive in the minds of people. I have nothing to do with the commercial aspect. What I do is to exhibit a selection of some of the more unusual curios that are *not* for sale. I allow them to be seen and studied, while I give a little lecture on the subject. That has its publicity value, too.

"Needless to say, it is necessary to keep a sharp eye on all the exhibits. Most of them have no intrinsic value to speak of, but they are enormously valuable to me and sometimes, I'm afraid, to the fans. While the vast majority of them wouldn't think of appropriating any of the items, there are bound to be occasional individuals who, out of a natural dishonesty or, more likely, an irresistible desire, would try to make off with one or more items. We have to watch for that.

"I am even the target for more desperate felons. On two different occasions, there have been attempts to break into my museum; attempts that, I am glad to say, were foiled by our rather sophisticated security system. I see you are smiling, Mr. Avalon, but actually my memorabilia, however trivial they might seem, could be disposed of quietly for a considerable sum of money.

"One item I have *does*, in fact, have a sizable intrinsic value. It is a Batman ring in which the bat-symbol is cut out of an emerald. I was given it under circumstances

Isaac Asimov

that, if I may say so, reflected well on the real Batman—myself—and it has always been much dearer to me for that reason than because of the value of the emerald itself. It is the pièce de resistance of my collection, and I put it on display only very occasionally.

"A year or so ago, though, I had promised to appear at a convention in Minneapolis, and I did not quite feel up to going. As you see, I am getting on in age, and for all my fitness program, my health and my sense of well-being is not what it once was. After all, I may be the real Batman in a manner of speaking, but I am also human.

"I therefore asked Cecil Pennyworth to attend the convention as my substitute. On occasion, I have asked him to fill in for me, though, till then, not at a major convention. I had promised an interesting display, but I had to cut that to Cecil's measure. I chose small items that could all be packed systematically—so they could be quickly checked to make sure the display was intact—in a single good-size suitcase. I sent Cecil off with the usual unnecessary admonition to keep a close eye on everything.

"He called me from Minneapolis to assure me of his safe arrival and, again, a few hours later, to apprise me of the fact that an attempt had been made to switch suitcases."

"'And failed, I hope,' I said.

"He assured me that he had the right suitcase and that the display was safe and intact, but asked me if I really felt he should display the ring. You see, since I was sending only small items, I felt that I was, in a way, cheating my public, and I therefore included my ring so that at least they could see this rarest and most valuable of all my curios. I told Cecil, therefore, that he should certainly display the ring but keep the sharpest eyes upon it.

"I heard from him again two mornings later, when the convention was drawing to a close. He was breathless and sounded strained.

"'Everything is safe, Mr. Wayne,' he said, 'but I think I am being followed. I can duck them, though. I'm going northwest, and I'll see you soon.'

"I said, rather alarmed, 'Are you in danger?'

"He only said, 'I must go now.' and hung up.

"I was galvanized into activity—it's the Batman in me, I suppose. I threw off all trace of my indisposition and made ready for action. It seemed to me that I knew what was happening. Cecil was being tracked by someone intent on that suitcase, and he was not, himself, a strong person of the heroic mold. It seemed to him, therefore, that he ought to do the unexpected. Instead of returning to New York, he would try to elude those who were after him, and quietly head off in another direction altogether. Once he had gotten away from his pursuers, he could then return to New York in safety.

"What's more, I knew where he was going. I have several homes all over the United States, which is the privilege of one who, like myself, is quite well off. One of my homes is a small and unobtrusive place in North Dakota, where I sometimes go when I feel the need to isolate myself from the too-unbearable insinuations of the world into my private life.

"It made good sense to go there. No one but Cecil and I and some legal representatives know that the house in question belongs to me. If he got there safely, he could feel secure. He knew that to indicate to me that he was going northwestward would have complete meaning to me, and would mean nothing to anyone who might be overhearing him. That was clever. He had to hang up quickly because, I presume, he was aware of enemies in the vicinity. He had said, 'I'll see you soon' by which, it seemed to me, he was begging me to come to my North Dakota home to join him. Clearly, he wanted me to take over the responsibility of defense. As I said, he was not the heroic type.

"He had called me in the morning and, before night fell, I was at my North Dakota home. I remember being grateful that it was early fall. I would have hated to have to come there with two feet of snow on the ground and the temperature forty below."

Rubin, who was listening intently, said, "I suppose that your butler, in weather like that, would have chosen some other place as a hideout. He would have told you he was going southeastward and you would have gone to your home in Florida, if you have one."

"I have a home in Georgia," said Wayne, "but you are correct otherwise. I suppose that is what he would have done. In any case, when I arrived in North Dakota, I found that Cecil was not yet there. I got in touch with the people who care for the place in my absence (and who knew me only as a 'Mr. Smith'), and they assured me that nobody, to their knowledge, had arrived. There were no signs of any very recent occupancy, so he could not have arrived and been waylaid in the house. Of course, he might have been interrupted en route.

"I spent the night in the house, a very wakeful night, as you can imagine, and an uncomfortable one. In the morning, when he still had not arrived, I called the police. There were no reports of any accidents to planes, trains, buses, or cars that could have possibly be applied to Cecil.

"I decided to wait another day or so. It was possible, after all, that he might have taken a circuitous route or paused on the way, 'holed up,' one might say, to mislead his pursuers, and would soon take up the trip again. In short, he might arrive a day late, or even two days late.

"On the third morning, however, I could wait no more. I was certain, by then, that something was very wrong. I called my New York home, feeling he might have left a message there, and was rather berating myself for not having made the call earlier for that purpose, or, if no message had been received, to have left the number at which I could be reach when the message came.

"At any rate, on the third morning I called, and it was Cecil who answered. I was thunderstruck. He had arrived on the afternoon of the day I had left. I simply said I would be home that night and, of course, I was. So you see my difficulty, gentlemen."

There was a short silence at the rather abrupt ending to the story, and then Rubin said, "I take it that Cecil was perfectly safe and sound."

"Oh, yes, indeed. I asked him about the pursuers, and he had smiled faintly and said, 'I believe I eluded them, Mr. Wayne. Or I may even have been entirely mistaken and they did not really exist. At least, I wasn't bothered in the least on my way home.'"

"So that he got home safely?"

"Yes, Mr. Rubin."

"And the exhibition curios were intact?"

"Entirely."

"Even the ring, Mr. Wayne?"

"Absolutely."

Rubin threw himself back in the chair with an annoyed expression on his face, "Then, no, I don't see your difficulty."

"But why did he tell me he was going northwestward. He told me that distinctly. There is no question of my having misheard."

Halsted said, "Well, he thought he was being followed, so he told you he was going to the North Dakota place.

Isaac Asimov

Then he decided that either he had gotten away from the pursuers, or that they didn't exist, and he thereupon switched his plans, and went straight to New York without having time to call you again and warn you of that."

"Don't you think that, in that case," said Wayne, with some heat, "he might have apologized to me. After all, he had misled me, sent me on an unnecessary chase into North Dakota, subjected me to a little over two days of uncertainty during which I not only feared for my collection, but also felt that he might be lying dead or badly injured somewhere. All this was the result of his having told me, falsely, that he was heading northwestward. And then, having arrived in New York, he might have known, since I wasn't home, that I had flown to the North Dakota home to be with him, and he might have had the kindness to call me there and tell me he was safe. He knew the North Dakota number. But he didn't call me, and he didn't apologize to me or excuse himself when I got home."

"Are you sure he knew that you were in North Dakota?" asked Halsted.

"Of course, I'm sure he knew. For one thing, I told him. I had to account for the fact that I had been away from home for three days. I said, 'Sorry I wasn't home when you arrived, Cecil. I had to make a quick and unexpected trip to North Dakota.' It would have taken a heart of forged steel not to have winced at that, and not to have begun apologizing, but it didn't seem to bother him at all."

There was another pause at this point, and then Avalon cleared his throat in a deep rumble and said, "Mr. Wayne, you know your butler better than any of us do. How do you account for this behavior."

"The logical feeling is that it was just callousness," said Wayne, "but I don't know him as a callous man. I have evolved the following thought, though: What if he had been tempted by the ring and the other curios himself? What if it was his plan to dispose of them for his own benefit? He could tell me that he was being pursued, and that would send me off on my foolish mission to North Dakota so that he would have a period of time to put away his ill-gotten gains somewhere and pretend he had been robbed. See?"

Rubin said, "Do you know Cecil to be a dishonest man?"

"I wouldn't have said so, but anyone can yield to temptation."

"Granted. But if he did, he resisted. You have everything. He didn't steal anything."

"That's true, but his telling me he was going northwestward and then never explaining why he had changed his mind, tells me that he was up to skullduggery. Just because he was too faint-hearted to go through with it this time doesn't excuse him. He might be bolder the next time."

Rubin said, "Have you asked him to explain the northwestward business?"

Wayne hesitated. "I don't like to. Suppose there is some explanation. The fact that I would ask him about it would indicate that I didn't trust him, and that would spoil our relationship. My having waited so long makes it worse. If I ask now, it would mean I have brooded about it all year, and I'm sure he would resign in resentment. On the other hand, I can't think what explanation he might have, and my not asking him leaves me unable to relax in his presence. I find I am always keyed up and waiting for him to try again."

Rubin said, "Then it seems that if you don't ask him, but convince yourself he's guilty, your relationship is ruined. And if you do ask him and he convinces you he's innocent, your relationship is ruined....What if you don't ask him, but convince yourself he is innocent?"

"That would be fine," said Wayne, "but how? I would love to do so. When I think of my long and close association with Alfred Pennyworth, Cecil's uncle, I feel I owe something to the nephew—but I must have an explanation and I don't dare ask for it."

Drake said, "Since Tom Trumbull knows about all this—what do you say about it, Tom?"

Wayne interposed. "Tom says I should forget all about it."

Trumbull said, "That's right. Cecil might have been so ashamed of his needless panic that he just can't talk about it."

"But he *did* talk about it," said Wayne, heatedly. "He casually admitted that he might have been mistaken about being pursued, and did so as soon as I got home. Why didn't he apologize to me and express regret for the trouble he had put me to."

"Maybe *that's* what he can't talk about," said Trumbull.

"Ridiculous. What do I do? Wait for a deathbed confession? He's twenty-two years younger than I am, and he'll outlive me."

"Then," said Avalon, "if we're to clear the air between you, we must find some natural explanation that would account for his having told you he was heading northwestward and that would also acount for his having failed to express regret over the trouble he put you to."

"Exactly," said Wayne, "but to explain both at once is impossible. I defy you to."

The silence that followed endured for quite a while until Rubin said, "And you won't accept embarrassment as an explanation for his failure to express regret."

"Of course not."

"And you won't ask him."

"No, I won't," said Wayne, biting off the remark with decision.

"And you find having him in your employ under present conditions is wearisome and nerve-wracking."

"Yes, I do."

"But you don't want to fire him, either."

"No. For old Alfred's sake, I don't."

"In that case," said Rubin, gloomily, "you have painted yourself into a corner, Mr. Wayne. I don't see how you can get out of it."

"I still say," growled Trumbull, "that you ought to forget about it, Bruce. Pretend it never happened."

"That's more than I can do, Tom," said Wayne, frowning.

"Then Manny is right," said Trumbull. "You can't get out of the hole you're in."

Rubin looked about the table. "Tom and I say Wayne can't get out of this impasse. What about the rest of you?"

Avalon said, "What if a third party—"

"No," said Wayne, instantly. "I won't have anyone else discussing this with Cecil. This is strictly between him and me."

Avalon shook his head. "Then I'm stuck, too."

"It would appear," said Rubin, looking about the table, "that none of the Black Widowers can help you."

"None of the Black Widowers seated at the table," said Gonzalo, "but we haven't asked Henry yet. He's our waiter, Mr. Wayne, and you'd be surprised at his ability to work things out. Henry!"

"Yes, Mr. Gonzalo," said Henry, from his quiet post at the sideboard.

"You heard everything. What do you think Mr. Wayne ought to do?"

"I agree with Mr. Trumbull, sir. I think that Mr. Wayne should forget the matter."

Wayne rolled his eyes upward and shook his head firmly.

"However," Henry went on. "I have a specific reason for suggesting it, one that perhaps Mr. Wayne will agree with."

"Good," said Gonzalo. "What is it, Henry?"

"Mr. Pennyworth, under the impression he had told you he was flying to New York, said he would see you soon—meaning, in New York. And he hung up suddenly because his plane probably announced, at that moment, that it was ready for boarding."

"Good Lord!" said Wayne.

"Exactly, sir. Then when Mr. Pennyworth got home and found you had been to North Dakota, he could honestly see no connection between that and anything he might have done, so that it never occurred to him to apologize for his actions. He couldn't have asked you why you had gone to North Dakota; as a servant, it wasn't his place to. Had you explained of your own accord, he would have understood the confusion and would undoubtedly have apologized for contributing to it, but you remained silent."

"Good Lord!" said Wayne, a second time. Then, energetically, "I have spent over a year making myself miserable over nothing at all. There's no question about it. Batman has made a terrible mistake."

"Batman," said Henry, "has, as you yourself have pointed out, the great advantage, and the occasional disadvantage, of being only human."

Daddy's Girl

WILLIAM F. NOLAN

From Robin's Casebook...

It was a solo night job.

Bruce had gone to Washington to deliver a lecture on the economic affairs at a business convention, and had asked me to stay here in Gotham. My job was nailing the Tomcat, a very sharp jewel thief who was hitting all the wealthy West Side mansions in the hours past midnight, one each night, and cleaning them out. There were a lot of very angry Gotham City citizens demanding his arrest, but the police had never been able to catch sight of him let alone arrest him. Nabbing the fellow, with Batman gone, was my responsibility.

"As you know, a prowling cat tends to follow a proscribed route," Batman had reminded me. "So all we have to do, in order to figure out where our Tomcat will prowl next, is to counter-triangulate the area of his previous robberies, feed in the fixed coordinates of his probable strike area, and we'll have it narrowed to a one-block target."

When Batman pulls off stuff like this he reminds me of Sherlock Holmes— but ol' Sherlock never had a Bat-

Daddy's Girl

computer to work with. Ours produced a one-block area readout, mansion by mansion, so all we had to do was to set up a stakeout in that area and wait for the Tomcat to show.

"Up to you to nail this Tomcat's tail to the fence," he told me.

"Don't worry, I'll make him yowl," I promised.

So here I was on my solo night job. I'd come in the Batmobile, but had sent it back to the Batcave; I didn't want our catman to spot it in the area. The directional computer took it back without any problem—like sending a good horse home to the stable.

Now I was on the hunt, hugging the tree shadows along Forest Avenue, using the InfraBatscope to scan the buildings for possible Tomcat activity. A full spring moon was riding above Gotham City, painting rooftops and sidewalks with glimmering sliver. A lovely night for action.

I was glad to be out here under the sky on a hunt instead of being stuck in Washington the way Batman was. Despite all the years of crook-catching the thrill of the hunt had never diminished. On a night like this my blood raced and my whole body was on alert—every muscle tensed and ready for combat. For a true crimefighter, what else was there to live for?

That was when I saw him—the Tomcat, clawing his way up a vine toward the roof of a mansion, a big Victorian structure set well back from the street and almost buried in trees.

I muttered "Gotcha!"—heading for the mansion's black iron fence. I was up and over, sprinting for the tall side of the house rising ahead of me like a white iceberg under the moon. I moved over the grass, shadow-quick, without sound, and he had no idea I was coming for him.

I scrambled up to the roof, reaching it just in time to spot Mr. Tomcat crouched next to a skylight, trying to jimmy the lock with a crowbar. He was a tall string-bean of a guy, all in black, sporting a black stovepipe hat and black leather gloves—and he had a sharp, beaked profile that reminded me of the Penguin. Apparently he figured nobody was home since he sure wasn't trying to be subtle about getting inside.

I padded across the roof, smiling, sure of the game. Bagging this particular feline was going to be a cinch.

I was wrong. When I was just two feet away from him he whipped up his head, let out a venomous cat hiss, and lunged at me with the heavy crowbar—which wouldn't have given me any trouble if my right foot hadn't snagged on a loose shingle, throwing me off balance.

The Tomcat's crowbar slammed into me across the chest, and I went crashing, head first, through the glass skylight. I felt myself falling through space. Then, a big crash, and darkness.

Pitch-black darkness.

What I saw next was a delicate white face floating above me—the face of a beautiful young woman with round, dark, startled eyes like the eyes of a fawn in the forest.

"Hello," she said in a voice as soft as her eyes. "Does your body flesh hurt?"

An odd question. "My...body flesh?" Things were coming into focus around me. I was in a large bedroom, her bedroom most likely, since it was all pink and flouncy. And the young lady was also in pink, the kind of wide-skirted lacy Victorian dress you'd wear to a costume ball.

Daddy's Girl

I tried to sit up. "Ouch!" I groaned, clutching my side. "It *does* hurt."

Which is when I realized I was wearing white silk pajamas. My cape and mask and clothes were gone! This was serious, since no one in Gotham City was ever supposed to see Robin without his mask. Batman was going to be plenty sore at me for this!

"Who are you?" I asked the girl.

"Sue-Ellen," she said softly.

"Sue-Ellen who?"

She flushed. "I don't have a last name. Sometimes I don't even feel like a real person. I mean, real people have last names—and Father has never told me what mine is."

"It would be the same as his," I pointed out.

"But I don't know that either. I just call him Father." She blinked at me. "What's *your* name?"

"I'm . . . I'm not authorized to reveal my true identity."

Her eyes were wide. "Are you with the FBI?"

"No. But I *do* fight crime."

"Is that why you were wearing a mask?" She had long blond hair framing the oval of her face; the moonlight from the window made it shine like a halo.

I adjusted the pillow, sitting up straight. "Haven't you seen my picture in the papers?"

"I don't ever see newspapers. Or magazines either. Father won't allow them in the house."

She'd caught me in full costume—and Robin had been on TV plenty of times. "You must have seen me on television?"

"We don't have television here," she said. Then she smiled for the first time and she was radiant. I was stunned by her pale beauty.

This surreal conversation was getting nowhere; it was time to end it. "I must leave now," I told her. "How long have I been here?"

William F. Nolan

"About ten hours. But you can't leave. Nobody ever leaves this house but Father. And he's away now. Far, far away."

"No, really," I said, "I must go. Just get me the clothes I had on when you found me."

She shook her head. "I want you to stay here with me. You're the first flesh person I've ever known, except for Father."

"Look, Sue-Ellen," I said, sliding my legs over the edge of the bed. "I really appreciate what you've done for me—fixing up my rib and all—but I have to leave immediately." I stood up. "Even if I have to walk out of here in a pair of silk pajamas."

"Gork will stop you," she declared. "I told him that you should stay." And she snapped her fingers.

A huge seven-footer appeared in the bedroom door. He had a flat gray face and eyes without pupils and wore a seamless gray uniform. He looked strong—but I was sure I could handle him.

"I'll have to clobber your big pal if he gets in my way." I told the girl. "Tell him to move back from the door."

"Gork is my friend. He does what I ask. He won't allow you to leave."

I was in no mood to argue the point. I just lowered my head and charged. Hitting him was like slamming into a brick wall. And trying to punch him was hopeless. My blows had no effect.

Then Gork put his hands on me. Like two steel meat hooks.

"Don't hurt him, Gork," said Sue-Ellen. "Just put him back in bed."

The big lug did that. And he tucked me in like a three-year-old. All without changing expression.

"You can go now," the girl told him.

He shambled out of the room.

"He's not human, is he?"

"Of course not," she said. "No one in this house is human, except for me. And Father—when he's home."

"What is Gork?"

"Mostly, he's made of metal. When I was very young Father got interested in the science of robotics. He's quite brilliant, and has many interests. He began to experiment with metal people. Robots. That's what Gork is—and he's identical to a dozen others that Father had constructed to take care of me. But Gork is the only one I really like." She moved very close, leaning over the bed. "May I touch your face?"

"Uh...sure, I guess so."

She reached out with tentative fingers to explore the planes of my face.

"It's warm—just like mine. The robots have cold faces, like wet fish." She gave me one of her radiant smiles. "I'm a flesh person, too. Just like you are."

This whole situation was totally bizarre; I couldn't figure it out.

"I need to talk to a friend," I told her. "Could I use your phone?"

"We don't have any phones here. Father says they'd just distract me—that I'd use them to try to call other flesh people." She giggled. "But that's silly because I don't know anyone but you and you're right here. I don't have to call you."

I looked at her intently. "Is it true...that I'm...the first boy you've ever met?"

"I said so, and I never lie."

"Where did you go to school?"

"Here. In this house. The robots taught me."

"You mean...you've never been to an outside school?"

"I've never been to an outside anything," she declared. "I've just been *here*, in Father's house. For my whole life."

I was shocked. "Are you saying your father has kept you prisoner?"

"Prisoner?" She frowned at the word. "No...I'm not a prisoner...I'm Daddy's girl. This is where he wants me to be—where he brought me as a tiny baby after Mother and Father quit living together."

"What happened to your mother?"

"I don't know. I never saw her again. Anyhow, after she left, Father told me I was 'too precious' to have the world 'pollute' me. He said he'd keep me here, always, safe from the 'harshness' of the world, that he didn't want me 'tarnished.' Father uses words like that all the time. He's a lot smarter than me."

"Did you ever get to play with other children?"

"Oh, no—never. Father had robot children made for me to play with. I never saw any real ones. I just grew up here—with the robots." She brightened. "I've even learned to make robots myself now. I'm very good at it, too."

"Who *is* your father?" I was angry at what the man had done to his daughter. "Tell me who he is."

"I've told you, I don't *know* his name. He's just...Father."

I walked over to her dresser. "You must have a picture of him...a photo. I want to see his face."

"He doesn't like pictures. There aren't any."

"What does he do for a living? How does he earn the money for all this?"

"He works in the circus. As a clown. I guess he always has. That's where he is right now, with a circus, way off in Washington. You know, the D.C. place."

Daddy's Girl

"Yes, that's where my friend is now—the one I need to contact."

She nodded. "Then maybe Father will see your friend there."

Something was very wrong. I sensed it—a rushing chill inside me, a prickly feeling that this crazy father of hers was a threat to Batman. I had no evidence to back it up, just a gut hunch. But it was strong.

I had to find out what was happening in Washington.

"When you found me," I said urgently to Sue-Ellen. "After I'd fallen through the skylight...I was wearing a wrist chron."

She looked confused.

"Like a watch," I said. "Where is it?"

"The robots took it away with your other clothing."

"I need it, Sue-Ellen! Badly."

"All right, I'll have Gork fetch it."

And she did. The big gray robot handed it to me, then shambled out again.

The Batchron was a communication device, featuring a mini-TV. I punched in the coordinates, and the face of a worried-looking newscaster flashed to life on the tiny screen. He was speaking with gravity: "...and the shocking attempt on the President's life was averted by Gotham City's Caped Crusader in a daring action when Batman suddenly appeared at the circus, throwing himself directly in the path of the killer clown, and managing to wrest a lethal dart-weapon from his grasp. Had just one of the deadly venom-coated darts struck the President he would have died instantly. In the subsequent melee the killer escaped from the circus tent, but Batman was unhurt..."

I switched it off. Sue-Ellen and I were staring at each other. "That clown...on the newscast," she said. "They only showed him from the back—but I'm sure it's Father."

"Then your father attempted to assassinate the President of the United States."

"I'm sorry," murmured Sue-Ellen softly, head down. "That's very wrong, isn't it?"

"Very," I said.

"I wonder why he'd *do* a thing like that," the girl said. "But then...he's not a very nice man. I have tried to love him, but I just can't. Gork has been much kinder to me than Father."

I was beginning to suspect a terrible truth about Sue-Ellen's father. But I needed to have her verify it.

"Describe him to me," I asked. "What does your father look like?"

"If you mean his features, I'm not sure. I mean, not really. He's always in his clown makeup. I've never seen him without it."

I nodded. "And what about his hair? What color is it?" My voice was intense.

"It's green," she said. "An ugly green color...and he always wears red on his lips."

I was right. Sue-Ellen's father was our old enemy, the Clown Prince of Crime himself....

"Surprise!" An oily voice from the doorway.

I looked up—and he was there, with his demonic smile distorting that dead-white face, the face of total evil.

"Joker!" I glared at him. Sue-Ellen drew back, as if from a snake. He ignored her, his eyes blazing into mine.

"Ah...it's Dick Grayson," he said slowly. "A known friend to Batman and Robin."

"And proud of it," I said tightly.

"Well, it seems your friend foiled me again," said the Joker. "I intend to make him pay for what he did to me in Washington!"

Daddy's Girl

We were face-to-face at the bed. His breath was foul, like rotten meat. "You're big at making empty threats, Joker," I told him. "But when the chips are down you always lose. Batman and Robin have defeated you time and again—and one of these days they'll put you permanently out of business."

"Never! My brain far surpasses the range of normal men."

"At least we both agree on that," I told him. "You're anything but normal."

During this entire exchange, from the moment her father had appeared in the room, Sue-Ellen had been silent, intent on the play of words between us. Now she spoke firmly, her small chin raised in defiance.

"Father, you are being very unkind. This is my first flesh friend and I don't like the mean way you've been talking to him. I think you should apologize."

"Apologize!" The Joker's laugh was bitter. "I'll apologize to no friend of Batman's. That bat-eared fool has been a plague in my life—continually thwarting my plans."

"If you have acted as wickedly in the past as you acted in Washington," declared the girl. "Then your plans *should* have been thwarted."

The clown glared at her. "What do you know of good and evil...of profit and gain...of besting authority...of the sheer power and joy in being a master of crime?"

"I know it's nothing to be proud of," she snapped. "From what I've learned here today, I would say you belong in jail."

"If Batman were here you'd see how he'd deal with your father," I told Sue-Ellen. "He'd put him out of action fast enough!"

"Oh, he'll be here," smiled the Joker. "I will see to that! I'll lead him to this very house...and there will be a present waiting for him...a present from the Joker to the Batman."

"What do you mean?" I demanded.

"I don't know what odd twist of fate brought you to this house," he said, "but I shall make good use of you. When Batman arrives—and I shall summon him personally—he shall find his society friend, Dick Grayson, waiting for him..." A fiendish cackle. "...with a cut throat!"

And he held up a long-bladed knife. Light trembled along the razored edge.

"And you, dear daughter," he said, turning to Sue-Ellen, "shall slice his throat neatly from ear to ear and we shall leave him for his bat-friend to find." His eyes glowed hotly. "It will be simply *delicious*—watching Batman's shock when he encounters Grayson's corpse!"

"How utterly *horrible!*" exclaimed Sue-Ellen. "You're a monster! You can never make me do such a..."

Her voice faltered. The Joker was standing above her, staring into her eyes. The tone of his voice was soft and compelling: "You shall obey your father in all things...You will do exactly as I command...You are Daddy's girl...Daddy's girl...Daddy's girl..." And his eyes burned like glowing coals in the dead white of his face.

"I...am...Daddy's...girl," Sue-Ellen murmured in a drugged voice. Her hands fell to her sides. She was blank-eyed and rigid, a victim of his dark powers.

That's when I jumped him, driving my right fist into the white of that grinning face—but before I could deliver a second blow I was jerked violently backward. Two gray-skinned house robots held my arms in a literal grip of steel. I was helpless.

"Don't try to fight them," said the clown. "They are far more powerful than any human." He reached into his striped coat and produced a small, jell capsule. "When she uses the knife on you," he said. "You'll never feel a thing."

And he snapped the capsule in two under my nose. A wave of sleeping gas spun me into blackness.

From the Batman's Casebook . . .

I had just returned from Washington—more enraged than ever at the Joker. His vicious attempt on the President's life was yet another act of total madness. I was grimly determined to run him into the ground in Gotham City.

When no word from Robin awaited me upon my return I was concerned as to his whereabouts. Cruising the West Side in the Batmobile, I scanned each section of the street, but found no sign of him. Where could Robin be?

Then, abruptly, the Joker's grinning face appeared directly ahead. The image was being beamed down from the sky above me—from the Joker's Clowncopter. I could see him at the controls as he hovered over me with his mocking devil's smile. He fired a burst from his laser nosecannon, blasting apart the road, and I veered sharply left to avoid a smoking crater. (More work for the street department.)

It was a short chase. The Joker brought his machine down on the roof of an old Victorian mansion on Forest Avenue, and I followed him through an open roof door.

The house was silent and lightless. The Clown Prince of Crime was hiding somewhere inside this gloomy building, and I was determined to find him. The silence seemed to deepen as I moved through the darkness, hunting from room to room, gliding down the main staircase.

William F. Nolan

I padded softly along a dimly lit hallway toward an open door just ahead. This was the main ballroom, immense and ornate, moonlight tinting its polished oak floor.

Then I gasped. Someone was spread-eagled on a table in the middle of the cavernous chamber. I moved closer.

And fell back in agonized shock. It was Robin! Unmasked, and dressed in white silk pajamas—spattered with blood! His head was twisted at a sharp angle—and his throat had been cut from ear to ear!

A searing white cone of light stabbed suddenly down from the ceiling and an amplified wave of ghoulish laughter crashed through the room. The Joker's laughter! Taunting, demonic, triumphant...

"He is dead, Batman. Your meddlesome little friend, Dick Grayson, is no more."

"Damn you, Joker, I'll tear you apart for this!" In a red rage, fists doubled, I swung around, raking the darkness for a glimpse of him. My fingers itched to close on his windpipe; I wanted to choke the life out of his foul body, to see his eyes bug and his tongue protrude from his swollen red lips...

"No use looking around for me, Batman. I'm in my second-floor study, enjoying this splendid show on my monitor screen."

I looked up. A shielded scanner rotated with my movements, providing the Joker with his image of my agony. Then the tall entrance door to the ballroom banged shut like an exploding cannon.

"There's no way out for you," the Joker informed me. "That door is steel-ribbed and the walls are rock solid."

"What's your game, Joker?"

Daddy's Girl

"Simple. I intend to leave you with your dead friend. No food. No water. Just you and a slowly-rotting corpse. I shall savor your death, Batman. Indeed, I shall."

And, again, the cackle of demonic laughter from the wall speakers.

I sprinted for the door, throwing my full weight against it, but the door held fast. The Joker was right; I was trapped like a fly in a web.

I slumped against the door, the full horror of Robin's death assaulting me. Tears ran down my cheeks behind the Batcowl, and I slammed the wall in pained frustration. Indeed, it seemed the Joker would have a good show.

Then, just beyond the viewing range of the scan unit, from the deep corner shadow, I saw a small white hand beckoning to me.

I didn't want to alert the Joker so I put on the act he was hoping for: I groaned aloud, turned in a hopeless circle, then staggered to the corner to beat both fists against the wall.

A young woman with frightened eyes was crouched there. Looking up at me, her words tumbled out in a desperate whisper.

"Your friend is alive," she said. "The figure on the table is a robot—to fool Father. He thought I was hypnotized, but I wasn't, I just pretended. Gork helped me. He's a robot, too. We modeled the machine boy after Dick Grayson. I made the face myself!"

Relief that Robin was still alive flooded through me. I leaned close to the girl. "Who are you?"

"I'm Sue-Ellen, the daughter of the person you call the Joker. He tried to force me to kill your friend, but I could never do that. I *love* him!"

"Where have you hidden him?"

William F. Nolan

"Below...in the basement. He's still unconscious from Father's sleeping gas. But the two of you can get away through a secret passage leading to the street."

"But how do I get out of this room?"

"Behind you...there's a trapdoor in the floor. It was bolted shut from below but I got it open."

"Where are you, Batman?" The Joker's taunting voice boomed from the speakers. "Come, come, this will never do." The tone became harsh. "Step back into the light or I shall be forced to send down some of my metallic friends to *drag* you out of that corner. And they won't be gentle about it. Now, do as I say!"

Sue-Ellen was gesturing to me; her voice was urgent: "Quickly! He'll send his robots if we don't hurry."

And she tugged open the trapdoor, revealing a square of pale yellow light from the basement below us. A twist of sagging wooden stairs led downward.

"This way," whispered the girl. "Follow me."

I slipped through the trapdoor, closing it behind me, and followed her rapidly down the stairs.

From Robin's Casebook...

I woke up, blinking, acrid powder fumes in my nostrils. Batman was leaning over me; he'd used a reviver vial from his utility belt to bring me around.

"You okay?"

"Yeah...a little dizzy is all." I gripped his arm. "How did you get here, Batman? And where's Sue-Ellen?"

The girl stepped forward, taking my hand. Her fingers felt warm and strong. "Here I am." She was smiling; my personal angel.

"I don't understand. I thought the Joker had—"

"Never mind what you thought," said Batman. "By now the Joker knows that his daughter tricked him. He'll be sending down his killer robots." He reached out a gloved hand. "On your feet. We need to get out of here."

I stood up. A bit shaky, but otherwise I was fine.

Then: wham!—the basement door crashed open.

Sue-Ellen screamed: "They're here!"

A half-dozen giant, gray-faced robots were pouring through the door, straight at us.

"Maybe this will slow them down," shouted Batman, tossing a Batpellet at the advancing tinmen. They staggered back as the pellet exploded into yellow fire.

"This way!" cried Sue-Ellen, taking the lead down a narrow rock-walled passageway. It was damp and cobwebby and smelled of dead rats.

The tunnel was as black as the Joker's soul—but we kept running full tilt behind the girl. Then we could make out a faint glow at the far end.

"That's the street light from the corner of Forest and Troost," Sue-Ellen informed us. "You're almost out."

But "almost" wasn't good enough; the robots were gaining fast. In another couple of seconds they'd catch us for sure.

"*Do* something, Batman!" I pleaded. "Or we're goners!"

The Caped Crusader spun around and flipped out another belt vial. Whoom! The whole roof caved in behind us, trapping the robots in rock and mud.

Then we were at the tunnel exit. Sue-Ellen stepped back. "Go quickly," she said.

I hesitated. "But we're taking you with us."

"Oh, no you're not!" rasped an oily voice—and the Joker leaped toward us, a gleaming .357 Magnum in his gloved hand.

Batman didn't say a word. It was time for action, not talk. He ducked under the Joker's gun arm to deliver a smashing blow to the clown's pointed chin.

The Joker fell back, dropping the Magnum. Then he pressed a button on his coat—and the Clowncopter, blades whirling, dropped to the pavement between us like a giant cat. Instantly, the Joker hopped to the controls, roaring the chopper skyward; it whip-sawed away over the trees.

My voice was intense: "Can we catch him in the Batcopter?"

"Afraid not," sighed Batman. "I left it on the roof. No doubt our green-haired friend disabled it. He wouldn't risk a pursuit."

We turned toward the girl. She was crouching inside the tunnel, peering out at us from the darkness.

"Come on, Sue-Ellen," I said. "Time to go."

She shook her head, "I can't."

I moved quickly to her. "But why not? You...you've said that you love me."

"I do...I really truly do," she declared. "But—"

I stopped her words with my lips.

"A kiss!" She gasped in delight. "I've never had one of those before."

"Sue-Ellen, I want you *with* me," I told her. "To share my life. I've never met a girl like you. I want to marry you."

Tears welled in her eyes. "Oh, that sounds...so wonderful. But it can't ever happen. Because..."

"Because why?"

She stepped forward into the light from the street lamp. "Because I'm dying."

Sue-Ellen was pale and her hands trembled; a crimson thread of blood ran from the corner of her mouth.

"Father made certain I'd never be able to go out into the world," she told us. "He gave me...injections. So long as I stayed indoors, in the house, I was all right.

But...those injections changed the chemistry of my body. I can't survive...on the outside. My coming out...set off a kind of...chain-reaction inside my body and nothing can save me now. Not even your love."

"But there must be an antidote," I gasped.

"No...too late..." She was moaning out the words. "Father was brilliant. He wanted to make sure that I'd always be...Daddy's girl."

She reached out, slowly, to clasp my hand. Her fingers were already turning cold. "Goodbye, Dick Grayson," she whispered. "Goodbye, my love!"

And she was gone.

I lowered her body to the ground.

Batman gripped my shoulder. "Dick, I...I'm sorry."

I'd lost the sweetest girl I'd ever known.

I loved her. Very much.

And I always will.

Command Performance

HOWARD GOLDSMITH

I

The Gotham City Department Store loomed before her. *What am I doing here?* she asked herself. Her brow wrinkled with the effort of recall. *Was it something The Man told me?* For a moment her eyes glazed. Then, suddenly remembering, Carol proceeded through the revolving door.

Her heart quickened as the security guard gave her the once over. Then he turned to answer a customer's question, and Carol relaxed. Dressed in a light blue sweater and designer jeans, she strode nimbly down the center aisle. She appeared about sixteen, with short dark hair and economical features.

What were my instructions? Carol halted momentarily, chewing her lower lip. A voice seemed to speak in her ear: *Walk to the back of the store.* Staring straight ahead, Carol glided past the cosmetics counter and maneuvered through a maze of dress racks. Not pausing to inspect the latest fashions, she proceeded with single-minded concentration.

As she approached the rear of the store, her step faltered. She glanced right and left, indecisive. The voice guided her again: *Turn right.* Carol turned mechanically. *The jewelry department is straight ahead.* Carol marched toward the counter.

Three customers clustered around the display cases. A middle-aged sales clerk approached them." May I help you?"

A woman asked to see a Longines watch. As the clerk brought it out, Carol sauntered over, her eyes seeking the diamond rings.

"I'll be with you in a minute," the clerk said, glancing at Carol.

"That's all right," Carol answered. "There's no hurry."

The customer standing next to Carol frowned at the watch's price tag. "I'll have to think it over," she said, drifting away.

Replacing the watch, the clerk turned her attention to Carol. Her eyes ran appraisingly over Carol, noting her age and dress. "Are you looking for anything in particular?" she asked.

Carol nodded. *Ask for the first ring on the bottom row,* the same inner voice instructed. Carol pointed to the ring. "I'd like to see that one, please."

The sales clerk made no attempt to conceal her surprise. How could a girl of Carol's age afford such an expensive diamond ring? She didn't appear wealthy. But looks are deceiving; some very wealthy families allowed their teenage children charge privileges. However, on a purchase of any magnitude, a parent's presence was required.

"I see you have a discerning eye," the clerk offered cheerfully, withdrawing the ring from the case. "This is a round one-carat diamond solitaire with a four-prong fourteen-carat yellow gold mounting. The list price is four thousand dollars. With a twenty percent discount, our price is three thousand two hundred."

Carol hesitated.

"Is it a gift for someone?"

"No, it's for me,"

The clerk's eyebrows rose. "Perhaps you'd like to see something else. The rings in this case are more moderately priced. They begin at two hundred dollars."

"All right. Could you show me that one?" Carol pointed to the tray in the middle of the case. "I'd like to compare the two rings side by side"

"Certainly. Of course this other one is a cocktail ring." As she bent over, Carol swiftly snatched the ring on the counter and replaced it with an imitation fished from her pocket. The facsimile was identical in all respects, except for the diamond which was paste—a cheap synthetic. The unsuspecting clerk brought out the cocktail ring and placed it beside the other. "This is a charming ring," she said. "A diamond cluster arranged in a sunburst pattern. Your friends will envy you."

"How much is it?" Carol asked.

"Only four hundred dollars."

"I like it," Carol said. "But I'll need my mother's permission. May I bring her in to look at it?"

"Of course," the clerk said, replacing the two rings.

"I'll see you soon," Carol said, turning on her heels. Her heart fluttered with the secret knowledge of the valuable ring concealed in her pocket. The saleslady hadn't suspected a thing. *Now just keep cool*, Carol told herself, feeling quivery. *You'll be out of this place in no time.*

She retraced her steps, trying to look as nonchalant as possible. But her heart pounded wildly as she saw the security guard eyeing her across the length of the store.

He couldn't have seen me at the jewelry counter. It was much too far and outside his field of vision.

The guard was stationed directly in front of the door with his arms folded sternly. He seemed to be following Carol's movements. *It must be my imagination,* she thought. *He's just staring straight ahead. Why should he single me out?* Had the saleslady detected the switch, after all, and tripped a silent alarm? An icy shudder ran through Carol's body. She searched for another exit. Spotting one at the right side of the store, she turned in that direction, her feet feeling heavy and numb. Her steps were leaden and agonizingly slow.

Approaching the side door, her heart fell. The door was bolted. A sign said, PLEASE USE FRONT ENTRANCE. Carol tugged furiously at the bolt, to no effect. *What am I doing?* she asked herself. *Even if I get the door open, an alarm will probably go off.* She realized that she had only succeeded in calling attention to herself. The guard was advancing rapidly toward her. *Just act natural,* she told herself. *Pretend you're a foreigner and can't read English. No, that won't work; my ID will give me away.*

Panicky, Carol searched for the ladies' room. *That's no good,* she realized. *I can't hide in there all day.* The guard was moving closer and closer. *Get rid of the ring!* But The Man would be furious if she returned without it. And the guard would see her reaching into her pocket. She was about to run, hoping to sidestep the guard and dash out the front door, when a man in plain clothes walked up to her. Seizing her arm in a firm grip, he identified himself as the chief security officer. "Please empty your pockets,"

A stab of terror cut through Carol like the point of a knife. Her body went limp and she began to reel.

"Get a hold of yourself," the officer said, steadying her. Her pupils were glassy-looking, her face white.

Propping her up against the wall, the officer reached into the left pocket of her jeans. His hand emerged with the ring.

"Do you have a receipt for this, Miss?" he asked.

"N-no," Carol stammered. Her throat was so dry she could barely talk. She couldn't think straight. She felt confused and paralyzed with fear.

"You took this off the jewelry counter."

"No, it's mine! It belongs to me!"

The officer gave a sarcastic laugh. "Enough of that, young lady. I saw you pocket this ring and substitute the imitation."

Carol's shoulders collapsed helplessly. "How could you see me?"

"On closed-circuit TV. We have a hidden monitor mounted above the jewelry counter. I observed you from the moment you approached the counter until you left. Come with me."

He marched her back to the jewelry department, where the sales clerk stood glaring at her, holding the fake ring in her hand.

"Is this the girl?" he asked.

"Yes, that's her," the clerk answered tartly. "She looked suspicious from the moment I first saw her. You should be ashamed of yourself, young lady. A nice girl like you. You can tell she comes from a good family," she added, turning to the officer.

"That's a positive identification. What's your name?"

Carol hesitated.

"Let's see some ID."

Carol produced a card case from her back pocket. The officer thumbed through the cards. "Carol Logan. Is that your real name? We can easily verify it."

"That's my name."

Command Performance

"All right, let's go upstairs to my office."

"Please," Carol pleaded. "Can't you let me go? You have the ring."

"Let you go? This is a serious offense, Carol: a planned theft. Do you realize that constitutes grand larceny? People go to jail for stealing much less. Come this way."

"Such a pretty thing too," the clerk said, shaking her head. "It's a shame."

"Sixteen years old," the officer remarked, leading Carol away. The clerk clucked her tongue.

Carol sobbed as she entered the security office. "I didn't know what I was doing. I couldn't help myself."

"You helped yourself to a four-thousand-dollar ring," the officer cracked. "You knew exactly what you were doing." He motioned her to a chair. Seating himself opposite her, he emptied the contents of her card case on his desk. "Is this your residence, 112 Milford Street, Westbury, Connecticut?"

She nodded miserably.

"What brings you to Gotham City?"

"I attend school here."

"Do you live with your parents?"

"No."

"You're a runaway, aren't you?"

Carol nodded.

"How long ago did you leave home?"

"Two months ago."

"Have you been in touch with your folks?"

"No."

"I'll have to contact them, let them know what their daughter has been up to."

"Oh no! Please, Mister, don't tell them. I'm so ashamed."

You should have thought of that before. What made you take the ring?"

"I needed money."

"Where did you get the imitation?"

"I bought it in a secondhand store."

"Where you happened to find an exact duplicate of a diamond solitaire. Don't con me. You said you couldn't help yourself. What did you mean?"

"I meant I did it for the money."

"Someone put you up to it. A professional thief with a knowledge of fine jewelry. Who was it?"

"No one!" Carol cried. "I planned the whole job myself."

"Someone gave you the imitation. The same person who acts as your fence for stolen property."

"I told you I bought the imitation. I was going to pawn the diamond ring."

"Whom are you protecting? If you don't come clean, the police will get the information out of you. If you cooperate with me, maybe we can work something out. I want to know who the main man is. This isn't the first time someone pulled this scam. We were ripped off a week ago."

The mention of the words "main man" sent a warning shock through Carol. She mustn't give away the The Man's identity. If she did, she would pay with her life.

"I can't tell you anything else," she said flatly.

"You're scared, aren't you? Afraid of what he'll do to you. All right, have it your way. I'm turning you over to the police."

"No, don't!" Carol began to weep.

The officer softened. "Is this your first offense?"

Carol nodded.

Command Performance

"How can I believe you? If you're telling the truth, the judge may go easy on you, considering your age. But this is grand larceny, Carol, not a shoplifting offense. He won't let you off with a slap on the wrist. Unless you turn state's evidence—disclose your confederate—you'll end up in a girls' reformatory. Is your partner worth it?"

Carol remained silent, her lips tight.

"All right, before I call the police, this is the procedure. A female security officer is going to search you. Then we'll take your photograph for our files. We don't want to see your face in this store again. Ever. Understand?"

Carol's lips quivered. "Yes,"

He buzzed the female security officer. "Helen, will you please step in here?"

A tall uniformed woman entered. Her straight black hair was drawn into a tight bun. Surveying Carol with a frosty expression, she asked, "What's up, Ted?"

The officer gave her a quick rundown. "She may be under the influence of drugs."

"Let me see your arms," she snapped, rolling up Carol's sleeves with a rough tug. "There are puncture marks, all right. What are you on?"

Carol shook her head, "Nothing."

"Which do you prefer, coke or heroin?"

"Neither," Carol answered.

"Come on, who are you kidding? Your eyes are glassy. You show all the signs."

A wave of dizziness swept over Carol. She wished she could shut out their prying questions.

"All right, take her into the other room," said the officer. "Make sure she isn't carrying anything else from the store, and take her picture."

"This way," the woman directed, conducting Carol into another room. The officer picked up the phone and dialed the police.

Satisfied that Carol had concealed nothing, the woman led Carol back to the office. "Stand back against the wall," she ordered.

She snapped several Polaroid pictures, waited for them to develop, and gave them to the officer. He put them in a folder marked with Carol's name.

Carol sat and cried until the police came.

II

Dick Grayson sat gazing out the window of the Gotham High *Clarion* office, where he worked as a reporter. It was a sunny spring afternoon, and Dick was itching to go outdoors, but the bell wouldn't ring for another twenty minutes.

Maybe I can scare up some news at the police station, he thought. He conceived a new column he would call "The Police Beat." He wanted to do a story on teenagers and younger kids who got into trouble with the law. Maybe a series of articles would help promote understanding between adults and young offenders.

At last the bell rang. Dick jumped up, grabbed a note pad and pencil, and locked the office door. He drove to the police station, which was toward the center of town.

As he stepped inside, two policemen led Carol Logan into the station.

Carol! Dick thought, startled. She was in his class at school. He wondered what she'd done. He didn't know her well, but she seemed a nice girl—serious, quiet, hardworking.

Carol choked back a sob as the police booked her. A detective took her into the examination room for questioning.

Dick stepped over to Sergeant Brady, an old acquaintance,

"Hi, Dick. How are you?" Brady asked.

Dick explained that he was doing an article on juvenile crime for the *Clarion* and wondered if he could sit in on the questioning. "I know Carol," he added.

"That's against department policy," Brady said, "But if you want to wait here, I'll see what I can find out for you. I'm glad to assist a budding young journalist in his career."

"Thanks," Dick said, smiling.

"It will take a while."

"That's all right."

After a half-hour, Lieutenant Rose emerged from his cross-examination of Carol. Dick overheard his remarks to Sergeant Brady.

"She wouldn't finger the ringleader," Ross said. "She's terrified of him. We're stymied. I tried every argument on her. She says he'll kill her if she gives him away. Looks like she pulled the job under the influence of some hypnotic drug like sodium pentothal.

"That would explain her dreamy, mechanical behavior in the store—" Brady said.

"As if she were following someone's commands."

Dick stood up and approached them. Brady introduced him.

"This is Dick Grayson. He's OK. A talented reporter for the Gotham High *Clarion*."

Dick smiled. "Maybe Carol would open up for me," he said. "We know each other. I think she'd welcome speaking to a friend."

Ross said, "Carol is under eighteen and we're not allowed to release any information about the case to the press."

"I understand, Lieutenant. I was more interested in general about teenage crime and how to prevent it. I promise I won't report any specific details fo the case."

"It might be a good idea at that to have Dick talk to the girl," Brady said. "He's a good man. You can trust him." He winked at Dick. "Dick's her own age and talks her language. She feels intimidated by police questioning—but she might confide in him."

Ross rubbed his chin. "O.K. Nothing to lose. She won't open up to me. But don't push her, Dick. The girl's desperate and close to cracking. Let her turn to you for sympathy and understanding."

"I'll go easy," Dick said.

The lieutenant conducted him to Carol's cell. "There's someone to see you," he said.

Carol glanced up at Dick with a dazed look.

"I'll leave you two alone," Ross said, closing the heavily barred door.

"Hello, Carol, how are you?"

"Hello," Carol murmured in a hollow voice. She made a place for him on her narrow cot. Sitting down beside her, Dick touched Carol's hand. Tears started from her eyes.

"I'm sorry to find you in a place like this, Carol. I happened to be at the station. It must be a terrible ordeal."

"I thought leaving home was rough—going out on my own. But this is the worst experience of my life."

"Do you want to talk about it?"

Carol hesitated, biting her lip.

"It will make you feel better if you get it all out," Dick coaxed. "It hurts to keep all that emotion bottled up inside."

Command Performance

Carol began to speak in a barely audible voice. "It all started at home. Dad was very strict, especially about dating. I got yelled at all the time. I was flunking courses in school and was miserable at home. So I made up my mind to leave home. I went down to the railroad depot. I had enough money to take me as far as Gotham City and still have a few dollars left. I wasn't thinking straight. I didn't know anyone in Gotham.

"When I got here, it was late in the day. I got on a bus and just rode up and down till the driver made me get off. I was hungry and peeked through a luncheonette window. Then I saw this man sitting on a bench, looking straight at me. He was middle-aged and distinguished-looking, with thick gray hair and expensive clothes. He stood up and started toward me. I got scared. I thought he wanted to pick me up.

"'Excuse me,' he said. He had a very smooth voice, with a trace of a foreign accent. 'I couldn't help noticing your interest in the diner. Are you hungry, down on your luck?'

"I said, 'Please leave me alone,' and started to walk away, but he followed.

"'Don't be afraid,' he said. 'I'm not making advances. You look hungry and lost. I know how it feels. I've been in the same predicament.' His voice was very soothing. It kind of made you want to trust him. 'You're hungry, I know you are. Won't you join me for dinner?' he kept saying over and over. 'No,' I said. 'Leave me alone.' He just answered, 'You *will* join me. I know you will.'"

Dick interrupted. "He sounds almost like a hypnotist, repeating the same phrases over and over. That's how a hypnotist works, you know."

"I guess so. Anyway, I finally accepted his offer, almost against my will. I was so hungry, and like I said, he had this way of making you want to trust him. His eyes were strange. He could stare straight through you, as if he read your thoughts.

"After we ate, he asked me if I had a place to stay. I said I didn't—" Carol broke off abruptly, turning to Dick with a look of alarm. "You're not going to tell any of this to the police, are you?"

"Not if you don't want me to," Dick assured her. Dick wished he could persuade Carol to talk to the police but was afraid of interrupting her story.

"Promise?"

"Please don't make me promise, Carol—for your own good and for the sake of others, too."

"If you don't promise I won't say any more."

"All right, I promise."

"Because he'd kill me if he found out I told anyone about him."

"Who, Carol? Won't you tell me his name?"

Carol shook her head vigorously.

"All right, go ahead, Carol. He asked you if you had a place to stay."

"Yeah—well, I told him I didn't and he said he ran a shelter for homeless kids like me. When he said that, I started to see him in a different light. Before I'd thought he wanted to take advantage of me. But now I thought he was just being kind. I was so relieved to hear the word 'shelter,' and I wanted so much to think that someone cared about me and wanted to help. So I went along with him to the 'shelter.' Some shelter! It was a place for stray kids, all right. I was shocked—some of them were hung over, some were smoking pot. A few were high. I couldn't understand why they were allowed to use drugs. They used them openly right before The Man's eyes. They didn't try to hide anything.

Command Performance

"'You let them use dope?' I asked.

"'Each to his own,' he answered. 'Many of the kids are addicts. They don't tell me how to live, I don't tell them. I'm here to help them in any way they choose. If they are going to use drugs, I prefer they use drugs openly instead of sneaking them in under the pretence that they're clean. It's more honest that way. Don't you agree?'

"When I first walked into the place, it seemed like a crazy way to rehabilitate young people. But I went along with him, even though part of my mind still questioned.

"The Man introduced me to the gang. 'This is a new recruit: Carol Logan,' he announced. I wondered what he meant by 'recruit,' but let it pass. I got to know some of the other kids. When a guy came and asked me if I'd like a snort, I thought he meant a drink. He gave me some white powder he called 'H.' I didn't know what to do with it, so he showed me how to sniff it through my nostrils. It was the first time I ever tried heroin. I got sick to my stomach and had to throw up. The guy told me that's how most people react the first time. He tried to get me to take another snort, but I felt so sick, I said no. I wanted to leave the place, but I was tired and sick, and had no place to go. I asked The Man if I could lie down. He acted very concerned, and showed me to the girls' sleeping quarters. 'You *will* like it here. I'm sure you will,' he kept saying.

"It wasn't a shelter at all. It was a dope ring. They didn't use the word 'ring,' of course. Insiders called it 'The Circle.' The Man lures other kids in the same way he did me. He gets them hooked on drugs—if they aren't already. Then he sends them out to steal jewelry and things. He promises drugs to the kids who do, and threatens to cut off the supply if they don't obey.

"That first night he offered me some medicine to help me sleep better. It wasn't dope, he said, just something to make me relax. His voice was so soothing that even when I saw he was going to inject me with a needle, it didn't bother me that much. I said 'All right,' and he injected me with the stuff."

"Do you know what drug it was?" Dick asked.

Carol shook her head. "It wasn't dope. I'm sure of that. All it did was put me to sleep."

"He never mentioned its name?"

"I can't remember."

"Try."

Carol twisted her lips. "I'm trying, but it doesn't come."

"Was it sodium pentothal?"

Carol's eyes widened. "Sodium something. That might be it."

"Sodium pentothal is the so-called 'truth serum.' I did a report on it once. It's a drug that puts you to sleep and makes you more suggestible. It's used to brainwash people; it lowers your resistance."

"You mean he was hypnotizing me? Planting ideas in my mind? While I was asleep?"

"I think so, Carol. Start with this morning. Tell me everything that happened before you walked into the department store."

"That's just it. I can't. It's all a blank."

"The man gave you the imitation diamond ring. Didn't he?"

"I guess so. He must've. I don't remember."

"How else could you have gotten it?"

"I don't know. Nothing makes any sense. I found myself standing in front of the store. I had no idea why I was there or how I got there. I remember hearing The Man's voice. It was like he was speaking to me, telling me what to do."

"I think you heard his post-hypnotic suggestions. He must have used the drug and put you to sleep, and then gave you instructions. When you walked into the store, you heard his voice exactly as you heard it under hypnosis. Part of your brain acted like a sleepwalker's, obeying his commands."

"In other words, he programmed me to steal the diamond ring and leave the phony."

"Sure."

"You know what that story's going to sound like? 'I didn't steal that ring, Your Honor, I was hypnotized.' I'll never be able to prove that."

"Not unless you tell the police who The Man is and where to find him. Right now we can't even prove he exists, much less that he hypnotized you. You've got to tell the police everything—it's your only way out of this mess."

"I told you, I can't" Carol shouted. "Won't you leave me alone? I thought you understood. I thought you were my friend." She buried her face in her hands, sobbing convulsively.

Dick put an arm around her shoulders. "I am your friend, Carol. I'm sorry I upset you. Maybe you ought to rest a while—try to calm down." He stood up.

"Don't go, please! I'm sorry I yelled at you. I know you mean the best for me. If only I could make you understand."

"I have to go, Carol. They won't let me stay much longer. But I'll come back tomorrow." He stepped outside the cell and walked down the corridor. Behind him the cell door gave a resounding clang.

"Did you find out anything?" Lieutenant Ross asked eagerly.

Dick hesitated. "I promised Carol I wouldn't repeat it to the police."

"Oh no!" Ross exclaimed. "Are you going to clam up on me too? Why did you make that promise?"

"It was the only way I could get her to talk."

Dick made a quick departure from the station.

Ross shouted after him. "Don't come back here until you change your mind! Boy reporter!"

III

"I just got here myself," Batman said as Dick arrived at Wayne Manor. "Police Commissioner Gordon thinks the Joker and Catwoman have teamed up again. I'll have to leave soon. Want to come along?"

"I'm working on a case of my own," Dick said. "As investigative reporter for the *Clarion*."

"Sounds impressive."

"It involves a classmate of mine, Carol Logan."

"Fill me in."

Dick quickly summarized Carol's account of her meeting with The Man, his use of injections to make her docile, and her trancelike state at the department store.

When he was through, Batman asked, "Are you sure she didn't drop a hint as to The Man's identity?"

"Not a one. And not a clue to the location of the hideout."

"Well, we know this much. It's probably in Gotham City because that's where the guy met Carol. Not necessarily, but let's start with that working assumption. Now what do we know about him? He's involved with the dope market and uses hypnotic drugs with skill. He's middle-aged, smooth, persuasive, distinguished-looking, apparently well educated. His speech is polished, with a trace of a foreign accent. Where would you look for a man of that description?"

"It could fit a lot of men. There's a range of possibilities. We're looking for a strong authority figure with a knowledge of psychoactive drugs—and the skill to use them. Maybe a doctor."

"Possibly, but not necessarily," Batman said. "It could be someone like a medical aide or orderly with experience in a psychological setting."

"Or even a lab technician or chemist," Dick suggested.

"Now there's an idea," Batman said. "How about a biochemistry professor?"

"What better front for illicit dealings?" Dick said. "A teaching post would give him the trappings of respectability—and contacts with a pool of young people. Who would suspect someone in his position?"

"Right. But it's a long shot. How many professors know hypnosis? That narrows it down considerably. Maybe we're dealing with a professional hypnotist, or someone who once was."

"You mean a stage performer?"

"Yes. Unless we consider a psychologist who knows hypnosis. But that's farfetched. It's hard to picture a psychologist as the head of a dope ring!"

"I agree. So I'll look for a hypnotist."

"If he ever performed professionally, he should be in our theatrical file. Take a look."

"All right."

They went down to the Batcave. Batman got in the Batmobile. "Good luck," he said. "I hope you find him. But be careful."

"I will."

Batman left, and Dick punched into the computer. He found the names of five hypnotists. However, phone calls to their agents disclosed that three of them were on tour. Another had just returned from an appearance at the Hawaii Hilton. Dick ruled him out.

Down to the last one, he thought, dialing Alexander Kurtz's theatrical agent.

"I'd like to know if you still handle Alexander Kurtz," Dick asked.

"Not at the present time. He's inactive."

"You mean retired?"

"I'm not sure. He's only about fifty. He just went on to other things. To be frank, I haven't heard from him in years. I'm not sure what he's doing these days."

"The man I have in mind has a slight foreign accent."

"Kurtz is from Austria. Came here after World War II."

"It sounds like him." Dick gave Carol's description of The Man.

"That fits Kurtz to a T." The agent offered to contact Kurtz but Dick said he'd rather talk to him first himself. "If he's the one I'm looking for, I'll get back to you."

"All right." The agent looked up Kurtz's phone number and address. "I hope he still lives there."

Dick thanked him and hung up. He dialed Information. The operator informed him that Kurtz's number was unlisted. So he still lived in Gotham City. If he performed, he would surely list his number, Dick reasoned. Someone might want to call him for an engagement.

Before driving to the address Kurtz's agent gave him, Dick left a note for Batman.

The address was at the other end of town. Dick wore his regular clothes, in his role as investigative reporter. He took along a miniature camera to snap Kurtz's picture. If he was The Man, Carol wouldn't be able to hide her reaction to it. He hoped she would break down and identify him.

The house was located in a residential neighborhood. Dick parked near a phone booth and dialed the number the agent had given him. He waited expectantly as the phone rang...and rang. Finally he hung up. Chances are that it was still Kurtz's number, and he wasn't at home.

Dick walked up to the building. The name on the mailbox was faded, but Dick detected a faint K. While neighboring houses were almost indistinguishable, this one had an eccentric, forbidding character, with old-fashioned gables and turrets. Vines ran along the weathered siding like sinuous snakes. An enclosed porch creaked and swayed as winds twisted through its aged supports.

Dick grimaced. *A real eyesore. It's a good thing I'm not here to do a story for House Beautiful.* He pulled out his camera and snapped a picture. Could it be the Circle's hideout? Not likely. In a residential neighborhood, their comings and goings would be too conspicuous.

Dick knocked on the door. As he expected, there was no response. He tried the doorbell, but it was broken.

Walking briskly around the house, as if on official business, he came to the back door. Several hard raps brought no reply. Stiff and rusty, the doorknob refused to turn. Dick pressed it hard and, to his surprise, a hinge broke off and the door fell open. He took a tentative step inside, pushing the door back in place. The interior was dark and musty, with a stale, airless smell. The floorboards groaned and creaked at the least pressure. With the shades drawn there was barely enough light to see by. He made out the outline of a lumpy old sofa, then stubbed his toe against something hard. Bending over to inspect it, he recoiled with a stifled cry. A head stared up at him— the head of a ferocious tiger forming the front end of a tiger's rug.

This place must have been decorated by Jungle Jim, Dick thought.

He examined one of the walls. It was entirely covered with scimitars, sabers, broadswords, and rapiers. The opposite wall boasted a huge elk's head with wide, flowing antlers. Kurtz was undoubtedly a hunter who liked to flaunt his marksmanship.

Finding no evidence of dope downstairs, Dick mounted the staircase. The banister swayed and lurched under his hand. There were four rooms upstairs. The first he entered was entirely bare.

As he entered the next room, he rocked back on his heels in surprise. A pair of eyes bore through him with a look of such intensity that he felt transfixed and defenseless. For a moment he was unable to move. Then he realized he was staring at the two-dimensional face of a man on a life-size poster. Switching on a lamp, he read the legend underneath.

ALEXANDER KURTZ

MASTER HYPNOTIST

His Magnetic Presence Will Stupefy
and Mesmerize You

The poster showed a man with jet-black hair, thick eyebrows, a straight nose, and ample lips. His jaw was square, and it thrust out defiantly. This was a younger Alexander Kurtz, in his prime. Allowing for age, the picture was consistent with Carol's description.

The walls were studded with photographs of Kurtz's stage performances. In one photo he stood gazing at a young woman in a deep trance. For a moment, Dick saw Carol's face in the picture, and his stomach twisted.

Command Performance

Various mementos of Kurtz's stage career covered the dresser, in addition to artifacts collected from around the world. Kurtz had traveled extensively. While the house was rundown, the room itself was neat, with everything in its proper place.

He looked in the closet. There were two tuxedos, both shiny from too many dry cleanings. Kurtz must have worn them for his performances. Two safari jackets and a tropical pith helmet gave further evidence of his interest in hunting. An automatic rifle stood upright in a corner of the closet. Then Dick came across an unexpected find: a black-and-red cape, like the one worn by Bela Lugosi in *Dracula*. It probably indicated nothing more than Kurtz's flair for the theatrical, Dick thought. Or perhaps his interest in the bizarre and the violent? Rummaging at the bottom of the closet, Dick uncovered a werewolf mask with long canines and wiry tufts of hair. There were some drops of dried blood around the mouth.

Dick suddenly heard a noise on the pavement below. Dashing to the window, he pulled the shade aside. A man was approaching the house. He kept his head down, and Dick couldn't see his face. But he had little doubt that it was Kurtz. He carried a walking stick, tapping it along the street.

Dick bolted down the stairs and ran to the back of the house. As he reached for the knob, the door suddenly heaved inward. Dick had assumed that Kurtz would use the front entrance. Now Kurtz would notice that someone had tampered with the back door. Dick didn't want to confront him as a housebreaker. He raced into the living room, ducking behind the sofa. The light was too dim for Kurtz to have seen Dick's sprint up the corridor, but he probably heard his steps.

"Who's there?" The words rang out in a deep baritone—a voice accustomed to command. "Who is in my house?"

Dick remained crouched behind the sofa.

Kurtz stomped heavily through the hallway, tapping with his stick. "You might as well come out. It's only a matter of time before I catch you." Dick noticed a slight European accent.

Kurtz snatched up a heavy board leaning against the stairwell, balancing it with one hand as if it were a pool cue. For a man of medium build, he possessed unusual strength. Dick watched him take a few steps down into the basement and return with a hammer and nails. What was he up to? He proceeded to the back of the house. Turning the board diagonally, he began pounding nails into it.

He's boarding up the back entrance! Dick realized. *Trapping me inside.*

"I said it was only a matter of time." Kurtz called, with a robust laugh that echoed down the hall.

Pound, pound, pound.

"Come out and let me take a look at you."

A drop of perspiration rolled down Dick's back.

Pound, pound, pound.

"No one will ever break in here again. I'm making certain of that."

The job completed, Kurtz lay down the hammer and walked into the living room. He lit an old-fashioned hurricane lamp. Shadows leaped across the walls as he crossed the room and placed it on a table.

"Of course I could phone the police," he said, "but I prefer dealing with problems directly. You, Sir, whoever you are, are a problem. My problem."

Command Performance

He pulled a rapier off the wall and tested its point. Kurtz parried with an invisible opponent. "*En garde!* Hup-hup-hup." The blade whistled through the air with razor-sharp menace.

"Or do you prefer the broadsword?" He pulled it down from the wall and swung it back and forth with both hands. "Choose your weapon, Sir. Speak up!"

Dick swallowed hard, perspiration beading his forehead. He was no expert with blades, and certainly didn't want to stab Kurtz.

"You have violated the privacy of my home. You are a trespasser, an interloper. Yet I offer you a contest, a choice of weapons. I treat you like a gentleman, a worthy adversary. You spurn my invitation. Don't you have a tongue? Can't you speak?"

Dick remained silent, huddled into a tight ball.

"Are you dumb? Or dumbstruck? Ha, ha, ha. I am not an American by birth, but I savor the paronomastic possibilities of the English language. Have you ever reflected upon the ambiguities of the English phonic structure?"

He's toying with me, Dick thought. *The cat and the mouse. Does he know I'm behind the sofa?*

Kurtz took down a halberd, a long-handled weapon with a sharp point. "A marvelous medieval weapon. One of the prize possessions of my collection. The Middle Ages was an era when men settled differences privately in hand-to-hand combat. Simpler and more primitive than our complicated system of jurisprudence. But lethally effective in resolving conflicts." He balanced the halberd on the palm of his hand, then suddenly drew it back, and let it fly. The point drove through the center of the sofa, emerging an inch at the back.

Dick leaped up involuntarily, recoiling at the sight of Kurtz leering at him.

Howard Goldsmith

"So there you are," Kurtz said, his eyes dancing with excitement. He picked up a rifle and pointed it at Dick.

"I never miss," he said with deadly coolness. "At this distance I can peg you right between the eyes."

He's loony, Dick thought. *I'm the game and he's the hunter.*

With lightning reflexes, Dick shouldered past Kurtz into the hall and up the stairs, taking the steps two at a time. A shot whistled past his right ear, making it ring. Dick searched for stairs leading to the roof, but found none. He heard Kurtz's footsteps mounting the staircase. Dick fled into Kurtz's bedroom. That would be the last place Kurtz would expect him to hide. Under the bed? No, in the closet. Dick ducked inside, wedging himself into a corner behind the clothes. He felt something cold against his face. The muzzle of Kurtz's rifle. Dick wondered if it was loaded. He couldn't check without giving his position away.

A ridiculous predicament, he thought. *I'm right where Kurtz wants me. In his own room!*

Kurtz's heavy tread sounded in the hallway.

"Come out, young man. It will do you no good to hide. I know this house like the back of my hand. You are in my territory. On my turf. Ha, ha, ha."

Dick heard him open the empty room. His shoes shuffled along the bare wood floor. Then he heard the door click shut.

"One room eliminated, that leaves three," Kurtz called. "Before there was a twenty-five percent probability of guessing correctly. One out of four. Now the odds have increased to one out of three."

Dick heard his shoes clumping past the bedroom. He wondered if he had time to dash down the stairs to the front door. Dick had observed that the door was chained and bolted. Kurtz could get off a shot before he managed to open all the locks.

"We're down to two rooms, young scholar. The guessing odds are fifty-fifty. Now which room is it? If I were a sportsman I would release you if I guess incorrectly. But I am not a sportsman. I'm a hunter. Now what were your thought processes when you selected your hiding place? You may have considered my bedroom the least likely place for me to look. So you ran straight into the lion's den. An audacious move on your part. I had better check the other room first, though, to make sure."

Dick heard him close the door and turn the key in the lock. He sprinted out of the closet and across the room. He tried to loosen the window lock. It was so old and rusty, he couldn't budge it.

Dick heard Kurtz unlock the door. He dove back into the closet, feeling like a trapped animal.

"So now we are down to one room," Kurtz said, entering the bedroom.I must thank you for affording me this unexpected sport. Now where are you? Under the bed or in the closet? I hope it's not the bed. That would reduce the entire exercise to slapstick. No, I won't even consider the possibility." He crossed to the closet. "Come out, come out wherever you are." He pushed aside the clothing, exposing the center of the closet. "Not there. You must be in one of the corners." He began poking into the closet with the barrel of his rifle.

"All right," Dick called. "I'll come out."

Kurtz slid the clothing to the other side. Dick sat curled up, eyes staring up at him.

"Now you want to come out," Kurtz taunted, poking his rifle at Dick. "Not so fast."

"Don't you think you've had enough fun?" Dick asked. "You have every right to be angry at finding me in your house. But I'm sure you did some dumb things when you were my age, too."

"You've found your tongue, have you?" Kurtz aimed his rifle at Dick's head. "Don't move a hair."

Dick flinched back. "Wait a minute! There's no need for a weapon."

"No need? For all I know, you may be a dangerous criminal. Breaking and entering is a crime, you know. I would be well within my rights to use this weapon against a burglar. I have to protect myself and my home. No jury would convict me."

"Mr. Kurtz, may I stand up and explain to you why I'm here? If you'll let me get my wallet, I'll show you my identification." He reached inside his pocket.

"Keep your hands out front where I can see them!"

Dick withdrew his hand from his pocket. "I'm an investigative reporter, Mr. Kurtz. Reporters often have to work outside official channels to get a story. You understand."

"A reporter! At your age? You can do better than that."

"I write for the Gotham High *Clarion*. My card's in my wallet. I'll show you if you don't believe me."

"All right, slowly reach into your pocket and remove the wallet. But remember, this rifle has a hair trigger. O.K., hand it to me. No, don't stand up!"

Dick gave him the wallet and fell back into his cramped position, knees pulled up to his chin. His muscles ached.

Kurtz flipped through Dick's ID cards. "Dick Grayson, eh? So you *are* on the *Clarion* staff. Why are you hounding me?"

"I'm not hounding you, Sir."

"Why do you want to invistigate me?"

Command Performance

"I wanted to do a close-up story about a hypnotist. It's a fascinating occupation. When I didn't find you home, I began poking around the back of the house, and the door fell open. I could see some of the things on the wall, and I was curious. So I went inside."

Kurtz sighed. "I was hoping you'd be honest with me. Instead you insult my intelligence with this transparent fabrication."

"I wanted to see Alexander Kurtz, 'master hypnotist' in person. It's no lie. I've never seen you before. I've never witnessed a performance."

Kurtz eyes grew bright. "I haven't performed publicly in years. You want me to give a demonstration of my powers?"

"Yes, Sir. That's just what I need for my story. May I stand up now?"

"Remain where you are!" Kurtz's finger curled around the trigger.

"Whatever you say."

"You don't want to get up, Dick. You want to sit in the closet. You feel more comfortable where you are, don't you?"

"No, Sir."

"But it's getting more and more comfortable. Your muscles are relaxing. Actually, you're not sitting on a wooden floor, but on a velvet carpet. Feel how thick and soft it is."

He's trying to hypnotize me, Dick realized. *Don't look into his eyes.*

"Look at me Dick."

Dick averted his eyes.

Kurtz jammed the rifle under Dick's nose. "Look at me, Dick!"

From his position, Dick couldn't risk knocking the rifle aside. It would explode at the slightest touch. He obeyed Kurtz's command.

"That's better. It's restful sitting on a velvet carpet," Kurtz droned. "You feel relaxed. Your tension is draining away. You're getting sleepy."

Dick's eyelids felt heavy. He caught himself and sat up straight, shaking off his growing drowsiness. Struggling to break Kurtz's grip on him, he silently recited a poem. But Kurtz's velvet smooth voice seemed to invade Dick's thoughts.

"You cannot fight me. Do not try to resist. You want to sleep. You feel drowsier and drowsier. Your eyelids are heavy. You cannot keep them open. Let your eyes close, Dick. You'll feel much better."

Kurtz's face swam before him in a mist, his eyes two beacons of light. *No, don't go to sleep* part of his mind whispered insistently. *Don't listen to him. Get up! Stand up!* Dick began to rise on wobbly legs, swaying back and forth.

"Sit down!" Kurtz commanded. "You're still fighting me. Sit down, I say!"

Dick inched forward on his feet. His hand touched something smooth and metallic. The rifle! Suddenly alert, his thoughts raced. "Get back!" he shouted, brandishing the rifle. "I don't want to use this."

Kurtz burst into laughter. "What a sight you make standing there with an empty gun."

"What makes you think it's empty?"

"Young man, it was empty when I placed it there a week ago." He raised his own rifle level with Dick's eyes.

"How do you know I didn't load it? See those cartridge boxes at the back of the closet?"

Kurtz's eyes narrowed. "You're bluffing."

"I had plenty of time to load the rifle while you were inspecting the other rooms."

Kurtz glared balefully at Dick. "Even if it's loaded, the moment you touch the trigger, I'll blast you. You don't have a chance against a marksman."

"Don't underestimate me," Dick said. He had no desire to fire the gun if it could be avoided.

Kurtz laughed derisively.

"There's no need for violence," Dick said. "I'll just walk out of the house and we'll forget the entire incident."

"Let you go unpunished for your brazen invasion of my house?"

"I explained my presence here, Mr. Kurtz. What more can I say?"

"You can say your prayers before you meet your maker."

Dick lunged for Kurtz's rifle, but felt his own slipping from his grasp.

"Ha!" Kurtz laughed triumphantly. "I've got you now."

Grasping the clothing rod, Dick swung his legs out, kicking with both feet. Kurtz stumbled back, but managed to steady himself. As Dick's fingers curled around the rod, it began to turn. To his surprise, the back wall of the closet slid to one side, creating an opening a little more than a foot wide.

A secret panel! Dick leaped headlong through the opening, as Kurtz snatched at him. Dick discovered a catch at the side of the panel. As he pressed it, the panel slid closed with a *whoosh*. Thinking swiftly, he removed his belt and jammed it into the space where the panel slid, preventing Kurtz from opening it.

Kurtz pounded on the panel, frustrated and enraged. "You won't get away!" he cried. "I'll get you!"

IV

As Kurtz pounded insanely on the back of the closet, Dick proceeded down a narrow, dark passageway. He felt his way carefully along the walls. Their texture had the coarseness of rough stones. Suddenly his right foot stepped out into space and he began to topple forward. With a gasp, he flung his hands outward, grasping at air. His arms struck an overhead arch that hurled him backward. He stood suspended on the brink of an unseen abyss, struggling to regain his footing. Clinging to the walls for support, he slowly recovered his balance. Then, cautiously, an inch at a time, he drew back into the safety of the passage.

Exhaling a long breath, Dick wiped sweat from his brow. It had been a close call. He felt as if he'd just stepped back from the brink of eternity. But he couldn't just stand there forever. He had the abyss in front of him, an armed Kurtz behind him.

Digging into his pocket for a coin, Dick tossed it into the void. It gave a *clunk*, and then a second *clunk*, as if rolling down a flight of stairs. The coin continued to echo down the abyss before it fell silent.

It must be a stairway. Dick pawed the ground with his shoe, feeling for the edge. He lowered one foot slowly and carefully. It came to rest on a step. He lowered the other foot and descended the stairs, haltingly, one at a time.

It seemed an hour before he reached the bottom. His shirt was soaked with perspiration. It felt good to plant his feet on solid ground again, but he still had no idea where he was. A dark labyrinth stretched before him, wrapped in silence and dust.

He continued forward, groping blindly through the passageway, his footsteps making a dull patter on the stone floor. As Dick turned a corner, he noticed a faint light flicker in the distance. The passage must lead to a secret chamber. Creeping catlike, on the balls of his feet, he drew steadily closer. The passage widened into a dimly

Command Performance

lit cavern. He found himself in a large, shadowy vault lit by an oil lamp. A heavy mixture of smoke and stagnant air filled the chamber.

Suddenly, with a creeping of his flesh, he saw something that made him reel backward with horror. It was a long coffinlike box with a round opening at one end. A women's head protruded through the opening, her hair hanging down in disarray. Dick drew a fist to his mouth. A heavy blade bisected the box in two. The woman's body had been severed in half.

Dick advanced closer—and drew a long sign of relief. He discovered that the woman was only a plaster dummy, lifelike in every detail. Dick realized that the "coffin" was a trick box used by magicians to saw a woman in two. He gazed about the chamber, his eyes lighting on other tools of the magician's trade. Caked with dust, they had laid unused for years. Yet Kurtz must come down occasionally, if only to replace the oil in the lamp.

As Dick crossed the chamber, it narrowed to a dark tunnel. He entered it with a sense of foreboding. He felt hemmed in, the walls closing around him. But he saw a light at the other end, and he inched his way forward. He was halfway through the tunnel when he heard a loud clang behind him. Whirling around, he saw a heavy steel grate slide down over the entrance, blocking his path of retreat. Kurtz was trying to trap him inside the tunnel. Dick raced toward the light at the other end and bounded through the opening. Gazing about, he found himself in another chamber. Behind him a grate slid down, closing the tunnel.

Kurtz let me escape from the tunnel, Dick reasoned. *He wants me inside this chamber. He knows exactly where I am.*

Howard Goldsmith

Dick walked around the chamber. It was completely empty. The walls were rough-hewn. Casting about for an exit, he found two ducts resembling ventilator shafts. They were identical in every respect. If he entered either one, it would mean crawling on hands and knees. The alternative was to remain buried in the chamber. But which duct?

He drew a coin from his pocket and tossed it in the air. *Heads it's left, tails right.* The coin came down heads. *Left it is then*, Dick decided, crawling into the narrow opening. It was a tight squeeze and slow going. Every foot of progress was an achievement. Dick thought of Alice falling through the hole in the ground, wondering where it would end. Of one thing he was certain; he would not end up in Wonderland—though Kurtz was as mad as the Mad Hatter. Kurtz could be toying with him, offering an avenue of escape, only to trap him alive in a narrow duct. Perhaps all his exertions were propelling him toward a dead end— a blank wall. Or he might be in a circular labyrinth without an exit. He would keep going around and around like a rat in a maze.

Dick came to two branches. Again he had to make a choice: left or right. A trickle of sweat rolled down his back. Without room to flip a coin, he decided to go right. After ten yards the tunnel widened and Dick had more room to maneuver. He heard a *swish*, and before he could react, an arm sprang out of the wall. It was long and hairy with an enormous fist. The fingers opened, clawlike, stretching toward him. Dick scurried back to safety. The fist continued opening and closing spasmodically. It couldn't be a human arm, Dick realized. It must belong to an ape. A gorilla. The arm groped back into the tunnel, reaching for Dick as he scampered away. Then, to his surprise, the arm suddenly went limp and fell to the ground, its fingers rigidly locked. Cautiously Dick inched toward it. It appeared stiff and lifeless, like the limb of a dead tree. Dick bent over it. He noticed coils where there should have been muscles and tendons. It was a mechanical arm whose coils had broken loose from its shoulder mounting.

"Nice stunt, Mr. Kurtz," Dick said out loud, wondering if Kurtz could hear him. "If you wanted to startle me, you succeeded. What next? King Kong?"

Dick took stock of his situation. Obviously, Kurtz had constructed a Chamber of Horrors, the kind seen at amusement parks. In fact, the whole building was a house of horror, consistent with Kurtz's bizarre personality. The hunter in Kurtz had constructed a giant trap, a maze to enmesh interlopers. He could toy with them like a spider playing with a fly.

Then again, perhaps he also had plans to revive his career as the morbid host of a creepy fun house—a kind of Vincent Price-type character. This would flatter his show biz ego. At the same time, it would bring a financial return from his investment in a Chamber of Horrors. Maybe Kurtz was giving the entire operation a trial run, with Dick as the subject.

Kurtz might be operating a panel of controls in the house above. The other possibility was that Dick had unwittingly triggered switches as he worked his way through the tunnels. If this was the case, Kurtz had no precise idea of Dick's location. The switches went off automatically in response to pressure. It was doubtful that Kurtz had installed photoelectric cells, his setup being too crude for sophisticated electronic equipment.

Dick continued inching forward through the duct. A strong breeze wafted toward him. It picked up in velocity, growing colder and colder as he advanced. The wind nipped at him with icy teeth, driving him back. But he saw a light at the end of the duct and pressed forward. He stepped out into a long, narrow room buffeted by polar gusts. *It must be a deep freeze,* Dick thought, his teeth chattering.

He started back toward the duct. He was within arm's length of it when a gate came down, barring his return. He rubbed his hands and hopped up and down, trying to maintain his circulation. He could see his breath in long frozen plumes. Dick began to jog, searching for an exit. Was there any way out of this room?

Without warning, he bumped into something unspeakably grotesque: a towering snow monster with icy tentacles and a cavernous mouth. Roaring and frothing, it shook up and down, tentacles whirling.

As Dick danced out of its way, it pivoted and lumbered after him with gargantuan, plodding steps. Dick ran in frantic circles, unable to find an exit. He spied a rectangular shape outlined against the farthest wall. It was no higher than his knees. As he moved toward it, the monster reared up before him, tentacles flailing. Dick ducked, sidestepped, and dove for the wall. The rectangle turned out to be a hinged door that swung open from the bottom. Scrambling through the opening, Dick plunged down a narrow chute.

He couldn't stifle a cry of "Help!" as he slid headfirst at dizzying speed. Unable to grab the smooth surface gliding past him, his efforts to check his rate of descent were futile.

He came to a sudden stop, his head colliding with something soft but solid like a pillow. He found himself in semidarkness, entangled with a cold sheetlike material. He thrashed about, unable to free himself. After tugging and wrestling for minutes, he managed to stand erect and pull the clinging material off him. Then he realized he was standing in a laundry bin! He had been fighting with a bed sheet after sliding down an ordinary laundry chute!

A rustling movement made him start. He ducked down, peering over the edge of the bin. Something was moving along the wall. It was too dim to distinguish clearly—but its hazy silhouette appeared human. Was it Kurtz waiting to pounce? Or some other monstrosity of his?

The figure moved again, close to the floor, flitting like a shadow.

I might as well break the ice, Dick decided. "Who is it?" he called.

The figure halted momentarily, then disappeared behind a packing crate.

I'm a stationary target inside this laundry bin, Dick thought, *A sitting duck.* He hoisted himself over the edge and vaulted down to the floor.

"Dick?" a voice called out.

"Bruce! Is that you?"

Batman stood up behind the crate.

"Bruce!" Dick exhaled a long breath. "How did you get in here?"

Batman stepped forward. "I read your note and decided to see how your investigative reporting was coming along. Are you all right?"

"Sure. But how did you get in here?" Dick repeated. "And where are we anyway?"

"Don't you know? We're in the basement. I just arrived. Did you find out anything about Kurtz?"

"The guy's batty. He tried to hypnotize me. I escaped through a secret panel—straight into a Chamber of Horrors."

"Sounds like fun."

"Chilling fun."

"Is he The Man Carol spoke of?"

"I don't think so. His mind is too scattered to run an operation like that. How do we get out of here?"

"The same way I came in. Through the crawlspace. Didn't you make a surveillance of the place? It leads into the basement."

"I overlooked it," Dick said, embarrassed.

The crawlspace was a tight squeeze, but they managed to crawl through, emerging directly below Kurtz's bedroom.

"It's good to breathe fresh air again," Dick said, standing erect.

He looked up at the window. Kurtz stood gazing down at them. He pulled open the window. "Why did you come here?" he cried, shaking a fist. "What do you want from me?"

"Take his picture," Batman suggested. "You're probably right about him. But it won't hurt to get Carol's reactions."

Dick snapped a picture. As the flash went off, Kurtz sprang back as if shot. "How dare you!" he bellowed. "I didn't give you permission to take my picture."

"That's a right included under freedom of the press, Mr. Kurtz," Dick answered.

"You had no right to invade my house," Kurtz shot back, "on the pretext of writing a story about me. I'll press charges against you, Dick Grayson."

"I don't think you'll call the police, Mr. Kurtz. Unless you're willing to face a charge of reckless endangerment. And the police might be interested in seeing your Chamber of Horrors."

Kurtz coughed and sputtered. "I never invited you to come here. Can't you see, I'm a has-been, a washed-up showman. Just leave me in peace."

Command Performance

Dick felt sorry for the shell of a man that once was Alexander Kurtz.

"Why are you standing there?" Kurtz shouted. "Get out and stay out!"

"He seems far around the bend," Batman said. "But all showmen are good actors. Take another picture for insurance."

"He's not The Man, Bruce."

"You're not absolutely certain. He may have hypnotized you more than you think."

"He didn't!"

"Then take his picture."

"All right." Dick snapped another shot.

Kurtz raised an arm in front of his face. "Get out, I told you!"

"Mr. Kurtz," Dick called, "I'm really sorry to have intruded on your privacy. You must have been an ingenious artist in your day. I'd like to keep these pictures to remind me of our meeting."

Kurtz's face took on a radiant glow. He squared his shoulders, gathering himself into a dignified pose. Raising his eyes to the horizon, he gazed out loftily, like an actor giving a command performance. "Keep them if you like. You may take your leave now, young man. Both of you."

"Thank you," Dick called.

"Come on, Dick. Let's go," Batman said. "It's getting late."

Dick got into his car behind the Batmobile. As Batman started the motor, Dick reached outside impulsively and waved. If Kurtz noticed, he gave no indication.

As Dick's car pulled away, he glanced back again. Kurtz stood framed in the window, stiff and regal, gazing into space, as if reliving the glories of his past performances.

V

Dick radioed Batman from his car. "I'm just going to stop off at the *Clarion* office."

"Now? What for?"

"I want to write that piece on the Circle for tomorrow's paper."

"You won't mention Carol's name or her arrest, will you?"

"No."

"It could endanger her if you did."

"I know. I'll be careful not to refer to her."

Batman rode off, and Dick parked in front of the *Clarion* office. After he typed his column, he left it at the printer's. Then he went home, ate, and developed the two photographs of Kurtz. It was soon time to turn in for the night.

The following day, the *Clarion* featured Dick's column. It created a sensation around Gotham High, where school authorities were waging a campaign against drug peddlers. The column was picked up by a city newspaper and reprinted in the afternoon edition. Dick found himself a campus celebrity.

After school, he went over to see Carol. Lieutenant Ross pulled in the welcome mat. "I told you I don't want to see you here until you're ready to cooperate."

Dick explained that he had photographs of a man he wanted to check out with Carol.

"So who is it?" Ross asked impatiently. "Don't pull that Sphinx routine again."

"Alexander Kurtz," Dick answered, handing Ross the photos.

"Kurtz the hypnotist? He's aged considerably since I last saw him. It's worth a shot. But I'll be standing outside the cell. This time you won't hold out on me."

Ross conducted Dick to Carol's cell. "There's a visitor to see you."

"I'm glad you came back," Carol said to Dick.

"I can only stay a few minutes."

Carol's face fell.

"I have something I want to show you." He held out the two photographs.

Carol glanced at them, expressionless.

"Does he look familiar to you?"

"Why, should he?" Carol studied the photographs intently. "I don't recognize him. Am I supposed to? As far as I know. I've never seen him before."

"Forget it then," Dick said.

"But who is he? Aren't you going to tell me?"

"His name is Alexander Kurtz. He used to be a professional hypnotist."

"A hypnotist!" Carol's eyes filled with sudden understanding. "And you thought he was The Man?"

"It was just an idea."

Carol looked upset. "He's not the one, Dick. I told you, I'm not free to identify him. You played a cheap trick on me."

"It wasn't, Carol. I'm just trying to get you out of this mess. I'm on your side."

"It was underhanded and sneaky. You're trying to trick me into telling you his name." She moved to the end of the cot, her back to Dick.

"I'm sorry you feel that way, Carol." Dick turned to leave.

As Ross opened the door, Carol sobbed softly to herself. Dick made a move toward her, then shrugged, turned, and left the cell.

"You made a good try," Ross said. "You did all you could. I'll take the photographs now."

"You can have them, for all they're worth," Dick said. He left the station feeling he had let Carol down.

VI

Alan Spencer stood in front of the Curtis jewelry store, working up the courage to enter. The gold-plated bracelet The Man had given him seemed alive and hot to the touch. He fingered it gingerly in his pocket. Then he withdrew his hand and ran it nervously through his sandy hair. Glancing at the door, a chill swept over him, though the weather was balmy.

As he hesitated, he realized he might look suspicious loitering in front of the shop. Pretending interest, he inclined his head toward the window display. He wanted to turn and run, but how could he ever face the Circle again? The Man would be furious and boot him out, at least for the night. Where would he sleep? He had no income, no family to shelter him. *By sundown I'll need a fix real bad*, he thought. *It's too late to find another connection.*

Unable to postpone the moment any longer, he approached the door and pushed it open. Now there was no turning back. A bell tinkled over the entrance.

Mr. Curtis shot a sharp, appraising look in his direction. He was a tall, stylishly dressed man with close-cropped hair and a cool expression. Alan swallowed and advanced toward him. His feet sank into the plush velour carpet. It was like walking through an Arabian bazaar, with precious trinkets glittering on every side. Alan buttoned his sport jacket and straightened his tie.

"May I help you?"

"I'd like to see some bracelets. I'm looking for a birthday present for my ahnt." He assumed a wealthy, upper crust accent.

"This way, please."

Curtis crossed to the other side of the store, with Alan at his elbow.

"What price range are you interested in?"

Alan replied exactly as The Man had instructed. "I'd like to see that bracelet: second row, third from the left."

Curtis looked surprised. "That's two thousand dollars," he said, with an edge of doubt.

"I expected as much," Alan replied evenly. "May I examine it?"

"Certainly." Curtis brought out the bracelet. "This is from our Regal collection, a fourteen-carat classic gold Cleopatra bracelet."

Alan raised it to the light, studying it.

"It's a beautifully crafted piece," Curtis went on. "Your aunt will treasure it forever."

Alan placed it on the counter. "May I see that bracelet also? In the case behind you?"

Curtis turned around. "You mean this one?"

"Yes."

As Curtis unlocked the case, Alan snatched the bracelet and swiftly substituted the cheap imitation. The entire operation took a split second, just as he had rehearsed it.

Unsuspecting, Curtis turned and placed the second bracelet on the counter. "This is a fourteen-carat gold tubular slip-on with twisted wire. It sells for one hundred dollars. Obviously there's no comparison between the two."

"I see what you mean," Alan said. "I'd like time to think it over."

"Of course. This slip-on is really suitable for a younger person. Your girlfriend, for example?"

"I'll drop by again tomorrow."

Howard Goldsmith

I knew he couldn't afford the Cleopatra, Curtis thought. *Trying to impress me with his phony Ivy League accent.*

Curtis was about to put away the bracelets when his eyes snapped wide open. He scooped up the Cleopatra imitation, his jaw gaping. "Hey, wait a minute!" he cried. "Come back here!"

Alan was almost at the door. He grabbed the doorknob, threw the door open, and plunged outside, his heart pounding.

"Stop, thief!"

Dick was driving home when he heard Curtis shouting outside the store. He spotted Alan charging into the midst of traffic.

Tires squealing, a Datsun ground to a stop, its driver screaming, "Watch where you're going! Are you crazy?"

Alan raced on without a backward look. The shrill clangor of Curtis's alarm pursued him up the street.

Dick got out of his car and asked Curtis what happened.

"He switched bracelets on me, ran off with the genuine one."

It sounded like The Man was behind this job, too. Dick ran after the thief, who was bounding up the steps of a library. Alan barreled into a line of borrowers and dashed out the back entrance. Puffing and gasping, he made for a bus that was just pulling out. Over his shoulder, he saw Dick pursuing him.

Alan pounded desperately on the side of the bus as it drew away from the curb. To his surprise, the driver brought it to a wheezing stop, and Alan ran for the entrance. Breathless, he leaped on board.

At that moment, Dick caught up with him and dragged him off the bus. Alan put up a fight, but Dick clamped a hammer lock on him, forcing him to his knees.

"Let go!" Alan cried in pain. "You're breaking my arm!"

"Not until you talk. Who put you up to this? Was it The Man?"

The color left Alan's cheeks. "I don't know what you're talking about. Ow!" he screamed as Dick tightened his hold.

"Spill it or you'll talk to the police."

"Ow! I can't. He'll kill me if he finds out."

"Who? What's his name?"

"All right! All right! Let go of my arm!"

Dick released him.

Alan rubbed his sore shoulder. "I didn't want to steal the damn bracelet. He made me."

"*Who?*"

A shot rang out from a car speeding by. Alan slumped to the ground, blood flowing from his scalp. The car zoomed off before Dick could get its license number. It turned a corner and disappeared.

Dick knelt down beside Alan, who was still conscious. He rolled out a handkerchief and pressed it firmly against Alan's wound. Then he looked inside Alan's wallet for his ID.

A man pushed his way through a gathering crowd. "I'm a doctor. Let me through." he examined the wound. "He's lucky. The bullet just grazed his skull. There could be a light concussion. He may be dizzy for a while."

Alan motioned to Dick to move closer. He spoke with difficulty. Dick bent over him, his ear close to Alan's mouth.

"Six—teen," Alan stammered.

"Sixteen?"

"Cr-Crescent."

"Sixteen Crescent? What about it, Alan?"

Alan struggled to speak. His eyes suddenly glazed and his head pitched forward. He was unconscious.

An ambulance soon arrived and took him to the hospital.

"Sixteen Crescent," Dick repeated to himself. "Was it The Man's address?"

Burning with curiosity, Dick got into his car and drove downtown.

VII

Crescent Street was in the heart of the business district. Sixteen Crescent turned out to be a restaurant. The Regency hardly looked like the headquarters for a dope ring. Maybe he'd misunderstood Alan's words. But having come this far, he was not about to leave without further investigation. He parked the car up the street and doubled back to the restaurant. Entering the lobby, he found himself in a well-appointed, though hardly plush establishment. The dining room was paneled in pale cypress and illuminated by apricot lights. Dick followed the headwaiter to a corner booth. Selecting the least expensive dish, he ordered a hot roast beef sandwich and a Coke.

As the waiter left, Dick glanced about the place. The patrons were mostly middle-aged, with a smattering of young couples in conventional dress. No one remotely resembling a drug addict. Snatches of conversation drifted over to his table. It consisted of the usual topics: family, friends, the mortgage, rising prices. Hardly a den of iniquity, Dick thought. Unless the operation was a front.

At the far end of the room, two swinging doors, IN and OUT led to the kitchen. To his left was the lounge and rest rooms; to his right, a short flight of stairs rising to a door marked PRIVATE. At the back of the room an ornamented doorway marked CLOSED led down a flight of steps to a lower level. Dick supposed it was the cellar. Everything seemed on the up-and-up. All very innocent-looking. Yet Dick wished he could look behind the closed doors, if only to put his mind at ease.

The waiter returned with his order. "The floor show will start soon," he remarked.

"Floor show?"

"Didn't you know? We have a show four times a week: Monday, Wednesday, Friday, and Saturday."

As the waiter was conversational, Dick tried a long shot, "A friend of mine recommended this place."

"Oh yeah? What's his name? Maybe I know him."

"Alan."

The man's eyebrows rose. *I may have hit pay dirt*, Dick thought.

"Alan who?"

"Spencer."

"Never heard of him," the waiter answered too quickly. He left abruptly.

He was lying. Dick was sure of it. He suppressed his excitement as the man walked up the short flight of steps and knocked on the door marked PRIVATE. Out of the corner of his eye, Dick saw the waiter turn in his direction. He felt the man's eyes on him.

He did know Alan. Though Alan didn't fit in with the surroundings, he somehow belonged. As unlikely as it seemed, Dick had found the correct address. The Regency. On the face of it, it made no sense. This was no sleazy dive off the main strip. It was a neat, respectable establishment.

If he'd really located The Man, Carol would finally be free of him. So would all the other kids under his thumb.

Howard Goldsmith

If only he could take a peek behind the doors marked PRIVATE and CLOSED. One of them might contain the answer. If the CLOSED door led to a cellar, it might be large enough to house a number of people. Dick looked down at the floor. He might be sitting right above them. There must be a cellar entrance at the back of the restaurant, Dick reasoned. He was about to leave, with the idea of returning to investigate the rear of the building, when a spotlight flashed on. It illuminated a slightly elevated stage in the center of the floor.

A dapper man dressed in dark evening clothes emerged from the PRIVATE room and crossed to the stage. Dick stiffened in his chair.

He was gray at the temples, of medium height, with an erect, self-confident bearing. He fitted Carol's description of The Man. But then so did a lot of men.

His speech was crisp and aggressive, his voice resonant. It easily penetrated the farthest reaches of the restaurant without a microphone. "How do you do, ladies and gentlemen. My name is Julian Richter. Regular patrons are familiar with my work. But to the uninitiated, let me introduce myself. I am co-owner of this restaurant and a sometime hypnotist. 'Sometime' meaning whenever people let me perform."

There were a few chuckles in the audience.

Dick sat riveted, his eyes following riveted, his eyes following Richter like a cobra.

"One of the advantages of being a co-owner is that I can hire myself at low wages. I don't have an 'act,' in popular parlance—but find that people are amused and instructed by my hypnotic demonstrations. Now—do we have a hardy soul among you who will volunteer as a subject?"

His invitation was met with nervous titters.

"Come, come, don't be afraid. I'm not going to eat you. How about you, young man? You there in the corner booth."

Everyone turned toward Dick, who was caught off guard. "No thanks," he answered.

"No? You disappoint me. You look strong and brave for someone your age. How old are you?"

"Sixteen."

"May I ask your name?"

He hesitated, "Dick Grayson."

"Dick Grayson," Richter repeated. "It seems to me I've heard that name just recently. Are you the same Dick Grayson who wrote the article about drug abuse?"

"Yes." *If this is The Man, I've fallen right into his lap,* Dick thought.

"For those of you who haven't seen the article, Dick is a reporter for the Gotham High *Clarion*. The paper is featuring a series of articles about drug traffic in Gotham City. Don't you think that's commendable? Give the boy a hand."

They all clapped good-humoredly.

"Your reticence is unbecoming in a fearless reformer. Let's see if we can coax Dick up to the stage." He gestured to the audience.

They obliged with more applause. When Dick shook his head, some people shouted:

"Come on, Dick."

"Don't be shy."

"Be a sport."

Richter stepped down from the platform and approached Dick's booth. Gripping Dick firmly by the arm, he said, "Come with me. I will escort you personally. Don't let us down, Dick."

Yielding, Dick stood up and accompanied Richter to the stage. The patrons laughed and cheered.

You're not going to hypnotize me, Dick silently vowed.

"Stand over here, Dick. I'd like to test your suggestibility." Richter stood behind Dick, his hands on both shoulders. "Now I'm going to blindfold you. Don't be alarmed. Just relax." Richter took a black handkerchief and wound it around Dick's eyes. "Can you see anything, Dick?"

Dick shook his head.

"I thought not." He gently pressed his fingertips to the center of Dick's back. "You're beginning to feel off-balance. Your body is swaying."

Dick stood ramrod-straight, refusing to yield to Richter's suggestion.

"At the count of five, you will fall forward. Have no fear, I will catch you. You won't be hurt. One...two. You're feeling slightly dizzy. You can't control your body's motion. Three. You're falling forward."

Lurching, Dick caught himself and snapped back on his heels. Perspiration broke out on his forehead.

"Four. You're about to fall, Dick. Don't be afraid. I'll catch you. You're teetering now, on the edge of a precipice."

Dick's entire body vibrated like a taut spring. *Don't listen to him. Block out his voice.*

"You're tipping over, Dick. Five. You're falling. Let go. Don't fight it. I'll catch you."

Dick began to tumble; at the last second, he pulled himself erect, standing at rigid attention. *How do you like that, Richter?*

"Obviously, Dick doesn't relish the prospect of falling off a precipice."

The audience laughed.

He removed the blindfold. "But the point is made, I think. In response to my verbal suggestions, Dick pitched forward, on the verge of falling. But he refused to yield to my final command, perhaps afraid I wouldn't catch him. You don't trust me, do you, Dick?" He grinned wolfishly.

Dick didn't answer.

"Well, we'll see if we can do something about that," Richter said. "You can trust me, Dick. Sit in this chair and make yourself comfortable. Relax and let your mind float. Your tension is dissolving."

Dick felt more tense than ever. An experienced hypnotist, Richter noted the rigidity of Dick's arms and decided to make use of it. "Extend your arms straight before you, with your hands tightly clasped."

Dick kept his arms at his sides.

"Come, come, Dick. Follow my directions. There's no need to convince me that you are still not hypnotized. I haven't attempted to put you under. Extend your arms, please."

Dick complied.

"I am going to recite the alphabet. When I reach the letter D—for Dick—you will be able to unclasp your hands, A...B. Tight, tight, tight. C. Tighter, tighter...."

Dick's hands were rigidly locked. He tried with all his might to separate them.

"D. Tighter still. You cannot unlock them. Try."

Flushed and perspiring, Dick struggled to open his hands, without success. They were welded together.

Triumphant, Richter chopped down on Dick's wrists. "Open."

Dick's hands slipped apart, as if greased with melted butter.

"I hope you learned a lesson, Dick. It's pointless to resist my commands."

Dick decided to play along with him, doubtful that he could stand up to Richter's repeated suggestions. But if he could simulate a trance, his mind would still be in control of his actions. *When he hypnotizes you, don't fight him. Make him think you've gone under very rapidly.*

Richter flashed a coin under Dick's eyes. "Concentrate on this golden coin. It's a talisman from the mystic Orient." Richter twirled the coin. "You see nothing but this coin. It occupies your entire field of vision. It is growing larger and larger. Keep staring at it. Its brilliance is dazzling. You cannot keep your eyes open. Your eyelids are growing heavy. A warm, drowsy sensation is creeping over your entire body." Dick's head nodded.

"When I snap my fingers, you will be asleep."

Snap. Dick's head fell forward against his chest.

"The subject is fully asleep now," Richter gloated.

Dick's body felt torpid, but his mind was still clear.

Richter held up a hatpin. "I'm going to stick a pin into your finger, Dick. Don't be afraid. You will feel no pain. You are armored against pain." He raised Dick's right hand—Dick steeled himself—and jabbed the pin into his thumb until it drew blood.

The pain was sharper than Dick expected—but his dreamy expression never wavered.

"This is an example of hypnotically induced analgesia," Richter told the audience. "Loss of pain sensitivity. Now, it has been demonstrated that a subject cannot lie under hypnosis. He becomes compulsively truthful. Let us test this. Dick, how old are you?"

"Sixteen."

"Do you like school, Dick?"

"Most of it."

"Do you like me?"

Dick hesitated. "No."

Everyone laughed.

Richter smiled thinly. "I guess I asked for that. This is your first visit here, isn't it, Dick? I don't remember seeing you here before."

"That's right."

"Did you discover us on your own, or did someone recommend you here before."

"Someone recommended it."

"Would you care to tell us who? Perhaps some of us know him. Or is it a secret?"

"No. It was Alan Spencer."

"A friend of yours?"

"An acquaintance. I hardly know him."

"Did he tell you anything about me?"

"No."

"He just mentioned the restaurant. Nothing else?"

"Nothing else."

"I see. Alan comes here often. I assure you he likes me."

The audience laughed.

"In time you'll come to like me, perhaps—once you become a part of my circle."

Circle! Keeping a tight lid on his emotions, Dick forced his features to remain impassive.

"Now we'll try some definitions," Richter said. "This is always fascinating to me, for it tells something about how the mind works. We may stumble upon some interesting subconscious associations. Dick, what is a circle?"

"A round shape. The area of a circle equals pi times the square of the radius."

"Very good. Does the word 'circle' mean anything else to you?"

"A social group."

"Any particular group?"

Dick hesitated. "Any social group could be called a circle."

At that moment a young man entered the restaurant and signaled to Richter. Richter nodded. "Ladies and gentlemen, I must end this demonstration now. Business calls. I trust you enjoyed yourselves."

They gave him a round of applause.

"I'll bring Dick out of it now. Dick, when I clap my hands, you'll be wide awake. You'll feel rested and perfectly relaxed, remembering nothing of our conversation." He clapped his hands.

Opening his eyes, Dick gazed about the restaurant, yawned, and stretched.

"How do you feel, Dick?"

"Just fine. Is it all over?"

"Yes."

"Was I hypnotized?"

Everyone laughed.

"I assure you, you were. You proved a good subject. Now return to your seat and order anything you like. It's on the house."

"Thank you," Dick said, stepping off the stage.

As Dick returned to his booth, Richter marched to the back of the restaurant, walked down a short flight, and entered the room marked CLOSED. He shut the door behind him, locked it, and entered a larger room, which was the headquarters for the Circle.

VIII

Soon afterward, Richter heard raised voices at the rear of the restaurant. As he moved toward the back door, it sprang open.

Two young men entered, prodding someone with their guns. "Come on, you!" they ordered, pushing their captive into the cellar.

"We found this guy poking around outside, boss," one of them said.

Richter's lips twisted into a predatory smile. His arms opened in a gesture of welcome. "How nice of you to join us, Dick Grayson."

Dick's eyes swept the cellar. "Carol!" he cried. She sat with her hands tied to the back of a chair.

Lashing out, Dick knocked the guns from both teenagers' hands. As he dove for a gun, a bullet exploded an inch from his outstretched hand. Dick straightened up to see a puff of smoke rising from a pistol in Richter's hand.

"Tsk, tsk. I had hoped you would become one of us, Dick. But you deceived me. You weren't hypnotized at all, were you?"

"Almost," Dick conceded.

"I give you credit—you had me completely fooled. It took poise to carry that off, plus unusual powers of resistance. It's a pity you didn't join our side. I could have used you."

"The way you've used the others."

Richter smiled. "Your fierce independence makes it impossible for me to release you. You see that, don't you? You know too much for your own good. Ergo, you must die, together with Carol."

"No!" Carol cried. "Please don't do it. I swear I didn't tell the police a thing!"

Richter looked at her contemptuously. "I realize that, or the police would have swooped down on us. We'll make sure your silence is permanent, my dear."

Carol cringed in her chair, her eyes wild with fear.

"How did you capture her?" Dick asked, with a flash of anger.

"As she was being escorted to the police psychologist's office a block from the jail. It was simply a matter of careful planning and waiting for the right opportunity. Unfortunately, a police officer was shot in the fray."

Richter reached for a hypodermic needle. "I hadn't bargained on a twin execution."

"Please!" Carol cried. She burst out sobbing.

"You will go first, you pathetic sheep. I'm sick of your whining. But I assure you, your deaths will be quite painless. The police will think you overdosed on morphine. Naturally, your bodies will be found far from this place."

"The police will connect us," Dick said. "I participated in your little demonstration, remember? There were witnesses. You gave my name to your audience."

"Quite right. But Julian Richter is a respectable restauranteur. Customers saw you leave this place in good health and good humor. So far as the police are concerned, The Man is still Mr. Anonymous. There's nothing to connect me with your rapidly approaching demise."

"Devil!" Carol cried.

"Shut up!" Richter exploded. "Let's get this over with." He turned to one of the gang members. "Fred, roll up their sleeves."

Fred cautiously unbuttoned Dick's sleeve, remembering how easily Dick had disarmed him before. His friend, Brad, pressed a gun to Dick's temple. Then Fred bent over Carol, huddled limply in her chair, and untied her hands. Carol collapsed weakly into Fred's arms.

There was a knock at the door leading to the restaurant.

"Who is it?" Richter demanded.

"It's Joe, the waiter."

"What do you want?" Richter growled. "I'm busy."
"There's a package for you. Registered mail. They need your signature."

"Sign it for me, idiot!"

They heard the waiter conferring with someone. "The guy says the sender requested your personal signature, boss. Or he has to take it back."

"Very well. One minute." Turning to Fred, he whispered, "Gag them. Brad, keep them covered."

Fred tied handkerchiefs around their mouths. Then Richter unlocked the door.

Dick cried out in a muffled voice. Brad jabbed a gun to his back. "Shut up," he whispered, "or I'll plug you."

"Hand it over," Richter said, reaching for the parcel. The waiter fell forward unexpectedly, and Richter reeled backward. Batman loomed up behind the waiter. A clubbing blow sent Richter crashing into Brad, who dropped his automatic. Dick swooped down, picked it up, and leveled it at Fred.

"All right, drop your gun!" Dick ordered Fred. Before he finished the sentence, Batman had already twisted the gun out of Fred's hand.

"Raise your hands and face the wall! All of you," Batman ordered. "You too, Richter."

Richter meekly obeyed.

They heard footsteps charging down the stairs to the cellar. Policemen appeared in the doorway, their guns drawn.

"I notified the police before barging in," Batman whispered to Dick.

The police searched and handcuffed the gang. "All right, take them away," Lieutenant Ross called out.

As the police led them out, Richter managed a defiant smile. "You can't prove a thing against me. I have witnesses who will swear I haven't left the restaurant all week. You'll never make the charges stick."

"Oh yes they will," Carol shot back. "With my testimony and Dick's."

Richter glared at her, his eyes full of menace.

"And I'll show the police where the junk is stashed," Carol added.

Richter's mouth fell open.

"For once he's speechless," Dick said, as a policeman led Richter outside.

"But how did you find this place?" Dick asked Batman.

"I did a little investigating on my own," Batman answered. "One of our first hunches was that The Man might be a professor adept at hypnosis. A teaching post would be the perfect cover. I looked up an instructor at Gotham U. who remembered a man fitting Carol's description. He was kicked off the faculty for illicit manufacture of psychedelic drugs. Afterward, Richter changed careers and bought an interest in the Regency, where he performed as hypnotist."

After the police put the gang in a van, they began a thorough search of the premises. Carol knew of glassine packets of heroin concealed in ceiling pipes. They found other packets in cans buried behind the brick and mortar walls of the cellar.

"This evidence will help put Richter away for life," Ross said.

"What about the rest of the gang?" Dick asked.

"The ones who abducted Carol will be held for kidnapping and attempted murder. We'll try to rehabilitate the others, beginning with medical treatment for their addictions. It won't be easy, but they're young, and there's always hope."

"What about me?" Carol asked.

"I haven't forgotten you, Carol. You'll be glad to learn that the department store has dropped its charges against you."

"That's great!" Dick said, hugging Carol.

"Your parents are waiting for you at the police station," Ross added.

"How can I ever thank you?" Carol said, clasping his hands. "And you too, of course, Dick and Batman. I'll never forget what you did for me."

"All in a day's police work," Ross said.

"All in a day's investigative reporting," Dick echoed.

Batman started for the door. "I have to leave now. Anyone want a lift?"

"Going my way?" Dick said, with a wink. "It's not every day a reporter gets chauffeured by Batman."

The Pirate of Millionaires' Cove

EDWARD D. HOCH

There was a full moon that night, only lightly obscured by mist, as Anton Bartizan strolled on the deck of his converted fishing schooner, the *Dragonfly*. The Fourth of July weekend was always a busy one at Milliton Cove, called Millionaires' Cove in the society pages of Gotham City's newspapers because of the large number of fabulous yachts that could usually be found at anchor there. Most had sailed out of the Cove earlier, positioning themselves for the following morning's big race, but Bartizan had been late, awaiting the arrival of his weekend traveling companion.

Now the sails were full, catching the breeze that drifted across the Cove like gentle fingers. Below deck, an auxiliary engine helped speed them along. Standing there at the railing, he saw the first of the night's fireworks going off along the opposite shore. He felt in his pocket for the flat box containing the diamond bracelet that was to be the weekend's surprise, then stepped to the hatchway and called down, "Come up on deck, darling. I have something to show you."

At almost the same instant there was a blast like a giant firecracker from a nearby vessel. Anton Bartizan looked up, startled, and saw the sky alive with fireflies streaking toward his schooner. He watched, unbelieving, as they punctured his sails, each one producing a tiny tongue of flame. Then he shouted for his two-man crew. "Fire! Fire on the sails!"

Jesse was at the wheel and had already seen the flames breaking out. He ran from the pilothouse as the other crewman, Luis, appeared from below deck carrying a fire extinguisher. But Bartizan was suddenly aware of another vessel moving closer without lights, until its side was almost touching the schooner. Bartizan tried to identify it, but not until the spreading flame from the sails had lit the scene did he make out the skull and crossbones flag fluttering from the mast.

Even when the first of the brawny men had leaped on board, Bartizan thought it must be some sort of tasteless practical joke. He saw their leader, with a bearded chin and a patch over one eye, brandishing a cutlass and looking like someone's costume-party version of a pirate, and he would have laughed had the flames at his back not felt quite so real.

Then Luis stepped in front of the pirate chief and took the cutlass through his midsection, and Anton Bartizan knew it was far from make-believe. Someone else fired a sort of flintlock pistol and Jesse went down too. The sails were burning out of control now, with bright red fire reflected off the water. To Bartizan it was like the worst of his nightmares.

As other boarders came over the side he remembered his passenger, the lovely young woman below deck who was to have been his companion for the long holiday weekend. He turned and ran for the hatchway with the eye-patched pirate in close pursuit.

She was waiting there for him, seemingly oblivious to the slaughter above deck. "Quick!" he shouted. "Over the side or we'll all be killed!"

She stood up calmly and smiled at him. "It's too late for that, dear Anton."

He turned and saw the pirate behind him, raising his cutlass one more time.

Two days later Gotham City's police commissioner, tough ex-patrolman James Gordon, sat alone in his office at headquarters, staring distastefully at the headlines in the local papers. *Pirate Ship Strikes Second Yacht at Millionaires' Cove*, screamed one, while the other—a bit more restrained—announced, *Police Believe Yacht Fire May Be Tied To Recent Sinking*.

Anton Bartizan had lived just long enough to babble out a lurid story of attack by a pirate ship, and now the whole thing was in the papers. They'd even managed to connect it with the unexplained sinking of a luxury yacht in the same cove two weeks earlier. The mayor was demanding action, and both their offices had been flooded with phone calls from frightened yachtsmen.

Commissioner Gordon needed help badly.

It was at this moment that the rear door of his office, leading to the private elevator, opened and closed. He heard the whisper of sound and whirled around in his chair.

"Batman!"

"At your service, Commissioner."

The tall hooded man in blue and gray tights and a blue batcape was a familiar figure to Commissioner Gordon.

The Pirate of Millionaires' Cove

Batman had come to his aid many times in the past when unspeakable crime menaced Gotham City. The Commissioner immediately felt as though a weight had been lifted from his shoulders. "You've read the papers, of course."

"Is it true," the Caped Crusader asked, "that a pirate ship has been attacking yachts in Milliton Cove?"

"All too true, Batman. We had a report of it two weeks ago when a young boy reported seeing a pirate ship alongside a yacht named the Trenchon. The yacht burned and sank in Milliton Cove that night. No one believed the boy, of course, and we had no other evidence of foul play. But now things are different."

"Exactly what did Anton Bartizan tell you before he died?" Batman asked.

Commissioner Gordon leaned forward on his desk, peering up at the mysterious caped figure who stood before him. "He said there were fireflies coming at him through the darkness, and then his sails caught fire."

"Fireflies!"

"Then they were boarded by men dressed as pirates. They slaughtered his two-man crew and he ran below decks to protect a young lady who was there."

"Was she killed too?" Batman asked.

"We found no trace of her. The crewmen, Jesse and Luis, were both dead and Bartizan was dying when police and firefighters reached the scene. The vessel's seacock had been opened and it would have sunk like the Trenchon if we hadn't gotten there in time to close it."

"Any idea of the motive behind these crimes, Commissioner?"

"The same as any pirate's—money and jewelry. Bartizan, for instance, purchased a diamond bracelet for twenty thousand dollars last week, possibly to give to the lady on the boat. It wasn't found anywhere. The jeweler supplied this photograph of it."

"Do you believe she's involved?" Batman asked, studying the photo.

"It would explain why she wasn't killed with the others."

"Pirates sometimes took captives, especially young women."

"There's been no missing person report of anyone who could possibly qualify. I think we'll find she's one of the gang."

But Batman wasn't willing to accept that. "Why would she help steal a diamond bracelet that was going to be hers anyhow?"

"We don't know that. Bartizan was divorced, but he may have had more than one lady friend. Or perhaps she didn't know she was getting the gift."

"What about the first sinking?" Batman asked. "Was there anyone on board?"

"The owner, a local banker named Brewster Hemmings, was alone on board. The seacock was opened in that case too, and until now it was classified as a suicide."

"Did he have money and jewels on board?"

"It's very possible. That place isn't called Millionaires' Cove for nothing."

"What line of investigation are you following at this point, Commissioner?"

"We're stumped, Batman," he admitted frankly. "Naturally I'm assigning more men to the Cove area, especially around the Yacht Club and marina. All we can hope for is to catch him in the act if he tries again."

"That might be too late to prevent the loss of more lives," Batman pointed out.

"Do you have any ideas?"

"Perhaps. I'll be in touch, Commissioner."

Without another word Batman wrapped the midnight blue cape around himself and stepped through the door by which he'd entered.

In a suburb within sight of Gotham City, the family mansion of multimillionaire Bruce Wayne stood alone and somewhat mysterious, not unlike its owner. Although lights shone through several of the leaded windows, the only activity in the mansion this evening was in the huge cavern beneath it, where Bruce Wayne was slipping the bat-eared mask and hood from his head. One man stood by watching—Bruce's friend and confidante Alfred Pennyworth, an aging British gentleman who ostensibly served as the butler in the Wayne mansion.

"You saw the police commissioner, sir?" Alfred asked.

"I saw him." Bruce hung up his bat cape and began removing the costume that had become the terror of Gotham City's underworld. "It was most unsatisfactory. The police know virtually nothing about the crimes. Even the commissioner seems content to wait until the next one in hopes this pirate gang can be caught in the act."

"What plan would you suggest, sir?"

"Almost anything but waiting. These crimes are audacious and well-planned. If this so-called pirate ship can appear and disappear at will, the gang won't wait long before they strike again." Bruce Wayne finished tying the sash of a silk dressing gown around his muscular body. "Alfred, I've decided to lease a yacht—something large and impressive. See about it first thing in the morning."

"Very good, sir."

The following morning Bruce drove out to the Gotham City Yacht Club, located not far from Milliton Cove. He'd

Edward D. Hoch

been there only a few times before, in the company of various members, but he knew no one except Rusty the bartender, a man whose weathered face hinted that he'd be
more at home on some tropical island than serving drinks
at an exclusive club.

"What can I get you, Mr. Wayne?" he asked, displaying
his legendary memory for faces.

"Nothing right now, Rusty. Is the membership secretary around?"

"That would be Mr. Ritter. He usually lunches here.
You might look out on the terrace."

Bruce found Herb Ritter eating alone at a table overlooking the water. Middle-aged, graying, but with a perfect
tan and infectious smile, he was the logical choice for a
position that required the skills of a social director as well
as a yachtsman.

"Bruce Wayne! What brings you out here? Sit down,
sit down!"

Bruce slipped into the chair opposite him. "I'm leasing
a yacht, Herb. Thought it was time I joined your club."

"Giving up the lonely life at last? We're happy to have
you, of course. I'm sure approval by our Board of Gover-
nors will be only a formality. I'll sponsor your application
personally."

"Thanks. I appreciate it." He glanced casually down
along the pier, where several large yachts were anchored.
"What happened to that big schooner? Looks like a fire."

"You must have read about it in the papers," Herb Ritter said. "That so-called pirate business over in Milliton
Cove."

"Oh, yes! So that's the yacht? Could we go down and
have a look?"

Ritter led the way along the pier to the gangplank.
"Careful, now! I don't know how sturdy this deck is."

"I'll watch my step," Bruce assured him.

"It belonged to Anton Bartizan, the man who was killed. The police just finished their investigation and took away the guard this morning."

"What is this—a schooner?"

"A fishing schooner that Bartizan converted to a pleasure yacht. I understand it cost him a small fortune. He enjoyed entertaining young women on it, so I suppose it was worth it to him."

"Oh?" Bruce showed the expected interest of an eligible man-about-town. "Who was his latest conquest?"

"Well, there were rumors he was seeing Amanda Royce."

"The man had good taste."

"The entire affair is a tragedy, and not just for Bartizan. Coupled with that earlier sinking at the Cove, it's making people very uneasy. When they're uneasy it's bad for business, bad for property values."

Bruce Wayne's gaze was attracted to something on the scarred deck. He bent to pick up a small nail that looked as if it had never been used. There were others on the deck too. He saw at least a dozen near their feet. "Looks as if the conversion work wasn't quite finished," he commented.

"Oh, Bartizan was always adding on something. He was never quite satisfied, with his yachts or his women."

They strolled back to the club and the membership secretary promised there'd be quick action on Bruce's application.

His next visit to the Gotham City Yacht Club came about ten days later. By this time he'd taken possession of a 54-foot cabin cruiser with sleek lines and an engine to match.

Edward D. Hoch

It was outfitted for fishing but Bruce was thinking of using it more as bait. Alfred was drafted as a one-man crew, with a firm promise that such a degradation would be only temporary.

"I feel out of my element here, sir," the Englishman complained. "I'm much more at ease acting as your butler."

They'd taken a morning cruise around Millionaires' Cove, getting the feel of the place, and then docked at the Yacht Club marina. While Alfred busied himself with an intense inspection of the fuel line, Bruce strolled up to the main club building. A few people were beginning to arrive for lunch, and he asked for a table by the window, taking a stool at the bar until it was ready.

"Good to see you again, Mr. Wayne," Rusty said, putting down the book he was reading. "Guess it's time for me to be on the job."

"What are you reading?"

"Book on the American Revolution. I like history. You read much of it?"

Bruce lit his pipe and drew on it. "When I have time, Rusty. Right now I'm learning all about yachts."

"Mr. Ritter told me you had a new 54-footer. Looks like a dandy."

"I'm pleased with it," Bruce told him. "Only leasing it, of course, with an option to buy."

The bartender fussed with his bottles, arranging them for the noonday trade. "You want a drink with lunch, Mr. Wayne?"

"A glass of white wine will do nicely." He drew on his pipe again, staring out the big picture window at the hulk of the burned yacht. "Did you know Anton Bartizan very well, Rusty?"

The Pirate of Millionaires' Cove

"I served him a few times. He didn't usually come to the bar, though. He'd sit over at that little corner table by the windows with his favorite drink, Courvoisier in a brandy snifter. He seemed like a nice man. Too bad what happened to him."

"Is the yacht going to stay out there?"

"Only till the insurance company finishes with it."

Bruce's table was ready and he carried the wine over to it. His waitress was Millie, a buxom young woman in her mid-twenties. He'd noticed her once before but never spoken to her. It was obvious she was popular with the other male diners, several of whom spoke to her as they came in. There were more waiters than waitresses working the dining room, but Bruce could see the waitresses' tables were much in demand.

After Millie brought his lunch he asked casually, "Has Amanda Royce been around lately?"

"Mrs. Royce." Bruce knew she was divorced but still used her married name. "I had her one night last week."

"She was probably pretty broken up about Bartizan's death, wasn't she?"

Millie didn't change expression. "I wouldn't know about that."

Bruce returned to the yacht to find Alfred munching on a sandwich he'd brought from home. "You should have come in with me. The food was quite good."

"That wouldn't have looked good, sir."

"Well, let's head for home. We've done enough sailing for the first day."

"What's your next move?"

"To find a way to meet Amanda Royce."

That weekend an opportunity presented itself. There was a midsummer dance at the Yacht Club to which a number of Gotham City's leading citizens had been invited. Even Commissioner Gordon and his wife were attending, and Gordon answered a late-night call from Batman with the news that Amanda Royce would be at the dance in the company of Simon Butterfield, the local real estate developer. It had not taken her long after Bartizan's death to move on to other game.

"Have there been any further incidents in Milliton Cove?" Batman asked into the phone.

"Not since the Bartizan killing. But we've had patrol boats out every night. They'll be coming off after this weekend. We can't afford to do it permanently."

"Thank you for the information about Amanda Royce, Commissioner."

"Will you be at the Yacht Club, Batman?"

"I'll be in the area," he answered vaguely.

Bruce Wayne managed to linger at the bar on the evening of the dance, observing the arrival of Amanda Royce and her escort. Since her divorce she'd been quite the woman-about-town, displaying her shapely body and winning smile at all the best social events. He wondered how a woman like that could possibly be involved with a gang of modern-day pirates.

Bruce did know her escort, Simon Butterfield, slightly, and managed to strike up a conversation with the man as they were returning to their table from the dance floor. Butterfield obliged with an introduction. "Amanda, do you know Bruce Wayne?"

"I don't believe I've had the pleasure," she said with her patented smile. "How do you do, Mr. Wayne."

The conversation, casual and brief as it was, drifted around to the incidents at Milliton Cove. "It's terrible for property values," Butterfield confirmed. "The yachtsmen are staying away from there in droves. One more pirate attack and the bottom will fall out of the real estate market. Just this week I've had two men from the Midwest drop their plans for a restaurant over there."

"The police seem to be protecting the Cove."

"Right now they are, but that can't go on. I understand they haven't a clue as to the gang's identity."

Bruce Wayne tried a smile himself, in Amanda's direction. "What do you think about it, Ms. Royce?"

"I believe Anton was high on drugs or something when he told the police about those pirates. I think he imagined the entire thing."

"They say he may have had a witness on board—a woman."

Amanda Royce shrugged. "If that's so, let her come forward."

Bruce lingered until the end of the dance at midnight, hoping for a few more words with her, but the opportunity never came. Butterfield's party was large and she was surrounded by admiring males the entire night. By the time he finally gave up the attempt it was nearly twelve-thirty. The dining room lights had dimmed and some of the waiters and waitresses were beginning to leave. He saw Millie in her street clothes heading for the door.

At that instant something clicked in his mind. He must have jumped an inch or two because Herb Ritter, the membership secretary, was passing at that moment and said, "I hope I didn't startle you, Bruce."

"No, no—it wasn't that."

"Did you enjoy the dance?"

"As much as I could without a date."

Ritter chuckled. "I'll try to introduce you to a few people. An extra man is always in demand for dinner parties."

Bruce excused himself and hurried to the door, but Millie was already out of sight. The memory of what he'd seen stayed with him, though. As she'd left the club she'd been wearing a sparkling bracelet on her right wrist. From a distance it looked identical to the one in the photograph Commissioner Gordon had shown to Batman, the diamond bracelet Anton Bartizan had purchased shortly before his death.

It was not difficult, the following week, for Bruce Wayne to entice Millie on board his yacht. He arranged to have lunch at one of her tables on Monday and Tuesday, and by Wednesday he extended the invitation in casual conversation. The following day, on which she was free, they set out on board Bruce's cabin cruiser with Alfred loyally at the helm.

"I don't think I even know your last name," Bruce said as they pulled away from the dock. "It just says Millie on your uniform."

"Millie Steiner," she replied. "It's German."

"How long have you worked at the Yacht Club, Millie?"

"Two years now." She shielded her eyes from the sun and watched shoreline passing by. "I like it. You meet lots of interesting people."

"I saw you leaving work the other night wearing a pretty fancy bracelet. Was that a gift from someone you met at the club?"

She blushed slightly and turned away. "He told me not to wear it. I could get in trouble if he knew you saw that."

"Ah! You have a secret admirer."

"Sort of," she admitted.

"Somebody told me you were with Anton Bartizan before he was killed. Is that true?"

For a moment she seemed on the verge of leaping overboard to escape his questions. Then she calmed down and found herself a seat in one of the swivel chairs that were fixed to the deck for deep-sea fishing. "What do you want from me, Mr. Wayne?" she asked, all traces of her smile gone. "Are you a detective or something?"

"Heavens, no! I'm only making conversation. I like to know all about the women I date."

"I think I'd better go back."

"Have a drink first and then we'll swing around."

She agreed with some reluctance and Bruce shifted the conversation into less dangerous waters. Her whole manner had changed, though, and she was on her guard. He noticed her obvious nervousness when she realized the yacht was headed into Milliton Cove. "Why did you bring me here?" she asked.

Before he could answer, Alfred shouted from the helm, "Speedboat bearing down on us, Mr. Wayne."

Bruce saw it off the starboard side, coming up fast. Almost by instinct he pulled Millie from her chair and fell to the deck. There was a burst of fire from an automatic weapon as the pursuer passed them by. The bulkhead above Bruce's head splintered under the force of the bullets.

"My God!" Millie gasped. "They're trying to kill me!"

"Who, Millie? Who's trying to kill you?"

"Are you all right, sir?" Alfred called out.

"So far. Let's get out of here, fast!"

Later, in a safe harbor, finally able to unwind a bit with a drink in her hand, Millie Steiner began to talk. "They tried to kill me," she repeated. "Maybe next time they'll succeed. I have to tell someone about it."

"About Bartizan?"

She nodded. "They paid me to lure him out to Millionaires' Cove. It was an anniversary of sorts for us—one month since we'd first gone out—and he bought me that diamond bracelet. I brought him a bottle of Courvoisier from the club. He'd never had it before but he liked it. I was waiting for him to give me the bracelet when they attacked—" There were tears in her eyes. "The fireflies. They burnt his sails and boarded us, just like in pirate days. That's why he calls himself the Pirate."

"Who does, Millie?"

But she ignored the question, speaking as if to herself. "He came down into the cabin to protect me, and the Pirate followed him with that cutlass. I thought they were only going to scare him and steal his money. I didn't know the Pirate would kill him. It was the most awful thing I ever saw. Then he went through Anton's pockets and tossed me the bracelet. I almost threw it overboard, but I knew Anton had bought it to give me and I decided I should keep it."

"Who is the Pirate?" Bruce asked again.

But she'd fallen silent, as if a spring had run down. She stared out at the water and he realized the sun had grown low in the sky. It would be evening soon. "What are his plans?" he asked softly.

"There'll be another attack. He said there have to be at least three."

"Why? For the money?"

"It's more than just money. It's real estate. I don't understand it all, but I'm afraid. If he sent them to kill me it means he saw me wearing the bracelet too. He thinks I can't be trusted anymore."

"We've got to get the police after this gang. Can't you understand that?"

"Yes," she said quietly, staring off at the low clouds reflecting the sunset.

"Who is to be the third victim?"

"You are. He picked you when you started noticing me."

Bruce Wayne smiled slightly. "When?"

"I was to lure you out to the Cove with your yacht, any night this week. Now that they've tried to kill me I don't know what to think."

"If they're still watching let's go there tonight."

"You're not afraid of anything, are you?"

"I have friends in the right places."

They'd been cruising Milliton Cove for nearly an hour and Bruce was beginning to think it was all for nothing. If they no longer trusted Millie it wasn't too likely that they'd walk into so obvious a trap. He decided to give it another half hour and then head for home. About ten minutes later he spotted a large craft running without lights some distance away, and turned to Millie. "You'd better get below. They might be coming." She didn't need to be warned twice.

"What about you?" she asked from the top of the hatch.

"I'll be right down. I have to warn Alfred."

He hurried up to the helm where Alfred was already turning the wheel to avoid the other vessel. "He's running without lights, sir!"

"And flying the skull and crossbones, I dare say. Kill the engine and get below. It's time we had a little help from Batman."

"But how can you—? The young woman will know."

There was a roar like a cannon from close off the port side, and suddenly the air seemed filled with fireflies streaking toward them. "Below decks—quickly! I'll handle the woman."

There was a clatter as the first of the fireflies struck the cabin cruiser. "What are they?" Alfred asked, terrified.

"Small nails heated red-hot and then fired from a cannon. If we had sails they'd be on fire by now." He shoved the Englishman ahead of him down the steps to where Millie Steiner waited.

"What'll we do?" she asked, trembling with fright. "This time they'll kill me too! I know they will."

"Quick! You get into this locker. Alfred and I'll take the next one." He pushed her into the narrow enclosure and closed the door.

Above deck, the darkened attacker edged closer. Within minutes it crunched against the side of Bruce's yacht as grappling hooks lashed them together. A half dozen armed men boarded quickly, led by a bearded pirate with a black patch over one eye.

That was when Batman swooped down upon them, swinging himself from the radio mast to land feet first in their midst. "It's Batman!" one man shouted, firing a wild shot with his weapon as he toppled backward over the side.

Two men threw themselves at Batman and managed to wrestle him to the deck, but only for an instant. He kicked out with his feet, catching one in the face with his blue boot. Then he rolled over and yanked the other's legs out from under him. A fourth man came at him with a deadly grappling hook held high, but Batman pulled another of the attackers off balance into the weapon's path.

The Pirate himself had retreated onto his ship, where he was bringing the small cannon to bear on Batman's chest. "You meddled with the wrong person this time!" he snarled.

"Not so fast, friend," Batman said, leaping the widening gap between the vessels. He grabbed at the barrel and swung it around just as the Pirate yanked on the lanyard. Another blast of nails was loosed, but this time they splintered the wood of the Pirate's own ship, a ketch with black sails and darkened running lights.

"Run him through!" the Pirate shouted to the only remaining crewman on his feet.

The man ran at the caped figure with his cutlass drawn, but Batman leaped up, caught the boom above his head, and swung his feet into the attacker's chest. He came down firmly and turned to face the Pirate. "These are better odds," he said. "Just the two of us, Pirate!"

"I won't be stopped by you, Batman! Where's Wayne and the girl?"

"Below deck, safe from you."

The Pirate raised his sword, just as a blinding beam of light hit him full in the face. "What's that?"

"Commissioner Gordon and the police, arriving just in time."

"Damn you!"

He hurled the cutlass at Batman and turned to flee, but Batman was on him with a flying leap, pinning him to the deck, ending the battle with a hard right fist to the Pirate's jaw.

A moment later Commissioner Gordon and his men were boarding the yacht from their patrol boat. "Your tip was certainly on target, Batman. I'm only sorry we were a few minutes late."

"No harm done, Commissioner. Here's the Pirate and his entire gang."

"But who is he? Why did he carry out these crimes?"

"I don't need to remove his false beard and eye patch to know his identity. There were enough clues to that."

Edward D. Hoch

The Pirate struggled to rise, but Batman shoved him back to the deck, pulling away his disguise until they could see the face of Rusty the bartender.

"You see," Batman told the commissioner a few minutes later, when the Pirate and his gang had been handcuffed and transferred to the police boat, "the robbery part of the attacks was always secondary. What he really wanted to do was drive people away from the Cove and bring down real estate values. It was happening already—plans for a new restaurant were abandoned. That was exactly what Rusty wanted, because once the land values were low enough he planned to buy up several parcels himself and open a restaurant and marina. I think you'll find that the members of his gang are all waiters at the Yacht Club."

"My God!"

"Figuring Rusty for the ringleader wasn't difficult. The Pirate launched his attacks by firing a small cannon loaded with a charge of nails heated red-hot. The technique was especially effective in setting sails on fire, and was used not just by pirates but in the Revolutionary War as well. Rusty liked to read books about the American Revolution, so he would have known about it. He also made the remark that Anton Bartizan's favorite drink was Courvoisier cognac, but Bartizan never had that before the night he died. If Rusty knew he drank it, he must have been on board the *Dragonfly*. He must have been the Pirate."

"You've done Gotham City a great service, Batman," Commissioner Gordon told him.

"It was my duty."

"Where are Bruce Wayne and the others who were on board?"

"Down below, hiding in the supply lockers. You'd better tell them it's all right to come out now." And with those words Batman swung himself over the railing and dropped to the dark water below.

While the commissioner made his way down to the cabin, Batman quickly shed his costume in the water and boosted himself through a porthole in one of the lockers, helped by Alfred. It was the same way he'd left the locker earlier.

The commissioner freed Millie and then opened their door. "Come out, Mr. Wayne. I hope you haven't been too inconvenienced."

"What's been happening?" Bruce asked, wrapping a jumpsuit around his damp body and hoping the commissioner wouldn't notice his wet hair.

"Batman has captured the gang for us. It's all over."

Bruce Wayne nodded. "Millie here has been telling me some things. I believe she may be willing to testify against them if you need more evidence."

The commissioner scowled at her. "You'd better come along with me, young lady."

"Thank you for everything," Millie told Bruce.

He smiled. "Good luck, and I hope you get back to the Yacht Club soon. I think they'll have a shortage of help for a while."

The Origin of The Polarizer

GEORGE ALEC EFFINGER

How ironic, Bertram Waters thought, that I, one of the most promising researchers in the field of plasmonics, should be denied Ivy University's facilities because of something as trivial as money. Until he'd found a job with Jennings Radio Supply in the summer of 1957, Waters despaired that he'd ever be able to complete his graduate studies at the college. He had a tedious job as a stock and shipping clerk, but he realized that his meager wages wouldn't entirely cover his expenses. He was already exploring other means of augmenting his income.

Waters was a brilliant young man who had grown frustrated with his poverty and the stubborn ignorance of Ivy University's bursar. His coworkers at Jennings knew little about him because he rarely spoke except as required by his duties. In his presence, one was always aware that his powerful brain was constantly observing, cataloging, evaluating, and deciding. He was a tall, slender man, strong, but not in a bulky way. He had black hair with a sharp widow's peak, a narrow, straight nose, deep dark eyes that people unfailingly described as "magnetic," and promi-

The Origin of The Polarizer

nent cheekbones that gave his face a long, somewhat sinister appearance. He had one affectation—a carefully trimmed mustache of the sort film stars had worn fifteen or twenty years earlier. Someone had once remarked, quite accurately, that Bertram Waters looked like Satan as played by Errol Flynn.

The shipping department was a wire cage separated from the rest of the Jennings warehouse. During the summer, there had been two employees to handle the stock and two in shipping. Now that school had begun again, however, three of the young men had quit their jobs, leaving only Waters to keep up with the never ending stream of orders. Again and again, he would grab the next purchase form, run to the warehouse and pull the stock, then run back to the shipping department to box it, address it, and get it ready for delivery. Mr. Jennings promised every day to hire more help, but as the year slipped from late summer into autumn, Waters was still all alone, doing the work of four men.

One day, while Waters was eating lunch alone and reading Vance Packard's new bestseller, *The Hidden Persuaders*, Joe Sampson, the deliveryman, came into the shipping cage. Waters and he were not really friends—Bertram Waters did not encourage friendship in anyone—but sometimes in odd moments they talked about the few interests they had in common. Both were ardent baseball fans, for instance, and they often discussed the chances that the Gotham City club might follow the Brooklyn Dodgers and the New York Giants to the West Coast.

Today, however, the subject wasn't baseball. "It never fails," complained Sampson. "Whenever I have to make a big delivery on one end of town, the next one will be clear over on the other side. What do you have for me after lunch?"

George Alec Effinger

Waters put down his book and his fried egg sandwich. He glanced at a clipboard hanging on the wire enclosure near him. "Just one," he said. "Another big order from Bruce Wayne."

"Jeez," said Sampson, "that guy again! Well, I guess he can afford it."

"That's what I hear," said Waters.

"He's one of Jennings' best accounts. I know for a fact that he gets as much electrical gear as some of the biggest factories and scientific outfits in Gotham City. What do you think he does with it all?"

Waters wasn't terribly interested. He only shrugged and picked up his book again.

"I hope he's around when I drop the stuff off," Sampson went on. "That butler of his never gives me any trouble or anything, but when the Wayne guy himself is there, he always gives me a healthy tip."

"Uh huh," said Waters absently. He kept on reading.

"Listen, pal. How about if I give you a hand filling the Wayne order? The sooner you get done, the sooner I can run it out to his mansion. Then I'll be done for the day. And I'll tell you what: if he slips me a few bucks, I'll come back here and split it with you. What do you say?"

Waters sighed. He was sure now that although he hadn't finished eating, his lunch break had come to an end. "Fine." he said. "Take one of those order form pages and find the electrical components in the bins. Bring them here to my desk because I have to check them all off."

"Whatever you say." Sampson slid the top sheet of paper free of the clipboard. Before he went to collect the parts, he switched on the maroon plastic AM radio above Waters' desk. The radio had been forgotten and left behind by one of the shipping clerks who had quit his job at Jennings to go back to school. Waters never turned it on because he hated pop music, and the radio did not receive Gotham City's FM classical music station. "Jeez, I'm getting sick of this song," said Sampson, listening to Pat Boone crooning "Love Letters in the Sand." Nevertheless, he left the radio on and went off in search of the electrical components Bruce Wayne had ordered.

Waters marked his place and closed *The Hidden Persuaders*. He watched Sampson wander off toward the vacuum tubes. "There should be a higher law," he muttered. "Something that would bring to justice all the double-digit IQs like Sampson." He took a deep breath and let it out, then stood and took the second page of the Wayne order. He began pulling boxes of resistors. He could tell that, once again, Wayne had ordered a small mountain of them.

Half an hour later, Sampson returned with a puzzled look on his face.

"This guy wants *two thousand* tubes," he said. "What can anybody do with two thousand vacuum tubes?"

"He can build a radio the size of your garage," said Waters irritably. "Maybe he has a crazy passion for Chinese music."

"Anyway, we're all out of some of these." He showed the order form to Waters.

"You can substitute for most of these tubes. Where it says 2A3, you can use a 2A3W, and it will be even more reliable."

"Yeah, easy for you to say, Waters. *I* haven't memorized the code numbers of every tube in the world."

Waters just stared at Sampson until he got himself under control again. "There's a big yellow chart on the wall, right in front of you," he said in a dangerous tone of voice, "and it gives all the tube numbers and all the permissible substitutions. It's probably been there since before you were born. You've seen it every time you've come into the cage."

Sampson grinned sheepishly, "I guess I never really noticed it before."

"That figures," said Waters sourly. "All right, I'll finish the vacuum tubes. You work on the resistors."

Sampson swapped pages with him and started to leave the shipping department. Then he stopped and turned back to Waters. "I always forget," he said. "What do the colored bands on the resistors mean again?"

It was all Waters could do to keep from punching him. "Forget it!" he said. "I'll finish the whole thing by myself. You just sit there and listen to the radio and don't touch anything."

Sampson shrugged. "All right, if you say so." He sat down and began munching on Waters' unfinished sandwich. "Listen," he said happily, "they're playing 'The Banana Boat Song.'"

Late that afternoon, Bruce Wayne bent over his work in the Batcave's superbly equipped laboratory. In addition to being in top physical condition to fight criminals on the streets of Gotham City, Wayne also found it necessary to keep current with all the latest advances in such fields as chemistry and electronics. What he had read in recent scientific journals had persuaded him that it was time to make improvements on the Batcave's Crime Data Analyzer. Wayne was convinced that he could build a new computer that could store and process information with even greater speed and efficiency.

New technology meant learning new techniques, but Bruce Wayne—the Batman—was never dismayed by such a challenge. As the day wore on, he worked with intense

The Origin of The Polarizer

concentration, unaware that both Dick Grayson, his ward, and his faithful butler, Alfred, were concerned about him. Alfred, in particular, was unhappy that his master had eaten little of his lunch and then hurried back to his experiment. He was worried that Wayne might be overtiring himself.

At four o'clock, Dick Grayson entered the Batcave and greeted the older man. "Gosh, Bruce," he said, "I'm sorry that I couldn't get out of that social engagement. I would much rather have been here, helping you with our project."

Wayne looked up, startled. "Hello, Dick. How was the matinee concert?"

"I've never heard the Gotham Philharmonic sound better. I explained to everyone that you had an important business matter that prevented you from accompanying me. But now I'm ready to get to work. Oh, and Alfred said to tell you that dinner will be served promptly at six."

Wayne glanced at his wristwatch and reacted with surprise. "I had no idea that I'd been working here so long."

Grayson came closer to the workbench to see what Wayne was doing. "Tell me, Bruce," he said, "what is that board? It's plastic on one side, and copper on the other. Is it going to be part of the new BATIVAC Crime Computer?"

Wayne smiled. "Yes, Dick. This is the prototype of the sort of printed circuit I've devised for the BATIVAC."

Grayson looked bewildered. "Printed circuit?"

"The printed circuit board will make building the BATIVAC much simpler. The plastic board will become the base onto which we will mount the necessary electrical components. After the board is properly processed, the remaining copper on the other side will serve as the 'wiring.' It will save us many hours of tedious wiring and difficult soldering. The BATIVAC will consist of hundreds of these printed circuit boards, and if a component or a circuit should fail, it will be much easier to remove the entire board and replace it with an identical one."

Grayson examined the unfinished circuit board in admiration. "This is wonderful, Bruce," he said, "but I suppose you won't be needing me and my soldering iron anymore."

Wayne laughed. "Oh, there will still be plenty of connections to make, Dick," he said. "We'll place the components on the plastic side of the board, with their leads pushed through properly spaced holes. Then it will be a simple matter to fasten them down to copper pathways on the other side with a bit of solder."

"What about the excess copper?"

Wayne indicated the copper-clad side of the board. "I'm just about to remove it now. I've masked the outline of the circuit I want with a resistant ink. Now I merely dip the board into this pan of ferric chloride solution, which will etch away all the excess copper. When it's finished, I'll rinse the board in clear water and remove that resistant ink with lacquer thinner. All that will be left on the copper side is a map of the circuit I designed."

"Wow, Bruce," said Grayson excitedly. "No more fumbling with copper wire!"

"Exactly, Dick. And this process will enable us to build our equipment more quickly and will reduce the overall size of it, too. We've entered the modern age of miniaturization. The BATIVAC will require several thousand vacuum tubes, and without miniaturization, it would take up much of the area of the Batcave."

Grayson understood the possibilities immediately. "Maybe later we could build a smaller version of the BATIVAC for the crime lab aboard the Batplane. And think of the new miniature devices we could carry in our utility belts."

"First things first, Dick," said Wayne, amused by his ward's enthusiasm. "And I think I've worked hard enough for tonight, although the sooner the BATIVAC is finished, the sooner all of Gotham City can sleep more securely."

It would be many days before the BATIVAC was completed, but both Bruce Wayne and Dick Grayson knew that there was no point in working to exhaustion. Together the two left the Batcave and went upstairs where Alfred had prepared them both a light but nutritious snack.

It was already after five o'clock when Bertram Walters drove the Jennings Radio Supply delivery truck up the long, curved driveway leading to Wayne Manor. Joe Sampson had said something that got Walters thinking, and when he'd finished locating all of the electrical components to fill Wayne's order, Waters had volunteered to make the delivery himself. Sampson had only shrugged, thankful to be going home early. He hadn't questioned why Waters would do him such a favor.

What Sampson had said was that Bruce Wayne bought as many electrical supplies as some of the largest factories in town. What *did* he do with it all? It seemed like too great a quantity for a mere hobbyist, someone who enjoyed puttering around in his basement workshop building homemade burglar alarms and electric-eye garage door openers. Unless, of course, Wayne were an electronics genius, just as Bertram Walters was. That seemed highly unlikely, too. Wayne was very well-known in Gotham City, but his reputation was as a wealthy playboy and socialite, not as a new Thomas Edison.

Waters switched off the truck's engine, opened the door, and jumped down to the gravel drive. He had a few not-so-innocent questions for whoever came to the door, and if the answers to those questions suited him, Waters might soon be embarked on an entirely new career—one that promised to be much more lucrative than his current job. Holding a clipboard and a box of vacuum tubes, Waters rang the doorbell and waited.

"Yes?" The man who opened the front door wasn't Bruce Wayne, whose photograph Waters had seen often enough in the newspaper. This must be the butler that Sampson mentioned, thought Waters.

"Jennings Radio," said Waters, trying to sound bored.

"Yes, of course," said the butler. He paused and examined Waters briefly. "Another gentleman usually delivers Mr. Wayne's orders."

"Yeah?" said Waters. "Well, today he didn't."

"Indeed, sir. Shall I sign?" he took the clipboard holding the invoice and packing list from Waters.

"Right. Top copy is yours."

The butler was shrewed enough not to return the clipboard until he'd examined the invoice thoroughly. "Pardon me, sir," he said at last, "but unless you have quite a few more parcels in your truck, this order is incomplete."

"Yeah, well, the stuff's on back order. It should be in tomorrow. I'll make a special trip out just as soon as it comes in."

"Thank you," said the butler. "I'm sure Mr. Wayne will be most appreciative."

"Uh huh. So tell me, this boss of yours, does he do a lot of electrical work around the house or what?"

The butler permitted himself a tiny smile. "Oh no, I wouldn't say that. Everyone knows that Mr. Wayne certainly doesn't need to attend to his own wiring difficulties."

"Well, he sure orders enough junk. All those vacuum tubes and everything."

"I believe, sir, that Mr. Wayne is planning to build a television set. He finds that sort of thing relaxing."

"Then he's not some sort of brilliant inventor, huh?"

Again, the butler favored Waters with a brief smile. "Oh, my goodness, no. He finds the plans in those home mechanic's magazines, but to be brutally honest, he's never yet finished a project. Now, good day to you, sir." He closed the great oak door quickly and firmly.

Well, Mr. Wayne, you have a clever and quick-witted butler, thought Waters, as he headed back to the delivery truck. A television set with two thousand tubes! You'll be able to tune in Mars if you want. But Waters was sure now that the components from Jennings Radio Supply would never form the inside of a television receiver. There was only one private citizen in all of Gotham City who would use such a great quantity of sophisticated electronic gear, and at the same time be so cautious about hiding the fact—the Batman!

Mr. Wayne, thought Waters as he drove the delivery truck to his own apartment, you'll receive the remainder of your order tomorrow, but first I want to put my own stamp of approval on every single part. And then I'll be ready for you when we meet at last.

Several weeks later, Bruce Wayne and Dick Grayson were putting the finishing touches on the newly completed BAT-IVAC, the Batman Algorithmic Tabular Integrated Vector Analzyer and Calculator. They had both enjoyed constructing the mammoth machine because the practical

George Alec Effinger

experience had taught them a great deal about the latest developments in electronics and data processing. There still remained the task of entering Batman's vast library of crime information. However, much of that was stored on punch cards for use with the non-obsolete Crime Data Analyzer, and the cards were also compatible with the BATIVAC. New information would have to be recorded on still more punch cards, and that job fell to the reliable Alfred, who, it should be obvious, was far more than a butler to his ever-vigilant masters.

Shortly before midnight, the red warning light far underground in the Batcave began flashing, indicating that the Bat-Signal was blazing through the night sky over Gotham City, invisible to Wayne and Grayson. They changed into their costumes as they raced to the Bat-mobile, as they had on innumerable occasions in the past. "I wonder what dangers we'll face tonight, Batman," said Robin.

"We'll learn soon enough," replied the Caped Crusader. "We'll report first to Commissioner Gordon. There are no urgent calls on the emergency radio frequency, so whatever the trouble is, no citizens or police officers are in a life-threatening situation."

"I suppose we can be grateful for that, but there are certainly plenty of other ways for crooks to cause trouble without using deadly force. And I'll bet we've fought every one."

Batman laughed ruefully. "Yet every time we think we've seen it all, Robin," he said, "some misguided mastermind comes up with an entirely new avenue of attack.

"We've been shot at, gassed, and trapped in burning buildings. The one thing we'll never have to worry about is being *bored* to death."

The Origin of The Polarizer

They drove at high speed through the rain-slicked city streets. It was late enough that there was little traffic about. Just before they reached police headquarters, Batman glanced at Robin. "Something's been bothering me about the Bat-Signal, Robin," he said. "Have you noticed it, too?"

"It seems to be flickering, Batman. Do you think it needs repair?"

"That's what I thought at first, but observe it carefully. The flickers aren't occurring at random."

"Gosh, you're right! It's a message in Morse Code! Let's see: B-A-T-M-A-N-! Y-O-U A-R-E H-E-L-P-L-E-S-S A-G-A-I-N-S-T T-H-E- A-W-E-S-O-M-E M-E-N-A-C-E O-F T-H-E P-O-L-A-R-I-Z-E-R-! But who or what is The Polarizer?"

"Perhaps the commissioner knows," said Batman. He had an ominous feeling that although the city's law enforcement chief had not seen fit to give the matter top priority, the case would soon prove to be one of the most bizarre and dangerous in the Batman's long career.

Leaving the Batmobile in a parking place reserved for police vehicles, the Dynamic Duo went inside to meet with the police commissioner. They hurried into the building and up to the commissioner's office.

"We got here as quickly as we could, Commissioner Gordon," said Batman.

"Good evening, Batman, Robin," said Gordon. He looked slightly perplexed. "Is there something I can do for you?"

Batman and Robin exchanged glances. "We came as soon as our warning light in the Batcave notified us that you'd activated the Bat-Signal, Commissioner," said Batman.

Gordon stood up behind his deck and looked levelly at the costumed crimefighters. "I don't know what you mean, Batman," he said. "I haven't turned on the Bat-Signal this evening. You know that the control switch is right here on my desk. I haven't used it, and I haven't been out of this room at all tonight, so that no one else could have used it, either. And even if the Bat-Signal had been operated without my knowledge, how could that help a crook in his criminal activity?"

"Hmm," said Batman. "It may be just an electrical problem, but perhaps it's something much more sinister. I think we'd better go up to the roof of Police Headquarters and examine the Bat-Signal itself."

When they all arrived there, the rooftop was deserted, but the Bat-Signal was still flashing its message in Morse Code across the clouds over Gotham City. "What does it mean, Batman?" asked Commissioner Gordon.

"I'm not sure, Commissioner," said Batman. "It seems to be a taunting threat, but I don't know of any criminal who calls himself The Polarizer. Perhaps it's just a demented hoax, but until we know for certain, we'll have to stay on guard."

"Look, Batman!" called Robin. "I've found a note."

"Is it in Morse Code, too?" asked Gordon.

"Let me see it," said Batman, taking the paper from Robin. "No it's in plain English. It's addressed to me. 'Dear Batman: Sorry I couldn't wait around to meet you in person, but while I lured you here, I've been robbing Shattuck Brothers Jewelry. For quite a while I've been admiring a sapphire and diamond necklace in their display window. Don't worry, though—we'll meet in person soon enough. At that time, you'll learn what it means to pit your meager skills against my power!' It's signed 'The Polarizer.'"

Commissioner Gordon took the note from Batman and studied it for a moment. "He sounds quite mad."

The Origin of The Polarizer

"Yes, that may be so," said Batman. "But he certainly knows enough about electricity to control the Bat-Signal from some remote location. And he has a strange sense of humor, as well, to use the Bat-Signal itself as a diversion to lure us here while he committed his robbery elsewhere. Somehow, I have no doubt that The Polarizer has made good on his boast. It's time for Robin and me to investigate the break-in at the jewelry store."

With Batman and Robin otherwise occupied at Police Headquarters, it was relatively simple for The Polarizer to break into the Gotham Ritz Jewelry Exchange. "Ha ha," he gloated, "even if those costumed fools decipher the Bat-Signal's message and find my note, they'll rush off in the wrong direction!" Although all the most elegant and luxurious jewelry had been put away in a safe for the night, there was still a large quantity of expensive merchandise left in the Jewelry Exchange's glass showcases. The Polarizer moved from one to another, stealing only the most exquisite and valuable pieces. I must hurry, he thought, aware that silent alarms must be sounding in a nearby police station. I can't afford to be greedy. I'll take only enough to pay my expenses for another year of graduate study.

When he estimated that he'd taken enough, he climbed back out through the plate-glass window he'd shattered only a few minutes before. He paused a moment to glance down the street in both directions, but he saw no one. He turned and sprinted down a narrow alley, where he'd parked the Jennings Radio Supply delivery truck. Already he could hear the howling shriek of sirens as police patrols began to converge on the neighborhood.

George Alec Effinger

The Polarizer threw his bag of loot carelessly into the back of the delivery truck and climbed in, pulling down the overhead door behind him. Hurriedly, he stripped off the stark black and white costume and the grotesque mask that hid his features. He had become Bertram Waters once again. Kittlemeier did a great job with this suit, he thought. I wonder if he could give me some advice about hiring henchmen. I could've gotten away with a lot more jewelry if I'd had a henchman or two. But you can't just put an ad in the Help Wanted section of the newspaper for somebody like that.

Waters hid his loot and The Polarizer's costume in the false bottom of a toolbox filled with needle-nose pliers and vacuum-tube extractors. The suit was close-fitting yet comfortable, and hadn't restricted his movements in the least. It was midnight black leather on the right side and snowy white on the left, separated by a jagged lightning bolt blazing diagonally down from the right shoulder to the left hip. He wore a white P in a black starburst on his chest, black gauntlets and high black boots, and a grimacing leather mask also divided into black and white halves.

When Waters was satisfied that everthing was safely stowed away, he pushed up the truck's sliding door and jumped down to the street. Once again behind the wheel, he turned the key in the truck's ignition and headed across town toward his own apartment. He would be many blocks from the crime scene before the police arrived.

Rain began to fall again, and Waters felt a damp chill in the air. He realized that he was driving too fast, fleeing in fear as though the Police might suspect the driver of a battered delivery truck to be Gotham City's most audacious jewel thief. He smiled at his own nervousness and slowed down, telling himself that it would be foolish to be stopped now for speeding. "I left no clues behind," he told himself, "There were no witnesses, and not even Batman will be able to find me."

Waters pulled the truck into his apartment building's parking area, then carried the toolbox holding the stolen gems and the costume of The Polarizer up to his apartment. He felt a peculiar excitement as he unlocked his front door. He had done it! He'd planned and executed a simple crime, taken enough valuable jewelry to pay for his needs, and gotten away cleanly. Now he could quit his boring job at Jennings Radio and take up again his studies in plasmonics.

Yet there was an intoxicating headiness about it all, and Waters realized that his ideas had changed. He'd planned at first to commit only one or two small thefts, just to pay for his further studies and enable him to get along without a regular job. But why should he limit himself? Tonight's crime had been so easy! Surely with a little more preparation, a large-scale robbery would be just as easy. Waters looked forward to working out the details of The Polarizer's second strike.

And there was one further matter that he did not want to let go of: the matter of Batman. It seemed likely to Waters that Bruce Wayne were one and the same, but Bertram Waters' scientific training required clear and unambiguous proof. He could not abandon his new life of crime until he knew for certain whether his hypothesis was true or false.

He took a cold bottle of Coca-Cola from his refrigerator, turned on his boxy, small-screen Muntz television, and sat down on his living room couch. As the opening theme of *Maverick* filled the room, Waters lifted the bottle in a toast. "Here's to you, Batman," he said. "Here's to your defeat and your unmasking...at the hands of The Polarizer!"

George Alec Effinger

Three days later, the entire punch card library had been fed into the BATIVAC, and Bruce Wayne and Dick Grayson were busily adding further information to the computer's memory. Grayson sat at the keypunch machine, while Wayne sat near him at the computer console's keyboard. "We must explore even the most unlikely hypothesis," said Wayne thoughtfully. "I don't think The Polarizer is one of our old enemies in a new guise, but we have to investigate that possibility nevertheless."

"I've recorded every detail of The Polarizer's *modus operandi* on these cards, Bruce. At least, as much as we could learn from our first encounter with him."

"We never actually saw The Polarizer, Dick," Wayne reminded him. "All we have to gone on is the Bat-Signal message and the unsolved thefts from the Gotham Ritz Jewelry Exchange. Does any of that match the known methods of the criminals in our Crime File?"

Grayson got up from the keypunch machine. "Let me feed these last few cards into the BATIVAC," he said, "and then we can let it sort all the information. Our answer will appear on the teletype."

"Good," said Wayne. "I hope the computer tells us something we can use. I haven't mentioned it before, Dick, but there's something about The Polarizer's attitude that worries me."

His young ward finished his task and looked up. "I think I know what you mean," he said. "It's almost as if The Polarizer were watching over our shoulders, right here in the Batcave. Of course, that's impossible."

Before Wayne could say any more, the BATIVAC began its operation. There was a loud hum of machinery and whirring of fans, as well as the rapid riffling of the punch cards. "I'll have it select all those criminals in our files who have the necessary knowledge and skills to use the Bat-Signal to send a coded message," said Wayne.

They waited and watched as the BATIVAC considered each past villain in turn. More than half an hour later, the computer had produced a stack of punch cards eighteen inches high. Grayson collected them from the output tray and returned them to the input tray. "What characteristic do you want to look for next, Bruce?" he asked.

Wayne considered the problem carefully. "If The Polarizer was known to us before, under another name, then his card must be in that stack. But many of those cards belong to criminals who are dead or in prison or can otherwise be accounted for. So next we should eliminate—"

Just then, the teletype started chattering. "How can it be typing, Bruce?" asked Grayson, startled by the machine. "We haven't even finished the sorting routine. It couldn't possibly have the answer yet!"

Wayne moved quickly to the teletype, which had once again fallen silent. He ripped the yellow paper free and read the single paragraph that had been typed on it. "Batman, it is time that we met in person. I am at this moment robbing the payroll of the Gotham *Daily Gazette*. Your friend, Vicki Vale, is waiting to photograph us together. Please don't keep us waiting! (Signed) The Polarizer."

"Come on, Bruce!" cried Grayson. "This time, innocent people may be in danger!"

"Right, Dick," said Wayne. "And now we have something else to bear in mind."

"What's that, Bruce?"

"We must face the possibility that The Polarizer has guessed our secret identities. He may have deduced the truth after learning that Bruce Wayne recently ordered a large quantity of electronic equipment. He may only be toying with us."

As if to underscore Wayne's suggestion, there came a rapid series of loud popping sounds from the BATIVAC. Grayson hurried to remove a panel from the back of the computer. "Bruce!" he cried. "The vacuum tubes! They're exploding! The BATIVAC—and our entire Crime File—may be useless now!"

They looked at each other in grim silence for a moment. "Don't worry about the Crime File," said Wayne. "I kept a duplicate set of punch cards as a backup. But we've got to put an end to The Polarizer's mischief. He's the cause of this, I'm sure of it."

As he and his young ward quickly completed their transformation into Batman and Robin, they each gave some thought to this new demonstration of The Polarizer's electronic wizardry.

"How could he get the teletype to print out that message?" asked Robin, as the fearsome Batmobile raced through the streets of Gotham City. "And how could he destroy the vacuum tubes in the computer? No one but Alfred and the two of us have ever been near the BATIVAC."

"We don't have the answers yet," said Batman in a low voice. "But we can't rest until we have them all. The Polarizer has discovered that we are somehow vulnerable, Robin, and therefore he's become a serious threat to our effectiveness as crime fighters in Gotham City. Our very future is at stake."

A crowd of spectators had already formed on the sidewalk outside the Gotham *Daily Gazette* building, drawn by the piercing alarm sounding in the newspaper's payroll office. The Polarizer, in his bizarre mask and black-and-white costume, pushed his way through the onlookers. He was carrying a heavy sack of stolen money and a box with several switches, meters, and a large antenna. He seemed to be in good spirits.

Vicki Vale, the famed photographer, accompanied him, snapping one picture after another. "Turn this way, sir," she called to The Polarizer. "And look menacing!"

"Ah, but my dear Miss Vale," he added, "I don't *feel* menacing today. I feel exhilarated and happy and full of all the warmest wishes for you and all mankind. Look at this lovely day. The sky is clear and the sun is bright, I've stolen enough money to indulge even my most fantastic whims, and soon I shall defeat this city's most cherished heroes. What more could any man ask?"

"Time for one more picture?" asked Vicki Vale.

The Polarizer nodded pleasantly. "I'm not going anywhere until Batman and Robin get here."

"You sound confident, Mr. Polarizer," said a man in the crowd.

"I *am* confident," he replied. "After all, I know something the Caped Crusaders don't know."

"What's that, you cowardly masked hoodlum?" shouted another spectator.

"Please," said The Polarizer. "Let's not start hurling personal insults. I only meant that I understand the full significance of my Terror Ray, and Batman and Robin couldn't even imagine the danger they're facing."

"They'll beat you," cried the first man, "Terror Ray or no Terror Ray!" The Polarizer only chuckled pleasantly.

A few moments later, the powerful thrumming sound of the Batmobile's engine signaled the arrival of the Dynamic Duo. Batman surveyed the scene and spotted The Polarizer. Vicki Vale was beside him, still clicking off one roll of film after another. "Robin," said Batman in a low voice, "we can't fight him here. An innocent bystander in this crowd might be injured."

"Gosh, you're right, Batman. What are we going to do?"

"Everyone, please move back!" called Batman in a loud, clear voice.

"Don't worry about them, Batman," said The Polarizer cheerfully. "They're in no danger from me. It's you who has to worry."

"Look out, Batman!" shouted someone in the crowd, "He has a Terror Ray!"

The Polarizer shook his head sadly. "Now, see that?" he chided. "You've given away my little surprise."

"Come on, Robin," urged Batman. "There's no such thing as a Terror Ray. That box he's holding looks like a remote-control unit of the type commonly used by model airplane hobbyists who fly radio-operated planes."

"Right, Batman! Let's get him!"

They ran toward The Polarizer, who dropped the sack of money and turned his attention to his Terror Ray box. He flipped two switches and turned a dial all the way to the right. "All right," he said, picking up the sack again, "I suppose this isn't really terror. But 'Consternation Ray' just doesn't have the same ring, don't you agree?"

Loud explosions came first from Robin's utility belt, and then from Batman's. Flames licked up, threatening to burn them, and they quickly unfastened the famed belts and dropped them to the ground. "Robin," said Batman without panic, "get the fire extinguisher from the Batmobile."

"But The Polarizer is using this diversion to make his getaway!" Robin said.

Indeed, the Radio Wizard had already loaded the stolen payroll into a brand-new Ford Edsel convertible

The Origin of The Polarizer

parked illegally at the curb, and was getting behind the steering wheel. He put the Edsel in gear and drove away.

Vicki Vale had run to the edge of the sidewalk to photograph The Polarizer's escape. Robin held her back. "Please, Miss Vale," he said, "there are potentially dangerous materials in some of the compartments of our utility belts. Until we have the fire under control, we have to ask you to stand back for your own safety."

"I understand, Robin," said the glamorous red-headed photographer. "But you *will* catch him, won't you? I want to get a picture of that egotistical maniac being brought to justice."

"We'll get him," said Batman grimly, "but we'll have to do it without our utility belts. Come on, Robin. To the Batmobile!"

As they sped off in pursuit, Batman thought over what little they knew about The Polarizer. "I'm beginning to understand how he's managed to wreck our equipment," he said. "And just as he may have applied logic to guess our secret identities, he may also have unknowingly revealed a clue to his own."

The fleeing Edsel appeared ahead of them, racing recklessly through Gotham City's afternoon traffic. "Look, Batman," said Robin. "We're beginning to shorten the distance between us. His car's engine sure doesn't have the power of the Batmobile. The license plate on the Edsel will probably give us no useful information. No doubt he's also stolen that car."

"Nevertheless, make a note of it, Robin. I think the Batmobile will catch up to him soon. In addition to being much slower, he's not a very good driver."

Robin grinned in anticipation. "I can't wait to see if he's immune to a right cross!" he said.

George Alec Effinger

The Polarizer steered the stolen Edsel onto the new Gotham Crosstown Expressway. He glanced into the rearview mirror and saw the Batmobile following some distance behind. Don't worry, Batman, he thought. Or should I say, Bruce Wayne? I'm not trying to evade you in this traffic. Indeed, I fully intend to let you catch me, but not until we reach the place I've chosen. And then I've got one final surprise for you!

He reached out and switched on the car's AM Radio, hoping to find a station broadcasting a news report of his daring daylight payroll robbery. As The Polarizer tuned the radio from one end of the band to the other, all he heard were the raucous and simpleminded pop tunes he hated so much. He felt it was horribly unfair for a genius such as he to be immersed against his will in the cesspool that was American culture in 1957.

The money he had stolen—the money that he would continue to steal—would help to shelter him from those demeaning influences. With money, he could live and work in a world unmarred by the cheap trash that passed nowadays for music and art and literature. He wanted to surround himself with the finer things, and carry on his own sophisticated research in the field of plasmonics. He had no desire to inflict harm, or to hurt people or wreak vengeance. He wanted only to be left alone with an awful lot of money.

He left the expressway and headed out beyond Gotham City's suburbs into a wooded, hilly area. "Only a little farther, you hapless heroes," he muttered. Beside him on the seat was the homemade remote-control unit. The Polarizer glanced over at it and reassured himself that all of its telltale lights were burning green. The unit was functioning perfectly. There was still one more switch to throw, but the time for that hadn't quite arrived.

The road wound around in sharp hairpin turns, leading up to the heights where The Polarizer planned to prove to Batman and Robin that they could never defeat him. "Shall I let them die?" he asked himself. "Or shall I let them live, knowing that I can take their lives any time I wish?" He decided to leave the matter in the hand of Fate. Once again he glanced into the mirror, and saw that the Batmobile had surged ahead on the empty road and was now following close behind. In another minute it would overtake the Edsel.

"It's time to say goodbye, Batman," said The Polarizer. He saw that the road was now little more than a broad ledge along the sheer rock wall to the left. On the right, there was a sharp drop leading down into a steep, rocky gorge. The Polarizer shrugged and flipped the final switch. He could hear the muted explosions behind him, as many of the elements of the Batmobile's electrical systems burst and shattered.

He watched the Batmobile swerve dangerously close to the edge of the cliff, and then, as Batman struggled to maintain control, it came to a halt across the middle of the road. Thick black smoke poured from beneath the Batmobile's hood and from underneath the chassis. The Polarizer braked the Edsel to a stop far enough away so that the costumed heroes wouldn't be able to capture him easily. He let the engine run, but got out of the car, carrying the remote-control unit and the bag of money.

"You've faced many ingenious foes, Batman," The Polarizer called, "but none so clever as I. Who else has been able to manipulate you at will? Who else has discovered the means to defeat you through your own oversight?

George Alec Effinger

Who else has been able to prove that you are, in fact, Bruce Wayne and Dick Grayson?"

Robin looked at Batman in surprise. "Batman, you were right! He knows our identities! But what does he mean about an oversight?"

"Quite simple, Robin," said Batman. "It must have occurred to him that Batman must need to purchase large quantities of electronic components and other materials in order to build his many crime-fighting aids. Think how much time we spend maintaining the Batplane and the Batmobile in top working order, as well as keeping them up-to-date with all the latest instruments and weapons."

"Of course, Mr. Wayne," said the Polarizer. "It would take someone with a personal fortune as large as yours to pay for all that."

Robin shook his head. "Then The Polarizer had some way of knowing which wealthy individuals in Gotham City were always buying electronic components and other parts."

"Yes," said Batman. "I think that behind that hideous mask is someone who, until a short time ago, worked for one of the city's major supply companies."

The Polarizer laughed. "I salute you, Batman. You're quite as shrewd as legend has it. But you must give me some credit, as well. After all, I certainly don't wish to draw unwanted attention to myself. If I did work for such a company, I wouldn't be foolish enough to quit just as I began my career as The Polarizer."

"Perhaps not," said Robin. "But I don't understand how you've wrecked the BATIVAC and the Batmobile."

The Polarizer laughed again. "Forgive me for keeping that a trade secret," he said.

"It's simple enough, Robin," said Batman. "Before delivering the components to us, he merely rigged them all with small amounts of plastic explosive, which he could detonate at will with his remote-control unit. In that way, he seemed to reach down into the very Batcave itself. As for the Bat-signal, that was even simpler. He didn't need to destroy anything, but merely control one or more key components from a distance, to make the Bat-signal flash in dots and dashes."

"And now I must leave you here," said The Polarizer. "Replace the tens of thousands of components in your computer if you wish, although it would take years to examine them all one at a time, to guarantee that each one is safe. And remember, you rely on other complicated hardware, too. Someday, perhaps, every electronic system in the Batplane will fail when you're flying over the ocean at 25,000 feet. You will never be able to trust your sophisticated machinery again." He threw back his head and laughed. It was a sound that was not altogether sane.

"I'm not frightened." said Batman. "We'll soon have you out of circulation. I placed a Bat-Tracer on your car back at the *Daily Gazette* building. When you drive home, it will let me know exactly where you are. If you abandon the car when you get back to Gotham City, then you'll be very conspicuous on foot. The police department will pick you up in a very short time."

The Polarizer laughed again. "Why, I'll merely destroy your tracer the same way I destroyed the Batmobile," he said.

"I used a Bat-Tracer that I constructed more than a year ago," said Batman. "That was before you began sabotaging the electronic components. Your remote-control unit will have no effect at all."

The Polarizer stared at his enemies for a few seconds, realizing that Batman had spoken the truth. If the Dynamic Duo were stranded on this little-traveled hill-

George Alec Effinger

side, so was he. He dropped the remote-control unit to the ground, and began running up the road, still clutching the bag of money.

"After him, Robin!" shouted Batman. While the Boy Wonder sprinted after The Polarizer, Batman took a rope Batarang from the damaged Batmobile. He flung it with practiced skill, and the Batarang looped through the air and twisted its rope around the bag containing the *Daily Gazette*'s payroll. When the Batarang returned to Batman's hand, he gave a hard yank on the rope, and the bag pulled free of The Polarizer's grasp.

"What?—" huffed The Polarizer, short of breath. "We're going to end this adventure the old-fashioned way," said Robin. He struck The Polarizer hard in the solar plexus, doubling him over. Then Robin landed a single massive blow to the point of The Polarizer's chin, and the costumed villain went down in a heap.

"Need any help, Robin?" called Batman, who had put the payroll money safely inside the Batmobile.

"I think he's under control. I'll just tie him securely to be sure—"

The Polarizer had regained his breath, however, and rolled away a short distance. He staggered to his feet, obviously confused and in pain.

"We're placing you under arrest," said Batman. "I've already called Commissioner Gordon on the radio in the Batmobile, and the police will be here in a few minutes."

"No jail," muttered The Polarizer, panting for breath and backing away across the shoulder of the road. "I won't go the jail."

Robin tried to wrap him with his strong silken cord, but again The Polarizer retreated. "You might as well give up now and make it easy on yourself," said Robin.

The Origin of The Polarizer

"There's a nice, warm cell waiting for you in Gotham City Jail."

Behind his mask, The Polarizer's eyes grew large. "I told you," he said, "I won't go to jail." He held his hands out in front of him, as if he were trying to ward off something terrifying.

"Robin," said Batman quietly, "obviously this man is mentally disturbed. Don't say or do anything to upset him further."

The Polarizer made a cackling sound. "Disturbed, am I? Are you calling me mad? Is that what you say about all the villains who defeat you? Well, I'm not mad. Is it mad to refuse to be locked up in some horrible penal institution?

"Be careful, you're near the edge!" warned Batman, but it was already too late.

The Polarizer had backed up as he delivered his final speech, and finally his foot slipped over the unguarded brink. He tottered there helplessly for the space of a heartbeat, and his terrified eyes flicked from Batman to Robin. Then, suddenly, he was gone. He did not utter a sound as he fell, but Batman and Robin both heard the sickening dull thud as The Polarizer's body hit the rocks far below.

"Should we go down after him, Batman?" asked Robin.

"I don't see his body," said the solemn Caped Crusader. "But I don't think anyone could have survived that fall. In any event, the police team will scour the area when they get here."

Batman and Robin moved away from the edge of the cliff. They sat in the Batmobile while they waited for the Gotham City Police units to arrive. "He must have been a brilliant man," mused Robin. "After all, he did figure out our secret identities, but they're safe again now."

For a few moments, Batman seemed lost in thought. When he spoke up, there was a sadness in his voice. "How ironic, Robin," he said, "that such a genius should have forgotten one of mankind's oldest proverbs: A sound mind in a sound body. The Polarizer couldn't hope to defeat us because he had followed only half of that ancient advice. It wasn't enough for him to wreck our modern devices because in the end it was that centuries-old piece of wisdom that conquered him. Wisdom, Robin! When all is said and done, the greatest force on Earth is still the human mind.

—*With thanks to Doug Wirth*

Idol

ED GORMAN

1984

Knock.

"Hi, hon. Just wanted to tell you that—"

His mother peeks around the edge of his bedroom door and says, "Gosh, hon. You're kind of old for that, aren't you?"

Her voice and eyes say she wishes she had not seen her seventeen-year-old son doing what he's doing.

Pause, then: "Are you OK, hon?"

"Why wouldn't I be OK?"

"Well—"

"I'm fine. Now get the hell out of here."

"Hon, I've asked you not to talk to me that way. I'm your own mother. I'm—"

"You heard me."

She knows this tone. Is afraid of it. Has been afraid of it ever since he was seven or eight years old.

He is not like other boys. Never has been.

"Yes, hon," she says, already starting to cry useless tears. "Yes, hon."

they don't know my loneliness. they see only my stren-gth. they don't know my loneliness.

1986

Open window. Autumn. Smell of leaves burning. In the distance a marching band practicing on the edge of campus. Smell of leaves rich as marijuana smoke.

He lies in his white undershorts on bed in this tiny off-campus apartment. Next to him girl sits stroking his chest. She is naked except for pink bikini panties.

"It's all right. Really."

"Sure," he says.

"It's happened to me a lot. You're probably just tired."

"Just shut up."

"Please," she says. "I really like you. Isn't that all that really matters?"

He slaps her, startling her as much as hurting her. Startling her.

i am beginning to understand my problem. i don't cause the headaches. he does. the impostor.
the impostor

1987

"So how do you feel about this man?"

"You know how I feel, doctor."

"Angry? Resentful?"

"Of course. Wouldn't you?"

Pause. "Tell me about the headaches."

"What time is it?"

"Pardon me?"

"The time, doctor. The time. I forgot my watch."

Sigh. "Two-ten. Why?"

"I'm in sort of a hurry today."

"We're not through till three."

"You, maybe. I'm in a hurry."

"You know your mother wants you to stay here for the entire session."

"Screw my mother."

"Please. Tell me about the headaches."

"What about them?"

"Do you know what triggers them?"

"No."

"Think about it a moment. Please."

Sigh. "Him."

"Him?"

"The impostor."

"Ah."

"Whenever I see him on tv or in the paper, the headaches start."

Writes quickly in his notebook. "What do you feel when you see him?"

"Nothing."

"Nothing?"

"Literally, nothing. People think he's me. It's as if I don't exist."

He thinks: how seriously can you take a shrink who has three big warts on his face and who wears falling-down socks with battered old Hush-Puppies?

Anyway, he is beginning to suspect that the shrink may well be a friend of the impostor's.

Yes. Of course.

My God, why didn't he think of that before?

He stands up.

"It's only two-fifteen. It's only—"

But he's already going out the door. "Goodbye, doctor."

1988

He sits in his room with the white kitten his mother bought him to cheer him up after he quit college a few months ago. He lazes warm and drifting in the soft May sunlight the same way the white kitten with the damp black nose and the quick pink tongue lazes.

"Kitty," he says, stroking her, You're my only friend. My only friend."

He starts crying then—sobbing really. He doesn't know why.

i saw him on TV last night. waving. accepting their applause. he's convinced them now. everybody. they really think he's me. they really believe it.

1989

"I'd like to talk to you."

"I'm in a hurry."

"I'm serious about this."

He's never seen his mother like this. No "hon." No backing down. Almost angry.

"All right."

"Upstairs."

"Why?"

"Your room, come on."

What is going on here? She seems almost...crazed.

So up the stairs.

So past where the white kitty with the damp black nose and quick pink tongue lies on the landing in the sunlight.

Into his room.

Throwing open the closet door.

Pointing.

Voice half-hysterical.

Ed Gorman

"I thought you told me you were getting rid of all this stuff."

Feeling himself flush. "This is none of your business. You have no right—"

"I have every right. I've put up with this since you were eight years old and I can't handle it any more. You're a man now, or supposed to be. Get rid of this silly junk and get rid of it now!"

Instead of becoming angry, he just stands there, allowing himself to understand the truth of this moment. The *real* truth.

So the impostor has gotten to her, too.

His own mother.

Sensing this shift in his mood, she seems less certain of herself. Backs away from the closet.

"What's wrong with you?" she says.

"Did you let him touch you?"

"Who? What are you *talking* about?"

"You know, mother. You know very well what I'm talking about." Pause. Stares at her. For a forty-two-year old woman she is quite attractive. All those aerobic shows on daytime tv. All that eating of fruit and lean meat and almost never any bread. Certainly no desserts. "You did let him touch you, didn't you?"

"My God, are you—"

But then she stops herself, obviously realizing that would be the wrong thing to say. The very wrongest thing to say. (Are...you...crazy?)

He grabs her, then.

By the throat.

Choking her before she has time to scream and alert the neighbors.

It is so easy.

His thumbs press down on her trachea.

Her eyes roll white.

Spittle silver and useless runs down the sides of her mouth as she tries to form useless words.

He watches the way her breasts move so gracefully inside the cotton of her housedress.

Harder harder.

"Please," she manages to say.

Then drops to the floor.

He has no doubt she is dead.

the impostor has taken over every aspect of my life. i have no friends (sometimes i even suspect that it was really he who put the white kitty here) i have no prospects for a career because nobody believes me when i tell them who i am i have no—

he leaves me no choice

no choice whatsoever

Same Day (Afternoon)

He has never flown before. He is frightened at takeoff, having heard that the two most dangerous times aboard a plane are takeoff and landing.

Once in the air—except for those brief terrifying moments of turbulence, anyway—he starts to enjoy himself.

He had never realized before what a burden she'd been, his mother.

His thinks of her back there in his room, crumpled and dead in a corner. He wonders how many days it will be before they find her. Will she be black? Will maggots be crawling all over her? He hopes so. That will teach the impostor to mess with him.

He spends the rest of the flight watching a dark-haired stewardess open a very red and exciting mouth as she smiles at various passengers.

Ed Gorman

Very red.
Very exciting.

Same Day (Evening)

The city terrifies him. He has checked into a good hotel. Thirty-sixth floor. People below so many ants.

Stench and darkness of city.

All those people in the thrall of the impostor.

Terrifying.

He has come here without an exact plan, but as he lies on the firm hotel bed eating donuts and drinking milk the late news comes on and the very first story gives him a beautiful plan. A wonderful plan.

Tomorrow the impostor will receive an award from the mayor.

So easy to—
so easy

tomorrow the world will know. my long struggle will be over and i will be able to assume my rightful place. tomorrow.

Next Day (Morning)

Warm spring day. The rear of the city jail where the impostor often brings the criminals he apprehends.

Smell of city—gasoline and smoke and filth and loneliness—sight of city: the helpless, the arrogant, the predatory.

His room, he wants to be back in his room...(the gun sweatily in his hand as he hides behind a parked car)

but suddenly now the impostor is here—

—leading a prisoner into the rear metal door—

—the impostor; so confident-looking—

—in full costume—

—going into the door as —
—the gunfire starts
Two quick cracks on the soft still air
Two quick cracks
(you bastard—father-of-mine—you've been fooling people too long; I exist now and you do not)
crack of pistol . . .
(and you do not . . .)

Same Day (Afternoon)

Around noon the story was on all the news media, bulletins on the networks, even.

And the would-be assassin (shot to death by police) was identified.

So a neighbor came over to see how his mother was doing after hearing such horrible news
and knocked and knocked
and went and called police
and

They find the body with no problem. Good-looking fortyish woman strangled to death, stuffed into a corner of the bedroom.

One cop, the mournful sort, shakes his head.

What a waste.

He sees the closet door partially open and, being a cop, curious and all, edges it open with a pencil (you've got to be extra careful at a crime scene; evidence can be destroyed so easily).

He looks inside.

"What the hell," he says.

His partner, who has been directing the lab man and the man from the coroner's office and the ambulance attendants, walks over next to him. "What?"

"Look inside."

So the second cop looks inside. And whistles. "All these costumes. They're just like—"

"Just like the guy he tried to kill."

"But if he had all these costumes you'd think he would have respected the guy, not wanted to kill him."

The first cop shakes his head. "It's a strange old world. A strange old world."

Same Afternoon (Later)

"Hey. Look at this," the first cop says.

"What?"

"Some kind of diary."

"Let's see."

They flip through pages. Open at a spot and read.

"*it is no longer tolerable. the impostor must be killed because there can't be two of us. one is real, one is false. and after today, the real one will assume the throne of power.*"

"Now what the hell could he have meant by that?"

The second cop shrugs. "You got me, partner. You sure got me."

THE MAN OF BRONZE

FOUR FABULOUS DOC ADVENTURES

☐ **DOC SAVAGE OMNIBUS #8**
27861-4 $4.95
THE MENTAL MONSTER
THE PINK LADY
WEIRD VALLEY
TROUBLE ON PARADISE

☐ **DOC SAVAGE OMNIBUS #9**
28000-7 $4.95
THE INVISIBLE-BOX MURDERS
THE WEE ONES
BIRDS OF DEATH
TERROR TAKES 7

Look for them at your bookstore or use this page to order:

- -

Special Offer
Buy a Bantam Book
for only 50¢.

Now you can have Bantam's catalog filled with hundreds of titles plus take advantage of our unique and exciting bonus book offer. A special offer which gives you the opportunity to purchase a Bantam book for only 50¢. Here's how!

By ordering any five books at the regular price per order, you can also choose any other single book listed (up to a $5.95 value) for just 50¢. Some restrictions do apply, but for further details why not send for Bantam's catalog of titles today!

Just send us your name and address and we will send you a catalog!

BANTAM BOOKS, INC.
P.O. Box 1006, South Holland, Ill. 60473

Mr./Mrs./Ms. _____
(please print)

Address _____

City _____ State _____ Zip _____

FC(A)—10/87

Please allow four to six weeks for delivery.